PENGUIN ⟨🐧⟩ CLASSICS

THE JUNGLE BOOKS

SERIES EDITOR: JAN MONTEFIORE

RUDYARD KIPLING, born in December 1865 in Bombay (now Mumbai), was taken to England in 1871 with his younger sister Alice and left for five years with an abusive foster-family in Southsea, after which he was sent to the United Services College in Devon, the public school affectionately recalled in *Stalky & Co.* (1899). He returned to India in the autumn of 1882 to work as a reporter. The poems, sketches and stories which he wrote during his 'Seven Years' Hard' in India, especially the series 'Plain Tales from the Hills', published as a book in 1888, won him immediate acclaim and, from his arrival in London in 1889, worldwide literary celebrity. This was increased by the powerful stories collected in *Life's Handicap* and the originality of *Barrack-Room Ballads* (1892), whose poems 'Mandalay', 'Tommy' and 'Gunga Din' became immensely popular performance items in music-halls – which, like hymns and ballads, were a lasting influence on Kipling's verse.

In 1892 Kipling married the American Caroline Balestier and lived with her in Vermont for four happy years, during which their daughters Josephine and Elsie were born and Kipling wrote some of his best work, including the two *Jungle Books* (1894, 1895). They moved to England in 1896, settling in Rottingdean, East Sussex, where their son John was born, and eventually at the house Batemans, at Burwash. Kipling continued to travel widely with his family, spending nearly all the winters from 1898 to 1908 in South Africa. On a trip to New York in 1899, his six-year-old daughter Josephine died of pneumonia, which Kipling himself narrowly survived.

Kipling published his masterpiece, *Kim*, in 1901, and the *Just So Stories* in 1902. He turned to the theme of Englishness and history in his children's books *Puck of Pook's Hill* (1906) and *Rewards and Fairies* (1910), interweaving poems and stories to subtle intertextual effect. His stories for adults after 1900 focus on the lives of ordinary people, uniquely combining a creative response to the new twentieth-century technologies of communication with a strong imaginative feeling for the strange and the numinous, intensified by his pared-down, understated style. His public poems, including 'Recessional', 'The White Man's Burden' and 'The Islanders', all printed in *The Times*, preached the virtues of patriotism and duty.

From the outset, Kipling identified with the rulers and officials of the British Empire, although he was never their servant (he refused both a knighthood and the Order of Merit). Yet he sympathized deeply with children, outlaws and outsiders, who often engaged his best energies as a writer, as witnessed by the vitality and subtlety of the *Jungle Books* and *Kim*. He was a strong supporter of the Boer War, for which he wrote journalism and propaganda; this, together with the hardening of his conservative political views after 1900, made him increasingly unpopular with liberals and anti-imperialists. Kipling returned their dislike. His books continued to sell and to be read widely and he was awarded honorary doctorates by many universities and the Nobel Prize in 1907, but he never again enjoyed the brilliant reputation which he had held in the 1890s.

In the First World War, Kipling remained a strongly patriotic writer, but after the blow of losing his son John at the Battle of Loos in 1915 he became a more private man. He none the less played a major role in the War Graves Commission, arguing successfully for equality of treatment for all ranks and choosing the inscriptions for the memorial stones. He commemorated the dead in his own moving 'Epitaphs of the War' and his *History of the Irish Guards in the Great War* (1923), an account of his son's regiment. His late stories of loss and bereavement are written with an acuteness and subtlety not always perceived by their contemporary readers.

Kipling died in 1936.

KAORI NAGAI teaches at the University of Kent. She is the author of *Empire of Analogies: Kipling, India and Ireland* (2006) and of many articles on colonial discourses in the nineteenth century. She has edited Kipling's *Plain Tales from the Hills* for Penguin Classics and has co-edited a collection of essays on Rudyard Kipling entitled *Kipling and Beyond* (2010).

JAN MONTEFIORE is Professor of Twentieth-Century English Literature at the University of Kent at Canterbury. Her books include *Rudyard Kipling* (2007).

RUDYARD KIPLING

The Jungle Books

Edited and with an Introduction and Notes by
KAORI NAGAI

PENGUIN BOOKS

PENGUIN CLASSICS

Published by the Penguin Group
Penguin Books Ltd, 80 Strand, London WC2R ORL, England
Penguin Group (USA) Inc., 375 Hudson Street, New York, New York 10014, USA
Penguin Group (Canada), 90 Eglinton Avenue East, Suite 700, Toronto, Ontario, Canada M4P 2Y3
(a division of Pearson Penguin Canada Inc.)
Penguin Ireland, 25 St Stephen's Green, Dublin 2, Ireland (a division of Penguin Books Ltd)
Penguin Group (Australia), 707 Collins Street, Melbourne, Victoria 3008, Australia
(a division of Pearson Australia Group Pty Ltd)
Penguin Books India Pvt Ltd, 11 Community Centre, Panchsheel Park, New Delhi – 110 017, India
Penguin Group (NZ), 67 Apollo Drive, Rosedale, Auckland 0632, New Zealand
(a division of Pearson New Zealand Ltd)
Penguin Books (South Africa) (Pty) Ltd, Block D, Rosebank Office Park,
181 Jan Smuts Avenue, Parktown North, Gauteng 2193, South Africa

Penguin Books Ltd, Registered Offices: 80 Strand, London WC2R ORL, England

www.penguin.com

The Jungle Book first published in Great Britain 1894
The Second Jungle Book first published in Great Britain 1895
'In the Rukh' first published in Great Britain [in *Many Inventions*] in 1893; this version first published
[in vol. 5 of the Sussex Edition] in 1937
The Jungle Books first published in Penguin Classics 1987
This edition published 2013
004

Chronology and General Preface copyright © Jan Montefiore, 2011
Other editorial materials © Kaori Nagai, 2013
All rights reserved

The moral right of the editors has been asserted

Set in 10.25/12.25pt Postscript Adobe Sabon
Typeset by Jouve (UK), Milton Keynes
Printed in Great Britain by Clays Ltd, St Ives plc

Except in the United States of America, this book is sold subject
to the condition that it shall not, by way of trade or otherwise, be lent,
re-sold, hired out, or otherwise circulated without the publisher's
prior consent in any form of binding or cover other than that in
which it is published and without a similar condition including this
condition being imposed on the subsequent purchaser

ISBN: 978-0-141-19665-7

www.greenpenguin.co.uk

MIX
Paper from
responsible sources
FSC® C018179
www.fsc.org

Penguin Books is committed to a sustainable
future for our business, our readers and our planet.
This book is made from Forest Stewardship
Council™ certified paper.

Contents

THE JUNGLE BOOKS

The Jungle Book

The Second Jungle Book

Chronology

1865 Joseph Rudyard Kipling born 30 December in Bombay, India, to Alice and John Lockwood Kipling, teacher of Art and Crafts at the Sir Jamesetjee Jejeeboy School of Art and Industry.

1868 Sister Alice ('Trix') born.

1871–7 Rudyard and Alice taken to England and left in the care of the Holloway family in Lorne Lodge, Southsea (the 'House of Desolation').

1878–82 Attends United Services College at Westward Ho!, Devon.

1880 Falls in love with Florence ('Flo') Garrard and corresponds with her for four years.

1881 *Schoolboy Lyrics* privately printed in Lahore, India, by Alice Kipling.

1882 Leaves school to join his family in Lahore (where Lockwood Kipling has been Principal of the Lahore School of Art and Curator of the Lahore Museum since 1875); 'unofficially' engaged to Flo Garrard.

1882–7 Junior reporter on *Civil and Military Gazette* in Lahore at a starting salary of 150 rupees a month, rising to 200 after six months and 400 after a year.

1884 Indian National Congress founded. Flo Garrard breaks off their connection. *Echoes*, a book of parodies and spoof poems written jointly with his sister, privately printed and published.

1885 In Lahore, publishes *Departmental Ditties* and *Quartette*, a supplement to the *Civil and Military Gazette* written by the Kipling family, including 'The Phantom 'Rickshaw' and 'The Strange Ride of Morrowbie Jukes'.

1886 *Departmental Ditties* published in London. November 1886–June 1887: 'Plain Tales from the Hills' appear as 'turn-overs' in the *Civil and Military Gazette*; negotiates with Thacker Spink in Bombay about publishing them as a book.

1887 Moves to Allahabad to write for the *Pioneer* newspaper, with increased salary of 600 rupees a month. Writes travel sketches of Native States entitled 'Letters of Marque' (later reprinted in *From Sea to Sea*, 1899).

1888 Thacker Spink publish *Plain Tales from the Hills*, revised and enlarged, in Bombay and England. *Soldiers Three*, *Wee Willie Winkie*, *Under the Deodars*, *The Phantom 'Rickshaw*, *In Black and White* and *The Story of the Gadsbys* published by A. D. Wheeler in the Indian Railway Library series.

1889 Leaves India to become a full-time freelance writer, travelling through China, Japan and the USA, as described in *From Sea to Sea*. Arrives in England, settles in London near Charing Cross, and achieves spectacular early literary success. Macmillan become his London publisher, publishing all his works apart from his poetry.

1890 Elected to Savile Club. Publishes 'Barrack-Room Ballads' in *Scots Observer*, and many poems and short stories in *Macmillan's Magazine*, *St James's Gazette* and *Lippincott's Monthly Magazine* in New York. Suffers a breakdown and recovers; meets Flo Garrard, again falls in love and is again rejected, fictionalizing the experience in *The Light That Failed*. Becomes a close friend of Wolcott Balestier, American literary agent, and with him begins their joint novel, *The Naulahka*.

1891 *The Light That Failed* and *Life's Handicap: Stories of Mine Own People* published. In October sets out by ship for South Africa, New Zealand and Australia, revisiting India for what proves to be the last time. On 7 December learns by telegram from Caroline (Carrie) Balestier of her brother Wolcott Balestier's death and on 27 December leaves Lahore for England.

1892 10 January: marries Carrie Balestier at All Souls, Langham Place, London. 3 February: the couple set out for

Brattleboro, Vermont, to meet the Balestier family. March: they continue their honeymoon journey via Vancouver to Japan. 9 June: Kipling loses his savings of nearly £2,000 when his bank (New Oriental Banking Co.) goes broke; they return to the USA, and settle in Brattleboro, in Bliss Cottage. 29 December: their daughter Josephine ('Best Beloved') is born. *The Naulahka* published. *Barrack-Room Ballads* (Methuen) sells 7,000 copies in its first year.

1893 The Kiplings move into their own house, Naulakha. *Many Inventions* published.

1894 *The Jungle Book* published. Lockwood and Alice Kipling leave India, retiring to Tisbury, Wiltshire.

1895 *The Second Jungle Book*, *Soldiers Three and Other Stories*, *Wee Willie Winkie and Other Stories* published. Anti-English feeling between the USA and Great Britain over Venezuela makes Kipling uncomfortable. He is approached about becoming Poet Laureate on the death of Tennyson and indicates refusal.

1896 A second daughter, Elsie, born on 3 February. Quarrel with Carrie's brother Beatty Balestier, followed by an embarrassing court action, decides Kipling to return to England. In September they take a house in Torquay, Devon.

1897 Family moves to Rottingdean, East Sussex. In June, Queen Victoria's Diamond Jubilee is celebrated; Kipling writes the admonitory 'Recessional', which appears in *The Times* on 17 July. Son John Kipling born on 17 August. *Captains Courageous* and *The Seven Seas* (poems) published.

1898 Kitchener killed at Omdurman. *The Day's Work* published. The Kipling family visits Cape Town, South Africa, from January to April. Kipling becomes a friend of Cecil Rhodes and Alfred Milner.

1899 *Stalky & Co.* published. February: 'The White Man's Burden', encouraging US annexation of the Philippines, appears in *The Times* and in *McClure's Journal* in the USA. Kipling and his family set out on a disastrous visit to the USA. Arriving in New York, Kipling becomes critically ill with pneumonia; his near-death and recovery is global headline news. 6 March: his daughter Josephine dies. His sister

'Trix' suffers her first mental breakdown. Travel writings collected in *From Sea to Sea* (2 vols.) published. 11 October: Boer War begins. Kipling, a strong supporter of the Government, writes 'The Absent-minded Beggar' which, set to music by Arthur Sullivan for the Soldiers' Families Fund, nets £300,000.

1900 January–April: Kipling and family visit South Africa, staying in Cape Town; Kipling visits the army to raise morale. Later he works on *Kim*, discussing its progress with his father. From 1900 to 1908 Kipling and his family spend their winters in Cape Town at The Woolsack, a house built specially for them by Cecil Rhodes.

1901 *Kim* published.

1902 Cecil Rhodes dies. Treaty of Vereeniging ends the Boer War. 2 January: *The Times* publishes Kipling's 'The Islanders', a poem rebuking the British for military unpreparedness. Kipling purchases his house Batemans in Burwash, East Sussex, and moves in on 3 September. *Just So Stories* published.

1903 *The Five Nations* (poems) published.

1904 *Traffics and Discoveries* published.

1906 *Puck of Pook's Hill* published.

1907 Kipling awarded Nobel Prize for literature and Hon. D.Litt. by Oxford and Durham universities.

1909 *Actions and Reactions* published.

1910 *Rewards and Fairies* published. Death of Edward VII. Union of South Africa created, to Kipling's disgust. 23 November: Alice Kipling dies.

1911 26 January: Lockwood Kipling dies. C. L. R. Fletcher's *History of England*, with poems by Kipling, published. Public agitation for women's suffrage; Kipling publishes 'The Female of the Species' in hostile response.

1912 'Marconi scandal' of insider dealing by Liberal Cabinet members, including Rufus Isaacs, outrages Kipling. *Songs from Books* (poems) published.

1913 Rufus Isaacs appointed Attorney General: Kipling writes and privately circulates the anti-Semitic poem 'Gehazi', attacking him. Home Rule Bill for Ireland passes the Commons twice, to be rejected by the Lords. Edward Carson foments rebellion in Ulster, supported by Kipling in speeches.

1914 Home Rule Bill for Ireland passes its third reading in the House of Commons, infuriating Ulster Protestants. April: Kipling's poem 'Ulster' supporting Edward Carson's sedition published in the *Morning Post*; he makes a speech in Tunbridge Wells attacking Liberals and Home Rule. 4 August: Britain declares war on Germany. 1 September: Kipling's call to arms, 'For All We Have and Are', published in *The Times*. 10 September: Kipling's son John joins the Irish Guards.

1915 Kipling writes war stories, including 'Mary Postgate'. John Kipling's battalion moves to France to take part in Battle of Loos (25–8 September). 27 September: Second Lieutenant John Kipling is reported 'wounded and missing'. Kipling begins to suffer the serious stomach pains that will trouble him for the next nineteen years. Writes naval sketches and poems published as *The Fringes of the Fleet*; four of the poems are set to music by Edward Elgar.

1916 Easter Rising in Dublin quashed by British Army; execution of its leaders. *Sea Warfare*, including the poem 'My Boy Jack', published.

1917 Kipling is asked to write the regimental history of the Irish Guards, and agrees. *A Diversity of Creatures* published. His poem 'Mesopotamia', protesting at the losses in the mishandled Mesopotamian campaign, published in the *Morning Post*. September: Kipling is appointed to War Graves Commission. Begins writing 'Epitaphs of the War'.

1918 End of the First World War. Election of Sinn Féin in Ireland, leading to unrest suppressed by British troops ('Black and Tans'). Kipling writes the poem 'Gods of the Copybook Headings'. *The Years Between*, a book of poems including 'Epitaphs of the War', published.

1921 Irish Free State established.

1922 Kipling falls ill with stomach pains, wrongly thought to be cancer.

1923 Elected Rector of St Andrews University. *History of the Irish Guards in the Great War* and *Land and Sea Tales for Scouts and Guides* published.

1924 Elsie Kipling marries Captain George Bambridge.

1926 *Debits and Credits* published.

1930 *Thy Servant a Dog* published, becoming an instant best-seller.

1932 *Limits and Renewals* published. Kipling writes the text of the first royal Christmas message to the Empire, broadcast by King George V.

1934 Kipling's stomach pain finally diagnosed as a duodenal ulcer and properly treated. His health improves.

1935 August: Kipling begins writing *Something of Myself*.

1936 12 January: Kipling falls ill with a perforated duodenal ulcer. 16 January: dies. He is cremated at Golders Green. 23 January: his ashes are interred in Poets' Corner, Westminster Abbey; pall-bearers include the Prime Minister, his cousin Stanley Baldwin.

1937 *Something of Myself* published.

1937–9 Sussex Edition of Kipling's works in 35 volumes issued.

Jan Montefiore 2011

General Preface

Rudyard Kipling (1865–1936) was a Victorian and an early modernist, a preacher of the imperialist virtues of discipline and duty whose imaginative sympathies lay with children and outlaws, and a lover of the stability of 'Old England' who much enjoyed travelling outside it. He was a world-famous author, the most genuinely popular English writer since Dickens, and his poem 'If –' is to this day read and admired by people who do not otherwise read poetry; yet when his ashes were interred in Westminster Abbey he was considered by many intellectuals as barely worth serious reading, even though he was admired by T. S. Eliot, Bertolt Brecht, W. H. Auden and André Gide. The 35-volume Sussex Edition of his work represents an extraordinary diversity: *Kim* and three other long prose fictions including *The Light That Failed*; eleven collections of stories, from *Plain Tales from the Hills* (1888) to *Limits and Renewals* (1932); seven books for children (the two *Jungle Books,* the *Just So Stories,* the two *Puck* books, *Stalky & Co.* and *Land and Sea Tales for Scouts and Guides*); journalism, propaganda, public speeches and travel writing, the little-read classic *History of the Irish Guards in the Great War*, a great deal of verse and the posthumous memoir *Something of Myself.* A virtuoso of the short story, he wrote ironic comedies and tragic dramas, tales of adventure and of work, ghost stories, revenge farces, psychological studies, animal fables and machine fables. D. H. Lawrence is the only English writer of the twentieth century who can match his record for brilliant and diverse writing which escapes conventional classifications, and as a storyteller he has no contemporary English rival.

Kipling's work is as much energized as fissured by these contradictions, the roots of which lie in his own childhood experiences of dislocation and exile. Born in Bombay, where his first language was the 'vernacular' Hindi spoken by the servants, who would remind him on visits to the drawing room to 'Speak English to Papa and Mamma', he was as a small child taken to England with his sister and left with a foster-family in Southsea, to endure six years of bullying and abuse culminating in near-blindness and 'some sort of nervous breakdown'. After four years at a tough public school which he came to enjoy, he returned to his family and a gruelling job as reporter, which reintroduced him both to India's rich glamour and to a colonial world where life was cheap and death common. He insisted that his harsh childhood had proved an asset to his career in that it taught him to survive by inventing stories and entering other imaginative worlds, while observing others' behaviour with due wariness and maintaining his independence. But the unforgotten rage, hatred and despair of the dark years in the 'House of Desolation', mitigated by a delight in imaginative play, continued to shadow his work in his identification with the stern wisdom of just authority, and in his fascination by the strange worlds beyond its understanding.

After Kipling's initial enthusiastic reception in London as the young genius from India, responses to his work became divided. In the 1890s Mrs Oliphant praised him for showing how the Indian Empire was 'defended and fought for every day against the Powers of Darkness', while Robert Buchanan condemned him as a jingo who spoke for 'all that is ignorant, selfish, base and brutal in the instincts of humanity'. Both writers defined Kipling in terms of a politicized split between defence of order and a daemonic abyss, one identifying him with the civilized side of the barrier, the other with the powers of darkness. This opposition is itself obviously conditioned by imperialist forms of thought, yet these writers correctly sense a connection between Kipling's political allegiance with Authority and the potentially anarchic energies of his work. The knowing young writer's ironic stories and poems insisted on the frustration, danger and misunderstanding that formed the conditions of colonial life, where 'two thousand pounds of education / Drops to a ten-rupee *jezail*' and British soldiers in barracks endured a monotonous life relieved by comradeship and the occasional prospect of action. Yet he was also fascinated by the unknowable strangeness of the 'life of the peoples of the land, a life as full of impossibilities and wonders as the Arabian Nights', just as he loved the idea of the sea, whose uncontrollable turbulence and endless horizons can be challenged but never subdued by human courage and skill.

But to take the sea as social metaphor meant identifying imperialism with the natural world; and this raises the problem of Kipling's politics. Despite his genuine respect for the humanity as well as the 'otherness' of Indian Muslims, Sikhs and Hindus, his 'anthropological' insistence on cultural difference as a social fact, and his fellow-feeling for private soldiers, Kipling's wide-ranging sympathies are based on the assumption of an unbreakable class, race and gender hierarchy. Defiance of the property-owning class by socialists, of all-male rule by feminists, and above all of the British Empire by nationalist subjects, whether Boers, Irish or Indian, all provoked him to splenetic writing, while his patronizing, uneasy or downright contemptuous attitudes to the Irish, to Jews and to Africans are no more defensible than those of his Victorian and Edwardian contemporaries. These opinions, articulated with his characteristic candour and vividness, have made Kipling's work a mine for postcolonial historians of imperialist thought from Edward Said's *Orientalism* onwards.

Yet although Kipling's writing is certainly informed, and sometimes deformed, by his political views, it is by no means reducible to these. This can be seen in his masterpiece *Kim* (1901) and to a lesser extent in the two *Jungle Books*, colonial fictions in which 'otherness' is regarded with pleasure, not anxiety, just as the *Just So Stories* deal with the 'other' world of the animal fable and the *Puck* books with the differences as well as the continuity of English history. The orphaned heroes Kim and Mowgli, never disciplined to the life of labour and duty whose virtues Kipling so often preached, are made free of the Jungle and the street-life of Lahore, apparently threatening places which are really magical worlds and whose citizens, whether human or animal, speak the richly rhetorical, archaized idiom that Kipling invented for Indian 'vernacular' speakers. This 'vernacular' equivalent signals its own difference by its obvious distance from the narrator's modern English, and yet is equally intelligible, and on the printed page indistinguishable from it, unlike cockney or Irish dialect with their dropped *g*s and aitches. These enchanted Indian worlds have their own cultures; the Jungle, far from being a place of raw terror, is ruled by a Law 'which never forbids anything without a good reason', while Akela the wolf and Bagheera the panther are models of nobility, unlike the cruel and superstitious villagers. The enchantment of *Kim* lies in the way the hero's double story, as spy in the Government's 'Great Game' and *chela* (disciple) to a Buddhist priest in quest of salvation, is lived through a rich variety of lovingly recreated and sensuously evoked Indian social worlds. Colonial racism is mocked in the persons of the fat drummer-boy who calls all natives 'niggers' and the parson who observes the holy and innocent Teshoo Lama 'with the triple-ringed uninterest of the creed that lumps nine-tenths of the world under the title "heathen"', while *Kim*'s Indian characters are far more complex and interesting than the English. Colonel Creighton may be significant for his joint role as ethnologist and intelligence boss, but as a character he barely exists compared with his agents Mahbub Ali and Hurree Babu. That said, Kipling's conservative imperialism is obvious, not just in Kim's work as a spy or in the stereotyping of 'Orientals' as lazy or untruthful, but more subtly in the vividly realized and sympathetic Indian characters whose assumptions about the benevolence and legitimacy of British rule match Kipling's own, like the loyalist old soldier recalling the 'madness' of the Mutiny, or Hurree Babu deceiving the Russian spies by pretending to resent the British Government for having given him an education which he is not allowed to use. It is unthinkable in the world of *Kim* that nationalist claims or grievances might be justified.

But Kipling's achievement goes far beyond his 'Indian writings' and his books for children. His later stories and poems represent a substantial contribution to modernist literature, partly in the deep intuition of chaos underlying the 'Law', which Kipling shares with Eliot and Conrad, and partly in his response to the possibilities of modern communications technology, to which the stories 'Mrs Bathurst' and 'Wireless' are among the first and strongest creative responses in the twentieth century. Moreover, the scope and versatility of the early stories, written in styles ranging from understated irony to demotic dialect and the flowery archaized idiom of his 'vernacular' equivalent, developed in his later work into an irony and indeterminacy which are characteristically modernist. A similar modernist indeterminacy is discernible in Kipling's poetry, not just in the rare but very successful free-verse poems like the 'Song of the Galley-Slaves', but in what look like obviously 'traditional' forms; the cockney language and self-invented elaborate stanzas of *Barrack-Room Ballads*, admired by Eliot and Brecht, are instantly identifiable as 'Kiplingesque' yet not identifiable with Kipling's own voice. His poems are rarely or never spoken in his own person, just as the knowing 'I' who narrates so many of his stories is not identifiable with Kipling himself. Even the elegy for his son John, 'My Boy Jack', takes the form of a dialogue in which an anxious mother is repeatedly told that her son is lost to 'this wind blowing and this tide', a refrain suggesting the blast of trench mortars and the waves of troops advancing in battle while locating Kipling's own unspoken loss in that figurative ocean. Through the use of the monologue form which he learned from Browning, his use of 'impure' demotic language and his skill as a parodist (evident from the 1884 *Echoes,* written with his sister, to the 1904 'Muse among the Motors'), the modernity of Kipling's poems lies in the interpretative uncertainty generated by the multiple voices and registers that speak his poems.

There is evident traditionalism in Kipling's contributions both during and after the First World War to the literature of mourning, such as the motto he contributed to the war cemeteries, 'Their Name Liveth For Evermore', and the formal sequence 'Epitaphs of the War' – and yet the famous couplet 'Common Form' ('If any question why we died / Tell them, because our fathers lied') bitterly mocks its own mode of heroic elegy. His pared-down, understated stories of mourning deploy a characteristically modernist irony, especially his tales of bereaved women. 'Mary Postgate' is as ambiguously open to interpretation as Henry James's *The Turn of the Screw*, and like that story turns on perverse sexuality and death. In both this story and 'The Gardener', the drily matter-of-fact narrative participates in the bad faith revealed in the protagonist, achieving both deep feeling and ironic ambiguity.

Kipling continued to break ground in his late stories. Their varied subject matter, which includes psychosomatic illness, forgery and the journeys of St Paul, their length, complexity and unobtrusive use of motif and symbol, allowed him a new depth and range in his treatment of men and women. His writing had always insisted on gender difference, partly through its emphasis on the homosocial masculinity of soldiers in barracks, officers in their mess and experts talking in their clubs; but his dwelling on masculine solidarity becomes even more marked in the late stories of war veterans coping with their scars through the ritual and comradeship of freemasonry, or first-century Roman sailors talking shop over their wine. His women, conversely, are defined by sexuality and motherhood and are often associated in more or less complex ways with the numinous – like the Woman in the tale of 'The Cat That Walked by Himself' who domesticates Man and animals by her magic, and yet is responsible for letting in the untameable Cat. His late treatments of women, like the fiercely possessive yet selfless Grace Ashcroft in 'The Wish House', achieve a new psychological depth. As with the short-story form which he practised with such brilliance, Kipling is a writer whose limitations paradoxically allowed him an unsurpassed range.

Jan Montefiore 2011

Introduction

Writing Jungle Books is rather difficult. I have to translate out of beast talk and jungle talk into easy English and as the beasts use 'portmanteau words' like the ones Humpty-Dumpty said to Alice through the looking glass, there is a great deal of translation to be done. When a tiger or a bear says '*Wough*' in a high voice it means something quite different from '*Wough*' in a low voice and when he says '*Wough?*' as if he were asking a question it means something else: and the same when he [says] *Wough-ugh* with a stop in the middle.

Where I live now, in America, we have a great many animals but they are not Jungle-creatures. We have foxes, and now and then a bear kills a calf or a pig . . .[1]

I

The *Jungle Books* consist of two collections of stories, *The Jungle Book* (1894) and *The Second Jungle Book* (1895), which were the major fruits of Kipling's American period (1892–6), when he lived in Brattleboro, Vermont, the hometown of his newly wed wife Caroline ('Carrie'). Kipling, in his autobiography, *Something of Myself*, posthumously published in 1937, recalls how '[i]n the stillness, and suspense, of the winter of '92', his Daemon, his creative power, who was 'with him' throughout his writing of the *Jungle Books*, guided him to write 'Mowgli's Brothers': 'After blocking out the main idea in my head, the pen took charge, and I watched it begin to write stories about Mowgli and animals, which later grew into the *Jungle Books*.'[2] Importantly, the writing of the *Jungle Books* coincided with, and was inspired by, the magical and spontaneous flowering of his new family life. Initial ideas of the books came to him during Carrie's pregnancy with their first child, Josephine, and their second daughter, Elsie, was born in 1896, soon after the completion of *The Second Jungle Book*. His creativity was further enhanced by his quiet life in the mountainous region of Vermont, known for its great natural beauty and healthy climate, where he built his first house, 'Naulakha', in which most of the *Jungle Book* tales were written and edited.

It was during this happiest and most productive time in his life that Kipling, praised for his ability to identify with 'whatever and whoever he wrote about',[3] ventured into the world of animals, putting himself in their paws. Rosemary Sutcliff, a famous children's writer herself, in recalling her childhood experience of reading the *Jungle Books*, wonders 'how anyone who had not himself run on four paws inside a lithe ebony velvet skin, could know so surely what it feels like to be a black panther'.[4] The above extract from a letter Kipling wrote in response to a fan letter sent by a young boy in England in 1895 interestingly captures how, in 'translating' beast talk into English, he sounded almost like the beasts himself, while the *Jungle Books*, through the figure of Humpty-Dumpty, merge with the world of *Through the Looking-Glass*, which Kipling was sure that the boy had read. By writing on and as animals, then, Kipling sought to be readmitted into the magical and privileged fellowship of child readers; this can also be seen in the fraternal tone with which he addresses the boy. Some of the earlier *Jungle Book* stories were written for *St Nicholas* magazine, a popular American children's periodical edited by Mary Mapes Dodge, which Kipling had enjoyed reading as a child, and he relished the challenge of writing stories for children, whom he saw as 'a good deal more important and discriminating' an audience than adults.[5]

Kipling's reputation as the 'Bard of Empire' means that the *Jungle Books*, written at the height of British imperial power, inevitably invite readings of them as allegories of his imperialist ideologies. However, even those who detest Kipling for his imperialism are apt to make an exception for his two best-known children's books, the *Jungle Books* and *Just So Stories for Little Children* (1902), as the only ones of his texts 'worth reading'.[6] In particular, the *Jungle Books*, probably the best known of Kipling's masterpieces, have had a far-reaching impact on our imagination with the creation of Mowgli the wolf-boy. Their structure, which embeds the Mowgli saga within other more realistic animal stories, stages the meeting of dream and reality; Kipling there sought to carve out a child's sphere of play and imagination, separate from the adult world of work, in the shape of Mowgli's jungle. Even when Kipling's 'adult' works rapidly lost their popularity as the hegemony of the British Empire waned in the first part of the twentieth century, the *Jungle Books* remained on children's bookshelves; they have almost become synonymous with the joy of childhood and of reading. Modern readers may have first come across them through the Disney animated film version (1967) and its spin-offs, which, though they hardly capture the complexity of Kipling's original, have played a significant role in propagating the myth of Mowgli and the accompanying images of wild animals as an integral part of a happy childhood.

An early draft of 'Mowgli's Brothers' indicates that Kipling originally set the jungle in 'the Aravulli hills' in the state of Mewar in Rajputana (now Rajasthan), north-west India.[7] He knew this area well, having visited it in 1887 as a special correspondent for the *Pioneer*, the Indian newspaper for which he was then working. However, he soon moved the jungle's location to the 'Seeonee hills' in central India, which he had never visited, and is said to have taken the details of the place largely from Robert Armitage Sterndale's *Seonee or Camp Life on the Satpura Range* (1877).[8] In the process of writing the *Jungle Books*, therefore, Kipling made a deliberate decision to distance himself from his own experiences in India, by relocating Mowgli's jungle elsewhere, as if to echo his recent move to America. In this way, his intimate knowledge and experiences of India were rearranged to acquire new expressions, in which the Indian landscape became overlaid with that of America, both being populated by 'a great many animals'.

Significantly, the Indian setting and the creation of a boy

hero enabled Kipling to relive his own childhood in colonial India, where he had spent his early years. Just like Mowgli, Kipling, as an Anglo-Indian child, considered himself to be a denizen of two worlds. He belonged to the world of his English parents, from which his authority as an English child was derived, while enjoying the company of his native servants, with whom he explored the colourful and exotic Indian world with its 'strong light and darkness'.[9] John McBratney calls this a 'felicitous space' of childhood, a brief period in which an English child born in India, immersed in native languages and cultures, could enjoy true fellowship with natives, unmarred by the adult politics of racial hierarchy.[10] At the same time, the *Jungle Books*, which end with Mowgli leaving the jungle to enter the human world as he attains maturity, present the jungle as a place of nostalgia, a long-lost childhood which grown-ups fondly look back upon. Kipling's own blissful childhood in India abruptly ended when he was sent to England to be educated at the age of five. The trauma of being uprooted from India and the miserable time he spent at his foster-parents' place in Southsea, which he called the 'House of Desolation', is well fictionalized in his semi-autobiographical story 'Baa Baa Black Sheep' (1888), while, in the *Jungle Books*, his cherished memories of India and the irreparable sense of loss from which he never recovered were beautifully sublimated into a universal myth of childhood.

Vermont was Kipling's newfound Garden of Eden, which Mowgli's jungle in many ways mirrors. There, he was blissfully unaware of the impending woes and tragedies which were to befall him; this idyllic life in Vermont turned out to be even shorter-lived than Kipling's Indian childhood. The escalating tension with his brother-in-law and neighbour Beatty Balestier drove him to leave America with his family in August 1896. When the Kiplings revisited the country in 1899, he and his daughter Josephine fell seriously ill during the trip, and she died while he was still convalescing. After this tragedy, he never returned to America, and Vermont remained another of his lost paradises.

II

Kipling's early reputation was built on his role as a storyteller of Indian people: he wrote about not only a wide variety of 'natives' from different races and walks of life, but also Anglo-Indians who served in India. Kipling calls all of these 'mine own people', with much affection and a strong sense of camaraderie. This is beautifully captured in his epigraph to *Life's Handicap* (1891): 'I met a hundred men on the road to Delhi and they were all my brothers.'[11] In the *Jungle Books*, Kipling turns his gaze to animals, as further beloved 'brothers' whom he met on his journey through India and beyond. Just like the narrator of *Life's Handicap* who collected his tales 'from all places, and all sorts of people', the narrator of the *Jungle Books* in his Preface (p. 3) acknowledges 'his indebtedness' to the various animals who provided him with first-hand accounts of marvellous stories – elephants, a monkey, a porcupine, a bear, a mongoose and many others who 'desire to preserve the strictest anonymity'; he presents himself as a mere 'Editor' of these amazing stories. The *Jungle Books* therefore can be seen as an animal version of *Life's Handicap*; indeed Limmershin, the winter wren, 'a very quaint little bird' who 'knows how to tell the truth' and is identified as the informant of 'The White Seal', is somewhat reminiscent of Gobind, an old native storyteller in *Life's Handicap*, who always provides the narrator with 'true' tales, which are not necessarily printable.[12]

The *Jungle Books* are, first and foremost, stories of animals, and the lives of these are intimately connected with the human society and affairs of the British Empire. 'Toomai of the Elephants', for instance, gives us insights into the life of Kala Naga, who 'had served the Indian Government in every way that an elephant could serve it' (p. 103) during his long service of forty-seven years, and into how four generations of native mahouts, also loyal to the Government, had taken good care of him. Many of Kipling's animal characters are based on ones he had met in India. For instance, 'a perfectly wild mongoose', according to Kipling, 'used to come and sit on [his] shoulder in [his] office in India',[13] and he became the model of the eponymous hero of 'Rikki-Tikki-Tavi'. The mischievous *Bandar-log*, the 'Monkey People' in the Mowgli stories, recall an article Kipling wrote about a group of monkeys in Simla – 'The hill side is alive with their clamour' – who sent 'a deputation' to his verandah and interrupted his writing.[14] Kipling's own fox terrier, Vixen, also makes an appearance as the narrator's dog in 'Servants of the Queen'; she runs 'all through the camp' (p. 132) to find her master, bringing back happy memories of the time Kipling spent with her in India.

In many ways, the *Jungle Books* can be seen as an imaginative reworking of Kipling's father's book *Beast and Man in India* (1891) with its rich descriptions of Indian animals 'in their relations with the people'.[15] John Lockwood Kipling, a gifted artist and illustrator, worked in Bombay and then in Lahore from 1865 to 1893, as an art professor and curator. Father and son shared similar perceptions of and an adoring gaze towards animals, and there are significant overlaps between their works. Kipling had contributed nine verse epigraphs and two poems to his father's book – on monkeys, asses, buffaloes, oxen and so forth.[16] His proud father further showcased his son's animal writing by citing lengthily from Kipling's newspaper articles and also by printing one of his barrack-room ballads, 'Oonts!' (1890), in its entirety; this, according to him, 'vividly and truly' captures the British soldier's relationship with the camel.[17]

In turn, Kipling freely took inspiration and materials from his father's book in writing his animal stories. Furthermore, John Lockwood Kipling contributed illustrations to *The Jungle Book*, and went on to be the sole illustrator for *The Second Jungle Book*. The *Jungle Books* were therefore a fruit of family collaboration, like so many imperial projects.

In the nineteenth century, the representation of wild animals was popular in the form of natural history books or hunting literature, with the exploration and exploitation of nature being an integral part of British colonial expansion. Kipling, in writing the *Jungle Books*, draws much from these traditions; one of his sources is R. A. Sterndale's *Natural History of the*

Mammalia of India and Ceylon (1884), and Mowgli's encounter with the tiger Shere Khan is in line with colonial hunting
literature, which takes delight in the thrill of chasing big game.
There were also, in this period, many 'fantasy' tales that
involved animals, such as Lewis Carroll's *Alice's Adventures in
Wonderland* (1865) and its sequel *Through the Looking-Glass*
(1871), which, like the Mowgli stories, set a child's journey
towards adulthood in a world of talking animals. Kipling in
Something of Myself refers to 'some memory of the Masonic
Lions of [his] childhood's magazine' as a source of inspiration
for the *Jungle Books*, along with 'a phrase' in Rider Haggard's
Nada the Lily (1892), which contains the episode of two men
who become kings of ghost-wolves.[18] The former source has
been identified as James Greenwood's *King Lion*, serialized in
Boy's Own Magazine from January to December 1864.[19]

In the *Jungle Books*, Kipling combined the popular accounts
of exotic animals in the colonial space with the 'make-believe'
world of talking animals, and, in doing so, elevated the old genre
of beast tales to a new height. He was particularly applauded for
his vivid description of animals, which 'helps [the readers] to
enter, by the power of the imagination, into the very nature of the
creatures',[20] and he pioneered the representation of wild animals
as characters with recognizable names and many interesting stories to tell. There had been Anna Sewell's *Black Beauty* (1877), in
which human cruelty against horses is graphically described from
a horse's point of view, but no writer had offered a sympathetic
treatment of animals in the wild before. The *Jungle Books* created a market and an appetite for such stories, paving the way for
naturalist writers like Ernest Thompson Seton and Charles G. D.
Roberts to develop the genre of realistic animal fiction, while setting in motion the burgeoning of fantasy tales of talking wild
animals, including Beatrix Potter's Peter Rabbit books (1902–12)
and Kenneth Grahame's *The Wind in the Willows* (1908). As
Kipling recalls in *Something of Myself*, the *Jungle Books* 'begat
Zoos of [imitators]'; Kipling identifies the American writer Edgar
Rice Burroughs, the author of *Tarzan of the Apes* (1912), as one
such imitator, who 'had "jazzed" the motif of the *Jungle Books*
and, I imagine, had thoroughly enjoyed himself'.[21]

Kipling's animals have often been deemed inaccurate, or 'frankly humanised'.[22] As Seton puts it: 'Since Kipling had no knowledge of natural history, and makes no effort to present it, and since furthermore his animals talk and live like men, his stories are not animal stories in the realistic sense; they are wonderful, beautiful fairy tales.'[23] The true ingenuity of the *Jungle Books*, however, consists in the combination of realistic animal stories set in the modern world with the time-honoured tradition of animal fables. In an animal fable, particularly within the Western literary tradition, animals are made to represent human types, and their stories are implicitly commentaries on, or satires of, various aspects of human society. This doubling of the animal figure enables us to read the *Jungle Books* as an allegory of, for instance, imperialism, racial politics, childhood, or anything else we care to read into the text. Upon the publication of the *Jungle Books*, Kipling was immediately hailed as a modern-day Aesop.

Moreover, in the nineteenth century, 'beast fables', such as those in Oriental and African folklore, were regarded as vital anthropological documents, shedding light on human origins. They were thought to have been originally told by primitive savages, who had not yet distinguished themselves from other animals, and to whose minds 'the semi-human beast is no fictitious creature' but a reality.[24] Kipling wrote his jungle tales with the idea of the beast fable in mind, this 'seem[ing] to [him] new in that it is a most ancient and long forgotten idea'.[25] He was greatly influenced by the Jataka tales, Buddhist fables and parables which tell of Buddha's previous incarnations in both human and animal forms, as well as by the tales of 'native hunters in India today', most of whom, according to Kipling, thought 'pretty much along the lines of an animal's brain'; he had ' "cribbed" freely from their tales'.[26] Another source of inspiration was Joel Chandler Harris's *Uncle Remus* (1881), which is based on 'Negro' beast fables collected in the Southern States of America, and features the famous trickster Brer Rabbit. *Uncle Remus* was a bestseller when Kipling was a student, and according to Kipling in a letter to Harris, 'the sayings of the noble beasties' from *Uncle Remus* 'ran like wild fire through an English public school when [he] was about fifteen'.[27]

Kipling's borrowings from the ancient genre of beast fables endow his tales in the *Jungle Books* with a mythical quality, and he created them to explore, to quote J. M. S. Tompkins, 'the world of the wild and strange, the ancient and the far'.[28] The *Jungle Books* take us back to our primordial origin, 'unspeakably various and wild and old',[29] with wild beasts providing an essential link to man's animal nature and primitive stages while Mowgli is the expression of man's return to and exploration of the archaic. Moreover, by setting the *Jungle Books* mainly in India, Kipling places his stories in the Eastern tradition of universal brotherhood among living creatures. In Kipling's time, it was widely assumed that in Indian or Buddhist beast fables 'animals are allowed to act as animals', due to the Eastern belief in the transmigration of the soul through reincarnation, which 'effaces the distinction between man and the animal, and which in every living thing sees a brother'.[30] 'The Miracle of Purun Bhagat' is a beautiful example of this: a holy man forms friendships with wild creatures, who later warn him of the danger of an imminent landslide, thus enabling him to save the villagers. He addresses his animal friends as *'Bhai! Bhai!'* ('Brother! Brother!' – p. 170), and this call which connects Man and Beasts is echoed throughout the Mowgli tales, in which animals receive Mowgli as their Brother.

India is the home of the *Panchatantra*, one of the oldest-known collections of animal fables, which has spread far and wide to other parts of the world, being retold and changing shape along the way: La Fontaine, for instance, acknowledges his indebtedness to the ancient Indian sources in writing his fables.[31] A direct link between the *Jungle Books* and Indian beast fables can be seen in 'Rikki-Tikki-Tavi', which is reminiscent of 'The Loyal Mungoose' in the *Panchatantra*, in which a pet mongoose fights and kills a snake to defend his master's baby. Also, 'The King's Ankus', in which Mowgli witnesses men killing each other to obtain a jewelled elephant goad, echoes Chaucer's 'The Pardoner's Tale', the original source of which is said to be 'The Robbers and the Treasure-trove' in the Jataka tales. In fact, Kipling, writing in a 1905 letter, objected to a suggestion that 'The King's Ankus' was a reworking of 'The Pardoner's Tale', as he was familiar with an Indian version of the story: 'I don't remember when I didn't know the tale. Got it I suppose as a fairy tale from my nurse in Bombay.' For Kipling, 'Chaucer was a parvenu' to the ancient fable tradition originating in India, from which he himself took his inspiration directly.[32]

The *Jungle Books*, connected with the rest of the world through the tradition of travelling beast fables, are woven around a strong sense of cosmopolitanism, the awareness of, to quote the title of Kipling's 1917 collection of stories, 'a diversity of creatures' co-existing and sharing the same world. Kipling takes care to show how the seemingly mythic and timeless realms of animals are in fact closely connected with a modern and fast globalizing world. In 'The Undertakers', for example, the Adjutant-crane on an Indian river-bank describes his experience of swallowing 'a seven-pound lump of Wenham Lake ice' (p. 214) freshly delivered from Massachusetts by an American ice-ship, not knowing what it was. In 'Quiquern', an Inuit village on Baffin Island is likewise shown to be part of the wider international world: 'a kettle picked up by a ship's cook in the Bhendy Bazaar' (the most cosmopolitan area of Bombay) 'might end its days over a blubber-lamp somewhere on the cool side of the Arctic Circle' (p. 248). This story tells the adventure of Kotuko and an Inuit girl, a 'stranger' from another part of the Arctic Circle, who set out to find food for Kotuko's starving village. It ends with the girl's integration into the community by marrying him. The movement and energy of the dog-sleigh, which propels the pair's adventure, is implicitly juxtaposed with that of the steamers, which eventually bring the written account, passed from hand to hand by traders, of Kotuko's adventure to Colombo, where the narrator finds it. This sense of the interconnectedness of the world is overlapped with Man's oneness or partnership with nature, which is most succinctly captured by the fact that Kotuko shares the same name with his dog, who follows a parallel trajectory towards adulthood with his master and is indeed an integral part of his identity.

III

The story of human children reared by and among wolves has an ancient and mythic history, as in the legend of Romulus and Remus, twin brothers and founders of the city of Rome, who as babies were abandoned and thrown into a river, but were then rescued by a she-wolf who suckled them to health. In this myth, the wolf-children, expelled from a human community and reared by a wolf, go on to found what would become the Roman Empire. In the *Jungle Books*, Mowgli, an outcast from his native Indian society who has been adopted by a family of wolves, plays a similar role for the British Empire. The jungle, of which Mowgli eventually becomes the Master, is portrayed as an epitome of Empire with its spirit of fair play and lawfulness. Kipling also presents it as the very place in which a higher social Law is created through an interaction with, and integration of, nature. Mowgli the wolf-boy embodies this new Law, which the Indian village, with its antagonistic and superstitious attitude towards the jungle, cannot take part in.

The late nineteenth century saw a revival of interest in the stories of wolf-children as crucial to an exploration of the origin of Man – as well as of the borders between humans and animals, culture and nature – in anthropological investigations stimulated by Charles Darwin's *On the Origin of Species* (1859). India became the centre of attention as 'the cradle'[33] of such stories when a pamphlet entitled 'An Account of Wolves nurturing Children in their Dens' was published in 1852, by William Henry Sleeman (1788–1856), a British officer and administrator in India. This presents several cases of Indian wolf-children.[34] These children, discovered and 'rescued' by villagers, would walk on all fours, eat raw meat, and die soon after being captured. Sleeman's testimony was repeatedly quoted and reprinted in various places throughout the latter part of the nineteenth century, and was further reinforced by many other eye-witness accounts. Kipling, while working as a journalist in India, must have come across many such stories of wolf-children. Anthropologists, however, had difficulty determining to what extent these stories were fact or fabrication, and called for the need carefully to sift the evidence. For instance, when Friedrich Max Müller (1823–1900), an eminent comparative philologist and mythologist, wrote a short article on 'Wolf-children', he emphasized the likelihood that these so-called accounts were woven from myths and native superstitions, though he cordially accepted the evidence put forward by honourable 'English gentlemen and officers'. Müller even likens wolf-children to mythical creatures such as sea-serpents: 'Though scotched and killed, they turn up again and again, each time in fuller vigour and supported by more powerful witnesses.'[35] The figure of the wolf-child, then, provided a rich field of investigation, where facts and imagination, myths and Western anxiety about Man's place in nature, heightened by the colonial fear of natives as savage animals, all intersected. This may be why Kipling's father in his *Beast and Man in India* refrained from exploring the topic in detail, stating that the wolf was 'beyond the narrow scope of this sketch',[36] while his son grabbed hold of the fascinating material with both hands, and created out of it Mowgli, one of the most extraordinary of literary characters.

In the *Jungle Books*, Kipling engages with, and rewrites, the myths surrounding wolf-children. For one thing, Mowgli is, as Daniel Karlin points out, 'almost the exact inverse of Sleeman's typical wolf-child', who is 'dumb, savage, filthy and wretched', and cannot be reformed to adapt to the human condition.[37] Mowgli is clean and intelligent, and can quickly pick up the ways and manners of the villagers, including their language. Moreover, his adventures, fabulous and incredible in themselves, are sharply contrasted against native 'superstitions' about wolf-children and animals in the jungle. Mowgli dismisses the jungle tales of Buldeo, the village hunter, as 'cobwebs and moon-talk': 'All the evening I have lain here listening . . . and, except once or twice, Buldeo has not said one word of truth concerning the jungle, which is at his very doors. How then shall I believe the tales of ghosts, and gods, and goblins which he says he has seen?' (p. 55). Conversely, Buldeo, once he witnesses Mowgli command a wolf, brands him a 'jungle-demon' (p. 63) and incites the villagers to turn against him. Considering that Buldeo is a skilled storyteller, who can dazzle the children with his wonderful tales, a rivalry is perhaps discernible between him and Kipling in the art of storytelling: by inventing Mowgli, whose mastery over, and knowledge of, the jungle calls into question the authenticity of native tales, Kipling replaces Buldeo as a true Indian raconteur, and cannily transforms the Indian jungle into an imperial space.

Moreover, Mowgli is also different from the typical wolf-child in that the wolf is hardly the only 'totem' animal whose characteristics he shares. Mowgli is also a 'frog', as his animal friends affectionately call him, and this captures the jumpiness and lightness of his movements. Mowgli the Frog is the name given to him by Mother Wolf, on account of his nakedness and vulnerability as a little human child, calling for the jungle animals' protection. Ironically, the same name also symbolizes his privilege as a human child: his two-worldliness and ability to traverse the jungle and the human world, just as the frog as an amphibian operates both on land and in water. Indeed, Mowgli is above all a 'man-cub', blessed with the charm to attract, and win over, a wide variety of powerful animals; as Harry Rickett humorously puts it, there is 'a queue of would-be foster-parents, falling over each other to look after him'.[38] In particular, he forms strong ties with Baloo, Bagheera and Kaa, each of whom performs the role of his guide and teacher. The bull is also a special animal for Mowgli, as his rights in the wolf-pack are bought by Bagheera in exchange for a bull's life. He is thus commanded 'never [to] kill or eat any cattle young or old' (p. 14) by the Law of the Jungle, and another bull's life is needed to release him from the jungle at the very end of his journey. Some animals, on the other hand, figure as dangers and enemies which Mowgli the young hero has to overcome as part of his growing-up process. In the dramatic story 'Red Dog', for instance, he fights alongside the wolves against the invasion of a large pack of deadly dholes (wild dogs). The dholes represent a threat to the jungle society, and fighting against them helps Mowgli grow into a defender of justice and the Law.

Kipling added another dimension to Mowgli's hybridity as a wolf-child, by highlighting his relationship with two societies. As we have already seen, the Mowgli stories interweave two conflicting themes of childhood: the child's joy in a loving environment and his trauma of abandonment, both of which mirror Kipling's own childhood experience. Although the overall tone is the sense of happiness and fellowship among animals, Mowgli, even before his eventual departure from the jungle, suffers being cast out from it in 'Mowgli's Brothers' and he is expelled from the Indian village in 'Tiger-Tiger!'. Mowgli's double identity is defined by the belonging to, and the rejection by, these two worlds. This is succinctly captured in the song that he sings at the Council Rock (p. 67):

> [. . .] The Jungle is shut to me
>   and the village gates are shut. Why?
> As Mang flies between the beasts and birds, so fly I
>   between the village and the Jungle. Why?

The polarity of Mowgli's two homes is embodied by his two foster-mothers, Mother Wolf in the jungle and Messua in the Indian village. It is through his relationship to these two mothers that he gains membership of their respective communities. The milk with which they feed Mowgli not only symbolizes mother-love, but also facilitates, as a kind of magic potion, his movement from one home to the other: as Jan Montefiore points out, milk, given as food by both human and wolf mothers, 'crosses the divide between humanity and the Jungle'.[39] Ironically, both mothers also represent Mowgli's essential non-belonging to the place which he has made home. Mother Wolf, who loves Mowgli best of all her children, is painfully aware that he is destined to go to Man and does not belong to her. Messua on the other hand gives him the name Nathoo, half believing that he is her long-lost son who was taken by the tiger. It is highly unlikely that Mowgli, a woodcutter's child, is indeed Messua's son, considering that she is the wife of the richest villager. However, the narrator never explicitly denies such a possibility.[40] Their meeting constantly and uneasily draws attention to the ways in which Mowgli might indeed be her son, and this textual uncertainty turns Mowgli into a ghost of Nathoo, prohibiting him from truly settling in Messua's home. In 'The Spring Running', Mowgli is finally freed from this role, as he finds Messua with her new baby boy, who rightfully fills the void which the original Nathoo had left.

Importantly, Mowgli's killing of Shere Khan coincides with the moment in which he is made aware of his double identity. Shere Khan, the chief villain of the *Jungle Books*, represents transgression of the Law, as he repeatedly violates the greatest taboo in the jungle, namely the killing and eating of Man; Mowgli initially enters the jungle as his prey. The pairing of Mowgli and Shere Khan is Kipling's most original innovation on the myth of the wolf-child. They are structurally uncannily similar: just like Mowgli, Shere Khan, as the Man-eater, represents a nexus between the village and the jungle, between civilization and nature, humans and animals. Through their battle, Kipling explores this intersection, and dramatizes the tensions between the two worlds. Shere Khan, Mowgli's arch-enemy, is also his shadow self: just like the tiger, Mowgli is an ultimate outsider, doubly feared and rejected by the two worlds which he forms connections with.

In a sense, Kipling turned the myth of the wolf-child into a *Bildungsroman*, which, according to Elliot L. Gilbert, deals with 'the inner growth of a young person – with his efforts to come to terms with the world as he finds it and to discover his own real nature'.[41] Seen in this light, the wolf-child figures as an adolescent, who, being always an outsider, is compelled to embark on a journey to find his true identity and his place in the world. For Mowgli, the end of his journey ultimately takes the form of his realization of, and coming to terms with, the fact that he is Man. Mowgli's Edenic jungle, the mythical and animal world of fable, then becomes a fixed point against which we measure his steady progress. His education ends when he finally becomes Man in a triple sense (adult-male-human). As he leaves the jungle, he takes his wolf brothers with him as if to say that to command wolves/dogs is an integral part of his humanity.

IV

Mowgli's jungle is ruled by the Law of the Jungle, which is, according to the narrator, 'by far the oldest law in the world' (p. 143). It is made up of a series of rules and practical instructions, covering every aspect of an animal's life. Despite its heavy emphasis on tradition and custom, the rules in the Law are apparently flexible enough to accommodate a new situation. For instance, we are told that the 'real reason' why the Law of the Jungle forbids animals to eat Man is that this leads to 'the arrival of white men on elephants, with guns, and hundreds of brown men with gongs and rockets and torches' (p. 7), which clearly refers to the contemporaneous British rule in India. The Law negotiates tradition and modernity, to generate new codes which fit the living reality – that of the British Empire. Furthermore, Bagheera reinterprets the rules of the Law so that Mowgli can be accepted as a member of the wolf-pack, and this can be read as an interesting allegory of how the British negotiated their way into India eventually to rule its vast territory.

The Law's most striking aspect is its unusual emphasis on order and the virtue of submission: 'the head and the hoof of the Law and the haunch and the hump is – Obey!' (p. 161). Kipling attributes the same principles to the Indian Army in 'Servants of the Queen' ('Her Majesty's Servants' in the American edition), the last episode of *The Jungle Book* (pp. 136–7):

> [the beasts] obey, as the men do. Mule, horse, elephant, or bullock, he obeys his driver, and the driver his sergeant, and the sergeant his lieutenant, and the lieutenant his captain, and the captain his major, and the major his colonel, and the colonel his brigadier commanding three regiments, and the brigadier the general, who obeys the Viceroy, who is the servant of the Empress.

The story takes its inspiration from the Rawal Pindi Durbar, the meeting between the Viceroy Lord Dufferin and the Amir of Afghanistan in 1885, which Kipling reported on as a special correspondent. Afghanistan was a British protectorate, and the Amir was a key player in the 'Great Game' – the rivalry between British India and Russia for dominance in Central Asia. The above quote shows Kipling's desire to see him as part of the grand imperial chain of command, in which animals, and their personal attachment and loyalty to their owners, are made to represent the solidarity of the British Empire. Through the same injunction to 'Obey!', Kipling brings together, and even equates, two representations of animal life in India: one consisting of wild animals following nature's Law and the other figured as a military hierarchy which the domesticated animals willingly submit to. He thereby presents the Raj as the meeting of different spaces, separate yet sharing the same Law, while the uncanny affinity between Mowgli's jungle and British India allows us to see the former as a metonym of the British Empire, embodying Kipling's imperial ideals.

It is interesting that 'Servants of the Queen' deals with the British encounter with native chiefs, considering that the Native States of Rajputana were, as mentioned earlier, the original inspiration for Mowgli's jungle. For instance, the Cold Lairs, the main setting of 'Kaa's Hunting' and 'The King's Ankus', are modelled on the old deserted cities of Amber and Chitor, which Kipling visited during his trip to Rajputana in 1887. Ruined and deserted Indian cities held a special appeal for the British imagination and were popular tourist destinations; as Stephen Montagu Burrows in his 1887 article puts it: 'The two great deserted cities of India, Ambair [Amber] in Rajputana and Fathpur Sikri near Agra, attract every year an increasing swarm of visitors'[42] – and Kipling was one of them. The Native States thus represented a space of exoticism and fantasy embedded within the British Empire. Furthermore, they were powerful allies which the British had to 'tame' to keep. The character of Bagheera, born and raised in the 'King's Palace at Oodeypore' (p. 16), at once represents the power, nobility and exoticism of the Native States, and their brutal treatment of wild animals. He is based on an actual black panther Kipling saw in the king's menagerie in Udaipur (Oodeypore), and it was also in this state that he, to his horror, witnessed panthers being driven and wantonly killed for pleasure and as a show of the state's power in the king's game reserve.[43] These Native States, though subjected to British rule by separate treaties, were able to exercise absolute power over the animal life in their realm. In the Mowgli stories, Kipling liberates the panther from the cage and thereby the power of the Native States, and explores a more 'natural' relationship with wild animals which the British Empire can take pride in. In this way, the British Raj can claim its rights as protector over them, and over the immense land of India which they inhabit, in which the native princes themselves figure as wild animals and powerful allies to be subjugated.

The *Jungle Books* are predominantly presented as a boy's playground, inhabited by young heroes such as Mowgli, Toomai, Rikki-tikki-tavi, Kotick and Kotuko, and affinities between the *Jungle Books* and imperialist ideologies can also be seen in the fact that the Mowgli stories famously provided the basis for the 'Wolf Cubs' (now 'Cub Scouts'), the junior section of the Boy Scouting Movement, which was set up in 1916. The Boy Scouts has its origin in the British Empire, having been created in 1907 by Lieutenant-General Robert Baden-Powell – the hero of the siege of Mafeking, which took place during the Boer War – in order to train boys for future military operations through outdoor activities and play. In his *The Wolf Cub's Handbook* (1916), Baden-Powell, with Kipling's permission, makes extensive use of materials from the *Jungle Books*.[44] Young scouts, just like Mowgli, are required to become 'wolves' with strong and healthy bodies, to whom the Law of the Jungle teaches the practical rules and skills necessary for daily survival, as well as discipline and order. These scouts shared the same spirit with, and were expected eventually to become, 'the frontiersmen in the wilder parts of our Empire', who included the 'backwoodsmen, the hunters, the explorers, the map-makers, our soldiers and sailors, the Arctic navigators, the missionaries': 'all those men of our race who are living out in the wild, facing difficulties and dangers because it is their duty, enduring hardships, looking after themselves, keeping up the name of Britons for bravery, kindness, and justice all over the world – those are the scouts of the nation to-day – they are the "Wolves" '.[45] When Baden-Powell wrote these lines, the British Empire was suffering from the devastating effects of the First World War, but the *Jungle Books* could always offer an inspiration and hope for the renewed strength and vitality of imperial manhood.

Mowgli's jungle is presented as a space of friendship and hospitality, in which different nations and races co-exist harmoniously under the ultimate authority of the White Man. Mowgli's animal friends thus represent law-abiding colonial subjects who would not, and cannot, disobey the White Man whom Mowgli as Man (a species apart) stands in for. As John McClure puts it: 'To be above yet to belong, to be obeyed as a god and loved as a brother, this is Kipling's dream for the imperial ruler, a dream that Mowgli achieves.'[46] The use of animals, who can be tamed and who would not talk back in human tongues, facilitates the construction and perpetuation of such a colonial fantasy.

The Mowgli stories have been much criticized for their racialist characterization of natives. Not only are the villagers negatively represented, but there is also an uneasy slippage between them and Mowgli's demonized animal adversaries. Take, for example, the *Bandar-log*, the 'Monkey People', to whom Mowgli likens the Indian villagers: 'Chatter – chatter! Talk, talk! Men are blood-brothers of the *Bandar-log*' (p. 188). These monkeys are the outcasts of the jungle society, 'portrayed as idle and senseless because they lack any organization or any code of social conduct', almost, as Mark Paffard points out, in the same manner as the Yahoos in *Gulliver's Travels* (1726).[47] The *Bandar-log* have been interpreted as a political allegory of, to quote Green, 'the Americans or the Liberals, or such "lesser breeds without the Law" as [. . .] Kipling was most anxious to insult at the moment of writing'.[48] Seen in the colonial context, they symbolize the subversive and untameable side of colonial subjectivity: 'a colonial psyche, a maddening, or already maddened, form of identity that threatens the stability of colonial rule'.[49] For Nirad C. Chaudhuri, a famous Bengali writer, the *Bandar-log* are nothing but the caricature of Bengali intellectuals or Babus, who were, to Kipling's eyes, alarmingly anglicizing themselves to seek independence. Chaudhuri draws attention to the representation of the monkeys as 'evil, dirty, shameless', their only desire being to be 'noticed by the Jungle-People', who of course stand here for the British, and he argues that the *Bandar-log*'s lack of leaders, principles or perseverance reveals Kipling's awareness, and ridiculing, of the 'role that the Bengalis were playing' in their striving for independence.[50]

The *Bandar-log*, who are numerous, also represent the fear of the natives turning into an ungovernable mob, and Kaa, who can force them to walk into his mouth with his mesmerizing Hunger Dance, is invented as a guardian against such threat. The Indian village figures as another community of the *Bandar-log*, a dystopia sharply contrasted with the Edenic and utopian nature of the jungle. The villagers are characterized as much more 'savage' than the *Bandar-log*, precisely because they are 'human', and unlike jungle beasts are capable of trapping, torturing and killing each other for their superstitions and especially for money. Human avarice is the central theme of 'The King's Ankus', while in 'Letting in the Jungle', the villagers trap Messua and her husband with the intention of killing them in order to lay hands on their cattle and land. When Mowgli mobilizes the jungle animals and wipes out the village, Kipling conflates his misanthropic drive against the barbaric and corrupt side of human nature, which the natives are made to represent, with the colonial fantasy of driving the natives out of sight. Either way, this racist representation of natives serves as a justification for the presence of the White Man, as an embodiment of lawfulness, fairness and even humanity itself.

The 'Indian Mutiny' of 1857, the biggest crisis in the history of the Raj during which natives rose against the British, marked a significant turning point in British colonial rule: once suppressed, it contributed to consolidating the Raj, as the British Government immediately took over the Indian administration from the East India Company, and placed India under direct

Crown rule. Don Randall fittingly terms the *Jungle Books* 'Post-Mutiny Allegories of Empire';[51] in this context, the hunting of Shere Khan can be seen as the restaging and rewriting of the suppression of the Indian Mutiny as an imperial myth, especially given that tigers in the nineteenth century symbolized the ferocious and untameable side of India.[52] Mowgli's fight with Shere Khan becomes elevated into the eternal battle between Man and Beast, which, according to Hathi in 'How Fear Came', originated in the killing of Man by the first of the Tigers, just as the Indian Mutiny was always represented as British 'retaliation' against native atrocities. Hathi's story silently edits out any suggestion that the British/Man might have acted inappropriately to provoke the attack from the natives/tigers.

If many of the stories in the *Jungle Books* seem openly to celebrate the workings of Empire, however, 'The Undertakers' in *The Second Jungle Book* interestingly suggests the existence of many unofficial stories circulating among natives or even animals, which have to be suppressed by any means. The story takes the form of a conversation between three scavengers living on the periphery of British rule: the Mugger, a man-eating crocodile, the Jackal and the Adjutant-crane. Their version of the Indian Mutiny is given in the reminiscences of the Mugger, who toured around the affected area and made a feast of dead bodies during the event. The fact that he regrets the missed opportunity of eating a white child during the rebellion represents latent insubordination against British rule and the possibility of another mutiny. The story ends with the shooting of the Mugger by the white child, who has now grown up to be a bridge-builder, thereby 'safely' terminating the lingering native threat. Yet, the two other scavengers live on, and with them the native underworld which passes on the Mugger's version of the story. This story should be read in conjunction with another of Kipling's stories, 'The Bridge-Builders' (collected in *The Day's Work*, 1898), in which the Mugger represents Mother Ganga, the River Ganges personified, who resents having been harnessed by the British bridges. The Mugger is the embodiment of the power of Indian nature, which, like the Mutiny, the British had to suppress in order to consolidate their rule.

Mowgli is often compared to the eponymous hero of Kipling's novel *Kim* (1901), an Irish orphan brought up as an Indian among natives. Kim, just like Mowgli, leads a double life: on the one hand, a *chela* (disciple) to his beloved lama – whom he accompanies on the latter's quest to be freed from the Wheel of Life – and, on the other hand, an 'English' boy who delights in his role as a secret agent in the Great Game. Both Kim and Mowgli enjoy the privileged position of a favourite child among the 'native' people, Kim's whiteness and Mowgli's humanity endowing each with natural superiority; both, because of their double allegiance, experience an identity crisis as part of their growing-up process. A big difference, however, is that Kim, unlike Mowgli, never experiences open hostility from the two worlds he belongs to. Edward Said has noted 'the absence of conflict' in *Kim*, which he interprets as reflecting Kipling's absolute belief in the righteousness of British rule: 'not because Kipling could not face it, but because for Kipling *there was no conflict*' in British India.[53] In contrast, the *Jungle Books* are built around conflicts, which are naturalized by the jungle setting, where animals fight each other for survival and any disagreements are settled by violence. It may be that the fabulous use of talking animals enables the narrative to give expression to conflicts and contradictions within the British Raj, without directly admitting their existence. For instance, the casting out of Mowgli from both the village and the jungle can be read as an anxiety that British rule might be rejected by the majority of the populace. Though Mowgli has many powerful patrons in the jungle, only a handful of beasts see him off as he leaves, and Messua is the only person in the village whom he trusts.

V

Mowgli made his first appearance prior to the *Jungle Books*, in a story called 'In the Rukh', first collected in *Many Inventions* (1893). This tells how the grown-up Mowgli meets Indian

Forestry Officers, and impresses them with his thorough knowledge of the forest animals; he is consequently offered
employment in the Indian Forestry, which enables him to marry
and start a family. In postcolonial readings of the *Jungle Books*,
'In the Rukh' has been a key text which clearly demonstrates
Mowgli's place in the imperial order. It provides historical and
ideological contexts that are made obscure in the *Jungle Books*,
and gives a sense of closure to the Mowgli saga as an imperial
myth. On the other hand, many scholars have, as W. W. Robson
puts it, felt that 'In the Rukh' does not 'really belong to the
same imaginative or daemonic impulse' as other Mowgli
stories, 'without necessarily being able to articulate their reasons'.[54] For instance, J. M. S. Tompkins feels that 'the Mowgli
of "In the Rukh" does not quite tally with the Mowgli of *The
Jungle Books*',[55] while Karlin similarly argues that the story is
'a half-baked anticipation' of Mowgli in the *Jungle Books*, and
should be considered as only one of many other 'indifferent
writing[s] which contributed to the making of Mowgli'.[56]

'In the Rukh' can of course be read independently of the
Jungle Books and we have no obligation to accept Mowgli's
future as an imperial forest guard. Indeed, those who have
enjoyed the magical world of the *Jungle Books* might rather
not learn of Mowgli's concern with such mundane matters as
his pension. On the other hand, it is difficult to dismiss the fact
that Kipling considered the Mowgli of 'In the Rukh' to be the
same Mowgli that we find in the *Jungle Books*. Reprinting the
story in *McClure's Magazine* in 1896, Kipling, in his marginal
note, describes it as 'the first written of the Mowgli stories,
though it deals with the closing chapters of his career – namely,
his introduction to white men, his marriage and civilization'.[57]
He subsequently incorporated 'In the Rukh' in the 1897 'Outward Bound' edition of the *Jungle Books*, in which all the
Mowgli stories are collected and rearranged in one volume,
while the non-Mowgli stories are put together to form the
second volume (see the Note on the Texts).[58] 'In the Rukh' also
appears in *All the Mowgli Stories* of 1933 as the last in the
Mowgli saga. In this present edition, the story is included as an

appendix, in order to honour the supplementary relationship which it has with the *Jungle Books*. This arrangement has the advantage of showing visually that the two texts are located outside of each other, just as Mowgli has to leave the jungle to start his adult life.

'In the Rukh', in fact, has much in common with one of the 'non-Mowgli' stories, 'Toomai of the Elephants', in that both stories show the working of the Indian Government in full operation. 'Toomai of the Elephants' is set during the Government's yearly expedition to the Garo hills to capture wild elephants for its service. The hero of this tale is the native boy Little Toomai, who is the son of a mahout, and whose privileged relationship with Kala Naga the elephant can be likened to Mowgli's close ties with the animals in the jungle. He is carried deep into the forest on the back of Kala Naga and witnesses an elephant dance which no man has ever seen, just as Mowgli obtains a thorough knowledge of the jungle which no white man can be privy to. The success of the Indian Government greatly depends upon the inclusion of these native boys whom the animals willingly obey.

'Toomai of the Elephants' implicitly characterizes the British as benign and diligent rulers who strive to cultivate better relationships with the natural world in India. Notably, it showcases the new technique of catching a whole herd of elephants by driving them into a stockade (*keddah*), which was pioneered by George Peress Sanderson in the 1870s. The British way of elephant-catching not only created a great spectacle, but was thought to be more humane than the traditional and commonly used method of catching single elephants by pitfalls or traps; in 'Letting in the Jungle', for instance, we learn that Hathi was once badly injured by 'the sharpened stake in the pit' (p. 195) which he had fallen into, and this is the reason why he, with his three sons, 'let in the jungle' upon five Indian villages to drive men away. The British colonizer's new identity as the protector of nature is also the central theme of 'In the Rukh'. The word *rukh*, in the vocabulary of the local government of Punjab, where Kipling had worked as a journalist, referred to 'a forest

reserve', a land specially set apart by Government for the growing of grass or timber for fuel. It originally derived from the
Punjabi word *rakkhna*, to keep or set apart, as did the term
rakkha, a protector or guardian. The word well encapsulates
the Indian Government's new, conservational attitude to
nature. By the mid-nineteenth century, it had become clear that
natural resources, declining through rapid deforestation, would
not be able to meet the growing want of fuel, created by the
building of new railway systems and the accompanying devel-
opments. Thus plots of government land, or 'rukhs', were
selected for plantation and reforestation. It is therefore *in the
rukh* that both 'nature' and a new imperial subjectivity as a
guardian of nature were invented. Mowgli the wolf-boy,
'altogether of the jungle' (p. 320), magically emerges in this
rukh where he gives the new man-managed nature his seal of
approval and authenticity. More importantly, he is the embodiment of man's new relationship with nature: the vigilant and
constant gaze over nature as an enclosed space of protection. It
must have been with considerable pride and excitement that
Kipling emphasized that Mowgli's true and noble origin was
'in the rukh'.

The *Jungle Books* register the contemporaneous concern
over diminishing nature and animal life, and were read in that
context: one of the early reviewers observed that 'as the wild
animals of the world become rarer and fewer, the sentiment of
interest in them felt by civilized people grows keener'.[59] When
Kipling was writing the *Jungle Books*, the myth of a great
abundance of animals in nature, which had propelled the cult
of hunting in the colonies, and thus enabled imperialism to
be characterized throughout the nineteenth century as a masculine and heroic endeavour, began gradually to be dispelled as
the realities of overhunting and overexploitation of animals
were being brought to public attention.[60] Kipling, through the
figure of Mowgli, glamorizes a new type of hunter, who does
not kill unnecessarily. 'Good hunting' is the standard greeting
in the jungle, and the Law dictates that one should 'Hunt . . .
for food, but not for pleasure' (p. 26). Killing is otherwise

justified only when there is a threat to life or to the community, as in the case of Shere Khan or the dholes in 'Red Dog'. Kipling's hero is a new Man who has learned nature's law.

Kipling's awareness of the anthropocentric violence that Man exercises over animals and its devastating consequences can be most clearly seen in 'The White Seal', in which he attacks international sealing, which was driving fur seals to the brink of extinction. It tells the story of Kotick the White Seal, a native of a seal island off the coast of Alaska, who becomes determined to find a peaceful hiding-place for his people, after witnessing men's brutal clubbing of his friends to death. This story is a rewriting from a seal's point of view of Henry Wood Elliott's book *The Seal-Islands of Alaska* (1881), which includes a long list of rookeries (breeding colonies) in which fur seals were harvested to extinction. Kipling invites us to travel with Kotick across the Seven Seas to visit every one of them, only to hear the same devastating news: 'men had killed them all off' (p. 79). Kotick, guided by Sea Cow, eventually finds a perfect sanctuary, but this happy ending has been read as suggesting ironically the eventual destruction of seals, as the Sea Cow is an extinct species of manatee which had been exterminated soon after Europeans discovered it in the eighteenth century. As Karlin beautifully puts it, 'salvation has become a *figure of speech* for the seals' gradual extinction'.[61]

'The White Seal' was originally written in response to Anglo-American tension over the rights to hunt seals in the Bering Sea in the early 1890s, during which Elliott, who had previously advocated seal-hunting in Alaska, emerged as a vehement critic of the indiscriminate hunting of seals, after witnessing the drastic fall of the seal population of once abundant rookeries over a period of ten years.[62] Kipling clearly sides with Elliott in his campaign, and this explains the story's sensationalist tone regarding the imminent threat of extinction of seals. The story made a timely appearance in the *National Review*, a few weeks before the dispute was finally resolved by international arbitration in August 1893. It is also important to note the symbolism of the 'whiteness' of Kotick, who guides his people to safety.

This represents the importance of Anglo-American unity to end the dispute, as well as of the white men's leadership in the cause of safeguarding nature, making amends for the past in which they had been the major force in destroying nature in the first place.

In the *Jungle Books* we gain an insight into the complex and often contradictory relationships which Man has had with nature, especially because the books draw our attention to, and are built upon, the anthropocentric supposition that he is the absolute Master of the animals, while giving expression to the force and brutality with which he subjugates them. Mowgli's power as Man is most succinctly symbolized by the power of his gaze, which his animal friends cannot return when he stares at them. If Adam the first Man gains control over animals by the act of naming, Mowgli does the same by seeing and knowing them, thus striking fear into their hearts. His relationship with animals also echoes God's promise to Noah: 'the fear of you and the dread of you shall be upon every beast of the earth' (Genesis 9: 2); this promise informs the foundational myth of the jungle told by Hathi in 'How Fear Came', which explains why animals 'of all things . . . most fear Man' (p. 151). In a dramatic moment in 'Letting in the Jungle', Mowgli forces the rebellious Bagheera into submission by resorting to the power of his gaze and his human speech. This puts Bagheera in his place, turning him into Mowgli's loving companion ('I am only a black panther. But I love thee, Little Brother', p. 192), while also successfully consolidating Man's special position in the animal world ('Thou art of the Jungle and *not* of the Jungle', p. 192). Although this scene is often read straightforwardly as an allegorical illustration of the colonial relationship between the colonizer and the colonized, it should be seen primarily as illustrating that between Man and animals and as another proof of how Man's control over the animal kingdom is at the core of any colonial relationship. Here we see laid bare the limitation of Kipling's dream of a brotherhood of humans and animals, inspired by the Oriental religious tradition: it is only allowed to function within the biblical framework of man's absolute dominance over animals, and this gives Bagheera's plea to his 'Little Brother' a hollow and ironic ring.

Kipling's *Jungle Books* are a unique textual space in which conflicting worlds and discourses co-exist: India and Britain, Man and nature, the primordial origin of humanity and our modernity, a child's dream jungle and the adult world of Work, heartfelt adoration of the Orient and crude racism, among other things. Mowgli inhabits the intersections between these, and is characteristically marked by duality: through the figure of the wolf-boy, Kipling invents a new myth of the modern man. Moreover, Kipling recognizes the worlds of animals, both real and imaginary, as an integral part of his Empire, with which we form intimate connections. The books are ultimately a precious record of the human-animal relationships that existed in the Raj in the late nineteenth century. By the time Kipling was compiling his notes for the Sussex Edition of the *Jungle Books*, published posthumously in 1937, some of the descriptions had already become out of date. His note for 'the bullocks and elephants of the big-gun batteries of 40-pound Armstrong guns' informs us that they 'are not needed now that machinery has come into fashion, and the batteries were abolished long ago'.[63] These animals whom Kipling met in India had now disappeared, receding into the past and the imagination.

Kaori Nagai 2013

NOTES

1. Letter to Mr Bower, 28 November 1895, in Rudyard Kipling, *Two Christmas Letters*, ed. David Alan Richards (privately printed, 2011). The letter is part of the David Alan Richards Kipling Collection, at the Beinecke Rare Book and Manuscript Library, Yale University. I would like to thank Mr Richards and the Beinecke Library for permission to quote from the letter.

2. Rudyard Kipling, *Something of Myself and Other Autobio-graphical Writings*, ed. Thomas Pinney (Cambridge: Cambridge University Press, 1990), pp. 67–8 and 122.

3. Rosemary Sutcliff, 'Kipling for Children', *Kipling Journal* 156 (December 1965), p. 25.

4. Ibid.

5. Kipling's letter to Mary Mapes Dodge, 21 February 1892, in Thomas Pinney (ed.), *The Letters of Rudyard Kipling*, 6 vols. (Basingstoke: Macmillan, 1990–2004), vol. 2, p. 49.

6. Roger Lancelyn Green, *Kipling and the Children* (London: Elek Books, 1965), p. 9.

7. 'Manuscript page from "Mowgli's Brother"', February 1893, reproduced in Lucile Russell Carpenter, *Rudyard Kipling: A Friendly Profile* (Chicago: Argus Books, 1942). See also note 3 to 'Mowgli's Brothers' (p. 341).

8. For further discussion about Kipling's change of the location of Mowgli's jungle from Mewar to Seoni, see, for example, 'Mowgli's Other Jungle', *Kipling Journal* 167 (September 1968), pp. 2–3, and John Slater, 'Seeonee: The Site of Mowgli's Jungle?', and Rhona Ghate, 'Kipling's Jungle: Fact or Fancy?' (originally published in *The March of India* 12/12 (December 1960)), both of which can be found on the Kipling Society website: www.kipling.org.uk/rg_junglebooks.htm.

9. Kipling, *Something of Myself*, p. 5.

10. John McBratney, *Imperial Subjects, Imperial Space: Rudyard Kipling's Fiction of the Native-Born* (Columbus: Ohio State University Press, 2002).

11. A native proverb, quoted in Rudyard Kipling, *Life's Handicap: Being Stories of Mine Own People*, ed. P. N. Furbank (London: Penguin, 1987), p. 3.

12. Ibid., p. 26.

13. Rudyard Kipling, 'Author's Notes on the Names in *The Jungle Books*', in *The Sussex Edition of the Complete Works in Prose and Verse of Rudyard Kipling*, vol. 12, *The Jungle Books* (London: Macmillan, 1937), p. 267.

14. Rudyard Kipling, 'Simla Notes', *Civil and Military Gazette*, 24 June 1885, collected in Thomas Pinney (ed.), *Kipling's India: Uncollected Sketches 1884–88* (Basingstoke: Macmillan, 1986), pp. 104–8. Kipling's experience of the Simla monkeys was also fictionalized in 'Collar-Wallah and the Poison Stick', published in *St Nicholas* magazine in February 1893.

15. John Lockwood Kipling, *Beast and Man in India: A Popular Sketch of Indian Animals in Their Relations with the People*, 2nd edn. (London: Macmillan, 1904).

16. For his father's book, Kipling composed verse epigraphs for the following chapters: 'Of Monkeys', 'Of Asses', 'Of Goats and Sheep', 'Of Buffaloes and Pigs', 'Of Elephants', 'Of Camels', 'Of Reptiles', 'Animal Calls' and 'Of Animals and the Supernatural'. He also contributed a poem for 'Of Cows and Oxen' (later collected in *Songs from Books* (1912) under the title of 'The Oxen') and, for 'Of Horses and Mules', a stanza from his early poem 'The Sudder Bazaar' (1884), with a description of a pony pulling an *ekka* (a light carriage used in India). 'Of Cows and Oxen' also features two illustrations by John Lockwood Kipling, entitled 'In Time of Drought' and 'In a Good Season', both of which are framed by four lines of verse by his son. Those framing 'In a Good Season' are taken from Kipling's poem 'What the People Said' (1887).

17. John Lockwood Kipling, *Beast and Man in India*, p. 250.

18. Kipling, *Something of Myself*, pp. 67–8.

19. Lancelyn Green, *Kipling and the Children*, p. 117.

20. 'The Jungle Book', *Saturday Review* 77 (1894), p. 639.

21. Kipling, *Something of Myself*, p. 127.

22. Charles G. D. Roberts, *The Kindred of the Wild: A Book of Animal Life* (Boston: L. C. Page, 1907), p. 27.

23. Ernest Thompson Seton, *Trail of an Artist-naturalist* (New York: Charles Scribner's Sons, 1948), p. 353.

24. Edward B. Tylor, *Primitive Culture: Researches into the Development of Mythology, Philosophy, Religion, Language, Art, and Custom* (1871), 4th edn. (London: John Murray, 1903), p. 409.

25. Kipling's letter to Edward Everett Hale, 16 January 1895, in Pinney (ed.), *Letters*, vol. 2, p. 168.

26. Ibid.

27. Letter to Joel Chandler Harris, 6 December 1895, in Pinney (ed.), *Letters*, vol. 2, p. 217. Kipling later fictionalizes this episode in one of the Stalky stories, 'The United Idolaters', collected in *Debits and Credits* (1926).

28. J. M. S. Tompkins, *The Art of Rudyard Kipling*, 2nd edn. (London: Methuen, 1965), p. 68.

29. Ibid., p. 69.

30. 'Beast-fables', *Chamber's Encyclopaedia: A Dictionary of Universal Knowledge*, vol. 1 (London: William & Robert Chambers, 1908), pp. 821–2.

31. Friedrich Max Müller, 'On the Migration of Fables', in *Chips from a German Workshop*, vol. 4 (London: Longmans, Green & Co., 1875), p. 146.

32. Letter to Brander Matthews, 7 February 1905, in Pinney (ed.), *Letters*, vol. 3, p. 176.

33. John Lockwood Kipling, *Beast and Man in India*, p. 281.

34. *Account of Wolves Nurturing Children in Their Dens. By an Indian Official* (Plymouth: Jenkin Thomas, 1852). Sleeman's pamphlet, originally published anonymously, was an extract from his long official report to the Indian Government, which was later posthumously published as *A Journey through the Kingdom of Oude* (1858).

35. Friedrich Max Müller, 'Wolf-Children', *Academy*, 7 November 1874, pp. 512–13.

36. John Lockwood Kipling, *Beast and Man in India*, p. 281.

37. Daniel Karlin, 'Introduction' to Rudyard Kipling, *The Jungle Books* (London: Penguin Classics, 2000), pp. 17–18.

38. Harry Ricketts, *The Unforgiving Minute: A Life of Rudyard Kipling* (London: Chatto & Windus, 1999), p. 207.

39. Jan Montefiore, 'Kipling as a children's writer and the *Jungle Books*', in Howard Booth (ed.), *The Cambridge Companion to Rudyard Kipling* (Cambridge: Cambridge University Press, 2011), p. 106.

40. It is interesting to note that in Kipling's *The Jungle Play* (see the Note on the Texts) it is made very clear that Mowgli is *not* Nathoo; as the story explores Mowgli's romance with Messua's daughter Dulia, this is to avoid any hint of incest (*The Jungle Play* (London: Penguin Books, 2001), p. 30).

41. Elliot L. Gilbert, *The Good Kipling: Studies in the Short Story* (Manchester: Manchester University Press, 1972), p. 71.

42. S. M. Burrows, 'A City of Granite', *Macmillan's Magazine* 56 (1887), p. 354.

43. Rudyard Kipling, 'Letters of Marque', in *From Sea to Sea and Other Sketches: Letters of Travel* (London: Macmillan, 1900), vol. 1, p. 72.

44. For the relationship between Kipling and the Boy Scout Movement, see Hugh Brogan, *Mowgli's Sons: Kipling and Baden-Powell's Scouts* (London: Cape, 1987).

45. Lord Baden-Powell of Gilwell, *The Wolf Cub's Handbook*, 9th edn. (London: C. Arthur Pearson, 1938), p. 23.

46. John A. McClure, *Kipling and Conrad: The Colonial Fiction* (Cambridge, Mass., and London: Harvard University Press, 1981), p. 60.

47. Mark Paffard, *Kipling's Indian Fiction* (London: Macmillan, 1989), p. 93.

48. Lancelyn Green, *Kipling and the Children*, p. 120.

49. Jopi Nyman, *Postcolonial Animal Tale from Kipling to Coetzee* (New Delhi: Atlantic, 2003), p. 44.

50. Nirad C. Chaudhuri, *Thy Hand, Great Anarch! India: 1921–1952* (London: Chatto & Windus, 1987), p. 672.

51. The subtitle of chapter 2 in Don Randall, *Kipling's Imperial Boy: Adolescence and Cultural Hybridity* (Basingstoke: Palgrave Macmillan, 2000).

52. The tiger metaphor was repeatedly evoked during the Mutiny to paint the mutineers as ferocious and bloodthirsty villains. In a *Punch* cartoon entitled 'The British Lion's Vengeance on the Bengal Tiger', for instance, a male lion representing Britain pounces on a tiger preying on a white woman with a baby in her arms (*Punch* 33 (22 August 1857), pp. 76–7).

53. Edward W. Said, *Culture and Imperialism* (London: Vintage, 1994), p. 176.

54. W. W. Robson, 'Introduction' to Rudyard Kipling, *The Jungle Books* (Oxford: Oxford University Press, 1992), p. xiv.

55. Tompkins, *The Art of Rudyard Kipling*, p. 68.

56. Karlin, 'Introduction', p. 13.

57. Rudyard Kipling, 'In the Rukh: Mowgli's Introduction to White Men', *McClure's Magazine* 7 (June 1896), p. 23.

58. It is worth noting that the 'Outward Bound' edition does not include *Many Inventions*, as all the stories in that collection, including 'In the Rukh', were dispersed into different volumes, in accordance with the edition's policy of '[grouping] the stories by their subjects' (Rudyard Kipling, ' "Outward Bound" Edition: Preface', in *The Writings in Prose and Verse of Rudyard Kipling*, vol. 1 (New York: Charles Scribner's Sons, 1897), p. vii). For instance, the stories about Mulvaney, Kipling's famous Irish character, such as 'My Lord the Elephant' and ' "Love-o'-Women" ', in *Many Inventions*, were incorporated in *Soldiers Three and Military Tales* (vols. 2 and 3 of the 'Outward Bound' edition).

59. 'The Jungle Book', *Saturday Review* 77 (1894), p. 639.

60. For the significance of hunting in the imperial context, see, for instance, John M. MacKenzie, *The Empire of Nature: Hunting, Conservation and British Imperialism* (Manchester and New York: Manchester University Press, 1988), and his edited collection, *Imperialism and the Natural World* (Manchester and New York: Manchester University Press, 1990).

61. Karlin, 'Introduction', p. 11.
62. See Charles S. Campbell, Jr, 'The Anglo-American Crisis in the Bering Sea, 1890–1891', *Mississippi Valley Historical Review* 48/3 (December 1961), pp. 393–414.
63. Rudyard Kipling, 'Author's Notes on the Names in *The Jungle Books*', p. 478.

Note on the Texts

The text of this edition is based on the first English editions of *The Jungle Book* and *The Second Jungle Book*, published in May 1894 and November 1895 respectively by Macmillan in London. 'The King's Ankus' in this first edition of *The Second Jungle Book* abruptly ends with 'lay the ruby-and-turquoise ankus' (p. 241), making it about 500 words shorter than it should be. The missing text was restored in the first reprint in December 1895 and is incorporated here. Misprints present in the first English editions have been silently corrected in consultation with the later editions. The text for 'In the Rukh', first published in *Many Inventions* (1893) and included here as an appendix, is taken from the Sussex Edition of Rudyard Kipling's complete works (published by Macmillan in 1937–9), which incorporates Kipling's final corrections. Throughout this present edition, '-ise' spellings have been standardized to '-ize', according to Penguin house style.

The English editions appeared simultaneously with the first American editions of *The Jungle Book* and *The Second Jungle Book*, published in New York by Century. There are slight differences between the English and American texts, most notably in some of the animal characters' names: Chil (the kite), Sahi (the porcupine) and Mor (the peacock) are respectively Rann, Ikki and Mao in the American editions. 'Servants of the Queen' in *The Jungle Book* is entitled 'Her Majesty's Servants' in the American edition. These and other differences are recorded in the Notes.

All the stories in the *Jungle Books* were originally published as journal articles, many of which appeared in both Britain and

America. The first to be published was 'The White Seal' in the *National Review* in August 1893. *St Nicholas* magazine, a popular American children's periodical, published five of the stories collected in the *Jungle Books*, including 'Mowgli's Brothers' and 'Tiger-Tiger!', the first two Mowgli stories which Kipling wrote for the *Jungle Books*. Another American periodical, *McClure's Magazine*, published four of the stories, and also republished 'In the Rukh' in June 1896 with an introductory note by Kipling. In England, many of the stories appeared in the 'Pall Mall' publications, such as the *Pall Mall Magazine* and the *Pall Mall Gazette*. See Notes (pp. 339–81) for further information.

The first edition of *The Jungle Book* contained illustrations by John Lockwood Kipling, William Henry Drake and Paul Frenzeny, those of the latter two having originally appeared in the journal publications. John Lockwood Kipling was the sole illustrator of the first edition of *The Second Jungle Book*.

The 1897 'Outward Bound' edition of the *Jungle Books* incorporates 'In the Rukh' as the last story in the Mowgli saga, and rearranges the stories into two parts (see also note 59 to the Introduction). *The Jungle Book* of this edition contains all the Mowgli stories in the following order, tracing chronologically Mowgli's growth from childhood to adulthood: 'Mowgli's Brothers', 'Kaa's Hunting', 'How Fear Came', 'Tiger! Tiger!', 'Letting in the Jungle', 'The King's Ankus', 'Red Dog', 'The Spring Running' and 'In the Rukh'; this arrangement of the Mowgli stories was adopted in *All the Mowgli Stories* (1933). In *The Second Jungle Book*, all the other stories were collected in the following order: 'Rikki-Tikki-Tavi', 'The White Seal', 'Toomai of the Elephants', 'Quiquern', 'The Undertakers', 'The Miracle of Purun Bhagat', and 'Her Majesty's Servants'. This arrangement was followed in the Sussex Edition, except that it excludes 'In the Rukh' from part I of the *Jungle Books*. (In the Sussex Edition, 'In the Rukh' was collected in volume 5, *Many Inventions*.)

Kipling's manuscripts of the *Jungle Books* are held by the British Library, with strict instructions that they should not be used to collate any published edition. The manuscript for a play by Kipling, entitled *The Jungle Play*, was discovered comparatively recently and first published in 2001. Loosely based on the Mowgli stories in the *Jungle Books*, it was written around 1900–1901, 'evidently with serious intent for performance and publication, and then put away and forgotten for a century' (Thomas Pinney, 'Introduction' to Rudyard Kipling, *The Jungle Play* (London: Penguin Classics, 2001), p. ix).

Kaori Nagai 2013

Further Reading

SOME OTHER WORKS BY KIPLING

The Day's Work (1898), ed. Constantine Phipps (London: Penguin Books, 1988).

A Diversity of Creatures (1917), ed. Paul Driver (London: Penguin Books, 1987).

From Sea to Sea and Other Sketches: Letters of Travel, 2 vols. (London: Macmillan, 1900).

The Jungle Play, ed. Thomas Pinney (London: Penguin Books, 2001).

Just So Stories (1902), ed. Judith Plotz (London: Penguin Books, 2011).

Kim (1901), ed. Harish Trivedi (London: Penguin Books, 2011).

Kipling's India: Uncollected Sketches 1884–88, ed. Thomas Pinney (Basingstoke: Macmillan, 1986).

Life's Handicap: Being Stories of Mine Own People (1891), ed. P. N. Furbank (London: Penguin Books, 1987).

Many Inventions (London: Macmillan, 1893).

The Naulahka: A Story of East and West, written in collaboration with Wolcott Balestier (London: William Heinemann, 1892).

Land and Sea Tales for Scouts and Guides (London: Macmillan, 1923).

Something of Myself and Other Autobiographical Writings, ed. Thomas Pinney (Cambridge: Cambridge University Press, 1990).

BIBLIOGRAPHY AND REFERENCE

Harbord, R. E. (ed.), *The Readers' Guide to Rudyard Kipling's Work*, 8 vols. (Canterbury: Gibbs, 1961–72).

Martindell, Ernest Walter, *A Bibliography of the Works of Rudyard Kipling* (London: Bookman's Journal, 1922).

New Readers' Guide to the Works of Rudyard Kipling (available through the Kipling Society's website: www.kipling.org.uk).

Richards, David A., *Rudyard Kipling: A Bibliography* (New Castle, Delaware: Oak Knoll Press, 2010).

Stewart, James, *Rudyard Kipling: A Bibliographical Catalogue* (Toronto: Dalhousie University Press and University of Toronto Press, 1959).

BIOGRAPHY AND LETTERS

Allen, Charles, *Kipling Sahib: India and the Making of Rudyard Kipling* (London: Little, Brown, 2007).

Birkenhead, Lord, *Rudyard Kipling* (London: Weidenfeld & Nicolson, 1978).

Carrington, Charles, *Rudyard Kipling: His Life and Work* (London: Macmillan, 1955).

Gilmour, David, *The Long Recessional: The Imperial Life of Rudyard Kipling* (London: John Murray, 2002).

Kipling, Rudyard, *The Letters of Rudyard Kipling*, ed. Thomas Pinney, 6 vols. (Basingstoke: Macmillan, 1990–2004).

Lycett, Andrew, *Rudyard Kipling* (London: Weidenfeld & Nicolson, 1999).

Ricketts, Harry, *The Unforgiving Minute: A Life of Rudyard Kipling* (London: Chatto & Windus, 1999).

Wilson, Angus, *The Strange Ride of Rudyard Kipling* (London: Secker & Warburg, 1977).

HISTORICAL AND LITERARY
BACKGROUND

Brogan, Hugh, *Mowgli's Sons: Kipling and Baden-Powell's Scouts* (London: Cape, 1987).

Cosslett, Tess, *Talking Animals in British Children's Fiction, 1786–1914* (Aldershot: Ashgate Publishing, 2006).

MacKenzie, John M., *The Empire of Nature: Hunting, Conservation and British Imperialism* (Manchester and New York: Manchester University Press, 1988).

—— (ed.), *Imperialism and the Natural World* (Manchester and New York: Manchester University Press, 1990).

Morse, Deborah Denenholz, and Danahay, Martin A. (eds.), *Victorian Animal Dreams: Representations of Animals in Victorian Literature and Culture* (Aldershot: Ashgate Publishing, 2007).

Ritvo, Harriet, *The Animal Estate: The English and Other Creatures in the Victorian Age* (London: Penguin Books, 1990).

Said, Edward W., *Culture and Imperialism* (London: Vintage, 1994).

CRITICISM ON THE *JUNGLE BOOKS*

Benson, Stephen, 'Kipling's Singing Voice: Setting the Jungle Books', *Critical Survey* 13/3 (2001), pp. 40–60.

Butter, Francelia, Rosen, Barbara, and Plotz, Judith A. (eds.), *Children's Literature* 20 (1992), special issue on Rudyard Kipling.

Hagiioannu, Andrew, *The Man Who Would be Kipling: The Colonial Fiction and the Frontiers of Exile* (New York: Palgrave Macmillan, 2003).

Hotchkiss, Jane, 'The Jungle of Eden: Kipling, Wolf Boys, and the Colonial Imagination', *Victorian Literature and Culture* 29/2 (2001), pp. 435–49.

Islam, Shamsul, *Kipling's 'Law': A Study of His Philosophy of Life* (London: Macmillan, 1975).

Lancelyn Green, Roger, *Kipling and the Children* (London: Elek Books, 1965).

McBratney, John, *Imperial Subjects, Imperial Space: Rudyard Kipling's Fiction of the Native-Born* (Columbus: Ohio State University Press, 2002).

Montefiore, Jan, 'Kipling as a Children's Writer and the *Jungle Books*', in Howard Booth (ed.), *The Cambridge Companion to Rudyard Kipling* (Cambridge: Cambridge University Press, 2011), pp. 95–110.

Nyman, Jopi, *Postcolonial Animal Tale from Kipling to Coetzee* (New Delhi: Atlantic, 2003).

Randall, Don, *Kipling's Imperial Boy: Adolescence and Cultural Hybridity* (Basingstoke: Palgrave, 2000).

Stevenson, Laura C., 'Mowgli and His Stories: Versions of Pastoral', *Sewanee Review* 109/3 (Summer, 2001), pp. 358–78.

Walsh, Sue, *Kipling's Children's Literature: Language, Identity, and Constructions of Childhood* (Farnham: Ashgate Publishing, 2010).

GENERAL CRITICISM

Cornell, Louis L., *Kipling in India* (London: Macmillan, 1966).

Dobrée, Bonamy, *Rudyard Kipling: Realist and Fabulist* (Oxford: Oxford University Press, 1967).

Gilbert, Elliot L., *The Good Kipling: Studies in the Short Story* (Manchester: Manchester University Press, 1972).

—— (ed.), *Kipling and the Critics* (London: Peter Owen, 1965).

Havholm, Peter, *Politics and Awe in Rudyard Kipling's Fiction* (Aldershot: Ashgate Publishing, 2008).

Kemp, Sandra, *Kipling's Hidden Narratives* (Oxford: Blackwell, 1988).

Kutzer, Daphne M., *Empire's Children: Empire and Imperialism in Classic British Children's Books* (New York and London: Garland Publishing, 2000).

Lancelyn Green, Roger (ed.), *Kipling: The Critical Heritage* (London: Routledge & Kegan Paul, 1971).

Mallett, Philip, *Rudyard Kipling: A Literary Life* (Basingstoke: Palgrave Macmillan, 2003).

McClure, John A., *Kipling and Conrad: The Colonial Fiction* (Cambridge, Mass., and London: Harvard University Press, 1981).

Montefiore, Jan, *Rudyard Kipling* (Horndon: Northcote House, 2007).

—— (ed.), *'In Time's Eye': Essays on Rudyard Kipling* (Manchester: Manchester University Press, 2013).

Moore-Gilbert, B. J., *Kipling and 'Orientalism'* (London and Sydney: Croom Helm, 1986).

—— (ed.), *Writing India 1757–1990* (Manchester: Manchester University Press, 1996).

Nagai, Kaori, *Empire of Analogies: Kipling, India and Ireland* (Cork: Cork University Press, 2006).

Orel, Harold (ed.), *Kipling: Interviews and Recollections*, 2 vols. (London: Macmillan, 1983).

Rao, K. Bhaskara, *Rudyard Kipling's India* (Norman: University of Oklahoma Press, 1967).

Rooney, Caroline, and Nagai, Kaori (eds.), *Kipling and Beyond: Patriotism, Globalisation and Postcolonialism* (Basingstoke: Palgrave Macmillan, 2010).

Rutherford, Andrew (ed.), *Kipling's Mind and Art* (Edinburgh and London: Oliver & Boyd, 1965).

Suleri, Sara, *The Rhetoric of English India* (Chicago: University of Chicago Press, 1992).

Sullivan, Zohreh T., *Narratives of Empire: The Fictions of Rudyard Kipling* (Cambridge: Cambridge University Press, 1993).

Tompkins, J. M. S., *The Art of Rudyard Kipling*, 2nd edn. (London: Methuen, 1965).

Kaori Nagai 2013

THE JUNGLE BOOK

PREFACE

The demands made by a work of this nature upon the generosity of specialists are very numerous, and the Editor would be wanting in all title to the generous treatment he has received were he not willing to make the fullest possible acknowledgment of his indebtedness.

His thanks are due in the first place to the scholarly and accomplished Bahadur Shah, baggage elephant 174 on the Indian Register, who, with his amiable sister Pudmini,[1] most courteously supplied the history of 'Toomai of the Elephants' and much of the information contained in 'Servants of the Queen'. The adventures of Mowgli were collected at various times and in various places from a multitude of informants, most of whom desire to preserve the strictest anonymity. Yet, at this distance, the Editor feels at liberty to thank a Hindu gentleman of the old rock, an esteemed resident of the upper slopes of Jakko, for his convincing if somewhat caustic estimate of the national characteristics of his caste – the Presbytes.[2] Sahi, a savant of infinite research and industry, a member of the recently disbanded Seeonee Pack, and an artist well known at most of the local fairs of Southern India, where his muzzled dance with his master attracts the youth, beauty, and culture of many villages, have contributed most valuable data on people, manners, and customs.[3] These have been freely drawn upon, in the stories of 'Tiger-Tiger!' 'Kaa's Hunting', and 'Mowgli's Brothers'. For the outlines of 'Rikki-tikki-tavi' the Editor stands indebted to one of the leading herpetologists of Upper India, a fearless and independent investigator who, resolving 'not to live but know', lately sacrificed his life through over-application to the study of our Eastern Thanatophidia.[4] A happy accident of travel enabled the Editor, when a passenger on the *Empress of India*,[5] to be of some slight assistance to a fellow-voyager.[6] How richly his poor services were repaid, readers of the 'White Seal' may judge for themselves.

MOWGLI'S BROTHERS

Now Chil[1] the Kite brings home the night
    That Mang[2] the Bat sets free –
The herds are shut in byre and hut
    For loosed till dawn are we.
This is the hour of pride and power,
    Talon and tush and claw.
Oh hear the call! – Good hunting all
    That keep the Jungle Law!
Night-Song in the Jungle

It was seven o'clock of a very warm evening in the Seeonee hills[3] when Father Wolf woke up from his day's rest, scratched himself, yawned, and spread out his paws one after the other to get rid of the sleepy feeling in their tips. Mother Wolf lay with her big gray nose dropped across her four tumbling, squealing cubs, and the moon shone into the mouth of the cave where they all lived. 'Augrh!' said Father Wolf, 'it is time to hunt again'; and he was going to spring down hill when a little shadow with a bushy tail crossed the threshold and whined: 'Good luck go with you, O Chief of the Wolves; and good luck and strong white teeth go with the noble children, that they may never forget the hungry in this world.'

It was the jackal – Tabaqui, the Dish-licker[4] – and the wolves of India despise Tabaqui because he runs about making mischief, and telling tales, and eating rags and pieces of leather from the village rubbish-heaps. But they are afraid of him too, because Tabaqui, more than anyone else in the jungle, is apt to go mad, and then he forgets that he was ever afraid of anyone, and runs through the forest biting everything in his way. Even the tiger runs and hides when little Tabaqui goes mad, for madness is the most disgraceful thing that can overtake a wild creature. We call it hydrophobia, but they call it *dewanee*[5] – the madness – and run.

'Enter, then, and look,' said Father Wolf, stiffly; 'but there is no food here.'

'For a wolf, no,' said Tabaqui; 'but for so mean a person as myself a dry bone is a good feast. Who are we, the Gidur-log [the jackal people],[6] to pick and choose?' He scuttled to the back of the cave, where he found the bone of a buck with some meat on it, and sat cracking the end merrily.

'All thanks for this good meal,' he said, licking his lips. 'How beautiful are the noble children! How large are their eyes! And so young too! Indeed, indeed, I might have remembered that the children of kings are men from the beginning.'

Now, Tabaqui knew as well as anyone else that there is nothing so unlucky as to compliment children to their faces; and it pleased him to see Mother and Father Wolf look uncomfortable.

Tabaqui sat still, rejoicing in the mischief that he had made, and then he said spitefully:

'Shere Khan,[7] the Big One, has shifted his hunting-grounds. He will hunt among these hills for the next moon, so he has told me.'

Shere Khan was the tiger who lived near the Waingunga River,[8] twenty miles away.

'He has no right!' Father Wolf began angrily – 'By the Law of the Jungle he has no right to change his quarters without due warning. He will frighten every head of game within ten miles, and I – I have to kill for two, these days.'

'His mother did not call him Lungri[9] [the Lame One] for nothing,' said Mother Wolf, quietly. 'He has been lame in one foot from his birth. That is why he has only killed cattle. Now the villagers of the Waingunga are angry with him, and he has come here to make *our* villagers angry. They will scour the jungle for him when he is far away, and we and our children must run when the grass is set alight. Indeed, we are very grateful to Shere Khan!'

'Shall I tell him of your gratitude?' said Tabaqui.

'Out!' snapped Father Wolf. 'Out and hunt with thy master.[10] Thou hast done harm enough for one night.'

'I go,' said Tabaqui, quietly. 'Ye can hear Shere Khan below in the thickets. I might have saved myself the message.'

Father Wolf listened, and below in the valley[11] that ran down to a little river, he heard the dry, angry, snarly, singsong whine of a tiger who has caught nothing and does not care if all the jungle knows it.

'The fool!' said Father Wolf. 'To begin a night's work with that noise! Does he think that our buck are like his fat Waingunga bullocks?'

'H'sh. It is neither bullock nor buck he hunts tonight,' said Mother Wolf. 'It is Man.' The whine had changed to a sort of humming purr that seemed to come from every quarter of the compass. It was the noise that bewilders woodcutters and gipsies sleeping in the open, and makes them run sometimes into the very mouth of the tiger.

'Man!' said Father Wolf, showing all his white teeth. 'Faugh! Are there not enough beetles and frogs in the tanks that he must eat Man, and on our ground too!'

The Law of the Jungle, which never orders anything without a reason, forbids every beast to eat Man except when he is killing to show his children how to kill, and then he must hunt outside the hunting-grounds of his pack or tribe. The real reason for this is that man-killing means, sooner or later, the arrival of white men on elephants, with guns, and hundreds of brown men with gongs and rockets and torches. Then everybody in the jungle suffers. The reason the beasts give among themselves is that Man is the weakest and most defenceless of all living things, and it is unsportsmanlike to touch him. They say too – and it is true – that man-eaters become mangy,[12] and lose their teeth.

The purr grew louder, and ended in the full-throated 'Aaarh!' of the tiger's charge.

Then there was a howl – an untigerish howl – from Shere Khan. 'He has missed,' said Mother Wolf. 'What is it?'

Father Wolf ran out a few paces and heard Shere Khan muttering and mumbling savagely, as he tumbled about in the scrub.

'The fool has had no more sense than to jump at a woodcutters' camp-fire, and has burned his feet,' said Father Wolf, with a grunt. 'Tabaqui is with him.'

'Something is coming uphill,' said Mother Wolf, twitching one ear. 'Get ready.'

The bushes rustled a little in the thicket, and Father Wolf dropped with his haunches under him, ready for his leap. Then, if you had been watching, you would have seen the most wonderful thing in the world – the wolf checked in mid-spring. He made his bound before he saw what it was he was jumping at, and then he tried to stop himself. The result was that he shot up straight into the air for four or five feet, landing almost where he left ground.

'Man!' he snapped. 'A man's cub. Look!'

Directly in front of him, holding on by a low branch, stood a naked brown baby who could just walk – as soft and as dimpled a little atom as ever came to a wolf's cave at night. He looked up into Father Wolf's face, and laughed.

'Is that a man's cub?' said Mother Wolf. 'I have never seen one. Bring it here.'

A wolf accustomed to moving his own cubs can, if necessary, mouth an egg without breaking it, and though Father Wolf's jaws closed right on the child's back not a tooth even scratched the skin, as he laid it down among the cubs.

'How little! How naked, and – how bold!' said Mother Wolf, softly. The baby was pushing his way between the cubs to get close to the warm hide. 'Ahai! He is taking his meal with the others. And so this is a man's cub. Now, was there ever a wolf that could boast of a man's cub among her children?'

'I have heard now and again of such a thing, but never in our Pack or in my time,' said Father Wolf. 'He is altogether without hair, and I could kill him with a touch of my foot. But see, he looks up and is not afraid.'

The moonlight was blocked out of the mouth of the cave, for Shere Khan's great square head and shoulders were thrust into the entrance. Tabaqui, behind him, was squeaking: 'My lord, my lord, it went in here!'

'Shere Khan does us great honour,' said Father Wolf, but his eyes were very angry. 'What does Shere Khan need?'

'My quarry. A man's cub went this way,' said Shere Khan. 'Its parents have run off. Give it to me.'

Shere Khan had jumped at a woodcutters' camp-fire, as Father

Wolf had said, and was furious from the pain of his burned feet. But Father Wolf knew that the mouth of the cave was too narrow for a tiger to come in by. Even where he was, Shere Khan's shoulders and fore paws were cramped for want of room, as a man's would be if he tried to fight in a barrel.

'The Wolves are a free people,' said Father Wolf. 'They take orders from the Head of the Pack, and not from any striped cattle-killer. The man's cub is ours – to kill if we choose.'

'Ye choose and ye do not choose! What talk is this of choosing? By the bull that I killed, am I to stand nosing into your dog's den for my fair dues? It is I, Shere Khan, who speak!'

The tiger's roar filled the cave with thunder. Mother Wolf shook herself clear of the cubs and sprang forward, her eyes, like two green moons in the darkness, facing the blazing eyes of Shere Khan.

'And it is I, Raksha[13] [The Demon], who answer. The man's cub is mine, Lungri – mine to me! He shall not be killed. He shall live to run with the Pack and to hunt with the Pack; and in the end, look you, hunter of little naked cubs – frog-eater – fish-killer – he shall hunt *thee*! Now get hence, or by the Sambhur[14] that I killed (I eat no starved cattle), back thou goest to thy mother, burned beast of the jungle, lamer than ever thou camest into the world! Go!'

Father Wolf looked on amazed. He had almost forgotten the days when he won Mother Wolf in fair fight from five other wolves, when she ran in the Pack and was not called The Demon for compliment's sake. Shere Khan might have faced Father Wolf, but he could not stand up against Mother Wolf, for he knew that where he was she had all the advantage of the ground, and would fight to the death. So he backed out of the cave-mouth growling, and when he was clear he shouted:

'Each dog barks in his own yard! We will see what the Pack will say to this fostering of man-cubs. The cub is mine, and to my teeth he will come in the end, O bush-tailed thieves!'

Mother Wolf threw herself down panting among the cubs, and Father Wolf said to her gravely:

'Shere Khan speaks this much truth. The cub must be shown to the Pack. Wilt thou still keep him, Mother?'

'Keep him!' she gasped. 'He came naked, by night, alone and very hungry; yet he was not afraid! Look, he has pushed one of my babes to one side already. And that lame butcher would have killed him and would have run off to the Waingunga while the villagers here hunted through all our lairs in revenge! Keep him? Assuredly I will keep him. Lie still, little frog. O thou Mowgli – for Mowgli the Frog[15] I will call thee – the time will come when thou wilt hunt Shere Khan as he has hunted thee.'

'But what will our Pack say?' said Father Wolf.

The Law of the Jungle lays down very clearly that any wolf may, when he marries, withdraw from the Pack he belongs to; but as soon as his cubs are old enough to stand on their feet he must bring them to the Pack Council, which is generally held once a month at full moon, in order that the other wolves may identify them. After that inspection the cubs are free to run where they please, and until they have killed their first buck no excuse is accepted if a grown wolf of the Pack kills one of them. The punishment is death where the murderer can be found; and if you think for a minute you will see that this must be so.

Father Wolf waited till his cubs could run a little, and then on the night of the Pack Meeting took them and Mowgli and Mother Wolf to the Council Rock – a hilltop covered with stones and boulders where a hundred wolves could hide. Akela,[16] the great gray Lone Wolf, who led all the Pack by strength and cunning, lay out at full length on his rock, and below him sat forty or more wolves of every size and colour, from badger-coloured veterans who could handle a buck alone, to young black three-year-olds who thought they could. The Lone Wolf had led them for a year now. He had fallen twice into a wolf-trap in his youth, and once he had been beaten and left for dead; so he knew the manners and customs of men. There was very little talking at the rock. The cubs tumbled over each other in the centre of the circle where their mothers and fathers sat, and now and again a senior wolf would go quietly up to a cub, look at him carefully, and return to his place on noiseless feet. Sometimes a mother would push her cub far out into the moonlight, to be sure that he had not been overlooked. Akela from his rock would cry: 'Ye know the Law – ye know the Law. Look well, O Wolves!' and the anxious mothers would take up the call: 'Look – look well, O Wolves!'

At last – and Mother Wolf's neck-bristles lifted as the time came – Father Wolf pushed 'Mowgli the Frog', as they called him, into the centre, where he sat laughing and playing with some pebbles that glistened in the moonlight.

Akela never raised his head from his paws, but went on with the monotonous cry: 'Look well!' A muffled roar came up from behind the rocks – the voice of Shere Khan crying: 'The cub is mine. Give him to me. What have the Free People to do with a man's cub?' Akela never even twitched his ears: all he said was: 'Look well, O Wolves! What have the Free People to do with the orders of any save the Free People? Look well!'

There was a chorus of deep growls, and a young wolf in his fourth year flung back Shere Khan's question to Akela: 'What have the Free People to do with a man's cub?' Now the Law of the Jungle lays down that if there is any dispute as to the right of a cub to be accepted by the Pack, he must be spoken for by at least two members of the Pack who are not his father and mother.

'Who speaks for this cub?' said Akela. 'Among the Free People who speaks?' There was no answer, and Mother Wolf got ready for what she knew would be her last fight, if things came to fighting.

Then the only other creature who is allowed at the Pack Council – Baloo,[17] the sleepy brown bear who teaches the wolf cubs the Law of the Jungle: old Baloo, who can come and go where he pleases because he eats only nuts and roots and honey – rose up on his hind quarters and grunted.

'The man's cub – the man's cub?' he said. '*I* speak for the man's cub. There is no harm in a man's cub. I have no gift of words, but I speak the truth. Let him run with the Pack, and be entered with the others. I myself will teach him.'

'We need yet another,' said Akela. 'Baloo has spoken, and he is our teacher for the young cubs. Who speaks beside Baloo?'

A black shadow dropped down into the circle. It was Bagheera[18] the Black Panther, inky black all over, but with the panther markings showing up in certain lights like the pattern of watered silk. Everybody knew Bagheera, and nobody cared to cross his path; for he was as cunning as Tabaqui, as bold as the wild buffalo, and as reckless as the wounded elephant. But he had a voice as soft as wild honey dripping from a tree, and a skin softer than down.

'O Akela, and ye the Free People,' he purred, 'I have no right in your assembly; but the Law of the Jungle says that if there is a doubt which is not a killing matter in regard to a new cub, the life of that cub may be bought at a price. And the Law does not say who may or may not pay that price. Am I right?'

'Good! good!' said the young wolves, who are always hungry. 'Listen to Bagheera. The cub can be bought for a price. It is the Law.'

'Knowing that I have no right to speak here, I ask your leave.'

'Speak then,' cried twenty voices.

'To kill a naked cub is shame. Besides, he may make better sport for you when he is grown. Baloo has spoken in his behalf. Now to Baloo's word I will add one bull, and a fat one, newly killed, not half a mile from here, if ye will accept the man's cub according to the Law. Is it difficult?'

There was a clamour of scores of voices, saying: 'What matter? He will die in the winter rains. He will scorch in the sun. What harm can a naked frog do us? Let him run with the Pack. Where is the bull, Bagheera? Let him be accepted.' And then came Akela's deep bay, crying: 'Look well – look well, O Wolves!'

Mowgli was still deeply interested in the pebbles, and he did not notice when the wolves came and looked at him one by one. At last they all went down the hill for the dead bull, and only Akela, Bagheera, Baloo, and Mowgli's own wolves were left. Shere Khan roared still in the night, for he was very angry that Mowgli had not been handed over to him.

'Ay, roar well,' said Bagheera, under his whiskers; 'for the time comes when this naked thing will make thee roar to another tune, or I know nothing of man.'

'It was well done,' said Akela. 'Men and their cubs are very wise. He may be a help in time.'

'Truly, a help in time of need; for none can hope to lead the Pack for ever,' said Bagheera.

Akela said nothing. He was thinking of the time that comes to every leader of every pack when his strength goes from him and he gets feebler and feebler, till at last he is killed by the wolves and a new leader comes up – to be killed in his turn.

'Take him away,' he said to Father Wolf, 'and train him as befits one of the Free People.'

And that is how Mowgli was entered into the Seeonee wolf-pack for the price of a bull and on Baloo's good word.

Now you must be content to skip ten or eleven whole years, and only guess at all the wonderful life that Mowgli led among the wolves, because if it were written out it would fill ever so many books. He grew up with the cubs, though they, of course, were grown wolves almost before he was a child, and Father Wolf taught him his business, and the meaning of things in the jungle, till every rustle in the grass, every breath of the warm night air, every note of the owls above his head, every scratch of a bat's claws as it roosted for a while in a tree, and every splash of every little fish jumping in a pool, meant just as much to him as the work of his office means to a business man. When he was not learning he sat out in the sun and slept, and ate and went to sleep again; when he felt dirty or hot he swam in the forest pools; and when he wanted honey (Baloo told him that honey and nuts were just as pleasant to eat as raw meat) he climbed up for it, and that Bagheera showed him how to do. Bagheera would lie out on a branch and call, 'Come along, Little Brother,' and at first Mowgli would cling like the sloth, but afterward he would fling himself through the branches almost as boldly as the gray ape. He took his place at the Council Rock, too, when the Pack met, and there he discovered that if he stared hard at any wolf, the wolf would be forced to drop his eyes, and so he used to stare for fun. At other times he would pick the long thorns out of the pads of his friends, for wolves suffer terribly from thorns and burs in their coats. He would go down the hillside into the cultivated lands by night, and look very curiously at the villagers in their huts, but he had a mistrust of men because Bagheera showed him a square box with a drop-gate so cunningly hidden in the jungle that he nearly walked into it, and told him that it was a trap. He loved better than anything else to go with Bagheera into the dark warm heart of the forest, to sleep all through the drowsy day, and at night see how Bagheera did his killing. Bagheera killed right and left as he felt hungry, and so did Mowgli – with one exception. As soon as he was old enough to understand things, Bagheera told him that he must never touch cattle because he had been bought into the Pack at the price of a bull's life. 'All the jungle is thine,' said Bagheera, 'and thou canst kill everything that thou art strong enough to kill; but for the sake of the bull that bought thee thou must never kill or eat any cattle young or old.[19] That is the Law of the Jungle.' Mowgli obeyed faithfully.

And he grew and grew strong as a boy must grow who does not know that he is learning any lessons, and who has nothing in the world to think of except things to eat.

Mother Wolf told him once or twice that Shere Khan was not a creature to be trusted, and that some day he must kill Shere Khan; but though a young wolf would have remembered that advice every hour, Mowgli forgot it because he was only a boy – though he would have called himself a wolf if he had been able to speak in any human tongue.

Shere Khan was always crossing his path in the jungle, for as Akela grew older and feebler the lame tiger had come to be great friends with the younger wolves of the Pack, who followed him for scraps, a thing Akela would never have allowed if he had dared to push his authority to the proper bounds. Then Shere Khan would flatter them and wonder that such fine young hunters were content to be led by a dying wolf and a man's cub. 'They tell me,' Shere Khan would say, 'that at Council ye dare not look him between the eyes'; and the young wolves would growl and bristle.

Bagheera, who had eyes and ears everywhere, knew something of this, and once or twice he told Mowgli in so many words that Shere Khan would kill him some day; and Mowgli would laugh and answer: 'I have the Pack and I have thee; and

Baloo, though he is so lazy, might strike a blow or two for my sake. Why should I be afraid?'

It was one very warm day that a new notion came to Bagheera – born of something that he had heard. Perhaps Sahi[20] the Porcupine had told him; but he said to Mowgli when they were deep in the jungle, as the boy lay with his head on Bagheera's beautiful black skin: 'Little Brother, how often have I told thee that Shere Khan is thy enemy?'

'As many times as there are nuts on that palm,' said Mowgli, who, naturally, could not count. 'What of it? I am sleepy, Bagheera, and Shere Khan is all long tail and loud talk – like Mor the Peacock.'[21]

'But this is no time for sleeping. Baloo knows it; I know it; the Pack know it; and even the foolish, foolish deer know. Tabaqui had told thee, too.'

'Ho! ho!' said Mowgli. 'Tabaqui came to me not long ago with some rude talk that I was a naked man's cub and not fit to dig pig-nuts; but I caught Tabaqui by the tail and swung him twice against a palm-tree to teach him better manners.'

'That was foolishness; for though Tabaqui is a mischief-maker, he would have told thee of something that concerned thee closely. Open those eyes, Little Brother. Shere Khan dare not kill thee in the jungle;[22] but remember, Akela is very old, and soon the day comes when he cannot kill his buck, and then he will be leader no more. Many of the wolves that looked thee over when thou wast brought to the Council first are old too, and the young wolves believe, as Shere Khan has taught them, that a man-cub has no place with the Pack. In a little time thou wilt be a man.'

'And what is a man that he should not run with his brothers?' said Mowgli. 'I was born in the jungle. I have obeyed the Law of the Jungle, and there is no wolf of ours from whose paws I have not pulled a thorn. Surely they are my brothers!'

Bagheera stretched himself at full length and half shut his eyes. 'Little Brother,' said he, 'feel under my jaw.'

Mowgli put up his strong brown hand, and just under Bagheera's silky chin, where the giant rolling muscles were all hid by the glossy hair, he came upon a little bald spot.

'There is no one in the jungle that knows that I, Bagheera, carry that mark – the mark of the collar; and yet, Little Brother, I was born among men, and it was among men that my mother died – in the cages of the King's Palace at Oodeypore.[23] It was because of this that I paid the price for thee at the Council when thou wast a little naked cub. Yes, I too was born among men. I had never seen the jungle. They fed me behind bars from an iron pan till one night I felt that I was Bagheera – the Panther – and no man's plaything, and I broke the silly lock with one blow of my paw and came away; and because I had learned the ways of men, I became more terrible in the jungle than Shere Khan. Is it not so?'

'Yes,' said Mowgli; 'all the jungle fear Bagheera – all except Mowgli.'

'Oh, *thou* art a man's cub,' said the Black Panther, very tenderly; 'and even as I returned to my jungle, so thou must go back to men at last – to the men who are thy brothers – if thou art not killed in the Council.'

'But why – but why should any wish to kill me?' said Mowgli.

'Look at me,' said Bagheera; and Mowgli looked at him steadily between the eyes. The big panther turned his head away in half a minute.

'*That* is why,' he said, shifting his paw on the leaves. 'Not even I can look thee between the eyes, and I was born among men, and I love thee, Little Brother. The others they hate thee because their eyes cannot meet thine; because thou art wise; because thou hast pulled out thorns from their feet – because thou art a man.'

'I did not know these things,' said Mowgli, sullenly; and he frowned under his heavy black eyebrows.

'What is the Law of the Jungle? Strike first and then give tongue. By thy very carelessness they know that thou art a man. But be wise. It is in my heart that when Akela misses his next kill – and at each hunt it costs him more to pin the buck – the Pack will turn against him and against thee. They will hold a jungle Council at the Rock, and then – and then – I have it!' said Bagheera, leaping up. 'Go thou down quickly to the men's huts in the valley, and take some of the Red Flower which they grow there, so that when the time comes thou mayest have even a stronger friend than I or Baloo or those of the Pack that love thee. Get the Red Flower.'

By Red Flower Bagheera meant fire, only no creature in the jungle will call fire by its proper name. Every beast lives in deadly fear of it, and invents a hundred ways of describing it.

'The Red Flower?' said Mowgli. 'That grows outside their huts in the twilight. I will get some.'

'There speaks the man's cub,' said Bagheera, proudly. 'Remember that it grows in little pots. Get one swiftly, and keep it by thee for time of need.'

'Good!' said Mowgli. 'I go. But art thou sure, O my Bagheera' – he slipped his arm round the splendid neck, and looked deep into the big eyes – 'art thou sure that all this is Shere Khan's doing?'

'By the Broken Lock that freed me, I am sure, Little Brother.'

'Then, by the Bull that bought me, I will pay Shere Khan full tale for this, and it may be a little over,' said Mowgli; and he bounded away.

'That is a man. That is all a man,' said Bagheera to himself, lying down again. 'Oh, Shere Khan, never was a blacker hunting than that frog-hunt of thine ten years ago!'

Mowgli was far and far through the forest, running hard, and his heart was hot in him. He came to the cave as the evening mist rose, and drew breath, and looked down the valley. The cubs were out, but Mother Wolf, at the back of the cave, knew by his breathing that something was troubling her frog.

'What is it, Son?' she said.

'Some bat's chatter of Shere Khan,' he called back. 'I hunt among the ploughed fields tonight'; and he plunged downward through the bushes, to the stream at the bottom of the valley. There he checked, for he heard the yell of the Pack hunting, heard the bellow of a hunted Sambhur, and the snort as the buck turned at bay. Then there were wicked, bitter howls from the young wolves: 'Akela! Akela! Let the Lone Wolf show his strength. Room for the leader of the Pack! Spring, Akela!'

The Lone Wolf must have sprung and missed his hold, for

Mowgli heard the snap of his teeth and then a yelp as the Sambhur knocked him over with his fore foot.

He did not wait for anything more, but dashed on; and the yells grew fainter behind him as he ran into the crop-lands where the villagers lived.

'Bagheera spoke truth,' he panted, as he nestled down in some cattle-fodder by the window of a hut. 'To-morrow is one day both for Akela and for me.'

Then he pressed his face close to the window and watched the fire on the hearth. He saw the husbandman's wife get up and feed it in the night with black lumps; and when the morning came and the mists were all white and cold, he saw the man's child pick up a wicker pot plastered inside with earth, fill it with lumps of red-hot charcoal, put it under his blanket, and go out to tend the cows in the byre.

'Is that all?' said Mowgli. 'If a cub can do it, there is nothing to fear'; so he strode round the corner and met the boy, took the pot from his hand, and disappeared into the mist while the boy howled with fear.

'They are very like me,' said Mowgli, blowing into the pot, as he had seen the woman do. 'This thing will die if I do not give it things to eat'; and he dropped twigs and dried bark on the red stuff. Half-way up the hill he met Bagheera with the morning dew shining like moonstones on his coat.

'Akela has missed,' said the Panther. 'They would have killed him last night, but they needed thee also. They were looking for thee on the hill.'

'I was among the ploughed lands. I am ready. See!' Mowgli held up the fire-pot.

'Good! Now, I have seen men thrust a dry branch into that stuff, and presently the Red Flower blossomed at the end of it. Art thou not afraid?'

'No. Why should I fear? I remember now – if it is not a dream – how, before I was a Wolf, I lay beside the Red Flower, and it was warm and pleasant.'

All that day Mowgli sat in the cave tending his fire-pot and dipping dry branches into it to see how they looked. He found a branch that satisfied him, and in the evening when Tabaqui came to the cave and told him rudely enough that he was wanted at the Council Rock, he laughed till Tabaqui ran away. Then Mowgli went to the Council, still laughing.

Akela the Lone Wolf lay by the side of his rock as a sign that the leadership of the Pack was open, and Shere Khan with his following of scrap-fed wolves walked to and fro openly being flattered. Bagheera lay close to Mowgli, and the fire-pot was between Mowgli's knees. When they were all gathered together, Shere Khan began to speak – a thing he would never have dared to do when Akela was in his prime.

'He has no right,' whispered Bagheera. 'Say so. He is a dog's son. He will be frightened.'

Mowgli sprang to his feet. 'Free People,' he cried, 'does Shere Khan lead the Pack? What has a tiger to do with our leadership?'

'Seeing that the leadership is yet open, and being asked to speak—' Shere Khan began.

'By whom?' said Mowgli. 'Are we *all* jackals, to fawn on this cattle-butcher? The leadership of the Pack is with the Pack alone.'

There were yells of 'Silence, thou man's cub!' 'Let him speak. He has kept our Law'; and at last the seniors of the Pack thundered: 'Let the Dead Wolf speak.' When a leader of the Pack has missed his kill, he is called the Dead Wolf as long as he lives, which is not long.[24]

Akela raised his old head wearily:

'Free People, and ye too, jackals of Shere Khan, for twelve seasons[25] I have led ye to and from the kill, and in all that time not one has been trapped or maimed. Now I have missed my kill. Ye know how that plot was made. Ye know how ye brought me up to an untried buck to make my weakness known. It was cleverly done. Your right is to kill me here on the Council Rock, now. Therefore, I ask, who comes to make an end of the Lone Wolf? For it is my right, by the Law of the Jungle, that ye come one by one.'

There was a long hush, for no single wolf cared to fight Akela to the death. Then Shere Khan roared: 'Bah! what have we to do with this toothless fool? He is doomed to die! It is the man-cub who has lived too long. Free People, he was my meat from the first. Give him to me. I am weary of this man-wolf folly. He has troubled the jungle for ten seasons. Give me the man-cub, or I will hunt here always, and not give you one bone. He is a man, a man's child, and from the marrow of my bones I hate him!'

Then more than half the Pack yelled: 'A man! a man! What has a man to do with us? Let him go to his own place.'

'And turn all the people of the villages against us?' clamoured Shere Khan. 'No; give him to me. He is a man, and none of us can look him between the eyes.'

Akela lifted his head again, and said: 'He has eaten our food. He has slept with us. He has driven game for us. He has broken no word of the Law of the Jungle.'

'Also, I paid for him with a bull when he was accepted. The worth of a bull is little, but Bagheera's honour is something that he will perhaps fight for,' said Bagheera, in his gentlest voice.

'A bull paid ten years ago!' the Pack snarled. 'What do we care for bones ten years old?'

'Or for a pledge?' said Bagheera, his white teeth bared under his lip. 'Well are ye called the Free People!'

'No man's cub can run with the people of the jungle,' howled Shere Khan. 'Give him to me!'

'He is our brother in all but blood,' Akela went on; 'and ye would kill him here! In truth, I have lived too long. Some of ye are eaters of cattle, and of others I have heard that, under Shere Khan's teaching, ye go by dark night and snatch children from the villager's door-step. Therefore I know ye to be cowards, and it is to cowards I speak. It is certain that I must die, and my life is of no worth, or I would offer that in the man-cub's place. But for the sake of the Honour of the Pack – a little matter that by being without a leader ye have forgotten – I promise that if ye let the man-cub go to his own place, I will not, when my time comes to die, bare one tooth against ye. I will die without fighting. That will at least save the Pack three lives. More I cannot do; but if ye will, I can save ye the shame that comes of killing a brother against whom there is no fault – a brother spoken for and bought into the Pack according to the Law of the Jungle.'

'He is a man – a man – a man!' snarled the Pack; and most of the wolves began to gather round Shere Khan, whose tail was beginning to switch.

'Now the business is in thy hands,' said Bagheera to Mowgli. '*We* can do no more except fight.'

Mowgli stood upright – the fire-pot in his hands. Then he stretched out his arms, and yawned in the face of the Council; but he was furious with rage and sorrow, for, wolf-like, the wolves had never told him how they hated him. 'Listen you!' he cried. 'There is no need for this dog's jabber. Ye have told me so often tonight that I am a man (and indeed I would have been a wolf with you to my life's end), that I feel your words are true. So I do not call ye my brothers any more, but *sag* [dogs],[26] as a man should. What ye will do, and what ye will not do, is not yours to say. That matter is with *me*; and that we may see the matter more plainly, I, the man, have brought here a little of the Red Flower which ye, dogs, fear.'

He flung the fire-pot on the ground, and some of the red coals lit a tuft of dried moss that flared up, as all the Council drew back in terror before the leaping flames.

Mowgli thrust his dead branch into the fire till the twigs lit and crackled, and whirled it above his head among the cowering wolves.

'Thou art the master,' said Bagheera, in an undertone. 'Save Akela from the death. He was ever thy friend.'

Akela, the grim old wolf who had never asked for mercy in his life, gave one piteous look at Mowgli as the boy stood all naked, his long black hair tossing over his shoulders in the light of the blazing branch that made the shadows jump and quiver.

'Good!' said Mowgli, staring round slowly.[27] 'I see than ye are dogs. I go from you to my own people – if they be my own people. The Jungle is shut to me, and I must forget your talk and your companionship; but I will be more merciful than ye are. Because I was all but your brother in blood, I promise that when I am a man among men I will not betray ye to men as ye have betrayed me.' He kicked the fire with his foot, and the sparks flew up. 'There shall be no war between any of us in the Pack.[28] But here is a debt to pay before I go.' He strode forward to where Shere Khan sat blinking stupidly at the flames, and caught him by the tuft on his chin. Bagheera followed in case of accidents. 'Up, dog!' Mowgli cried. 'Up, when a man speaks, or I will set that coat ablaze!'

Shere Khan's ears lay flat back on his head, and he shut his eyes, for the blazing branch was very near.

'This cattle-killer said he would kill me in the Council because he had not killed me when I was a cub. Thus and thus, then, do we beat dogs when we are men. Stir a whisker, Lungri, and I ram the Red Flower down thy gullet!' He beat Shere Khan over the head with the branch, and the tiger whimpered and whined in an agony of fear.

'Pah! Singed jungle-cat – go now! But remember when next I come to the Council Rock, as a man should come, it will be with Shere Khan's hide on my head. For the rest, Akela goes free to live as he pleases. Ye will *not* kill him, because that is not my will. Nor do I think that ye will sit here any longer, lolling out your tongues as though ye were somebodies, instead of dogs whom I drive out – thus! Go!' The fire was burning furiously at the end of the branch, and Mowgli struck right and left round the circle, and the wolves ran howling with the sparks burning their fur. At last there were only Akela, Bagheera, and perhaps ten wolves that had taken Mowgli's part. Then something began to hurt Mowgli inside him, as he had never been hurt in his life before, and he caught his breath and sobbed, and the tears ran down his face.

'What is it? What is it?' he said. 'I do not wish to leave the jungle, and I do not know what this is. Am I dying, Bagheera?'

'No, Little Brother. That is only tears such as men use,' said Bagheera. 'Now I know thou art a man, and a man's cub no longer. The Jungle is shut indeed to thee henceforward. Let them fall, Mowgli. They are only tears.' So Mowgli sat and cried as though his heart would break; and he had never cried in all his life before.

'Now,' he said, 'I will go to men. But first I must say farewell to my mother'; and he went to the cave where she lived with

Father Wolf, and he cried on her coat, while the four cubs howled miserably.

'Ye will not forget me?' said Mowgli.

'Never while we can follow a trail,' said the cubs. 'Come to the foot of the hill when thou art a man, and we will talk to thee; and we will come into the crop-lands to play with thee by night.'

'Come soon!' said Father Wolf. 'Oh, wise little frog, come again soon; for we be old, thy mother and I.'

'Come soon,' said Mother Wolf, 'little naked son of mine; for, listen, child of man, I loved thee more than ever I loved my cubs.'

'I will surely come,' said Mowgli; 'and when I come it will be to lay out Shere Khan's hide upon the Council Rock. Do not forget me! Tell them in the jungle never to forget me!'

The dawn was beginning to break when Mowgli went down the hillside alone,[29] to meet those mysterious things that are called men.

Hunting-Song of the Seonee Pack

As the dawn was breaking the Sambhur belled
   Once, twice and again!
And a doe leaped up and a doe leaped up
From the pond in the wood where the wild deer sup.
This I, scouting alone, beheld,
   Once, twice and again!

As the dawn was breaking the Sambhur belled
   Once, twice and again!
And a wolf stole back and a wolf stole back
To carry the word to the waiting pack,
And we sought and we found and we bayed on his track
   Once, twice and again!

As the dawn was breaking the Wolf Pack yelled
   Once, twice and again!
Feet in the jungle that leave no mark!
Eyes that can see in the dark – the dark!
Tongue – give tongue to it! Hark! O hark!
   Once, twice and again!

KAA'S HUNTING

His spots are the joy of the Leopard: his horns are the Buffalo's pride.
Be clean, for the strength of the hunter is known by the gloss of his hide.
If ye find that the bullock can toss you, or the heavy-browed Sambhur
    can gore;
Ye need not stop work to inform us: we knew it ten seasons before.
Oppress not the cubs of the stranger, but hail them as Sister and
    Brother,
For though they are little and fubsy,[1] it may be the Bear is their mother.
'There is none like to me!' says the Cub in the pride of his earliest kill;
But the jungle is large and the Cub he is small. Let him think and
    be still.

Maxims of Baloo

All that is told here happened some time before Mowgli was turned out of the Seeonee wolf-pack, or revenged himself on Shere Khan the tiger.[2] It was in the days when Baloo was teaching him the Law of the Jungle. The big, serious, old brown bear was delighted to have so quick a pupil, for the young wolves will only learn as much of the Law of the Jungle as applies to their own pack and tribe, and run away as soon as they can repeat the Hunting Verse: 'Feet that make no noise; eyes that can see in the dark; ears that can hear the winds in their lairs, and sharp white teeth, all these things are the marks of our brothers except Tabaqui the Jackal and the Hyæna whom we hate.' But Mowgli, as a man-cub, had to learn a great deal more than this. Sometimes Bagheera, the Black Panther, would come lounging through the jungle to see how his pet was getting on, and would purr with his head against a tree while Mowgli recited the day's lesson to Baloo. The boy could climb almost as well as he could swim, and swim almost as well as he could run; so Baloo, the Teacher of the Law, taught him the Wood and Water Laws: how to tell a rotten branch from a sound one; how to speak politely to the wild bees when he came upon a hive of them fifty feet above ground; what to say to Mang the Bat when he disturbed him in the branches at midday; and how to warn the water-snakes in the pools before he splashed down among them. None of the Jungle-People like being disturbed, and all are very ready to fly at an intruder. Then, too, Mowgli was taught the Strangers' Hunting Call, which must be repeated aloud till it is answered, whenever one of the Jungle-People hunts outside his own grounds. It means, translated: 'Give me leave to hunt here because I am hungry'; and the answer is: 'Hunt then for food, but not for pleasure.'

All this will show you how much Mowgli had to learn by heart, and he grew very tired of saying the same thing over a hundred times; but, as Baloo said to Bagheera, one day when Mowgli had been cuffed and run off in a temper: 'A man's cub is a man's cub, and he must learn *all* the Law of the Jungle.'

'But think how small he is,' said the Black Panther, who would have spoiled Mowgli if he had had his own way. 'How can his little head carry all thy long talk?'

'Is there anything in the jungle too little to be killed? No. That is why I teach him these things, and that is why I hit him, very softly, when he forgets.'

'Softly! What dost thou know of softness, old Iron-feet?' Bagheera grunted. 'His face is all bruised today by thy – softness. Ugh.'

'Better he should be bruised from head to foot by me who love him than that he should come to harm through ignorance,' Baloo answered very earnestly. 'I am now teaching him the Master Words of the Jungle that shall protect him with the birds and the Snake-People, and all that hunt on four feet, except his own pack. He can now claim protection, if he will only remember the words, from all in the jungle. Is not that worth a little beating?'

'Well, look to it then that thou dost not kill the man-cub. He is no tree-trunk to sharpen thy blunt claws upon. But what are those Master Words? I am more likely to give help than to ask it' – Bagheera stretched out one paw and admired the steel-blue, ripping-chisel talons at the end of it – 'still I should like to know.'

'I will call Mowgli and he shall say them – if he will. Come, Little Brother!'

'My head is ringing like a bee-tree,' said a sullen little voice over their heads, and Mowgli slid down a tree-trunk very angry and indignant, adding as he reached the ground: 'I come for Bagheera and not for *thee*, fat old Baloo!'

'That is all one to me,' said Baloo, though he was hurt and grieved. 'Tell Bagheera, then, the Master Words of the Jungle that I have taught thee this day.'

'Master Words for which people?' said Mowgli, delighted to show off. 'The jungle has many tongues. *I* know them all.'

'A little thou knowest, but not much. See, O Bagheera, they never thank their teacher. Not one small wolfling has ever come back to thank old Baloo for his teachings. Say the word for the Hunting-Peoples then – great scholar.'

'We be of one blood, ye and I,' said Mowgli, giving the words the Bear accent which all the hunting-people use.

'Good. Now for the birds.'

Mowgli repeated, with the Kite's whistle at the end of the sentence.

'Now for the Snake-People,' said Bagheera.

The answer was a perfectly indescribable hiss, and Mowgli kicked up his feet behind, clapped his hands together to applaud himself, and jumped on to Bagheera's back, where he sat sideways, drumming with his heels on the glossy skin and making the worst faces he could think of, at Baloo.

'There – there! That was worth a little bruise,' said the brown bear tenderly. 'Some day thou wilt remember me.' Then he turned aside to tell Bagheera how he had begged the Master Words from Hathi[3] the Wild Elephant, who knows all about these things, and how Hathi had taken Mowgli down to a pool to get the Snake Word from a water-snake, because Baloo could not pronounce it, and how Mowgli was now reasonably safe against all accidents in the jungle, because neither snake, bird, nor beast, would hurt him.

'No one then is to be feared,' Baloo wound up, patting his big furry stomach with pride.

'Except his own tribe,' said Bagheera, under his breath; and then aloud to Mowgli: 'Have a care for my ribs, Little Brother! What is all this dancing up and down?'

Mowgli had been trying to make himself heard by pulling at Bagheera's shoulder fur and kicking hard. When the two listened to him he was shouting at the top of his voice: 'And so I shall have a tribe of my own, and lead them through the branches all day long.'

'What is this new folly, little dreamer of dreams?' said Bagheera.

'Yes, and throw branches and dirt at old Baloo,' Mowgli went on. 'They have promised me this. Ah!'

'*Whoof!*' Baloo's big paw scooped Mowgli off Bagheera's back, and as the boy lay between the big fore paws he could see the Bear was angry.

'Mowgli,' said Baloo, 'thou hast been talking with the *Bandar-log*[4] – the Monkey-People.'

Mowgli looked at Bagheera to see if the Panther was angry too, and Bagheera's eyes were as hard as jade-stones.

'Thou hast been with the Monkey-People – the gray apes – the people without a Law – the eaters of everything. That is great shame.'

'When Baloo hurt my head,' said Mowgli (he was still on his back), 'I went away, and the gray apes came down from the trees and had pity on me. No one else cared.' He snuffled a little.

'The pity of the Monkey-People!' Baloo snorted. 'The stillness of the mountain stream! The cool of the summer sun! And then, man-cub?'

'And then, and then, they gave me nuts and pleasant things to eat, and they – they carried me in their arms up to the top of the trees and said I was their blood-brother except that I had no tail, and should be their leader some day.'

'They have *no* leader,' said Bagheera. 'They lie. They have always lied.'

'They were very kind and bade me come again. Why have

I never been taken among the Monkey-People? They stand on their feet as I do. They do not hit me with hard paws. They play all day. Let me get up! Bad Baloo, let me up! I will play with them again.'

'Listen, man-cub,' said the Bear, and his voice rumbled like thunder on a hot night. 'I have taught thee all the Law of the Jungle for all the peoples of the jungle – except the Monkey-Folk who live in the trees. They have no law. They are outcaste.[5] They have no speech of their own, but use the stolen words which they overhear when they listen, and peep, and wait up above in the branches. Their way is not our way. They are without leaders. They have no remembrance. They boast and chatter and pretend that they are a great people about to do great affairs in the jungle, but the falling of a nut turns their minds to laughter and all is forgotten. We of the jungle have no dealings with them. We do not drink where the monkeys drink; we do not go where the monkeys go; we do not hunt where they hunt; we do not die where they die. Hast thou ever heard me speak of the *Bandar-log* till to-day?'

'No,' said Mowgli in a whisper, for the forest was very still now Baloo had finished.

'The Jungle-People put them out of their mouths and out of their mind. They are very many, evil, dirty, shameless, and they desire, if they have any fixed desire, to be noticed by the Jungle-People. But we do *not* notice them even when they throw nuts and filth on our heads.'

He had hardly spoken when a shower of nuts and twigs spattered down through the branches; and they could hear coughings and howlings and angry jumpings high up in the air among the thin branches.

'The Monkey-People are forbidden,' said Baloo, 'forbidden to the Jungle-People. Remember.'

'Forbidden,' said Bagheera; 'but I still think Baloo should have warned thee against them.'

'I – I? How was I to guess he would play with such dirt. The Monkey-People! Faugh!'

A fresh shower came down on their heads and the two trotted away taking Mowgli with them. What Baloo had said

about the monkeys was perfectly true. They belonged to the
tree-tops, and as beasts very seldom look up, there was no
occasion for the monkeys and the Jungle-People to cross each
other's path. But whenever they found a sick wolf, or a wounded
tiger, or bear, the monkeys would torment him, and would
throw sticks and nuts at any beast for fun and in the hope of
being noticed. Then they would howl and shriek senseless
songs, and invite the Jungle-People to climb up their trees and
fight them, or would start furious battles over nothing among
themselves, and leave the dead monkeys where the Jungle-People
could see them. They were always just going to have a leader,
and laws and customs of their own, but they never did, because
their memories would not hold over from day to day, and so
they compromised things by making up a saying: 'What the
Bandar-log think now the jungle will think later,'[6] and that
comforted them a great deal. None of the beasts could reach
them, but on the other hand none of the beasts would notice
them, and that was why they were so pleased when Mowgli
came to play with them, and they heard how angry Baloo was.

They never meant to do any more – the *Bandar-log* never
mean anything at all; but one of them invented what seemed to
him a brilliant idea, and he told all the others that Mowgli
would be a useful person to keep in the tribe, because he could
weave sticks together for protection from the wind; so, if they
caught him, they could make him teach them. Of course
Mowgli, as a woodcutter's child, inherited all sorts of instincts,
and used to make little huts of fallen branches without thinking
how he came to do it, and the Monkey-People, watching in the
trees, considered his play most wonderful. This time, they said,
they were really going to have a leader and become the wisest
people in the jungle – so wise that everyone else would notice
and envy them. Therefore they followed Baloo and Bagheera
and Mowgli through the jungle very quietly till it was time for
the mid-day nap, and Mowgli, who was very much ashamed of
himself, slept between the Panther and the Bear, resolving to
have no more to do with the Monkey-People.

The next thing he remembered, was feeling hands on his legs
and arms – hard, strong, little hands – and then a swash of

branches in his face, and then he was staring down through the swaying boughs as Baloo woke the jungle with his deep cries and Bagheera bounded up the trunk with every tooth bared. The *Bandar-log* howled with triumph and scuffled away to the upper branches where Bagheera dared not follow, shouting: 'He has noticed us! Bagheera has noticed us. All the Jungle-People admire us for our skill and our cunning.' Then they began their flight; and the flight of the Monkey-People through tree-land is one of the things nobody can describe. They have their regular roads and cross-roads, up hills and down hills, all laid out from fifty to seventy or a hundred feet above ground, and by these they can travel even at night if necessary. Two of the strongest monkeys caught Mowgli under the arms and swung off with him through the tree-tops, twenty feet at a bound. Had they been alone they could have gone twice as fast, but the boy's weight held them back. Sick and giddy as Mowgli was he could not help enjoying the wild rush, though the glimpses of earth far down below frightened him, and the terrible check and jerk at the end of the swing over nothing but empty air brought his heart between his teeth. His escort would rush him up a tree till he felt the thinnest topmost branches crackle and bend under them, and then with a cough and a whoop would fling themselves into the air outwards and downwards, and bring up, hanging by their hands or their feet to the lower limbs of the next tree. Sometimes he could see for miles and miles across the still green jungle, as a man on the top of a mast can see for miles across the sea, and then the branches and leaves would lash him across the face, and he and his two guards would be almost down to earth again. So, bounding and crashing and whooping and yelling, the whole tribe of *Bandar-log* swept along the tree-roads with Mowgli their prisoner.

For a time he was afraid of being dropped: then he grew angry but knew better than to struggle, and then he began to think. The first thing was to send back word to Baloo and Bagheera, for, at the pace the monkeys were going, he knew his friends would be left far behind. It was useless to look down, for he could only see the top-sides of the branches, so he stared upwards and saw, far away in the blue, Chil the Kite balancing and wheeling as he kept watch over the jungle waiting for things to die. Chil saw that the monkeys were carrying something, and dropped a few hundred yards to find out whether their load was good to eat. He whistled with surprise when he saw Mowgli being dragged up to a tree-top and heard him give the Kite call for – 'We be of one blood, thou and I.' The waves of the branches closed over the boy, but Chil balanced away to the next tree in time to see the little brown face come up again. 'Mark my trail,' Mowgli shouted. 'Tell Baloo of the Seeonee Pack and Bagheera of the Council Rock.'

'In whose name, Brother?' Chil had never seen Mowgli before, though of course he had heard of him.

'Mowgli, the Frog. Man-cub they call me! Mark my tra-il!'

The last words were shrieked as he was being swung through the air, but Chil nodded and rose up till he looked no bigger than a speck of dust, and there he hung, watching with his telescope eyes the swaying of the tree-tops as Mowgli's escort whirled along.

'They never go far,' he said with a chuckle. 'They never do what they set out to do. Always pecking at new things are the *Bandar-log*. This time, if I have any eyesight, they have pecked down trouble for themselves, for Baloo is no fledgling and Bagheera can, as I know, kill more than goats.'

So he rocked on his wings, his feet gathered up under him, and waited.

Meantime, Baloo and Bagheera were furious with rage and grief. Bagheera climbed as he had never climbed before, but the thin branches broke beneath his weight, and he slipped down, his claws full of bark.

'Why didst thou not warn the man-cub?' he roared to poor Baloo, who had set off at a clumsy trot in the hope of overtaking the monkeys. 'What was the use of half slaying him with blows if thou didst not warn him?'

'Haste! O haste! We – we may catch them yet!' Baloo panted.

'At that speed! It would not tire a wounded cow. Teacher of the Law – cub-beater – a mile of that rolling to and fro would burst thee open. Sit still and think! Make a plan. This is no time for chasing. They may drop him if we follow too close.'

'*Arrula! Whoo!* They may have dropped him already, being tired of carrying him. Who can trust the *Bandar-log*? Put dead bats on my head! Give me black bones to eat! Roll me into the hives of the wild bees that I may be stung to death, and bury me with the Hyæna, for I am the most miserable of bears! *Arulala! Wahooa!* O Mowgli, Mowgli! why did I not warn thee against the Monkey-Folk instead of breaking thy head? Now perhaps I may have knocked the day's lesson out of his mind, and he will be alone in the jungle without the Master Words.'

Baloo clasped his paws over his ears and rolled to and fro moaning.

'At least he gave me all the Words correctly a little time ago,' said Bagheera, impatiently. 'Baloo, thou hast neither memory, nor respect. What would the jungle think if I, the Black Panther, curled myself up like Sahi the Porcupine, and howled?'

'What do I care what the jungle thinks? He may be dead by now.'

'Unless and until they drop him from the branches in sport, or kill him out of idleness, I have no fear for the man-cub. He is wise and well-taught, and above all he has the eyes that make the Jungle-People afraid. But (and it is a great evil) he is in the power of the *Bandar-log*, and they, because they live in trees, have no fear of any of our people.' Bagheera licked one fore-paw thoughtfully.

'Fool that I am! Oh fat, brown, root-digging fool that I am,' said Baloo, uncoiling himself with a jerk, 'it is true what Hathi the Wild Elephant says: "*To each his own fear*"; and they, the *Bandar-log*, fear Kaa the Rock Snake. He can climb as well as they can. He steals the young monkeys in the night. The whisper of his name makes their wicked tails cold. Let us go to Kaa.'

'What will he do for us? He is not of our tribe, being footless – and with most evil eyes,' said Bagheera.

'He is very old and very cunning. Above all, he is always hungry,' said Baloo hopefully. 'Promise him many goats.'

'He sleeps for a full month after he has once eaten. He may be asleep now, and even were he awake what if he would rather kill his own goats?' Bagheera, who did not know much about Kaa, was naturally suspicious.

'Then in that case, thou and I together, old hunter, might make him see reason.' Here Baloo rubbed his faded brown shoulder against the Panther, and they went off to look for Kaa the Rock-python.

They found him stretched out on a warm ledge in the afternoon sun, admiring his beautiful new coat, for he had been in retirement for the last ten days changing his skin, and now he was very splendid – darting his big blunt-nosed head along the ground, and twisting the thirty feet of his body into fantastic knots and curves, and licking his lips as he thought of his dinner to come.

'He has not eaten,' said Baloo, with a grunt of relief, as soon as he saw the beautifully mottled brown and yellow jacket. 'Be careful, Bagheera! He is always a little blind after he has changed his skin, and very quick to strike.'

Kaa was not a poison-snake – in fact he rather despised the poison-snakes as cowards – but his strength lay in his hug, and when he had once lapped his huge coils round anybody there was no more to be said. 'Good hunting!' cried Baloo, sitting up on his haunches. Like all snakes of his breed Kaa was rather deaf, and did not hear the call at first. Then he curled up ready for any accident, his head lowered.

'Good hunting for us all,' he answered. 'Oho, Baloo, what dost thou do here? Good hunting, Bagheera. One of us at least needs food. Is there any news of game afoot? A doe now, or even a young buck? I am as empty as a dried well.'

'We are hunting,' said Baloo carelessly. He knew that you must not hurry Kaa. He is too big.

'Give me permission to come with you,' said Kaa. 'A blow more or less is nothing to thee, Bagheera or Baloo, but I – I have to wait and wait for days in a wood-path and climb half a night on the mere chance of a young ape. Psshaw! The branches are not what they were when I was young. Rotten twigs and dry boughs are they all.'

'Maybe thy great weight has something to do with the matter,' said Baloo.

'I am a fair length – a fair length,' said Kaa, with a little pride. 'But for all that, it is the fault of this new-grown timber.

I came very near to falling on my last hunt – very near indeed – and the noise of my slipping, for my tail was not tight wrapped round the tree, waked the *Bandar-log*, and they called me most evil names.'

'Footless, yellow earth-worm,' said Bagheera under his whiskers, as though he were trying to remember something.

'Sssss! Have they ever called me *that*?' said Kaa.

'Something of that kind it was that they shouted to us last moon, but we never noticed them. They will say anything – even that thou hast lost all thy teeth, and wilt not face anything bigger than a kid, because (they are indeed shameless, these *Bandar-log*) – because thou art afraid of the he-goats' horns,' Bagheera went on sweetly.

Now a snake, especially a wary old python like Kaa, very seldom shows that he is angry, but Baloo and Bagheera could see the big swallowing-muscles on either side of Kaa's throat ripple and bulge.

'The *Bandar-log* have shifted their grounds,' he said quietly. 'When I came up into the sun today I heard them whooping among the tree-tops.'

'It – it is the *Bandar-log* that we follow now,' said Baloo, but the words stuck in his throat, for that was the first time in his memory that one of the Jungle-People had owned to being interested in the doings of the monkeys.

'Beyond doubt then it is no small thing that takes two such hunters – leaders in their own jungle I am certain – on the trail of the *Bandar-log*,' Kaa replied, courteously, as he swelled with curiosity.

'Indeed,' Baloo began, 'I am no more than the old and sometimes very foolish Teacher of the Law to the Seeonee wolf-cubs, and Bagheera here—'

'Is Bagheera,' said the Black Panther, and his jaws shut with a snap, for he did not believe in being humble. 'The trouble is this, Kaa. Those nut-stealers and pickers of palm leaves have stolen away our man-cub, of whom thou hast perhaps heard.'

'I heard some news from Sahi (his quills make him presumptuous) of a man-thing that was entered into a wolf-pack, but I did not believe. Sahi is full of stories half heard and very badly told.'

'But it is true. He is such a man-cub as never was,' said Baloo. 'The best and wisest and boldest of man-cubs – my own pupil, who shall make the name of Baloo famous through all the jungles; and besides, I – we – love him, Kaa.'

'Ts! Ts!' said Kaa, weaving his head to and fro. 'I also have known what love is. There are tales I could tell that—'

'That need a clear night when we are all well fed to praise properly,' said Bagheera, quickly. 'Our man-cub is in the hands of the *Bandar-log* now, and we know that of all the Jungle-People they fear Kaa alone.'

'They fear me alone. They have good reason,' said Kaa. 'Chattering, foolish, vain – vain, foolish, and chattering, are monkeys. But a man-thing in their hands is in no good luck. They grow tired of the nuts they pick, and throw them down. They carry a branch half a day, meaning to do great things with it, and then they snap it in two. That man-thing is not to be envied. They called me also – yellow fish was it not?'

'Worm – worm – earth-worm,' said Bagheera, 'as well as other things which I cannot now say for shame.'

'We must remind them to speak well of their master. Aaa-ssp![7] We must help their wandering memories. Now, whither went they with the cub?'

'The jungle alone knows. Towards the sunset, I believe,' said Baloo. 'We had thought that thou wouldst know, Kaa.'

'I? How? I take them when they come in my way, but I do not hunt the *Bandar-log*, or frogs – or green scum on a water-hole for that matter. Hsss!'

'Up, Up! Up, Up! Hillo! Illo! Illo, look up, Baloo of the Seeonee Wolf Pack!'

Baloo looked up to see where the voice came from, and there was Chil the Kite, sweeping down with the sun shining on the upturned flanges of his wings. It was near Chil's bed-time, but he had ranged all over the jungle looking for the Bear and missed him in the thick foliage.

'What is it?' said Baloo.

'I have seen Mowgli among the *Bandar-log*. He bade me tell you. I watched. The *Bandar-log* have taken him beyond the river to the monkey city – to the Cold Lairs.[8] They may stay there for a night, or ten nights, or an hour. I have told the bats to watch through the dark time. That is my message. Good hunting, all you below!'

'Full gorge and a deep sleep to you, Chil,' cried Bagheera. 'I will remember thee in my next kill, and put aside the head for thee alone – oh best of kites!'

'It is nothing. It is nothing. The boy held the Master Word. I could have done no less,' and Chil circled up again to his roost.

'He has not forgotten to use his tongue,' said Baloo, with a chuckle of pride. 'To think of one so young remembering the Master Word for the birds too while he was being pulled across-trees!'

'It was most firmly driven into him,' said Bagheera. 'But I am proud of him, and now we must go to the Cold Lairs.'

They all knew where that place was, but few of the Jungle-People ever went there, because what they called the Cold Lairs was an old deserted city, lost and buried in the jungle, and beasts seldom use a place that men have once used. The wild boar will, but the hunting-tribes do not. Besides, the monkeys lived there as much as they could be said to live anywhere, and no self-respecting animal would come within eye-shot of it except in times of drouth, when the half-ruined tanks and reservoirs held a little water.

'It is half a night's journey – at full speed,' said Bagheera, and Baloo looked very serious. 'I will go as fast as I can,' he said, anxiously.

'We dare not wait for thee. Follow, Baloo. We must go on the quick-foot – Kaa and I.'

'Feet or no feet, I can keep abreast of all thy four,' said Kaa, shortly. Baloo made one effort to hurry, but had to sit down panting, and so they left him to come on later, while Bagheera hurried forward, at the quick panther-canter. Kaa said nothing, but, strive as Bagheera might, the huge Rock-python held level with him. When they came to a hill-stream, Bagheera gained, because he bounded across while Kaa swam, his head and two feet of his neck clearing the water, but on level ground[9] Kaa made up the distance.

'By the Broken Lock that freed me,' said Bagheera, when twilight had fallen, 'thou art no slow goer!'

'I am hungry,' said Kaa. 'Besides, they called me speckled frog.'

'Worm – earth-worm, and yellow to boot.'

'All one. Let us go on,' and Kaa seemed to pour himself along the ground, finding the shortest road with his steady eyes, and keeping to it.

In the Cold Lairs the Monkey-People were not thinking of Mowgli's friends at all. They had brought the boy to the Lost City, and were very pleased with themselves for the time. Mowgli had never seen an Indian city before, and though this was almost a heap of ruins it seemed very wonderful and splendid. Some king had built it long ago on a little hill. You could still trace the stone causeways that led up to the ruined gates where the last splinters of wood hung to the worn, rusted hinges. Trees had grown into and out of the walls; the battlements were tumbled down and decayed, and wild creepers hung out of the windows of the towers on the walls in bushy hanging clumps.

A great roofless palace crowned the hill, and the marble of the courtyards and fountains was split, and stained with red and green, and the very cobblestones in the courtyard where the king's elephants used to live had been thrust up and apart by grasses and young trees. From the palace you could see the rows and rows of roofless houses that made up the city looking like empty honeycombs filled with blackness; the shapeless block of stone that had been an idol, in the square where four roads met; the pits and dimples at street-corners where the public wells once stood, and the shattered domes of temples with wild figs sprouting on their sides. The monkeys called the place their city, and pretended to despise the Jungle-People because they lived in the forest. And yet they never knew what the buildings were made for nor how to use them. They would sit in circles on the hall of the king's council chamber, and scratch for fleas and pretend to be men; or they would run in and out of the roofless houses and collect pieces of plaster and old bricks in a corner, and forget where they had hidden them, and fight and cry in scuffling crowds, and then break off to play up and down the terraces of the king's garden, where they would shake the rose trees and the oranges in sport to see the fruit and flowers fall. They explored all the passages and dark tunnels in the palace and the hundreds of little dark rooms, but they never remembered what they had seen and what they had not; and so drifted about in ones and twos or crowds telling each other that they were doing as men did. They drank at the tanks and made the water all muddy, and then they fought over it, and then they would all rush together in mobs and shout: 'There is no one in the jungle so wise and good and clever and strong and gentle as the *Bandar-log*.' Then all would begin again till they grew tired of the city and went back to the tree-tops, hoping the Jungle-People would notice them.

Mowgli, who had been trained under the Law of the Jungle, did not like or understand this kind of life. The monkeys dragged him into the Cold Lairs late in the afternoon, and instead of going to sleep, as Mowgli would have done after a long journey, they joined hands and danced about and sang their foolish songs. One of the monkeys made a speech and told his companions that Mowgli's capture marked a new thing in the history of the *Bandar-log*, for Mowgli was going to show them how to weave sticks and canes together as a protection against rain and cold. Mowgli picked up some creepers and began to work them in and out, and the monkeys tried to imitate; but in a very few minutes they lost interest and began to pull their friends' tails or jump up and down on all fours, coughing.

'I wish to eat,' said Mowgli. 'I am a stranger in this part of the jungle. Bring me food, or give me leave to hunt here.'

Twenty or thirty monkeys bounded away to bring him nuts and wild pawpaws; but they fell to fighting on the road, and it was too much trouble to go back with what was left of the fruit. Mowgli was sore and angry as well as hungry, and he roamed through the empty city giving the Strangers' Hunting Call from time to time, but no one answered him, and Mowgli felt that he had reached a very bad place indeed. 'All that Baloo has said about the *Bandar-log* is true,' he thought to himself. 'They have no Law, no Hunting Call, and no leaders – nothing but foolish words and little picking thievish hands. So if I am starved or killed here, it will be all my own fault. But I must try to return to my own jungle. Baloo will surely beat me, but that is better than chasing silly rose leaves with the *Bandar-log*.'

No sooner had he walked to the city wall than the monkeys pulled him back, telling him that he did not know how happy he was, and pinching him to make him grateful. He set his teeth and said nothing, but went with the shouting monkeys to a terrace above the red sandstone reservoirs that were half-full of rain water. There was a ruined summer-house of white marble in the centre of the terrace, built for queens dead a hundred years ago. The domed roof had half fallen in and blocked up the underground passage from the palace by which the queens used to enter; but the walls were made of screens of marble tracery – beautiful milk-white fret-work, set with agates and cornelians and jasper and lapis lazuli, and as the moon came up behind the hill it shone through the open work, casting shadows on the ground like black velvet embroidery. Sore, sleepy, and hungry as he was, Mowgli could not help laughing when the *Bandar-log* began, twenty at a time, to tell him how great and wise and strong and gentle they were, and how foolish he was to wish to leave them. 'We are great. We are free. We are wonderful. We are the most wonderful people in all the jungle! We all say so, and so it must be true,' they shouted. 'Now as you are a new listener and can carry our words back to the Jungle-People so that they may notice us in future, we will tell you all about our most excellent selves.' Mowgli made no objection, and the monkeys gathered by hundreds and hundreds on the terrace to listen to their own speakers singing the praises of the *Bandar-log*, and whenever a speaker stopped for want of breath they would all shout together: 'This is true; we all say so.' Mowgli nodded and blinked, and said 'Yes' when they asked him a question, and his head spun with the noise. 'Tabaqui, the Jackal, must have bitten all these people,' he said to himself, 'and now they have the madness. Certainly this is *dewanee*, the madness. Do they never go to sleep? Now there is a cloud coming to cover that moon. If it were only a big enough cloud I might try to run away in the darkness. But I am tired.'

That same cloud was being watched by two good friends in the ruined ditch below the city wall, for Bagheera and Kaa, knowing well how dangerous the Monkey-People were in large numbers, did not wish to run any risks. The monkeys never fight unless they are a hundred to one, and few in the jungle care for those odds.

'I will go to the west wall,' Kaa whispered, 'and come down swiftly with the slope of the ground in my favour. They will not throw themselves upon *my* back in their hundreds, but—'

'I know it,' said Bagheera. 'Would that Baloo were here; but we must do what we can. When that cloud covers the moon I shall go to the terrace. They hold some sort of council there over the boy.'

'Good hunting,' said Kaa, grimly, and glided away to the west wall. That happened to be the least ruined of any, and the big snake was delayed awhile before he could find a way up the stones. The cloud hid the moon, and as Mowgli wondered what would come next he heard Bagheera's light feet on the terrace. The Black Panther had raced up the slope almost without a sound and was striking – he knew better than to waste time in biting – right and left among the monkeys, who were seated round Mowgli in circles fifty and sixty deep. There was a howl of fright and rage, and then as Bagheera tripped on the rolling, kicking bodies beneath him, a monkey shouted: 'There is only one here! Kill him! Kill.' A scuffling mass of monkeys, biting, scratching, tearing, and pulling, closed over Bagheera, while five or six laid hold of Mowgli, dragged him up the wall of the summer-house and pushed him through the hole of the broken dome. A man-trained boy would have been badly bruised, for the fall was a good fifteen feet, but Mowgli fell as Baloo had taught him to fall, and landed on his feet.

'Stay there,' shouted the monkeys, 'till we have killed thy friends, and later we will play with thee – if the Poison-People leave thee alive.'

'We be of one blood, ye and I,' said Mowgli, quickly giving the Snake's Call. He could hear rustling and hissing in the rubbish all round him and gave the Call a second time, to make sure.

'Even ssso! Down hoods all!' said half a dozen low voices (every ruin in India becomes sooner or later a dwelling-place of snakes, and the old summer-house was alive with cobras). 'Stand still, Little Brother, for thy feet may do us harm.'

Mowgli stood as quietly as he could, peering through the open work and listening to the furious din of the fight round the Black Panther – the yells and chatterings and scufflings, and Bagheera's deep, hoarse cough as he backed and bucked and twisted and plunged under the heaps of his enemies. For the first time since he was born, Bagheera was fighting for his life.

'Baloo must be at hand; Bagheera would not have come alone,' Mowgli thought; and then he called aloud: 'To the tank, Bagheera. Roll to the water-tanks. Roll and plunge! Get to the water!'

Bagheera heard, and the cry that told him Mowgli was safe gave him new courage. He worked his way desperately, inch by inch, straight for the reservoirs, hitting in silence. Then from the ruined wall nearest the jungle rose up the rumbling war-shout of Baloo. The old Bear had done his best, but he could not come before. 'Bagheera,' he shouted, 'I am here. I climb! I haste! *Ahuwora!* The stones slip under my feet! Wait my coming, oh most infamous *Bandar-log*!' He panted up the terrace only to disappear to the head in a wave of monkeys, but he threw himself squarely on his haunches, and, spreading out his fore-paws, hugged as many as he could hold, and then began to hit with a regular *bat-bat-bat*, like the flipping strokes of a paddle-wheel. A crash and a splash told Mowgli that Bagheera had fought his way to the tank where the monkeys could not follow. The Panther lay gasping for breath, his head just out of water, while the monkeys stood three deep on the red steps, dancing up and down with rage, ready to spring upon him from all sides if he came out to help Baloo. It was then that Bagheera lifted up his dripping chin, and in despair gave the Snake's Call for protection – 'We be of one blood, ye and I' – for he believed that Kaa had turned tail at the last minute. Even Baloo, half smothered under the monkeys on the edge of the terrace, could not help chuckling as he heard the Black Panther asking for help.

Kaa had only just worked his way over the west wall, landing with a wrench that dislodged a coping-stone into the ditch. He had no intention of losing any advantage of the ground, and coiled and uncoiled himself once or twice, to be sure that every foot of his long body was in working order. All that while the fight with Baloo went on, and the monkeys yelled in the tank round Bagheera, and Mang, the Bat, flying to and fro, carried the news of the great battle over the jungle, till even Hathi the Wild Elephant trumpeted, and, far away, scattered bands of the Monkey-Folk woke and came leaping along the tree-roads to help their comrades in the Cold Lairs, and the noise of the fight roused all the day-birds for miles round. Then Kaa came straight, quickly, and anxious to kill. The fighting-strength of a python is in the driving blow of his head backed by all the strength and weight of his body. If you can imagine a lance, or a battering ram, or a hammer weighing nearly half a ton driven by a cool, quiet mind living in the handle of it, you can roughly imagine what Kaa was like when he fought. A python four or five feet long can knock a man down if he hits him fairly in the chest, and Kaa was thirty feet long, as you know. His first stroke was delivered into the heart of the crowd round Baloo – was sent home with shut mouth in silence, and there was no need of a second. The monkeys scattered with cries of – 'Kaa! It is Kaa! Run! Run!'

Generations of monkeys had been scared into good behaviour by the stories their elders told them of Kaa, the night-thief, who could slip along the branches as quietly as moss grows, and steal away the strongest monkey that ever lived; of old Kaa, who could make himself look so like a dead branch or a rotten stump that the wisest were deceived, till the branch caught them. Kaa was everything that the monkeys feared in the jungle, for none of them knew the limits of his power, none of them could look him in the face, and none had ever come alive out of his hug. And so they ran, stammering with terror, to the walls and the roofs of the houses, and Baloo drew a deep breath of relief. His fur was much thicker than Bagheera's, but he had suffered sorely in the fight. Then Kaa opened his mouth for the first time and spoke one long hissing word, and the far away monkeys, hurrying to the defence of the Cold Lairs, stayed where they were, cowering, till the loaded branches bent and crackled under them. The monkeys on the walls and the empty houses stopped their cries, and in the stillness that fell upon the city Mowgli heard Bagheera shaking his wet sides as he came up from the tank. Then the clamour broke out again. The monkeys leaped higher up the walls; they clung round the necks of the big stone idols and shrieked as they skipped along the battlements, while Mowgli, dancing in the summer-house, put his eye to the screen work and hooted owl-fashion between his front teeth, to show his derision and contempt.

'Get the man-cub out of that trap; I can do no more,' Bagheera gasped. 'Let us take the man-cub and go. They may attack again.'

'They will not move till I order them. Stay you sssso!' Kaa hissed, and the city was silent once more. 'I could not come before, Brother, but I *think* I heard thee call' – this was to Bagheera.

'I – I may have cried out in the battle,' Bagheera answered. 'Baloo, art thou hurt?'

'I am not sure that they did not pull me into a hundred little bearlings,' said Baloo, gravely shaking one leg after the other. 'Wow! I am sore. Kaa, we owe thee, I think, our lives – Bagheera and I.'

'No matter. Where is the manling?'

'Here, in a trap. I cannot climb out,' cried Mowgli. The curve of the broken dome was above his head.

'Take him away. He dances like Mor, the Peacock. He will crush our young,' said the cobras inside.

'Hah!' said Kaa with a chuckle, 'he has friends everywhere, this manling. Stand back, manling; and hide you, O Poison-People. I break down the wall.'

Kaa looked carefully till he found a discoloured crack in the marble tracery showing a weak spot, made two or three light taps with his head to get the distance, and then lifting up six feet of his body clear of the ground, sent home half-a-dozen full-power smashing blows, nose-first. The screen-work broke and fell away in a cloud of dust and rubbish, and Mowgli leaped through the opening and flung himself between Baloo and Bagheera – an arm round each big neck.

'Art thou hurt?' said Baloo, hugging him softly.

'I am sore, hungry, and not a little bruised; but oh they have handled ye grievously my Brothers! Ye bleed.'

'Others also,' said Bagheera, licking his lips and looking at the monkey-dead on the terrace and round the tank.

'It is nothing, it is nothing if thou art safe, oh my pride of all little frogs!' whimpered Baloo.

'Of that we shall judge later,' said Bagheera, in a dry voice that Mowgli did not at all like. 'But here is Kaa to whom we owe the battle and thou owest thy life. Thank him according to our customs, Mowgli.'

Mowgli turned and saw the great Python's head swaying a foot above his own.

'So this is the manling,' said Kaa. 'Very soft is his skin, and he is not unlike the *Bandar-log*. Have a care, manling, that I do not mistake thee for a monkey some twilight when I have newly changed my coat.'

'We be one blood, thou and I,' Mowgli answered. 'I take my life from thee tonight. My kill shall be thy kill if ever thou art hungry, O Kaa.'

'All thanks, Little Brother,' said Kaa, though his eyes twinkled. 'And what may so bold a hunter kill? I ask that I may follow when next he goes abroad.'

'I kill nothing – I am too little – but I drive goats towards such as can use them. When thou art empty come to me and see if I speak the truth. I have some skill in these' – he held out his hands – 'and if ever thou art in a trap, I may pay the debt which I owe to thee, to Bagheera, and to Baloo, here. Good hunting to ye all, my masters.'

'Well said,' growled Baloo, for Mowgli had returned thanks very prettily. The Python dropped his head lightly for a minute on Mowgli's shoulder. 'A brave heart and courteous tongue,' said he. 'They shall carry thee far through the jungle, manling. But now go hence quickly with thy friends. Go and sleep, for the moon sets, and what follows it is not well that thou shouldst see.'

The moon was sinking behind the hills and the lines of trembling monkeys huddled together on the walls and battlements looked like ragged shaky fringes of things. Baloo went down to the tank for a drink and Bagheera began to put his fur in order, as Kaa glided out into the centre of the terrace and brought his jaws together with a ringing snap that drew all the monkeys' eyes upon him.

'The moon sets,' he said. 'Is there yet light enough to see?'

From the walls came a moan like the wind in the tree-tops – 'We see, O Kaa.'

'Good. Begins now the dance – the Dance of the Hunger of Kaa. Sit still and watch.' He turned twice or thrice in a big circle, weaving his head from right to left. Then he began making loops and figures of eight with his body, and soft, oozy triangles that melted into squares and five-sided figures, and coiled mounds, never resting, never hurrying, and never stopping his low humming song. It grew darker and darker, till at last the dragging, shifting coils disappeared, but they could hear the rustle of the scales.

Baloo and Bagheera stood still as stone, growling in their throats, their neck-hair bristling, and Mowgli watched and wondered.

'*Bandar-log*,' said the voice of Kaa at last, 'can ye stir foot or hand without my order? Speak!'

'Without thy order we cannot stir foot or hand, O Kaa!'

'Good! Come all one pace nearer to me.'

The lines of the monkeys swayed forward helplessly, and Baloo and Bagheera took one stiff step forward with them.

'Nearer!' hissed Kaa, and they all moved again.

Mowgli laid his hands on Baloo and Bagheera to get them away, and the two great beasts started as though they had been waked from a dream.

'Keep thy hand on my shoulder,' Bagheera whispered. 'Keep it there, or I must go back – must go back to Kaa. Aah!'

'It is only old Kaa making circles on the dust,' said Mowgli; 'let us go'; and the three slipped off through a gap in the walls to the jungle.

'*Whoof!*' said Baloo, when he stood under the still trees

again. 'Never more will I make an ally of Kaa,' and he shook himself all over.

'He knows more than we,' said Bagheera, trembling. 'In a little time, had I stayed, I should have walked down his throat.'

'Many will walk by that road before the moon rises again,' said Baloo. 'He will have good hunting – after his own fashion.'

'But what was the meaning of it all?' said Mowgli, who did not know anything of a python's powers of fascination. 'I saw no more than a big snake making foolish circles till the dark came. And his nose was all sore. Ho! Ho!'

'Mowgli,' said Bagheera, angrily, 'his nose was sore on *thy* account, as my ears and sides and paws, and Baloo's neck and shoulders are bitten on *thy* account. Neither Baloo nor Bagheera will be able to hunt with pleasure for many days.'

'It is nothing,' said Baloo; 'we have the man-cub again.'

'True; but he has cost us heavily in time which might have been spent in good hunting, in wounds, in hair – I am half plucked along my back – and last of all, in honour. For, remember, Mowgli, I, who am the Black Panther, was forced to call upon Kaa for protection, and Baloo and I were both made stupid as little birds by the Hunger-Dance. All this, man-cub, came of thy playing with the *Bandar-log*.'

'True; it is true,' said Mowgli, sorrowfully. 'I am an evil man-cub, and my stomach is sad in me.'

'Mf! What says the Law of the Jungle, Baloo?'

Baloo did not wish to bring Mowgli into any more trouble, but he could not tamper with the Law, so he mumbled: 'Sorrow never stays punishment. But remember, Bagheera, he is very little.'

'I will remember; but he has done mischief, and blows must be dealt now. Mowgli, hast thou anything to say?'

'Nothing. I did wrong. Baloo and thou are wounded. It is just.'

Bagheera gave him half a dozen love-taps from a panther's point of view (they would hardly have waked one of his own cubs), but for a seven-year-old boy they amounted to as severe a beating as you could wish to avoid. When it was all over Mowgli sneezed, and picked himself up without a word.

'Now,' said Bagheera, 'jump on my back, Little Brother, and we will go home.'

One of the beauties of Jungle Law is that punishment settles all scores. There is no nagging afterwards.

Mowgli laid his head down on Bagheera's back and slept so deeply that he never waked when he was put down[10] in the home-cave.

Road-Song of the Bandar-Log

Here we go in a flung festoon,
Half way up to the jealous moon!
Don't you envy our pranceful bands?
Don't you wish you had extra hands?
Wouldn't you like if your tails were – *so* –
Curved in the shape of a Cupid's Bow?
    Now you're angry, but – never mind,
    Brother, thy tail hangs down behind!

Here we sit in a branchy row,
Thinking of beautiful things we know,
Dreaming of deeds that we mean to do,
All complete, in a minute or two –
Something noble and wise and good,
Done by merely wishing we could.
    We've forgotten, but[1] – never mind,
    Brother, thy tail hangs down behind!

All the talk we ever have heard
Uttered by bat or beast or bird –
Hide or fin or scale or feather –
Jabber it quickly and all together!
Excellent! Wonderful! Once again!
Now we are talking just like men!
    Let's pretend we are – never mind,
    Brother, thy tail hangs down behind!
    This is the way of the monkey-kind.

Then join our leaping lines that scumfish[2] through the pines,
That rocket by where, light and high, the wild grape swings,
By the rubbish in our wake, and the noble noise we make,
Be sure, be sure, we're going to do some splendid things!

'TIGER-TIGER!'

What of the hunting, hunter bold?
Brother, the watch was long and cold.
What of the quarry ye went to kill?
Brother, he crops in the jungle still.
Where is the power that made your pride?
Brother, it ebbs from my flank and side.
Where is the haste that ye hurry by?
Brother, I go to my lair to die.

When Mowgli left the wolf's cave after the fight with the Pack at the Council Rock, he went down to the ploughed lands where the villagers lived, but he would not stop there because it was too near to the jungle, and he knew that he had made at least one bad enemy at the Council.[1] So he hurried on, keeping to the rough road that ran down the valley, and followed it at a steady jog-trot for nearly twenty miles, till he came to a country that he did not know. The valley opened out into a great plain dotted over with rocks and cut up with ravines. At one end stood a little village, and at the other the thick jungle came down in a sweep to the grazing-grounds, and stopped there as though it had been cut off with a hoe. All over the plain, cattle and buffaloes were grazing, and when the little boys in charge of the herds saw Mowgli they shouted and ran away, and the yellow pariah dogs that hang about every Indian village barked. Mowgli walked on, for he was feeling hungry, and when he came to the village gate he saw the big thornbush that was drawn up before the gate at twilight, pushed to one side.

'Umph!' he said, for he had come across more than one such barricade in his night rambles after things to eat. 'So men are afraid of the People of the Jungle here also.' He sat down by the gate, and when a man came out he stood up, opened his mouth, and pointed down it to show that he wanted food. The man stared, and ran back up the one street of the village shouting for the priest, who was a big, fat man dressed in white, with a red and yellow mark on his forehead.[2] The priest came to the gate, and with him at least a hundred people, who stared and talked and shouted and pointed at Mowgli.

'They have no manners, these Men Folk,' said Mowgli to himself. 'Only the gray ape would behave as they do.' So he threw back his long hair and frowned at the crowd.

'What is there to be afraid of?' said the priest. 'Look at the marks on his arms and legs. They are the bites of wolves. He is but a wolf-child run away from the jungle.'

Of course, in playing together, the cubs had often nipped Mowgli harder than they intended, and there were white scars all over his arms and legs. But he would have been the last person in the world to call these bites, for he knew what real biting meant.

'*Arré! arré!*' said two or three women together. 'To be bitten by wolves, poor child! He is a handsome boy. He has eyes like red fire. By my honour, Messua,[3] he is not unlike thy boy that was taken by the tiger.'

'Let me look,' said a woman with heavy copper rings on her wrists and ankles, and she peered at Mowgli under the palm of her hand. 'Indeed he is not. He is thinner, but he has the very look of my boy.'

The priest was a clever man, and he knew that Messua was wife to the richest villager in the place. So he looked up at the sky for a minute, and said solemnly: 'What the jungle has taken the jungle has restored. Take the boy into thy house, my sister, and forget not to honour the priest who sees so far into the lives of men.'

'By the Bull that bought me,' said Mowgli to himself, 'but all this talking is like another looking over by the Pack! Well, if I am a man, a man I must be.'[4]

The crowd parted as the woman beckoned Mowgli to her hut, where there was a red lacquered bedstead, a great earthen grain-chest with funny raised patterns on it, half a dozen copper cooking-pots, an image of a Hindu god in a little alcove, and on the wall a real looking-glass, such as they sell at the country fairs for eight cents.[5]

She gave him a long drink of milk[6] and some bread, and then she laid her hand on his head and looked into his eyes; for she thought perhaps that he might be her real son come back from the jungle where the tiger had taken him. So she said: 'Nathoo, O Nathoo!' Mowgli did not show that he knew the name. 'Dost thou not remember the day when I gave thee thy new shoes?' She touched his foot, and it was almost as hard as horn. 'No,' she said, sorrowfully; 'those feet have never worn shoes, but thou art very like my Nathoo, and thou shalt be my son.'

Mowgli was uneasy, because he had never been under a roof before; but as he looked at the thatch, he saw that he could tear it out any time if he wanted to get away, and that the window had no fastenings. 'What is the good of a man,' he said to himself at last, 'if he does not understand man's talk? Now I am as silly and dumb as a man would be with us in the jungle. I must speak their talk.'

He had not learned while he was with the wolves to imitate the challenge of bucks in the jungle and the grunt of the little wild pig for fun. So, as soon as Messua pronounced a word Mowgli would imitate it almost perfectly, and before dark he had learned the name of many things in the hut.

There was a difficulty at bedtime, because Mowgli would not sleep under anything that looked so like a panther-trap as that hut, and when they shut the door he went through the window. 'Give him his will,' said Messua's husband. 'Remember he can never till now have slept on a bed. If he is indeed sent in the place of our son he will not run away.'

So Mowgli stretched himself in some long clean grass at the edge of the field, but before he had closed his eyes a soft gray nose poked him under the chin.

'Phew!' said Gray Brother (he was the eldest of Mother Wolf's cubs). 'This is a poor reward for following thee twenty miles. Thou smellest of wood-smoke and cattle – altogether like a man already. Wake, Little Brother; I bring news.'

'Are all well in the jungle?' said Mowgli, hugging him.

'All except the wolves that were burned with the Red Flower.

Now, listen. Shere Khan has gone away to hunt far off till his coat grows again, for he is badly singed. When he returns he swears that he will lay thy bones in the Waingunga.'

'There are two words to that. I also have made a little promise. But news is always good. I am tired tonight – very tired with new things, Gray Brother – but bring me the news always.'

'Thou wilt not forget that thou art a wolf? Men will not make thee forget?' said Gray Brother, anxiously.

'Never. I will always remember that I love thee and all in our cave; but also I will always remember that I have been cast out of the Pack.'

'And that thou may'st be cast out of another pack. Men are only men, Little Brother, and their talk is like the talk of frogs in a pond. When I come down here again, I will wait for thee in the bamboos at the edge of the grazing-ground.'

For three months after that night Mowgli hardly ever left the village gate, he was so busy learning the ways and customs of men. First he had to wear a cloth round him, which annoyed him horribly; and then he had to learn about money, which he did not in the least understand, and about ploughing, of which he did not see the use. Then the little children in the village made him very angry. Luckily, the Law of the Jungle had taught him to keep his temper, for in the jungle, life and food depend on keeping your temper; but when they made fun of him because he would not play games or fly kites, or because he mispronounced some word, only the knowledge that it was unsportsmanlike to kill little naked cubs kept him from picking them up and breaking them in two. He did not know his own strength in the least. In the jungle he knew he was weak compared with the beasts, but in the village, people said that he was as strong as a bull. He certainly had no notion of what fear was, for when the village priest told him that the god in the temple would be angry with him if he ate the priest's mangoes, he picked up the image, brought it over to the priest's house, and asked the priest to make the god angry and he would be happy to fight him. It was a horrible scandal, but the priest hushed it up, and Messua's husband paid much good silver to comfort the god.[7] And Mowgli had not the faintest idea of the difference that caste makes between man and man. When the potter's donkey slipped in the clay-pit, Mowgli hauled it out by the tail, and helped to stack the pots for their journey to the market at Khanhiwara.[8] That was very shocking, too, for the potter is a low-caste man, and his donkey is worse.[9] When the priest scolded him, Mowgli threatened to put him on the donkey, too, and the priest told Messua's husband that Mowgli had better be set to work as soon as possible; and the village head-man told Mowgli that he would have to go out with the buffaloes next day, and herd them while they grazed. No one was more pleased than Mowgli; and that night, because he had been appointed a servant of the village, as it were, he went off to a circle that met every evening on a masonry platform under a great fig-tree. It was the village club, and the head-man and the watchman and the barber, who knew all the gossip of the village, and old Buldeo,[10] the village hunter, who had a Tower musket,[11] met and smoked. The monkeys sat and talked in the upper branches, and there was a hole under the platform where a cobra lived, and he had his little platter of milk every night because he was sacred; and the old men sat around the tree and talked, and pulled at the big *huqas* (the water-pipes) till far into the night. They told wonderful tales of gods and men and ghosts; and Buldeo told even more wonderful ones of the ways of beasts in the jungle, till the eyes of the children sitting outside the circle bulged out of their heads. Most of the tales were about animals, for the jungle was always at their door. The deer and the wild pig grubbed up their crops, and now and again the tiger carried off a man at twilight, within sight of the village gates.

Mowgli, who naturally knew something about what they were talking of, had to cover his face not to show that he was laughing, while Buldeo, the Tower musket across his knees, climbed on from one wonderful story to another, and Mowgli's shoulders shook.

Buldeo was explaining how the tiger that had carried away Messua's son was a ghost-tiger, and his body was inhabited by the ghost of a wicked, old money-lender, who had died some years ago. 'And I know that this is true,' he said, 'because Purun

Dass[12] always limped from the blow that he got in a riot when his account-books were burned, and the tiger that I speak of *he* limps, too, for the tracks of his pads are unequal.'

'True, true, that must be the truth,' said the graybeards nodding together.

'Are all these tales such cobwebs and moon-talk?' said Mowgli. 'That tiger limps because he was born lame, as everyone knows. To talk of the soul of a money-lender in a beast that never had the courage of a jackal is child's talk.'

Buldeo was speechless with surprise for a moment, and the head-man stared.

'Oho! It is the jungle brat, is it?' said Buldeo. 'If thou art so wise, better bring his hide to Khanhiwara, for the Government has set a hundred rupees[13] on his life. Better still, talk not when thy elders speak.'

Mowgli rose to go. 'All the evening I have lain here listening,' he called back, over his shoulder, 'and, except once or twice, Buldeo has not said one word of truth concerning the jungle, which is at his very doors. How then shall I believe the tales of ghosts, and gods, and goblins which he says he has seen?'

'It is full time that boy went to herding,' said the head-man, while Buldeo puffed and snorted at Mowgli's impertinence.[14]

The custom of most Indian villages is for a few boys to take the cattle and buffaloes out to graze in the early morning, and bring them back at night; and the very cattle that would trample a white man to death allow themselves to be banged and bullied and shouted at by children that hardly come up to their noses.[15] So long as the boys keep with the herds they are safe, for not even the tiger will charge a mob of cattle. But if they straggle to pick flowers or hunt lizards, they are sometimes carried off. Mowgli went through the village street in the dawn, sitting on the back of Rama,[16] the great herd bull; and the slaty-blue buffaloes, with their long, backward-sweeping horns and savage eyes, rose out of their byres, one by one, and followed him, and Mowgli made it very clear to the children with him that he was the master. He beat the buffaloes with a long, polished bamboo, and told Kamya, one of the boys, to graze the cattle by themselves, while he went on with the buffaloes, and to be very careful not to stray away from the herd.

An Indian grazing-ground is all rocks, and scrubs, and tussocks, and little ravines, among which the herds scatter and disappear. The buffaloes generally keep to the pools and muddy places, where they lie wallowing or basking in the warm mud for hours. Mowgli drove them on to the edge of the plain where the Waingunga came out of the jungle; then he dropped from Rama's neck, trotted off to a bamboo clump and found Gray Brother. 'Ah,' said Gray Brother, 'I have waited here very many days. What is the meaning of this cattle-herding work?'

'It is an order,' said Mowgli; 'I am a village herd for a while. What news of Shere Khan?'

'He has come back to this country, and has waited here a long time for thee. Now he has gone off again, for the game is scarce. But he means to kill thee.'

'Very good,' said Mowgli. 'So long as he is away do thou or one of the four brothers sit on that rock, so that I can see thee as I come out of the village. When he comes back wait for me in the ravine by the *dhâk*-tree[17] in the centre of the plain. We need not walk into Shere Khan's mouth.'

Then Mowgli picked out a shady place, and lay down and slept while the buffaloes grazed round him. Herding in India is one of the laziest things in the world. The cattle move and crunch, and lie down, and move on again, and they do not even low.[18] They only grunt, and the buffaloes very seldom say anything, but get down into the muddy pools one after another,[19] and work their way into the mud till only their noses and staring china-blue eyes show above the surface, and then they lie like logs. The sun makes the rocks dance in the heat, and the herd-children hear one kite (never any more) whistling almost out of sight overhead, and they know that if they died, or a cow died, that kite would sweep down, and the next kite miles away would see him drop and follow, and the next, and the next, and almost before they were dead there would be a score of hungry kites come out of nowhere. Then they sleep and wake and sleep again, and weave little baskets of dried grass and put grasshoppers in them, or catch two praying mantises and make them fight; or string a necklace of red and black jungle-nuts, or watch a lizard basking on a rock, or a snake hunting a frog near the wallows. Then they sing long, long songs with odd native quavers at the end of them, and the day seems longer than most people's whole lives, and perhaps they make a mud castle with mud figures of men and horses and buffaloes, and put reeds into the men's hands, and pretend that they are kings and the figures are their armies, or that they are gods to be worshipped. Then evening comes and the children call, and the buffaloes lumber up out of the sticky mud with noises like gunshots going off one after the other, and they all string across the gray plain back to the twinkling village lights.

Day after day Mowgli would lead the buffaloes out to their wallows, and day after day he would see Gray Brother's back a mile and a half away across the plain (so he knew that Shere Khan had not come back), and day after day he would lie on the grass listening to the noises round him, and dreaming of old days in the jungle. If Shere Khan had made a false step with his lame paw up in the jungles by the Waingunga, Mowgli would have heard him in those long still mornings.

At last a day came when he did not see Gray Brother at the signal place, and he laughed and headed the buffaloes for the ravine by the *dhâk*-tree, which was all covered with golden-red flowers. There sat Gray Brother, every bristle on his back lifted.

'He has hidden for a month to throw thee off thy guard. He crossed the ranges last night with Tabaqui, hot-foot on thy trail,' said the Wolf, panting.

Mowgli frowned. 'I am not afraid of Shere Khan, but Tabaqui is very cunning.'

'Have no fear,' said Gray Brother, licking his lips a little. 'I met Tabaqui in the dawn. Now he is telling all his wisdom to the kites, but he told *me* everything before I broke his back. Shere Khan's plan is to wait for thee at the village gate this evening – for thee and for no one else. He is lying up now, in the big dry ravine of the Waingunga.'

'Has he eaten today, or does he hunt empty?' said Mowgli, for the answer meant life and death to him.

'He killed at dawn – a pig – and he has drunk too. Remember, Shere Khan could never fast, even for the sake of revenge.'

'Oh! fool, fool! What a cub's cub it is! Eaten and drunk too, and he thinks that I shall wait till he has slept! Now, where does he lie up? If there were but ten of us we might pull him down as he lies. These buffaloes will not charge unless they wind him, and I cannot speak their language. Can we get behind his track so that they may smell it?'

'He swam far down the Waingunga to cut that off,' said Gray Brother.

'Tabaqui told him that, I know. He would never have thought of it alone.' Mowgli stood with his finger in his mouth, thinking. 'The big ravine of the Waingunga. That opens out on the plain not half a mile from here. I can take the herd round through the jungle to the head of the ravine and then sweep down[20] – but he would slink out at the foot. We must block that end. Gray Brother, canst thou cut the herd in two for me?'

'Not I, perhaps – but I have brought a wise helper.' Gray Brother trotted off and dropped into a hole. Then there lifted up a huge gray head that Mowgli knew well, and the hot air was filled with the most desolate cry of all the jungle – the hunting-howl of a wolf at mid-day.

'Akela! Akela!' said Mowgli, clapping his hands. 'I might have known that thou wouldst not forget me. We have a big work in hand. Cut the herd in two, Akela. Keep the cows and calves together, and the bulls and the plough-buffaloes by themselves.'

The two wolves ran, ladies'-chain[21] fashion, in and out of the herd, which snorted and threw up its head, and separated into two clumps. In one, the cow-buffaloes stood with their calves in the centre, and glared and pawed, ready, if a wolf would only stay still, to charge down and trample the life out of him. In the other, the bulls and the young bulls snorted and stamped, but though they looked more imposing they were much less dangerous, for they had no calves to protect. No six men could have divided the herd so neatly.

'What orders!' panted Akela. 'They are trying to join again.'

Mowgli slipped on to Rama's back. 'Drive the bulls away to the left, Akela. Gray Brother, when we are gone, hold the cows together, and drive them into the foot of the ravine.'

'How far?' said Gray Brother, panting and snapping.

'Till the sides are higher than Shere Khan can jump,' shouted Mowgli, 'Keep them there till we come down.' The bulls swept off as Akela bayed, and Gray Brother stopped in front of the cows. They charged down on him, and he ran just before them to the foot of the ravine, as Akela drove the bulls far to the left.

'Well done! Another charge and they are fairly started. Careful, now – careful, Akela. A snap too much, and the bulls will charge. *Hujah!* This is wilder work than driving black-buck. Didst thou think these creatures could move so swiftly?' Mowgli called.

'I have – have hunted these too in my time,' gasped Akela in the dust. 'Shall I turn them into the jungle?'

'Ay! Turn. Swiftly turn them! Rama is mad with rage. Oh, if I could only tell him what I need of him today.'

The bulls were turned, to the right this time, and crashed into the standing thicket. The other herd-children, watching with the cattle half a mile away, hurried to the village as fast as their legs could carry them, crying that the buffaloes had gone mad and run away. But Mowgli's plan was simple enough. All he wanted to do was to make a big circle uphill and get at the head of the ravine, and then take the bulls down it and catch Shere Khan between the bulls and the cows; for he knew that after a meal and a full drink Shere Khan would not be in any condition to fight or to clamber up the sides of the ravine. He was soothing the buffaloes now by voice, and Akela had dropped far to the rear, only whimpering once or twice to hurry the rear-guard. It was a long, long circle, for they did not wish to get too near the ravine and give Shere Khan warning. At last Mowgli rounded up the bewildered herd at the head of the ravine on a grassy patch that sloped steeply down to the ravine itself. From that height you could see across the tops of the trees down to the plain below; but what Mowgli looked at was the sides of the ravine, and he saw with a great deal of satisfaction that they ran nearly straight up and down, while the vines and creepers that hung over them would give no foothold to a tiger who wanted to get out.

'Let them breathe, Akela,' he said, holding up his hand.

'They have not winded him yet. Let them breathe. I must tell Shere Khan who comes. We have him in the trap.'

He put his hands to his mouth and shouted down the ravine – it was almost like shouting down a tunnel – and the echoes jumped from rock to rock.

After a long time there came back the drawling, sleepy snarl of a full-fed tiger just wakened.

'Who calls?' said Shere Khan, and a splendid peacock fluttered up out of the ravine screeching.

'I, Mowgli. Cattle thief, it is time to come to the Council Rock! Down – hurry them down, Akela! Down, Rama, down!'

The herd paused for an instant at the edge of the slope, but Akela gave tongue in the full hunting yell, and they pitched over one after the other just as steamers shoot rapids, the sand and stones spurting up round them. Once started, there was no chance of stopping, and before they were fairly in the bed of the ravine Rama winded Shere Khan and bellowed.

'Ha! Ha!' said Mowgli, on his back. 'Now thou knowest!' and the torrent of black horns, foaming muzzles, and staring eyes whirled down the ravine just as boulders go down in flood-time; the weaker buffaloes being shouldered out to the sides of the ravine where they tore through the creepers. They knew what the business was before them – the terrible charge of the buffalo herd against which no tiger can hope to stand. Shere Khan heard the thunder of their hoofs, picked himself up, and lumbered down the ravine, looking from side to side for some way of escape, but the walls of the ravine were straight and he had to hold on, heavy with his dinner and his drink, willing to do anything rather than fight. The herd splashed through the pool he had just left, bellowing till the narrow cut rang. Mowgli heard an answering bellow from the foot of the ravine, saw Shere Khan turn (the tiger knew if the worst came to the worst it was better to meet the bulls than the cows with their calves), and then Rama tripped, stumbled, and went on again over something soft, and, with the bulls at his heels, crashed full into the other herd, while the weaker buffaloes were lifted clean off their feet by the shock of the meeting. That charge carried both herds out into the plain, goring and stamping and snorting. Mowgli watched his time, and slipped off Rama's neck, laying about him right and left with his stick.

'Quick, Akela! Break them up. Scatter them, or they will be fighting one another. Drive them away, Akela. *Hai*, Rama! *Hai! hai! hai!* my children. Softly now, softly! It is all over.'

Akela and Gray Brother ran to and fro nipping the buffaloes' legs, and though the herd wheeled once to charge up the ravine again, Mowgli managed to turn Rama, and the others followed him to the wallows.

Shere Khan needed no more trampling. He was dead,[22] and the kites were coming for him already.

'Brothers, that was a dog's death,' said Mowgli, feeling for the knife he always carried in a sheath round his neck now that he lived with men. 'But he would never have shown fight. *Wallah!* his hide will look well on the Council Rock. We must get to work swiftly.'

A boy trained among men would never have dreamed of skinning a ten-foot tiger alone, but Mowgli knew better than anyone else how an animal's skin is fitted on, and how it can be taken off. But it was hard work, and Mowgli slashed and tore and grunted for an hour, while the wolves lolled out their tongues, or came forward and tugged as he ordered them. Presently a hand fell on his shoulder, and looking up he saw Buldeo with the Tower musket. The children had told the village about the buffalo stampede, and Buldeo went out angrily, only too anxious to correct Mowgli for not taking better care of the herd. The wolves dropped out of sight as soon as they saw the man coming.

'What is this folly?' said Buldeo, angrily. 'To think that thou canst skin a tiger! Where did the buffaloes kill him? It is the Lame Tiger, too, and there is a hundred rupees on his head. Well, well, we will overlook thy letting the herd run off, and perhaps I will give thee one of the rupees of the reward when I have taken the skin to Khanhiwara.' He fumbled in his waist-cloth for flint and steel, and stooped down to singe Shere Khan's whiskers. Most native hunters always singe a tiger's whiskers to prevent his ghost from haunting them.

'Hum!' said Mowgli, half to himself as he ripped back the

skin of a forepaw. 'So thou wilt take the hide to Khanhiwara for the reward, and perhaps give me one rupee? Now it is in my mind that I need the skin for my own use. Heh! old man, take away that fire!'

'What talk is this to the chief hunter of the village? Thy luck and the stupidity of thy buffaloes have helped thee to this kill. The tiger has just fed, or he would have gone twenty miles by this time. Thou canst not even skin him properly, little beggar brat, and forsooth I, Buldeo, must be told not to singe his whiskers. Mowgli, I will not give thee one anna[23] of the reward, but only a very big beating. Leave the carcass!'

'By the Bull that bought me,' said Mowgli, who was trying to get at the shoulder, 'must I stay babbling to an old ape all noon? Here, Akela, this man plagues me.'

Buldeo, who was still stooping over Shere Khan's head, found himself sprawling on the grass, with a gray wolf standing over him, while Mowgli went on skinning as though he were alone in all India.

'Ye-es,' he said, between his teeth. 'Thou art altogether right, Buldeo. Thou wilt never give me one anna of the reward. There is an old war between this lame tiger and myself – a very old war, and – I have won.'

To do Buldeo justice, if he had been ten years younger he would have taken his chance with Akela had he met the wolf in the woods, but a wolf who obeyed the orders of this boy who had private wars with man-eating tigers was not a common animal. It was sorcery, magic of the worst kind, thought Buldeo, and he wondered whether the amulet round his neck would protect him. He lay as still as still, expecting every minute to see Mowgli turn into a tiger, too.

'Maharaj! Great King,' he said at last, in a husky whisper.

'Yes,' said Mowgli, without turning his head, chuckling a little.

'I am an old man. I did not know that thou wast anything more than a herdsboy. May I rise up and go away, or will thy servant tear me to pieces?'

'Go, and peace go with thee. Only, another time do not meddle with my game. Let him go, Akela.'

Buldeo hobbled away to the village as fast as he could, looking back over his shoulder in case Mowgli should change into something terrible. When he got to the village he told a tale of magic and enchantment and sorcery that made the priest look very grave.

Mowgli went on with his work, but it was nearly twilight before he and the wolves had drawn the great gay skin clear of the body.

'Now we must hide this and take the buffaloes home! Help me to herd them, Akela.'

The herd rounded up in the misty twilight, and when they got near the village Mowgli saw lights, and heard the conches and bells in the temple blowing and banging. Half the village seemed to be waiting for him by the gate. 'That is because I have killed Shere Khan,' he said to himself; but a shower of stones whistled about his ears, and the villagers shouted: 'Sorcerer! Wolf's brat! Jungle-demon! Go away! Get hence quickly, or the priest will turn thee into a wolf again. Shoot, Buldeo, shoot!'

The old Tower musket went off with a bang, and a young buffalo bellowed in pain.

'More sorcery!' shouted the villagers. 'He can turn bullets. Buldeo, that was *thy* buffalo.'

'Now what is this?' said Mowgli, bewildered, as the stones flew thicker.

'They are not unlike the Pack, these brothers of thine,' said Akela, sitting down composedly. 'It is in my head that, if bullets mean anything, they would cast thee out.'

'Wolf! Wolf's cub! Go away!' shouted the priest, waving a sprig of the sacred *tulsi*[24] plant.

'Again? Last time it was because I was a man. This time it is because I am a wolf. Let us go, Akela.'

A woman – it was Messua – ran across to the herd, and cried: 'Oh, my son, my son! They say thou art a sorcerer who can turn himself into a beast at will. I do not believe, but go away or they will kill thee. Buldeo says thou art a wizard, but I know thou hast avenged Nathoo's death.'

'Come back, Messua!' shouted the crowd. 'Come back, or we will stone thee.'

Mowgli laughed a little short ugly laugh, for a stone had hit him in the mouth. 'Run back, Messua. This is one of the foolish tales they tell under the big tree at dusk. I have at least paid for thy son's life. Farewell; and run quickly, for I shall send the herd in more swiftly than their brickbats. I am no wizard, Messua. Farewell!'

'Now, once more, Akela,' he cried. 'Bring the herd in.'

The buffaloes were anxious enough to get to the village. They hardly needed Akela's yell, but charged through the gate like a whirlwind, scattering the crowd right and left.

'Keep count!' shouted Mowgli, scornfully. 'It may be that I have stolen one of them. Keep count, for I will do your herding no more. Fare you well, children of men, and thank Messua that I do not come in with my wolves and hunt you up and down your street.'

He turned on his heel and walked away with the Lone Wolf; and as he looked up at the stars he felt happy. 'No more sleeping in traps for me, Akela. Let us get Shere Khan's skin and go away. No; we will not hurt the village, for Messua was kind to me.'

When the moon rose over the plain, making it look all milky, the horrified villagers saw Mowgli, with two wolves at his heels and a bundle on his head, trotting across at the steady wolf's trot that eats up the long miles like fire. Then they banged the temple bells and blew the conches louder than ever; and Messua cried, and Buldeo embroidered the story of his adventures in the jungle, till he ended by saying that Akela stood up on his hind legs and talked like a man.

The moon was just going down when Mowgli and the two wolves came to the hill of the Council Rock, and they stopped at Mother Wolf's cave.

'They have cast me out from the man Pack, Mother,' shouted Mowgli, 'but I come with the hide of Shere Khan to keep my word.' Mother Wolf walked stiffly from the cave with the cubs behind her, and her eyes glowed as she saw the skin.

'I told him on that day, when he crammed his head and shoulders into this cave, hunting for thy life, little frog – I told him that the hunter would be the hunted. It is well done.'

'Little Brother, it is well done,' said a deep voice in the thicket. 'We were lonely in the jungle without thee,' and Bagheera came running to Mowgli's bare feet. They clambered up the Council Rock together, and Mowgli spread the skin out on the flat stone where Akela used to sit, and pegged it down with four slivers of bamboo, and Akela lay down upon it, and called the old call to the Council, 'Look, look well, O Wolves,' exactly as he had called when Mowgli was first brought there.

Ever since Akela had been deposed, the Pack had been without a leader, hunting and fighting at their own pleasure. But they answered the call from habit; and some of them were lame from the traps they had fallen into, and some limped from shot-wounds, and some were mangy from eating bad food, and many were missing; but they came to the Council Rock, all that were left of them, and saw Shere Khan's striped hide on the rock, and the huge claws dangling at the end of the empty dangling feet.[25]

'Look well, O Wolves. Have I kept my word?'[26] said Mowgli; and the wolves bayed Yes, and one tattered wolf howled:

'Lead us again, O Akela. Lead us again, O man-cub, for we be sick of this lawlessness, and we would be the Free People once more.'

'Nay,' purred Bagheera, 'that may not be. When ye are full-fed, the madness may come upon ye again. Not for nothing are ye called the Free People. Ye fought for freedom, and it is yours. Eat it, O Wolves.'

'Man pack and wolf pack have cast me out,' said Mowgli. 'Now I will hunt alone in the jungle.'

'And we will hunt with thee,' said the four cubs.

So Mowgli went away and hunted with the four cubs in the jungle from that day on. But he was not always alone, because, years afterward, he became a man and married.[27]

But that is a story for grown-ups.

Mowgli's Song

That he sang at the Council Rock
when he danced on Shere Khan's hide

The Song of Mowgli – I, Mowgli am singing. Let the Jungle
    listen to the things I have done.
Shere Khan said he would kill – would kill! At the gates in the
    twilight he would kill Mowgli, the Frog!
He ate and he drank. Drink deep, Shere Khan, for when wilt
    thou drink again? Sleep and dream of the kill.
I am alone on the grazing-grounds. Gray Brother, come to me!
    Come to me, Lone Wolf, for there is big game afoot!
Bring up the great bull-buffaloes, the blue-skinned herd-bulls
    with the angry eyes. Drive them to and fro as I order.
    Sleepest thou still, Shere Khan? Wake, O wake! Here
    come I, and the bulls are behind.[1]
Rama the king of the buffaloes stamped with his foot. Waters
    of the Waingunga, whither went Shere Khan?
He is not Sahi to dig holes, nor Mor, the Peacock, that he should
    fly. He is not Mang, the Bat, to hang in the branches. Little
    bamboos that creak together, tell me where he ran?
Ow! he is there. *Ahoo!* he is there. Under the feet of Rama
    lies the Lame One! Up, Shere Khan! Up and kill! Here is
    meat; break the necks of the bulls!
Hsh! he is asleep. We will not wake him, for his strength is
    very great. The kites have come down to see it. The black
    ants have come up to know it. There is a great assembly
    in his honour.
Alala! I have no cloth to wrap me. The kites will see that I am
    naked. I am ashamed to meet all these people.
Lend me thy coat, Shere Khan. Lend me thy gay striped coat
    that I may go to the Council Rock.
By the Bull that bought me I made a promise – a little prom-
    ise. Only thy coat is lacking before I keep my word.

With the knife, with the knife that men use, with the knife of
the hunter,[2] I will stoop down for my gift.

Waters of the Waingunga, Shere Khan[3] gives me his coat for
the love that he bears me. Pull, Gray Brother! Pull, Akela!
Heavy is the hide of Shere Khan.

The Man Pack are angry. They throw stones and talk child's
talk. My mouth is bleeding. Let me run away.

Through the night, through the hot night, run swiftly with
me, my brothers. We will leave the lights of the village
and go to the low moon.

Waters of the Waingunga, the Man Pack have cast me out. I
did them no harm, but they were afraid of me. Why?

Wolf Pack ye have cast me out too. The Jungle is shut to me
and the village gates are shut. Why?

As Mang flies between the beasts and birds so fly I between
the village and the Jungle. Why?

I dance on the hide of Shere Khan, but my heart is very heavy.
My mouth is cut and wounded with the stones from the
village, but my heart is very light, because I have come
back to the Jungle. Why?

These two things fight together in me as the snakes fight in the
spring. The water comes out of my eyes: yet I laugh while
it falls. Why?[4]

I am two Mowglis, but the hide of Shere Khan is under my
feet.

All the Jungle knows that I have killed Shere Khan. Look,
look well, O Wolves!

Ahae! my heart is heavy with the things that I do not
understand.

THE WHITE SEAL

Oh! hush thee, my baby, the night is behind us,
    And black are the waters that sparkled so green.
The moon, o'er the combers, looks downward to find us
    At rest in the hollows that rustle between.
Where billow meets billow, there soft be thy pillow,
    Oh, weary wee flipperling curl at thy ease!
The storm shall not wake thee, nor shark overtake thee,
    Asleep in the arms of the slow-swinging seas!

Seal Lullaby

All these things happened several years ago at a place called Novastoshnah[1] or North East Point on the Island of St Paul,[2] away and away in the Bering Sea. Limmershin, the Winter Wren, told me the tale when he was blown on to the rigging of a steamer going to Japan, and I took him down into my cabin and warmed and fed him for a couple of days till he was fit to fly back to St Paul's again. Limmershin is a very quaint little bird,[3] but he knows how to tell the truth.

Nobody comes to Novastoshnah except on business, and the only people who have regular business there are the seals. They come in the summer months by hundreds and hundreds of thousands out of the cold gray sea; for Novastoshnah beach has the finest accommodation for seals of any place in all the world. Sea Catch[4] knew that, and every spring would swim from whatever place he happened to be in – would swim like a torpedo-boat straight for Novastoshnah and spend a month fighting with his companions for a good place on the rocks, as close to the sea as possible. Sea Catch was fifteen years old, a huge gray fur-seal with almost a mane on his shoulders, and long, wicked dog-teeth. When he heaved himself up on his front flippers he stood more than four feet clear of the ground, and his weight, if anyone had been bold enough to weigh him, was nearly seven hundred pounds. He was scarred all over with the marks of savage fights, but he was always ready for just one fight more. He would put his head on one side, as though he were afraid to look his enemy in the face; then he would shoot it out like lightning, and when the big teeth were firmly fixed on the other seal's neck, the other seal might get away if he could, but Sea Catch would not help him. Yet Sea Catch never chased a beaten seal, for that was against the Rules of the Beach. He only wanted room by the sea for his nursery; but as there were forty or fifty thousand other seals hunting for the same thing each spring, the whistling, bellowing, roaring, and blowing on the beach was something frightful. From a little hill called Hutchinson's Hill,[5] you could look over three and a half miles of ground covered with fighting seals; and the surf was dotted all over with the heads of seals hurrying to land and begin their share of fighting. They fought in the breakers, they fought in the sand, and they fought on the smooth-worn basalt rocks of the nurseries, for they were just as stupid and unaccommodating as men. Their wives never came to the island until late in May or early in June, for they did not care to be torn to pieces; and the young two, three, and four-year-old seals who had not begun housekeeping went inland about half a mile through the ranks of the fighters and played about on the sand-dunes in droves and legions, and rubbed off every single green thing that grew. They were called the holluschickie[6] – the bachelors – and there were perhaps two or three hundred thousand of them at Nova-stoshnah alone.

Sea Catch had just finished his forty-fifth fight one spring when Matkah,[7] his soft, sleek, gentle-eyed wife came up out of the sea, and he caught her by the scruff of the neck and dumped her down on his reservation, saying gruffly: 'Late as usual. Where *have* you been?'

It was not the fashion for Sea Catch to eat anything during the four months he stayed on the beaches, and so his temper was generally bad. Matkah knew better than to answer back. She looked round and cooed: 'How thoughtful of you. You've taken the old place again.'

'I should think I had,' said Sea Catch. 'Look at me!'

He was scratched and bleeding in twenty places; one eye was almost out, and his sides were torn to ribbons.

'Oh, you men, you men!' Matkah said, fanning herself with her hind-flipper. 'Why can't you be sensible and settle your places quietly? You look as though you had been fighting with the Killer Whale.'

'I haven't been doing anything *but* fight since the middle of May. The beach is disgracefully crowded this season. I've met at least a hundred seals from Lukannon Beach,[8] house-hunting. Why can't people stay where they belong?'

'I've often thought we should be much happier if we hauled out at Otter Island instead of this crowded place,' said Matkah.

'Bah! only the holluschickie go to Otter Island.[9] If we went there they would say we were afraid. We must preserve appearances, my dear.'

Sea Catch sunk his head proudly between his fat shoulders and pretended to go to sleep for a few minutes, but all the time he was keeping a sharp lookout for a fight. Now that all the seals and their wives were on the land you could hear their clamour miles out to sea above the loudest gales. At the lowest counting there were over a million seals on the beach – old seals, mother seals, tiny babies and holluschickie, fighting, scuffling, bleating, crawling and playing together – going down to the sea and coming up from it in gangs and regiments, lying over every foot of ground as far as the eye could reach, and skirmishing about in brigades through the fog. It is nearly always foggy at Novastoshnah, except when the sun comes out and makes everything look all pearly and rainbow-coloured for a little while.

Kotick,[10] Matkah's baby, was born in the middle of that confusion, and he was all head and shoulders, with pale, watery blue eyes, as tiny seals must be, but there was something about his coat that made his mother look at him very closely.

'Sea Catch,' she said, at last, 'our baby's going to be white!'

'Empty clam-shells and dry seaweed!' snorted Sea Catch. 'There never has been such a thing in the world as a white seal.'[11]

'I can't help that,' said Matkah; 'there's going to be now'; and she sang the low, crooning seal-song that all the mother seals sing to their babies:

> You mustn't swim till you're six weeks old,
>   Or your head will be sunk by your heels;
> And summer gales and Killer Whales
>   Are bad for baby seals.
>
> Are bad for baby seals, dear rat,
>   As bad as bad can be;
> But splash and grow strong,
>   And you can't be wrong,
> Child of the Open Sea!

Of course the little fellow did not understand the words at first. He paddled and scrambled about by his mother's side and learned to scuffle out of the way when his father was fighting with another seal, and the two rolled and roared up and down the slippery rocks. Matkah used to go to sea to get things to eat, and the baby was only fed once in two days, but then he ate all he could and throve upon it. The first thing he did was to crawl inland, and there he met tens of thousands of babies of his own age, and they played together like puppies, went to sleep on the clean sand, and played again. The old people in the nurseries took no notice of them, and the holluschickie kept to their own grounds and the babies had a beautiful playtime. When Matkah came back from her deep-sea fishing she would go straight to their play-ground and call as a sheep calls for a lamb, and wait until she heard Kotick bleat. Then she would take the straightest of straight lines in his direction, striking out with her fore-flippers and knocking the youngsters head over heels right and left. There were always a few hundred mothers hunting for their children through the play-grounds, and the babies were kept lively; but, as Matkah told Kotick, 'So long as you don't lie in muddy water and get mange; or rub the hard sand into a cut or scratch, and so long as you never go swimming when there is a heavy sea, nothing will hurt you here.'

Little seals can no more swim than little children, but they are unhappy till they learn. The first time that Kotick went down to the sea a wave carried him out beyond his depth, and his big head sank and his little hind-flippers flew up exactly as his mother had told him in the song, and if the next wave had not thrown him back again he would have drowned. After that, he learned to lie in a beach-pool and let the wash of the waves just cover him and lift him up while he paddled, but he always kept his eye open for big waves that might hurt. He was two weeks learning to use his flippers; and all that while he floundered in and out of the water and coughed and grunted and crawled up the beach and took cat-naps on the sand and went back again, until at last he found that he truly belonged to the water. Then you can imagine the times that he had with his companions, ducking under the rollers; or coming in on top of a comber and landing with a swash and a splutter as the big wave went whirling far up the beach; or standing up on his tail and scratching his head as the old people did; or playing 'I'm the King of the Castle' on slippery, weedy rocks that just stuck out of the wash. Now and then he would see a thin fin, like a big shark's fin, drifting along close to shore, and he knew that that was the Killer Whale, the Grampus, who eats young seals when he can get them, and Kotick would head for the beach like an arrow, and the fin would jig off slowly, as if it were looking for nothing at all.

Late in October the seals began to leave St Paul's for the deep sea, by families and tribes, and there was no more fighting over the nurseries, and the holluschickie played anywhere they liked. 'Next year,' said Matkah to Kotick, 'you will be a holluschickie; but this year you must learn how to catch fish.'

They set out together across the Pacific, and Matkah showed Kotick how to sleep on his back with his flippers tucked down by his side[12] and his little nose just out of the water. No cradle is so comfortable as the long, rocking swell of the Pacific. When Kotick felt his skin tingle all over, Matkah told him he was learning the 'feel of the water', and that tingly, prickly feelings meant bad weather coming, and he must swim hard and get away. 'In a little time,' she said, 'you'll know where to swim to, but just now we'll follow Sea Pig,[13] for he is very wise.' A school of porpoises were ducking and tearing through the water and little Kotick followed them as fast as he could. 'How do you know where to go to?' he panted. The leader of the school rolled his white eye and ducked under: 'My tail tingles, youngster,' he said. 'That means there's a gale behind me. Come along! When you're south of the Sticky Water (he meant the Equator) and your tail tingles, that means there's a gale in front of you and you must head north. Come along. The water feels bad here.'

This was one of the very many things that Kotick learned, and he was always learning. Matkah taught him to follow the cod and the halibut along the under-sea-banks and wrench the rockling out of his hole among the weeds; how to skirt the wrecks lying a hundred fathoms below water and dart like a rifle bullet in at one port-hole and out at another as the fishes ran; how to dance on the top of the waves when the lightning was racing all over the sky, and wave his flipper politely to the Stumpy-tailed albatross[14] and the man-of-war hawk[15] as they went down the wind; how to jump three or four feet clear of the water like a dolphin, flippers close to the side and tail curved; to leave the flying-fish alone because they are all bony; to take the shoulder-piece out of a cod at full speed ten fathoms deep, and never to stop and look at a boat or a ship, but particularly a row-boat.[16] At the end of six months what Kotick did not know about deep-sea fishing was not worth the knowing; and all that time he never set flipper on dry ground.

One day, however, as he was lying half asleep in the warm water somewhere off the Island of Juan Fernandez,[17] he felt faint and lazy all over, just as human people do when the Spring is in their legs, and he remembered the good firm beaches of Novastoshnah seven thousand miles away; the games his companions played, the smell of the sea-weed, the seal-roar and the fighting. That very minute he turned north, swimming steadily, and as he went on he met scores of his mates, all bound for the same place, and they said: 'Greeting, Kotick! This year we are all holluschickie, and we can dance the Fire Dance in the breakers off Lukannon and play on the new grass. But where did you get that coat?'

Kotick's fur was almost pure white now, and though he felt very proud of it he only said: 'Swim quickly! My bones are aching for the land.' And so they all came to the beaches where they had been born and heard the old seals, their fathers, fighting in the rolling mist.

That night Kotick danced the Fire Dance with the yearling seals. The sea is full of fire on summer nights all the way down from Novastoshnah to Lukannon, and each seal leaves a wake like burning oil behind him and a flaming flash when he jumps, and the waves break in great phosphorescent streaks and swirls. Then they went inland to the holluschickie-grounds and rolled up and down in the new wild wheat and told stories of what they had done while they had been at sea. They talked about the Pacific as boys would talk about a wood that they had been nutting in, and if anyone had understood them he could have gone away and made such a chart of that ocean as never was. The three and four-year-old holluschickie romped down from Hutchinson's Hill crying: 'Out of the way, youngsters! The sea is deep and you don't know all that's in it yet. Wait till you've rounded the Horn.[18] Hi, you yearling, where did you get that white coat?'

'I didn't get it,' said Kotick; 'it grew.' And just as he was going to roll the speaker over, a couple of black-haired men with flat red faces came from behind a sand-dune, and Kotick, who had never seen a man before, coughed and lowered his head. The holluschickie just bundled off a few yards and sat staring stupidly. The men were no less than Kerick Booterin,[19] the chief of the seal-hunters on the island, and Patalamon, his son. They came from the little village not a half a mile from the seal nurseries, and they were deciding what seals they would drive up to the killing-pens – for the seals were driven just like sheep – to be turned into sealskin jackets later on.

'Ho!' said Patalamon. 'Look! There's a white seal!'

Kerick Booterin turned nearly white under his oil and smoke, for he was an Aleut,[20] and Aleuts are not clean people. Then he began to mutter a prayer. 'Don't touch him, Patalamon. There has never been a white seal since – since I was born. Perhaps it is old Zaharrof's ghost. He was lost last year in the big gale.'

'I'm not going near him,' said Patalamon. 'He's unlucky. Do you really think he is old Zaharrof come back? I owe him for some gulls' eggs.'

'Don't look at him,' said Kerick. 'Head off that drove of four-year-olds. The men ought to skin two hundred today, but it's the beginning of the season and they are new to the work. A hundred will do. Quick!'

Patalamon rattled a pair of seal's shoulder-bones in front of a herd of holluschickie and they stopped dead, puffing and blowing. Then he stepped near and the seals began to move, and Kerick headed them inland, and they never tried to get back to their companions. Hundreds and hundreds of thousands of seals watched them being driven, but they went on playing just the same. Kotick was the only one who asked questions, and none of his companions could tell him anything, except that the men always drove seals in that way for six weeks or two months of every year.

'I am going to follow,' he said, and his eyes nearly popped out of his head as he shuffled along in the wake of the herd.

'The white seal is coming after us,' cried Patalamon. 'That's the first time a seal has ever come to the killing-grounds alone.'

'Hsh! don't look behind you,' said Kerick. 'It *is* Zaharrof's ghost! I must speak to the priest about this.'

The distance to the killing-ground was only half a mile, but it took an hour to cover, because if the seals went too fast Kerick knew that they would get heated and then their fur would come off in patches when they were skinned. So they went on very slowly, past Sea-Lion's Neck, past Webster House, till they came to the Salt House[21] just beyond the sight of the seals on the beach. Kotick followed, panting and wondering. He thought that he was at the world's end, but the roar of the seal-nurseries behind him sounded as loud as the roar of a train in a tunnel. Then Kerick sat down on the moss and pulled out a heavy pewter watch and let the drove cool off for thirty minutes, and Kotick could hear the fog-dew dripping off the brim of his cap. Then ten or twelve men, each with an iron-bound club three or four feet long, came up, and Kerick pointed out one or two of the drove that were bitten by their companions or too hot, and the men kicked those aside with their heavy boots made of the skin of a walrus's throat, and then Kerick said: 'Let go!' and then the men clubbed the seals on the head as fast as they could. Ten minutes later little Kotick did not recognize his friends any more, for their skins were ripped off from the nose to the hind-flippers, whipped off and thrown down on the ground in a pile. That was enough for Kotick. He turned and galloped (a seal can gallop very swiftly for a short time) back to the sea; his little new moustache bristling with horror. At Sea-Lion's Neck, where the great sea-lions sit on the edge of the surf, he flung himself flipper-overhead into the cool water and rocked there, gasping miserably. 'What's here?' said a sea-lion gruffly, for as a rule the sea-lions keep themselves to themselves.

'Scoochnie! Ochen Scoochnie!' ('I'm lonesome, very lonesome!') said Kotick. 'They're killing *all* the holluschickie on *all* the beaches!'

The Sea-Lion turned his head inshore. 'Nonsense,' he said, 'your friends are making as much noise as ever. You must have seen old Kerick polishing off a drove. He's done that for thirty years.'

'It's horrible,' said Kotick, backing water as a wave went over him, and steadying himself with a screw-stroke of his flippers that brought him up all standing within three inches of a jagged edge of rock.

'Well done for a yearling!' said the Sea-Lion, who could appreciate good swimming. 'I suppose it *is* rather awful from your way of looking at it, but if you seals will come here year after year, of course the men get to know of it, and unless you can find an island where no men ever come you will always be driven.'

'Isn't there any such island?' began Kotick.

'I've followed the *poltoos* (the halibut) for twenty years, and I can't say I've found it yet. But look here – you seem to have a fondness for talking to your betters – suppose you go to Walrus Islet and talk to Sea Vitch.[22] He may know something. Don't flounce off like that. It's a six-mile swim, and if I were you I should haul out and take a nap first, little one.'

Kotick thought that that was good advice, so he swam round to his own beach, hauled out and slept for half an hour, twitching all over, as seals will. Then he headed straight for Walrus Islet, a little low sheet of rocky island almost due north-east from Novastoshnah, all ledges of rock and gulls' nests, where the walrus herded by themselves.

He landed close to old Sea Vitch – the big, ugly, bloated, pimpled, fat-necked, long-tusked walrus of the North Pacific, who has no manners except when he is asleep – as he was then, – with his hind-flippers half in and half out of the surf.

'Wake up!' barked Kotick, for the gulls were making a great noise.

'Hah! Ho! Hmph! What's that?' said Sea Vitch, and he struck the next walrus a blow with his tusks and waked him up, and the next struck the next and so on till they were all awake and staring in every direction but the right one.

'Hi! It's me,' said Kotick, bobbing in the surf and looking like a little white slug.

'Well! May I be – skinned!' said Sea Vitch, and they all looked at Kotick as you can fancy a club full of drowsy old gentlemen would look at a little boy. Kotick did not care to hear any more about skinning just then; he had seen enough of it; so he called out: 'Isn't there any place for seals to go where men don't ever come?'

'Go and find out,' said Sea Vitch, shutting his eyes. 'Run away. We're busy here.'

Kotick made his dolphin-jump in the air and shouted as loud as he could: 'Clam-eater! Clam-eater!' He knew that Sea Vitch never caught a fish in his life but always rooted for clams and sea-weeds; though he pretended to be a very terrible person. Naturally the Chickies and the Gooverooskies and the Epatkas – the Burgomaster gulls, and the Kittiwakes, and the Puffins who are always looking for a chance to be rude – took up the cry, and – so Limmershin told me – for nearly five minutes you could not have heard a gun fired on Walrus Islet. All the population was yelling and screaming: 'Clam-eater! *Stareek* (old man)!' while Sea Vitch rolled from side to side grunting and coughing.

'*Now* will you tell?' said Kotick, all out of breath.

'Go and ask Sea Cow,'[23] said Sea Vitch. 'If he is living still he'll be able to tell you.'

'How shall I know Sea Cow when I meet him?' said Kotick, sheering off.

'He's the only thing in the sea uglier than Sea Vitch,' screamed a Burgomaster gull, wheeling under Sea Vitch's nose. 'Uglier, and with worse manners! *Stareek!*'

Kotick swam back to Novastoshnah, leaving the gulls to scream. There he found that no one sympathized with him in his little attempt to discover a quiet place for the seals. They told him that men had always driven the holluschickie – it was part of the day's work – and that if he did not like to see ugly things he should not have gone to the killing grounds. But none of the other seals had seen the killing, and that made the difference between him and his friends. Besides, Kotick was a white seal.

'What you must do,' said old Sea Catch, after he had heard his son's adventures, 'is to grow up and be a big seal like your father, and have a nursery on the beach, and then they will leave you alone. In another five years you ought to be able to fight for yourself.' Even gentle Matkah, his mother, said: 'You will never be able to stop the killing. Go and play in the sea, Kotick.' And Kotick went off and danced the Fire Dance with a very heavy little heart.

That autumn he left the beach as soon as he could, and set off alone because of a notion in his bullet-head. He was going to find Sea Cow, if there was such a person in the sea, and he was going to find a quiet island with good firm beaches for seals to live on, where men could not get at them. So he explored and explored by himself from the North to the South Pacific, swimming as much as three hundred miles in a day and night. He met with more adventures than can be told, and narrowly escaped being caught by the Basking shark,[24] and the Spotted shark and the Hammerhead, and he met all the untrustworthy ruffians that loaf up and down the seas; and the heavy polite fish, and the scarlet spotted scallops that are moored in one place for hundreds of years, and grow very proud of it; but he never met Sea Cow, and he never found an island that he could fancy. If the beach was good and hard, with a slope behind it for seals to play on, there was always the smoke of a whaler on the horizon, boiling down blubber, and Kotick knew what *that* meant. Or else he could see that seals had once visited the island and been killed off, and Kotick knew that where men had come once they would come again.

He picked up with an old Stumpy-tailed albatross, who told him that Kerguelen Island[25] was the very place for peace and quiet, and when Kotick went down there he was all but smashed to pieces against some wicked black cliffs in a heavy sleet storm with lightning and thunder. Yet as he pulled out against the gale he could see even there had once been a seal-nursery. And it was so in all the other islands that he visited.

Limmershin gave a long list of them, for he said that Kotick spent five seasons exploring, with a four months' rest each year at Novastoshnah, when the holluschickie used to make fun of him and his imaginary islands. He went to the Gallapagos, a horrid dry place on the Equator, where he was nearly baked to death; he went to the Georgia Islands, the Orkneys, Emerald Island, Little Nightingale Island, Gough's Island, Bouvet's Island, The Crossets, and even to a little speck of an island south of the Cape of Good Hope.[26] But everywhere the People of the Sea told him the same things. Seals had come to those islands once upon a time, but men had killed them all off. Even when he swam thousands of miles out of the Pacific and got to a place called Cape Corientes[27] (that was when he was coming back from Gough's Island) he found a few hundred mangy seals on a rock and they told him that men came there too. That nearly broke his heart, and he headed round the Horn back to his own beaches; and on his way north he hauled out on an island full of green trees, where he found an old, old seal who was dying, and Kotick caught fish for him and told him all his failures. 'Now,' said Kotick, 'I am going back to Novastoshnah, and if I am driven to the killing-pens with the holluschickie I shall not care.'

The old seal said: 'Try once more. I am the last of the Lost Rookery of Masafuera,[28] and in the days when men killed us by the hundred thousand there was a story on the beaches that some day a white seal would come out of the North and lead the seal-people to a quiet place. I am old, and I shall never live to see that day, but others will. Try once more.'

And Kotick curled up his moustache (it was a beauty) and said: 'I am the only white seal that has ever been born on the beaches, and I am the only seal, black or white, who ever thought of looking for new islands.'

This cheered him immensely; and when he came back to Novastoshnah that summer, Matkah, his mother, begged him to marry and settle down, for he was no longer a holluschick but a full-grown sea-catch, with a curly white mane on his shoulders, as heavy, as big, and as fierce as his father. 'Give me another season,' he said. 'Remember, mother, it is always the seventh wave that goes furthest up the beach.'

Curiously enough, there was another seal who thought that she would put off marrying till the next year, and Kotick danced the Fire Dance with her all down Lukannon beach the night before he set off on his last exploration. This time he went westward, because he had fallen on the trail of a great shoal of halibut, and he needed at least one hundred pounds of fish a day to keep him in good condition. He chased them till he was tired, and then he curled himself up and went to sleep on the hollows of the ground-swell that sets in to Copper Island.[29] He knew the coast perfectly well, so about midnight, when he felt himself gently bumped on a weed bed, he said: 'Hm, tide's running strong tonight,' and turning over under water opened his eyes slowly and stretched. Then he jumped like a cat, for he saw huge things nosing about in the shoal-water and browsing on the heavy fringes of the weeds.

'By the Great Combers of Magellan!'[30] he said, beneath his moustache. 'Who in the Deep Sea are these people?'

They were like no walrus, sea-lion, seal, bear, whale, shark, fish, squid or scallop that Kotick had ever seen before. They were between twenty and thirty feet long, and they had no hind-flippers, but a shovel-like tail that looked as if it had been whittled out of wet leather. Their heads were the most foolish-looking things you ever saw, and they balanced on the ends of their tails in deep water when they weren't grazing, bowing solemnly to each other and waving their front-flippers as a fat man waves his arm.

'Ahem!' said Kotick. 'Good sport, gentlemen?' The big things answered by bowing and waving their flippers like the Frog-Footman.[31] When they began feeding again Kotick saw that their upper lip was split into two pieces that they could twitch apart about a foot and bring together again with a whole bushel of sea-weed between the splits. They tucked the stuff into their mouths and chumped solemnly.

'Messy style of feeding that,' said Kotick. They bowed again, and Kotick began to lose his temper. 'Very good,' he said. 'If you *do* happen to have an extra joint in your front-flipper you needn't show off so. I see you bow gracefully, but I should like to know your names.' The split lips moved and twitched, and the glassy green eyes stared; but they did not speak.

'Well!' said Kotick, 'you're the only people I've ever met uglier than Sea Vitch – and with worse manners.'

Then he remembered in a flash what the Burgomaster Gull had screamed to him when he was a little yearling at Walrus Islet, and he tumbled backward in the water, for he knew that he had found Sea Cow at last! The sea-cows went on schloop-ing and grazing and chumping in the weed, and Kotick asked them questions in every language that he had picked up in his travels; and the Sea People talk nearly as many languages as human beings. But the sea-cows did not answer, because Sea Cow cannot talk. He has only six bones in his neck where he ought to have seven, and they say under the sea that that pre-vents him from speaking even to his companions; but, as you know, he has an extra joint in his fore-flipper, and by waving it up and down and about he makes what answers to a sort of clumsy telegraphic code.

By daylight Kotick's mane was standing on end and his tem-per was gone where the dead crabs go. Then the Sea Cow began to travel northward very slowly, stopping to hold absurd bow-ing councils from time to time, and Kotick followed them, saying to himself: 'People who are such idiots as these are, would have been killed long ago if they hadn't found out some safe island; and what is good enough for the Sea Cow is good enough for the Sea Catch. All the same, I wish they'd hurry.'

It was weary work for Kotick. The sea-cows' herd never went more than forty or fifty miles a day, and stopped to feed at night, and kept close to the shore all the time; while Kotick swam round them, and over them, and under them, but he could not hurry them up one mile. As they went further north they held a bowing council every few hours, and Kotick nearly bit off his moustache with impatience till he saw that they were following up a warm current of water, and then he respected them more. One night they sank through the shiny water – sank like stones – and for the first time since he had known them began to swim quickly. Kotick followed, and the pace astonished him, for he never dreamed that Sea Cow was anything of a swimmer. They headed for a cliff by the shore, a cliff that ran down into deep water, and plunged into a dark hole at the foot of it, twenty fathoms under the sea. It was a long, long swim, and Kotick badly wanted fresh air before he was out of the dark tunnel they led him through.

'My wig!' he said, when he rose, gasping and puffing, into open water at the farther end. 'It was a long dive, but it was worth it.'

The sea-cows had separated and were browsing lazily along the edges of the finest beaches that Kotick had ever seen. There were long stretches of smooth-worn rock running for miles, exactly fitted to make seal-nurseries, and there were playgrounds of hard sand sloping inland behind them, and there were rollers for seals to dance in, and long grass to roll in, and sand-dunes to climb up and down, and best of all, Kotick knew by the feel of the water, which never deceives a Sea Catch, that no men had ever come there. The first thing he did was to assure himself that the fishing was good, and then he swam along the beaches and counted up the delightful low sandy islands half hidden in the beautiful rolling fog. Away to the northward, out to sea, ran a line of bars and shoals and rocks that would never let a ship come within six miles of the beach, and between the islands and the mainland was a stretch of deep water that ran up to the perpendicular cliffs, and somewhere below the cliffs was the mouth of the tunnel.

'It's Novastoshnah over again, but ten times better,' said Kotick. 'Sea Cow must be wiser than I thought. Men can't come down the cliffs, even if there were any men; and the shoals to seaward would knock a ship to splinters. If any place in the sea is safe, this is it.' He began to think of the seal he had left behind him, but though he was in a hurry to go back to Novastoshnah, he thoroughly explored the new country, so that he would be able to answer all questions.

Then he dived and made sure of the mouth of the tunnel, and raced through to the southward. No one but a sea-cow or a seal would have dreamed of there being such a place, and when he looked back at the cliffs even Kotick could hardly believe that he had been there.[32]

He was ten days going home, though he was not swimming slowly; and when he hauled out just above Sea-Lion's Neck the first person he met was the seal who had been waiting for him, and she saw by the look in his eyes that he had found his island at last.

But the holluschickie and Sea Catch his father, and all the other seals, laughed at him when he told them what he had discovered, and a young seal about his own age said: 'This is all very well, Kotick, but you can't come from no one knows where and order us off like this. Remember *we*'ve been fighting for our nurseries, and that's a thing you never did. You preferred prowling about in the sea.' The other seals laughed at this, and the young seal began twisting his head from side to side. He had just married that year, and was making a great fuss about it.

'I've no nursery to fight for,' said Kotick. 'I only want to show you all a place where you will be safe. What's the use of fighting?'

'Oh, if you're trying to back out, of course I've no more to say,' said the young seal, with an ugly chuckle.

'Will you come with me if I win?' said Kotick; and a green light came into his eye, for he was very angry at having to fight at all.

'Very good,' said the young seal, carelessly. '*If* you win, I'll come.' He had no time to change his mind, for Kotick's head was out and his teeth sunk in the blubber of the young seal's neck. Then he threw himself back on his haunches and hauled his enemy down the beach, shook him and knocked him over. Then Kotick roared to the seals: 'I've done my best for you these five seasons past. I've found you the island where you'll be safe, but unless your heads are dragged off your silly necks you won't believe. I'm going to teach you now. Look out for yourselves!'

Limmershin told me that never in his life – and Limmershin sees ten thousand big seals fighting every year – never in all his little life did he see anything like Kotick's charge into the nurseries. He flung himself at the biggest sea catch he could find, caught him by the throat, choked him and bumped him and banged him till he grunted for mercy, and then threw him aside and attacked the next. You see, Kotick had never fasted for four months as the big seals did every year, and his deep-sea swimming trips kept him in perfect condition, and, best of all, he had never fought before. His curly white mane stood up with rage, and his eyes flamed, and his big dog-teeth glistened, and he was splendid to look at. Old Sea Catch, his father, saw him tearing past, hauling the grizzled old seals about as though they had been halibut, and upsetting the young bachelors in all directions; and Sea Catch gave a roar and shouted: 'He may be a fool, but he is the best fighter on the Beaches! Don't tackle your father, my son! He's with you!'

Kotick roared in answer, and old Sea Catch waddled in with his moustache on end, blowing like a locomotive, while Matkah and the seal that was going to marry Kotick cowered down and admired their men-folk. It was a gorgeous fight, for the two fought as long as there was a seal that dared lift up his head, and when there were none they paraded grandly up and down the beach side by side, bellowing.

At night, just as the Northern Lights were winking and flashing through the fog, Kotick climbed a bare rock and looked down on the scattered nurseries and the torn and bleeding seals. 'Now,' he said, 'I've taught you your lesson.'

'My wig!' said old Sea Catch, boosting himself up stiffly, for he was fearfully mauled. 'The Killer Whale himself could not have cut them up worse. Son, I'm proud of you, and what's more, *I'll* come with you to your island – if there is such a place.'

'Hear you, fat pigs of the sea. Who comes with me to the Sea Cow's tunnel? Answer, or I shall teach you again,' roared Kotick.

There was a murmur like the ripple of the tide all up and down the beaches. 'We will come,' said thousands of tired voices. 'We will follow Kotick, the White Seal.'

Then Kotick dropped his head between his shoulders and shut his eyes proudly. He was not a white seal any more, but red from head to tail. All the same he would have scorned to look at or touch one of his wounds.

A week later he and his army (nearly ten thousand hollus-chickie and old seals) went away north to the Sea Cow's tunnel, Kotick leading them, and the seals that stayed at Novastoshnah called them idiots. But next spring when they all met off the fishing-banks of the Pacific, Kotick's seals told such tales of the new beaches beyond Sea Cow's tunnel that more and more seals left Novastoshnah. Of course it was not all done at once, for the seals are not very clever, and they[33] need a long time to turn things over in their minds, but year after year more seals went away from Novastoshnah, and Lukannon, and the other nurseries, to the quiet, sheltered beaches where Kotick sits all the summer through, getting bigger and fatter and stronger each year, while the holluschickie play round him, in that sea where no man comes.[34]

Lukannon

This is a sort of sad Seal National Anthem.[1]

I met my mates in the morning (and oh, but I am old!)
Where roaring on the ledges the summer ground-swell rolled.
I heard them lift the chorus that drowned the breakers' song –
The Beaches of Lukannon two million voices strong.

The song of pleasant stations beside the salt lagoons,
The song of blowing squadrons that shuffled down the dunes –
The song of midnight dances that churned the swell to flame –
The Beaches of Lukannon – before the sealers came!

I met my mates in the morning (I'll never meet them more!).
They came and went in legions that darkened all the shore.
And o'er the foam-flecked offing as far as voice could reach
We hailed the landing-parties and we sang them up the beach.

The Beaches of Lukannon – the winter-wheat so tall,
The dripping, crinkled lichens, and the sea-fog drenching all!
The platforms of our playground, all shining smooth and worn!
The Beaches of Lukannon – the home where we were born!

I met my mates in the morning, a broken, scattered band,
Men shoot us in the water and club us on the land.
Men drive us to the Salt House like silly sheep and tame,
And still we sing Lukannon – before the sealers came.

Wheel down, wheel down to Southward – Oh, Gooverooska go!
And tell the Deep Sea Viceroys the story of our woe.
Ere, empty as the shark's-egg the tempest flings ashore,
The Beaches of Lukannon shall know their sons no more!

'RIKKI-TIKKI-TAVI'

At the hole where he went in
Red-Eye called to Wrinkle-Skin.
Hear what little Red-Eye saith:
'Nag,[1] come up and dance with death!'
Eye to eye and head to head
  (*Keep the measure, Nag*).
This shall end when one is dead
  (*At thy pleasure, Nag*).
Turn for turn and twist for twist
  (*Run and hide thee, Nag*).
Hah! The hooded Death has missed!
  (*Woe betide thee, Nag!*)

This is the story of the great war that Rikki-tikki-tavi fought single-handed, through the bath-rooms of the big bungalow in Segowlee[2] cantonment. Darzee,[3] the tailor-bird, helped him, and Chuchundra, the musk-rat,[4] who never comes out into the middle of the floor, but always creeps round by the wall, gave him advice; but Rikki-tikki did the real fighting.

He was a mongoose, rather like a little cat in his fur and his tail, but quite like a weasel in his head and his habits. His eyes and the end of his restless nose were pink; he could scratch himself anywhere he pleased with any leg, front or back, that he chose to use; he could fluff up his tail till it looked like a bottle-brush, and his war-cry as he scuttled through the long grass was: *Rikk-tikk-tikki-tikki-tchk!*

One day, a high summer flood washed him out of the burrow where he lived with his father and mother, and carried him, kicking and clucking, down a roadside ditch. He found a little wisp of grass floating there, and clung to it till he lost his senses. When he revived, he was lying in the hot sun on the middle of a garden path, very draggled indeed, and a small boy was saying: 'Here's a dead mongoose. Let's have a funeral.'

'No,' said his mother; 'let's take him in and dry him. Perhaps he isn't really dead.'

They took him into the house, and a big man picked him up between his finger and thumb and said he was not dead but half choked; so they wrapped him in cotton-wool, and warmed him over a little fire, and he opened his eyes and sneezed.

'Now,' said the big man (he was an Englishman who had just moved into the bungalow); 'don't frighten him, and we'll see what he'll do.'

It is the hardest thing in the world to frighten a mongoose, because he is eaten up from nose to tail with curiosity. The motto of all the mongoose family is, 'Run and find out'; and Rikki-tikki was a true mongoose. He looked at the cotton-wool, decided that it was not good to eat, ran all round the table, sat up and put his fur in order, scratched himself, and jumped on the small boy's shoulder.

'Don't be frightened, Teddy,' said his father. 'That's his way of making friends.'

'Ouch! He's tickling under my chin,' said Teddy.

Rikki-tikki looked down between the boy's collar and neck, snuffed at his ear, and climbed down to the floor, where he sat rubbing his nose.

'Good gracious,' said Teddy's mother, 'and that's a wild creature! I suppose he's so tame because we've been kind to him.'

'All mongooses are like that,' said her husband. 'If Teddy doesn't pick him up by the tail, or try to put him in a cage, he'll run in and out of the house all day long. Let's give him something to eat.'

They gave him a little piece of raw meat. Rikki-tikki liked it immensely, and when it was finished he went out into the veranda and sat in the sunshine and fluffed up his fur to make it dry to the roots. Then he felt better.

'There are more things to find out about in this house,' he said to himself, 'than all my family could find out in all their lives. I shall certainly stay and find out.'

He spent all that day roaming over the house. He nearly

drowned himself in the bath-tubs; put his nose into the ink on a writing-table, and burnt it on the end of the big man's cigar, for he climbed up in the big man's lap to see how writing was done. At nightfall he ran into Teddy's nursery to watch how kerosene lamps were lighted, and when Teddy went to bed Rikki-tikki climbed up too; but he was a restless companion, because he had to get up and attend to every noise all through the night, and find out what made it. Teddy's mother and father came in, the last thing, to look at their boy, and Rikki-tikki was awake on the pillow. 'I don't like that,' said Teddy's mother; 'he may bite the child.' 'He'll do no such thing,' said the father. 'Teddy's safer with that little beast than if he had a bloodhound to watch him. If a snake came into the nursery now—'

But Teddy's mother wouldn't think of anything so awful.

Early in the morning Rikki-tikki came to early breakfast in the veranda riding on Teddy's shoulder, and they gave him banana and some boiled egg; and he sat on all their laps one after the other, because every well-brought-up mongoose always hopes to be a house-mongoose some day and have rooms to run about in; and Rikki-tikki's mother (she used to live in the General's house at Segowlee) had carefully told Rikki what to do if ever he came across white men.

Then Rikki-tikki went out into the garden to see what was to be seen. It was a large garden, only half cultivated, with bushes, as big as summer-houses, of Marshal Niel[5] roses; lime and orange trees, clumps of bamboos, and thickets of high grass. Rikki-tikki licked his lips. 'This is a splendid hunting-ground,' he said, and his tail grew bottle-brushy at the thought of it, and he scuttled up and down the garden, snuffing here and there till he heard very sorrowful voices in a thorn-bush. It was Darzee, the tailor-bird, and his wife. They had made a beautiful nest by pulling two big leaves together and stitching them up the edges with fibres, and had filled the hollow with cotton and downy fluff. The nest swayed to and fro, as they sat on the rim and cried.

'What is the matter?' asked Rikki-tikki.

'We are very miserable,' said Darzee. 'One of our babies fell out of the nest yesterday and Nag ate him.'

'H'm!' said Rikki-tikki, 'that is very sad – but I am a stranger here. Who is Nag?'

Darzee and his wife only cowered down in the nest without answering, for from the thick grass at the foot of the bush there came a low hiss – a horrid cold sound that made Rikki-tikki jump back two clear feet. Then inch by inch out of the grass rose up the head and spread hood of Nag, the big black cobra, and he was five feet long from tongue to tail. When he had lifted one-third of himself clear of the ground, he stayed balancing to and fro exactly as a dandelion-tuft balances in the wind, and he looked at Rikki-tikki with the wicked snake's eyes that never change their expression, whatever the snake may be thinking of.

'Who is Nag?' said he. '*I* am Nag. The great God Brahm[6] put his mark upon all our people, when the first cobra spread his hood to keep the sun off Brahm as he slept. Look, and be afraid!'

He spread out his hood more than ever, and Rikki-tikki saw the spectacle-mark on the back of it that looks exactly like the eye part of a hook-and-eye fastening. He was afraid for the minute; but it is impossible for a mongoose to stay frightened for any length of time, and though Rikki-tikki had never met a live cobra before, his mother had fed him on dead ones, and he knew that all a grown mongoose's business in life was to fight and eat snakes. Nag knew that too and, at the bottom of his cold heart, he was afraid.

'Well,' said Rikki-tikki, and his tail began to fluff up again, 'marks or no marks, do you think it is right for you to eat fledgelings out of a nest?'

Nag was thinking to himself, and watching the least little movement in the grass behind Rikki-tikki. He knew that mongooses in the garden meant death sooner or later for him and his family; but he wanted to get Rikki-tikki off his guard. So he dropped his head a little, and put it on one side.

'Let us talk,' he said. 'You eat eggs. Why should not I eat birds?'

'Behind you! Look behind you!' sang Darzee.

Rikki-tikki knew better than to waste time in staring. He jumped up in the air as high as he could go, and just under him whizzed by the head of Nagaina,[7] Nag's wicked wife. She had crept up behind him as he was talking, to make an end of him; and he heard her savage hiss as the stroke missed. He came down almost across her back, and if he had been an old mongoose he would have known that then was the time to break her back with one bite; but he was afraid of the terrible lashing return-stroke of the cobra. He bit, indeed, but did not bite long enough, and jumped clear of the whisking tail, leaving Nagaina torn and angry.

'Wicked, wicked Darzee!' said Nag, lashing up as high as he could reach toward the nest in the thorn-bush; but Darzee had built it out of reach of snakes, and it only swayed to and fro.

Rikki-tikki felt his eyes growing red and hot (when a mongoose's eyes grow red, he is angry), and he sat back on his tail and hind legs like a little kangaroo, and looked all round him, and chattered with rage. But Nag and Nagaina had disappeared into the grass. When a snake misses its stroke, it never says anything or gives any sign of what it means to do next. Rikki-tikki did not care to follow them, for he did not feel sure that he could manage two snakes at once. So he trotted off to the gravel path near the house, and sat down to think. It was a serious matter for him. If you read the old books of natural history, you will find they say that when the mongoose fights the snake and happens to get bitten, he runs off and eats some herb that cures him. That is not true. The victory is only a matter of quickness of eye and quickness of foot – snake's blow against mongoose's jump – and as no eye can follow the motion of a snake's head when it strikes, this makes things much more wonderful than any magic herb. Rikki-tikki knew he was a young mongoose, and it made him all the more pleased to think that he had managed to escape a blow from behind. It gave him confidence in himself, and when Teddy came running down the path, Rikki-tikki was ready to be petted. But just as Teddy was stooping, something wriggled[8] a little in the dust, and a tiny voice said: 'Be careful. I am Death!' It was Karait,[9] the dusty brown snakeling that lies for choice on the dusty earth; and his bite is as dangerous as the cobra's. But he is so small that nobody thinks of him, and so he does the more harm to people.

Rikki-tikki's eyes grew red again, and he danced up to Karait with the peculiar rocking, swaying motion that he had inherited from his family. It looks very funny, but it is so perfectly balanced a gait that you can fly off from it at any angle you please; and in dealing with snakes this is an advantage. If Rikki-tikki had only known, he was doing a much more dangerous thing than fighting Nag, for Karait is so small, and can turn so quickly, that unless Rikki bit him close to the back of the head, he would get the return-stroke in his eye or his lip. But Rikki did not know: his eyes were all red, and he rocked back and forth, looking for a good place to hold. Karait struck out. Rikki jumped sideways and tried to run in, but the wicked little dusty gray head lashed within a fraction of his shoulder, and he had to jump over the body, and the head followed his heels close.

Teddy shouted to the house: 'Oh, look here! Our mongoose is killing a snake'; and Rikki-tikki heard a scream from Teddy's mother. His father ran out with a stick, but by the time he came up, Karait had lunged out once too far, and Rikki-tikki had sprung, jumped on the snake's back, dropped his head far between his fore-legs, bitten as high up the back as he could get hold, and rolled away. That bite paralysed Karait, and Rikki-tikki was just going to eat him up from the tail, after the custom of his family at dinner, when he remembered that a full meal makes a slow mongoose, and if he wanted all his strength and quickness ready, he must keep himself thin. He went away for a dust-bath under the castor-oil bushes, while Teddy's father beat the dead Karait. 'What is the use of that?' thought Rikki-tikki; 'I have settled it all'; and then Teddy's mother picked him up from the dust and hugged him, crying that he had saved Teddy from death, and Teddy's father said that he was a providence, and Teddy looked on with big scared eyes. Rikki-tikki was rather amused at all the fuss, which, of course, he did not understand. Teddy's mother might just as well have petted Teddy for playing in the dust. Rikki was thoroughly enjoying himself.

That night at dinner, walking to and fro among the wine-glasses on the table, he might have stuffed himself three times over with nice things; but he remembered Nag and Nagaina, and though it was very pleasant to be patted and petted by Teddy's mother, and to sit on Teddy's shoulder, his eyes would get red from time to time, and he would go off into his long war-cry of '*Rikk-tikk-tikki-tikki-tchk!*'

Teddy carried him off to bed, and insisted on Rikki-tikki sleeping under his chin. Rikki-tikki was too well bred to bite or scratch, but as soon as Teddy was asleep he went off for his nightly walk round the house, and in the dark he ran up against Chuchundra, the musk-rat, creeping round by the wall. Chuchundra is a broken-hearted little beast. He whimpers and cheeps all the night, trying to make up his mind to run into the middle of the room; but he never gets there.

'Don't kill me,' said Chuchundra, almost weeping. 'Rikki-tikki, don't kill me!'

'Do you think a snake-killer kills musk-rats?' said Rikki-tikki scornfully.

'Those who kill snakes get killed by snakes,' said Chuchundra, more sorrowfully than ever. 'And how am I to be sure that Nag won't mistake me for you some dark night?'

'There's not the least danger,' said Rikki-tikki; 'but Nag is in the garden, and I know you don't go there.'

'My cousin Chua,[10] the rat, told me—' said Chuchundra, and then he stopped.

'Told you what?'

'H'sh! Nag is everywhere, Rikki-tikki. You should have talked to Chua in the garden.'

'I didn't – so you must tell me. Quick, Chuchundra, or I'll bite you!'

Chuchundra sat down and cried till the tears rolled off his whiskers. 'I am a very poor man,' he sobbed. 'I never had spirit enough to run out into the middle of the room. H'sh! I mustn't tell you anything. Can't you *hear*, Rikki-tikki?'

Rikki-tikki listened. The house was as still as still, but he thought he could just catch the faintest *scratch-scratch* in the world – a noise as faint as that of a wasp walking on a window-pane – the dry scratch of a snake's scales on brickwork.

'That's Nag or Nagaina,' he said to himself; 'and he is crawling into the bath-room sluice. You're right, Chuchundra; I should have talked to Chua.'

He stole off to Teddy's bath-room, but there was nothing there, and then to Teddy's mother's bath-room. At the bottom of the smooth plaster wall there was a brick pulled out to make a sluice for the bath-water, and as Rikki-tikki stole in by the masonry curb where the bath is put, he heard Nag and Nagaina whispering together outside in the moonlight.

'When the house is emptied of people,' said Nagaina to her husband, '*he* will have to go away, and then the garden will be our own again. Go in quietly, and remember that the big man who killed Karait is the first one to bite. Then come out and tell me, and we will hunt for Rikki-tikki together.'

'But are you sure that there is anything to be gained by killing the people?' said Nag.

'Everything. When there were no people in the bungalow, did we have any mongoose in the garden? So long as the bungalow is empty, we are king and queen of the garden; and remember that as soon as our eggs in the melon-bed hatch (as they may tomorrow), our children will need room and quiet.'

'I had not thought of that,' said Nag. 'I will go, but there is no need that we should hunt for Rikki-tikki afterward. I will kill the big man and his wife, and the child if I can, and come away quietly. Then the bungalow will be empty, and Rikki-tikki will go.'

Rikki-tikki tingled all over with rage and hatred at this, and then Nag's head came through the sluice, and his five feet of cold body followed it. Angry as he was, Rikki-tikki was very frightened as he saw the size of the big cobra. Nag coiled himself up, raised his head, and looked into the bath-room in the dark, and Rikki could see his eyes glitter.

'Now, if I kill him here, Nagaina will know; and if I fight him on the open floor, the odds are in his favour. What am I to do?' said Rikki-tikki-tavi.

Nag waved to and fro, and then Rikki-tikki heard him drinking from the biggest water-jar that was used to fill the bath. 'That is good,' said the snake. 'Now, when Karait was killed, the big man had a stick. He may have that stick still, but when he comes in to bathe in the morning he will not have a stick. I shall wait here till he comes. Nagaina – do you hear me? – I shall wait here in the cool till daytime.'

There was no answer from outside, so Rikki-tikki knew Nagaina had gone away. Nag coiled himself down, coil by coil, round the bulge at the bottom of the water-jar, and Rikki-tikki stayed still as death. After an hour he began to move, muscle by muscle, towards the jar. Nag was asleep, and Rikki-tikki looked at his big back, wondering which would be the best place for a good hold. 'If I don't break his back at the first jump,' said Rikki, 'he can still fight; and if he fights – O Rikki!' He looked at the thickness of the neck below the hood, but that was too much for him; and a bite near the tail would only make Nag savage.

'It must be the head,' he said at last; 'the head above the hood; and, when I am once there, I must not let go.'

Then he jumped. The head was lying a little clear of the water-jar, under the curve of it; and, as his teeth met, Rikki braced his back against the bulge of the red earthenware to hold down the head. This gave him just one second's purchase, and he made the most of it. Then he was battered to and fro as a rat is shaken by a dog – to and fro on the floor, up and down, and round in great circles, but his eyes were red and he held on as the body cart-whipped over the floor, upsetting the tin dipper and the soap-dish and the flesh-brush, and banged against the tin side of the bath. As he held he closed his jaws tighter and tighter, for he made sure he would be banged to death, and, for the honour of his family, he preferred to be found with his teeth locked. He was dizzy, aching, and felt shaken to pieces when something went off like a thunderclap just behind him; a hot wind knocked him senseless and red fire singed his fur. The big man had been wakened by the noise, and had fired both barrels of a shot-gun into Nag just behind the hood.

Rikki-tikki held on with his eyes shut, for now he was quite sure he was dead; but the head did not move, and the big man picked him up and said: 'It's the mongoose again, Alice: the little chap has saved *our* lives now.' Then Teddy's mother came in with a very white face, and saw what was left of Nag, and Rikki-tikki dragged himself to Teddy's bedroom and spent half the rest of the night shaking himself tenderly to find out whether he really was broken into forty pieces, as he fancied.

When morning came he was very stiff, but well pleased with his doings. 'Now I have Nagaina to settle with, and she will be worse than five Nags, and there's no knowing when the eggs she spoke of will hatch. Goodness! I must go and see Darzee,' he said.

Without waiting for breakfast, Rikki-tikki ran to the thorn-bush where Darzee was singing a song of triumph at the top of his voice. The news of Nag's death was all over the garden, for the sweeper had thrown the body on the rubbish-heap.

'Oh, you stupid tuft of feathers!' said Rikki-tikki angrily. 'Is this the time to sing?'

'Nag is dead – is dead – is dead!' sang Darzee. 'The valiant Rikki-tikki caught him by the head and held fast. The big man brought bang-stick, and Nag fell in two pieces! He will never eat my babies again.'

'All that's true enough; but where's Nagaina?' said Rikki-tikki, looking carefully round him.

'Nagaina came to the bath-room sluice and called for Nag,' Darzee went on; 'and Nag came out on the end of a stick – the sweeper picked him up on the end of a stick and threw him upon the rubbish-heap. Let us sing about the great, the red-eyed Rikki-tikki!' and Darzee filled his throat and sang.

'If I could get up to your nest, I'd roll your babies out!' said Rikki-tikki. 'You don't know when to do the right thing at the right time. You're safe enough in your nest there, but it's war for me down here. Stop singing a minute, Darzee.'

'For the great, the beautiful Rikki-tikki's sake I will stop,' said Darzee. 'What is it, O Killer of the terrible Nag?'

'Where is Nagaina, for the third time?'

'On the rubbish-heap by the stables, mourning for Nag. Great is Rikki-tikki with the white teeth.'

'Bother my white teeth! Have you ever heard where she keeps her eggs?'

'In the melon-bed, on the end nearest the wall, where the sun strikes nearly all day. She hid them there weeks ago.'

'And you never thought it worth while to tell me? The end nearest the wall, you said?'

'Rikki-tikki, you are not going to eat her eggs?'

'Not eat exactly; no. Darzee, if you have a grain of sense you will fly off to the stables and pretend that your wing is broken, and let Nagaina chase you away to this bush. I must get to the melon-bed, and if I went there now she'd see me.'

Darzee was a feather-brained little fellow who could never hold more than one idea at a time in his head; and just because he knew that Nagaina's children were born in eggs like his own, he didn't think at first that it was fair to kill them. But his wife was a sensible bird, and she knew that cobra's eggs meant young cobras later on; so she flew off from the nest, and left Darzee to keep the babies warm, and continue his song about the death of Nag. Darzee was very like a man in some ways.

She fluttered in front of Nagaina by the rubbish-heap, and cried out, 'Oh, my wing is broken! The boy in the house threw a stone at me and broke it.' Then she fluttered more desperately than ever.

Nagaina lifted up her head and hissed, 'You warned Rikki-tikki when I would have killed him. Indeed and truly, you've chosen a bad place to be lame in.' And she moved toward Darzee's wife, slipping along over the dust.

'The boy broke it with a stone!' shrieked Darzee's wife.

'Well! It may be some consolation to you when you're dead to know that I shall settle accounts with the boy. My husband lies on the rubbish-heap this morning, but before night the boy in the house will lie very still. What is the use of running away? I am sure to catch you. Little fool, look at me!'

Darzee's wife knew better than to do *that*, for a bird who looks at a snake's eyes gets so frightened that she cannot move. Darzee's wife fluttered on, piping sorrowfully, and never leaving the ground, and Nagaina quickened her pace.

Rikki-tikki heard them going up the path from the stables, and he raced for the end of the melon-patch near the wall. There, in the warm litter about the melons, very cunningly hidden, he found twenty-five eggs, about the size of a bantam's eggs, but with whitish skins instead of shells.

'I was not a day too soon,' he said; for he could see the baby cobras curled up inside the skin, and he knew that the minute they were hatched they could each kill a man or a mongoose.

He bit off the tops of the eggs as fast as he could, taking care to crush the young cobras, and turned over the litter from time to time to see whether he had missed any. At last there were only three eggs left, and Rikki-tikki began to chuckle to himself, when he heard Darzee's wife screaming:

'Rikki-tikki, I led Nagaina toward the house, and she has gone into the veranda, and – oh, come quickly – she means killing!'

Rikki-tikki smashed two eggs, and tumbled backward down the melon-bed with the third egg in his mouth, and scuttled to the veranda as hard as he could put foot to the ground. Teddy and his mother and father were there at early breakfast; but Rikki-tikki saw that they were not eating anything. They sat stone-still, and their faces were white. Nagaina was coiled up on the matting by Teddy's chair, within easy striking distance of Teddy's bare leg, and she was swaying to and fro, singing a song of triumph.

'Son of the big man that killed Nag,' she hissed, 'stay still. I am not ready yet. Wait a little. Keep very still, all you three! If you move I strike, and if you do not move I strike. Oh, foolish people, who killed my Nag!'

Teddy's eyes were fixed on his father, and all his father could do was to whisper, 'Sit still, Teddy. You mustn't move. Teddy, keep still.'

Then Rikki-tikki came up and cried: 'Turn round, Nagaina; turn and fight!'

'All in good time,' said she, without moving her eyes. 'I will settle my account with *you* presently. Look at your friends, Rikki-tikki. They are still and white. They are afraid. They dare not move, and if you come a step nearer I strike.'

'Look at your eggs,' said Rikki-tikki, 'in the melon-bed near the wall. Go and look, Nagaina!'

The big snake turned half round, and saw the egg on the veranda. 'Ah-h! Give it to me,' she said.

Rikki-tikki put his paws one on each side of the egg, and his eyes were blood-red. 'What price for a snake's egg? For a young cobra? For a young king-cobra? For the last – the very last of the brood? The ants are eating all the others down by the melon-bed.'

Nagaina spun clear round, forgetting everything for the sake of one egg; and Rikki-tikki saw Teddy's father shoot a big hand, catch Teddy by the shoulder, and drag him across the little table with the tea-cups, safe and out of reach of Nagaina.

'Tricked! Tricked! Tricked! *Rikk-tck-tck!*' chuckled Rikki-tikki. 'The boy is safe, and it was I – I – I that caught Nag by the hood last night in the bath-room.' Then he began to jump up and down, all four feet together, his head close to the floor. 'He threw me to and fro, but he could not shake me off. He was dead before the big man blew him in two. I did it! *Rikki-tikki-tck-tck!* Come then, Nagaina. Come and fight with me. You shall not be a widow long.'

Nagaina saw that she had lost her chance of killing Teddy, and the egg lay between Rikki-tikki's paws. 'Give me the egg, Rikki-tikki. Give me the last of my eggs, and I will go away and never come back,' she said, lowering her hood.

'Yes, you will go away, and you will never come back; for you will go to the rubbish-heap with Nag. Fight, widow! The big man has gone for his gun! Fight!'

Rikki-tikki was bounding all round Nagaina, keeping just out of reach of her stroke, his little eyes like hot coals. Nagaina gathered herself together, and flung out at him. Rikki-tikki jumped up and backwards. Again and again and again she struck, and each time her head came with a whack on the matting of the veranda and she gathered herself together like a watch-spring. Then Rikki-tikki danced in a circle to get behind her, and Nagaina spun round to keep her head to his head, so that the rustle of her tail on the matting sounded like dry leaves blown along by the wind.

He had forgotten the egg. It still lay on the veranda, and Nagaina came nearer and nearer to it, till at last, while Rikki-tikki was drawing breath, she caught it in her mouth, turned to the veranda steps, and flew like an arrow down the path, with Rikki-tikki behind her. When the cobra runs for her life, she goes like a whip-lash flicked across a horse's neck. Rikki-tikki knew that he must catch her, or all the trouble would begin again. She headed straight for the long grass by the thorn-bush, and as he was running Rikki-tikki heard Darzee still singing his foolish little song of triumph. But Darzee's wife was wiser. She flew off her nest as Nagaina came along, and flapped her wings about Nagaina's head. If Darzee had helped they might have turned her; but Nagaina only lowered her hood and went on. Still, the instant's delay brought Rikki-tikki up to her, and as she plunged into the rat-hole where she and Nag used to live, his little white teeth were clenched on her tail, and he went down with her – and very few mongooses, however wise and old they may be, care to follow a cobra into its hole. It was dark in the hole; and Rikki-tikki never knew when it might open out and give Nagaina room to turn and strike at him. He held on savagely, and stuck out his feet to act as brakes on the dark slope of the hot, moist earth. Then the grass by the mouth of the hole stopped waving, and Darzee said: 'It is all over with Rikki-tikki! We must sing his death-song. Valiant Rikki-tikki is dead! For Nagaina will surely kill him underground.'

So he sang a very mournful song that he made up on the spur of the minute, and just as he got to the most touching part the grass quivered again, and Rikki-tikki, covered with dirt, dragged himself out of the hole leg by leg, licking his whiskers. Darzee stopped with a little shout. Rikki-tikki shook some of the dust out of his fur and sneezed. 'It is all over,' he said. 'The widow will never come out again.' And the red ants that live between the grass stems heard him, and began to troop down one after another to see if he had spoken the truth.

Rikki-tikki curled himself up in the grass and slept where he was – slept and slept till it was late in the afternoon, for he had done a hard day's work.

'Now,' he said, when he awoke, 'I will go back to the house. Tell the Coppersmith,[11] Darzee, and he will tell the garden that Nagaina is dead.'

The Coppersmith is a bird who makes a noise exactly like the beating of a little hammer on a copper pot; and the reason he is always making it is because he is the town-crier to every Indian garden, and tells all the news to everybody who cares to listen. As Rikki-tikki went up the path, he heard his 'attention' notes like a tiny dinner-gong; and then the steady '*Ding-dong-tock!* Nag is dead – *dong!* Nagaina is dead! *Ding-dong-tock!*' That set all the birds in the garden singing, and the frogs croaking; for Nag and Nagaina used to eat frogs as well as little birds.

When Rikki got to the house, Teddy and Teddy's mother (she looked very white still, for she had been fainting) and Teddy's father came out and almost cried over him; and that night he ate all that was given him till he could eat no more, and went to bed on Teddy's shoulder, where Teddy's mother saw him when she came to look late at night.

'He saved our lives and Teddy's life,' she said to her husband. 'Just think, he saved all our lives.'

Rikki-tikki woke up with a jump, for the mongooses are light sleepers.

'Oh, it's you,' said he. 'What are you bothering for? All the cobras are dead; and if they weren't, I'm here.'

Rikki-tikki had a right to be proud of himself; but he did not grow too proud, and he kept that garden as a mongoose should keep it, with tooth and jump and spring and bite, till never a cobra dared show its head inside the walls.

Darzee's Chaunt

Sung in honour of Rikki-tikki-tavi

Singer and tailor am I –
    Doubled the joys that I know –
Proud of my lilt to the sky,
    Proud of the house that I sew.
Over and under, so weave I my music – so weave I the house
    that I sew.

Sing to your fledglings again,
    Mother, O lift up your head!
Evil that plagued us is slain,
    Death in the garden lies dead.
Terror that hid in the roses is impotent – flung on the dunghill
    and dead!

Who has delivered us, who?
    Tell me his nest and his name.
Rikki, the valiant, the true,
    Tikki, with eyeballs of flame –
Rikk-tikki-tikki, the ivory-fanged, the hunter with eyeballs of
    flame!

Give him the Thanks of the Birds,
    Bowing with tail-feathers spread,
Praise him with nightingale words –
    Nay, I will praise him instead.
Hear! I will sing you the praise of the bottle-tailed Rikki with
    eyeballs of red!

(Here Rikki-tikki interrupted, so the rest of the song is lost.)

TOOMAI OF THE ELEPHANTS

I will remember what I was. I am sick of rope and chain.
  I will remember my old strength and all my forest affairs.
I will not sell my back to man for a bundle of sugar-cane:
  I will go out to my own kind, and the wood-folk in their lairs.

I will go out until the day, until the morning break –
  Out to the winds' untainted kiss, the waters' clean caress –
I will forget my ankle-ring and snap my picket-stake.
  I will revisit my lost loves, and playmates masterless!

Kala Nag, which means Black Snake, had served the Indian Government[1] in every way that an elephant could serve it for forty-seven years, and as he was fully twenty years old when he was caught, that makes him nearly seventy – a ripe age for an elephant.[2] He remembered pushing, with a big leather pad on his forehead, at a gun stuck in deep mud, and that was before the Afghan war of 1842,[3] and he had not then come to his full strength. His mother Radha Pyari – Radha the Darling – who had been caught in the same drive with Kala Nag, told him, before his little milk tusks had dropped out,[4] that elephants who were afraid always got hurt: and Kala Nag knew that that advice was good, for the first time that he saw a shell burst he backed, screaming, into a stand of piled rifles, and the bayonets pricked him in all his softest places. So, before he was twenty-five, he gave up being afraid, and so he was the best-loved and the best-looked-after elephant in the service of the Government of India. He had carried tents, twelve hundred pounds' weight of tents, on the march in Upper India: he had been hoisted into a ship at the end of a steam-crane and taken for days across the water, and made to carry a mortar on his back in a strange and rocky country very far from India, and had seen the Emperor Theodore lying dead in Magdala, and had come back again in the steamer entitled, so the soldiers said, to the Abyssinian War medal.[5] He had seen his fellow-elephants die of cold and epilepsy and starvation and sunstroke up at a place called Ali Musjid,[6] ten years later; and afterward he had been sent down thousands of miles south to haul and pile big baulks of teak in the timber-yards at Moulmein.[7] There he had half killed an insubordinate young elephant who was shirking his fair share of work.

After that he was taken off timber-hauling, and employed, with a few score other elephants who were trained to the business, in helping to catch wild elephants among the Garo hills.[8] Elephants are very strictly preserved by the Indian Government. There is one whole department which does nothing else but hunt them, and catch them, and break them in, and send them up and down the country as they are needed for work. Kala Nag stood ten fair feet at the shoulders, and his tusks had been cut off short at five feet, and bound round the ends, to prevent them splitting, with bands of copper; but he could do more with those stumps than any untrained elephant could do with the real sharpened ones. When, after weeks and weeks of cautious driving of scattered elephants across the hills, the forty or fifty wild monsters were driven into the last stockade, and the big drop-gate, made of tree-trunks lashed together, jarred down behind them, Kala Nag, at the word of command, would go into that flaring, trumpeting pandemonium (generally at night, when the flicker of the torches made it difficult to judge distances), and, picking out the biggest and wildest tusker[9] of the mob, would hammer him and hustle him into quiet while the men on the backs of the other elephants roped and tied the smaller ones. There was nothing in the way of fighting that Kala Nag, the old wise Black Snake, did not know, for he had stood up more than once in his time to the charge of the wounded tiger, and, curling up his soft trunk to be out of harm's way, had knocked the springing brute sideways in mid-air with a quick sickle-cut of his head, that he had invented all by himself; had knocked him over, and kneeled upon him with his huge knees till the life went out with a gasp and a howl, and there was only a fluffy striped thing on the ground for Kala Nag to pull by the tail.

'Yes,' said Big Toomai, his driver, the son of Black Toomai who had taken him to Abyssinia, and grandson of Toomai of the Elephants who had seen him caught, 'there is nothing that the Black Snake fears except me. He has seen three generations of us feed him and groom him, and he will live to see four.'

'He is afraid of *me* also,' said Little Toomai, standing up to his full height of four feet, with only one rag upon him. He was ten years old, the eldest son of Big Toomai, and, according to custom, he would take his father's place on Kala Nag's neck when he grew up, and would handle the heavy iron *ankus*, the elephant-goad, that had been worn smooth by his father, and his grandfather, and his great-grandfather. He knew what he was talking of; for he had been born under Kala Nag's shadow, had played with the end of his trunk before he could walk, had taken him down to water as soon as he could walk, and Kala Nag would no more have dreamed of disobeying his shrill little orders than he would have dreamed of killing him on that day when Big Toomai carried the little brown baby under Kala Nag's tusks, and told him to salute his master that was to be. 'Yes,' said Little Toomai, 'he is afraid of *me*,' and he took long strides up to Kala Nag, called him a fat old pig and made him lift up his feet one after the other.

'Wah!' said Little Toomai, 'thou art a big elephant,' and he wagged his fluffy head, quoting his father. 'The Government may pay for elephants, but they belong to us mahouts.[10] When thou art old, Kala Nag, there will come some rich Rajah, and he will buy thee from the Government, on account of thy size and thy manners, and then thou wilt have nothing to do but to carry gold earrings in thy ears, and a gold howdah[11] on thy back, and a red cloth covered with gold on thy sides, and walk at the head of the processions of the King. Then I shall sit on thy neck, O Kala Nag, with a silver *ankus*, and men will run before us with golden sticks, crying, "Room for the King's elephant!" That will be good, Kala Nag, but not so good as this hunting in the jungles.'

'Umph!' said Big Toomai. 'Thou art a boy, and as wild as a buffalo-calf. This running up and down among the hills is not the best Government service. I am getting old, and I do not love wild elephants. Give me brick elephant-lines, one stall to each elephant, and big stumps to tie them to safely, and flat, broad roads to exercise upon, instead of this come-and-go camping. Aha, the Cawnpore[12] barracks were good. There was a bazaar close by, and only three hours' work a day.'

Little Toomai remembered the Cawnpore elephant-lines and said nothing. He very much preferred the camp life, and hated those broad, flat roads, with the daily grubbing for grass in the forage-reserve, and the long hours when there was nothing to do except to watch Kala Nag fidgeting in his pickets. What Little Toomai liked was to scramble up bridle-paths that only an elephant could take; the dip into the valley below; the glimpses of the wild elephants browsing miles away; the rush of the frightened pig and peacock under Kala Nag's feet; the blinding warm rains, when all the hills and valleys smoked; the beautiful misty mornings when nobody knew where they would camp that night; the steady, cautious drive of the wild elephants, and the mad rush and blaze and hullaballoo of the last night's drive, when the elephants poured into the stockade like boulders in a landslide, found that they could not get out, and flung themselves at the heavy posts only to be driven back by yells and flaring torches and volleys of blank cartridge. Even a little boy could be of use there, and Toomai was as useful as three boys. He would get his torch and wave it, and yell with the best. But the really good time came when the driving out began, and the Keddah, that is, the stockade, looked like a picture of the end of the world, and men had to make signs to one another, because they could not hear themselves speak. Then Little Toomai would climb up to the top of one of the quivering stockade-posts, his sun-bleached brown hair flying loose all over his shoulders, and he looking like a goblin in the torchlight; and as soon as there was a lull you could hear his high-pitched yells of encouragement to Kala Nag, above the trumpeting and crashing, and snapping of ropes, and groans of the tethered elephants. '*Maîl, maîl, Kala Nag!* (Go on, go on,

Black Snake!) *Dant do!* (Give him the tusk!) *Somalo! Somalo!* (Careful, careful!) *Maro! Mar!* (Hit him, hit him!) Mind the post! *Arré! Arré! Hai! Yai! Kya-a-ah!*' he would shout, and the big fight between Kala Nag and the wild elephant would sway to and fro across the Keddah, and the old elephant-catchers would wipe the sweat out of their eyes, and find time to nod to Little Toomai wriggling with joy on the top of the posts.

He did more than wriggle. One night he slid down from the post and slipped in between the elephants, and threw up the loose end of a rope, which had dropped, to a driver who was trying to get a purchase on the leg of a kicking young calf (calves always give more trouble than full-grown animals). Kala Nag saw him, caught him in his trunk, and handed him up to Big Toomai, who slapped him then and there, and put him back on the post. Next morning he gave him a scolding, and said: 'Are not good brick elephant-lines and a little tent-carrying enough, that you must needs go elephant-catching on thy own account, little worthless? Now those foolish hunt-ers, whose pay is less than my pay, have spoken to Petersen Sahib[13] of the matter.' Little Toomai was frightened. He did not know much of white men, but Petersen Sahib was the greatest white man in the world to him. He was the head of all the Ked-dah operations – the man who caught all the elephants for the Government of India, and who knew more about the ways of elephants than any living man.

'What – what will happen?' said Little Toomai.

'Happen! the worst that can happen. Petersen Sahib is a madman; else why should he go hunting these wild devils? He may even require thee to be an elephant-catcher, to sleep any-where in these fever-filled jungles, and at last to be trampled to death in the Keddah. It is well that this nonsense ends safely. Next week the catching is over, and we of the plains are sent back to our stations. Then we will march on smooth roads, and forget all this hunting. But, son, I am angry that thou shouldst meddle in the business that belongs to these dirty Assamese jungle-folk. Kala Nag will obey none but me, so I must go with him into the Keddah, but he is only a fighting elephant, and he does not help to rope them. So I sit at my ease, as befits a mahout – not a mere hunter – a mahout, I say, and a man who gets a pension at the end of his service. Is the family of Toomai of the Elephants to be trodden underfoot in the dirt of a Keddah? Bad one! Wicked one! Worthless son! Go and wash Kala Nag and attend to his ears, and see that there are no thorns in his feet; or else Petersen Sahib will surely catch thee and make thee a wild hunter – a follower of elephants' foot-tracks, a jungle-bear. Bah! Shame! Go!'

Little Toomai went off without saying a word, but he told Kala Nag all his grievances while he was examining his feet. 'No matter,' said Little Toomai, turning up the fringe of Kala Nag's huge right ear. 'They have said my name to Petersen Sahib, and perhaps – and perhaps – and perhaps – who knows? Hai! That is a big thorn that I have pulled out!'

The next few days were spent in getting the elephants together, in walking the newly caught wild elephants up and down between a couple of tame ones, to prevent them giving too much trouble on the downward march to the plains, and in taking stock of the blankets and ropes and things that had been worn out or lost in the forest. Petersen Sahib came in on his clever she-elephant Pudmini;[14] he had been paying off other camps among the hills, for the season was coming to an end, and there was a native clerk sitting at a table under a tree, to pay the drivers their wages. As each man was paid he went back to his elephant, and joined the line that stood ready to start. The catchers, and hunters, and beaters, the men of the regular Keddah, who stayed in the jungle year in and year out, sat on the backs of the elephants that belonged to Petersen Sahib's permanent force, or leaned against the trees with their guns across their arms, and made fun of the drivers who were going away, and laughed when the newly caught elephants broke the line and ran about. Big Toomai went up to the clerk with Little Toomai behind him, and Machua Appa, the head-tracker, said in an undertone to a friend of his, 'There goes one piece of good elephant-stuff at least. 'Tis a pity to send that young jungle-cock to moult in the plains.'

Now Petersen Sahib had ears all over him, as a man must have who listens to the most silent of all living things – the wild elephant. He turned where he was lying all along Pudmini's back, and said, 'What is that? I did not know of a man among the plains-drivers who had wit enough to rope even a dead elephant.'

'This is not a man, but a boy. He went into the Keddah at the last drive, and threw Barmao there the rope, when we were trying to get that young calf with the blotch on his shoulder away from his mother.' Machua Appa pointed at Little Toomai, and Petersen Sahib looked, and Little Toomai bowed to the earth.

'He throw a rope? He is smaller than a picket-pin. Little one, what is thy name?' said Petersen Sahib. Little Toomai was too frightened to speak, but Kala Nag was behind him, and Toomai made a sign with his hand, and the elephant caught him up in his trunk and held him level with Pudmini's forehead, in front of the great Petersen Sahib. Then Little Toomai covered his face with his hands, for he was only a child, and except where elephants were concerned, he was just as bashful as a child could be.

'Oho!' said Petersen Sahib, smiling underneath his moustache, 'and why didst thou teach thy elephant *that* trick? Was it to help thee steal green corn from the roofs of the houses when the ears are put out to dry?'

'Not green corn, Protector of the Poor – melons,' said Little Toomai, and all the men sitting about broke into a roar of laughter. Most of them had taught their elephants that trick when they were boys. Little Toomai was hanging eight feet up in the air, and he wished very much that he were eight feet under ground.

'He is Toomai, my son, Sahib,' said Big Toomai, scowling. 'He is a very bad boy, and he will end in a jail, Sahib.'

'Of that I have my doubts,' said Petersen Sahib. 'A boy who can face a full Keddah at his age does not end in jails. See, little one, here are four annas[15] to spend in sweetmeats because thou hast a little head under that great thatch of hair. In time thou mayest become a hunter too.' Big Toomai scowled more than ever. 'Remember, though, that Keddahs are not good for children to play in,' Petersen Sahib went on.

'Must I never go there, Sahib?' asked Little Toomai, with a big gasp.

'Yes.' Petersen Sahib smiled again. 'When thou hast seen the elephants dance. That is the proper time. Come to me when thou hast seen the elephants dance, and then I will let thee go into all the Keddahs.'

There was another roar of laughter, for that is an old joke among elephant-catchers, and it means just never. There are great cleared flat places hidden away in the forests that are called elephants' ballrooms, but even these are only found by accident, and no man has ever seen the elephants dance.[16] When a driver boasts of his skill and bravery the other drivers say, 'And when didst *thou* see the elephants dance?'

Kala Nag put Little Toomai down, and he bowed to the earth again and went away with his father, and gave the silver four-anna piece to his mother, who was nursing his baby-brother, and they all were put up on Kala Nag's back, and the line of grunting, squealing elephants rolled down the hill-path to the plains. It was a very lively march on account of the new elephants, who gave trouble at every ford, and needed coaxing or beating every other minute.

Big Toomai prodded Kala Nag spitefully, for he was very angry, but Little Toomai was too happy to speak. Petersen Sahib had noticed him, and given him money, so he felt as a private soldier would feel if he had been called out of the ranks and praised by his commander-in-chief.

'What did Petersen Sahib mean by the elephant-dance?' he said, at last, softly to his mother.

Big Toomai heard him and grunted. 'That thou shouldst never be one of these hill-buffaloes of trackers. *That* was what he meant. Oh you in front, what is blocking the way?'

An Assamese driver, two or three elephants ahead, turned round angrily, crying: 'Bring up Kala Nag, and knock this youngster of mine into good behaviour. Why should Petersen Sahib have chosen *me* to go down with you donkeys of the rice-fields? Lay your beast alongside, Toomai, and let him prod with his tusks. By all the Gods of the Hills, these new elephants are possessed, or else they can smell their companions in the jungle.'

Kala Nag hit the new elephant in the ribs and knocked the

wind out of him, as Big Toomai said, 'We have swept the hills
of wild elephants at the last catch. It is only your carelessness
in driving. Must I keep order along the whole line?'

'Hear him!' said the other driver. '*We* have swept the hills!
Ho! ho! You are very wise, you plains-people. Any one but a
mud-head who never saw the jungle would know that *they*
know that the drives are ended for the season. Therefore all the
wild elephants tonight will – but why should I waste wisdom
on a river-turtle?'

'What will they do?' Little Toomai called out.

'*Ohé*, little one. Art thou there? Well, I will tell thee, for
thou hast a cool head. They will dance, and it behoves thy
father, who has swept *all* the hills of *all* the elephants, to
double-chain his pickets tonight.'

'What talk is this?' said Big Toomai. 'For forty years, father
and son, we have tended elephants, and we have never heard
such moonshine about dances.'

'Yes; but a plains-man who lives in a hut knows only the
four walls of his hut. Well, leave thy elephants unshackled
tonight and see what comes. As for their dancing, I have seen
the place where – *Bapree bap!*[17] how many windings has the
Dihang River?[18] Here is another ford, and we must swim the
calves. Stop still, you behind there.'

And in this way, talking and wrangling and splashing
through the rivers, they made their first march to a sort of
receiving-camp for the new elephants; but they lost their tem-
pers long before they got there.

Then the elephants were chained by their hind legs to their
big stumps of pickets, and extra ropes were fitted to the new
elephants, and the fodder was piled before them, and the
hill-drivers went back to Petersen Sahib through the afternoon
light, telling the plains-drivers to be extra careful that night,
and laughing when the plains-drivers asked the reason.

Little Toomai attended to Kala Nag's supper, and as evening
fell wandered through the camp, unspeakably happy, in search
of a tom-tom. When an Indian child's heart is full, he does not
run about and make a noise in an irregular fashion. He sits
down to a sort of revel all by himself. And Little Toomai had

been spoken to by Petersen Sahib! If he had not found what he wanted I believe he would have been ill. But the sweetmeat-seller in the camp lent him a little tom-tom – a drum beaten with the flat of the hand – and he sat down, cross-legged, before Kala Nag as the stars began to come out, the tom-tom in his lap, and he thumped and he thumped and he thumped, and the more he thought of the great honour that had been done to him, the more he thumped, all alone among the elephant-fodder. There was no tune and no words, but the thumping made him happy. The new elephants strained at their ropes, and squealed and trumpeted from time to time, and he could hear his mother in the camp hut putting his small brother to sleep with an old, old song about the great God Shiv, who once told all the animals what they should eat. It is a very soothing lullaby, and the first verse says:

> Shiv, who poured the harvest and made the winds to blow,
> Sitting at the doorways of a day of long ago,
> Gave to each his portion, food and toil and fate,
> From the King upon the *guddee*[19] to the Beggar at the gate.
>> All things made he – Shiva the Preserver.
>> Mahadeo! Mahadeo! he made all –
>> Thorn for the camel, fodder for the kine,
>> And mother's heart for sleepy head, O little son of mine!

Little Toomai came in with a joyous *tunk-a-tunk* at the end of each verse, till he felt sleepy and stretched himself on the fodder at Kala Nag's side. At last the elephants began to lie down one after another as is their custom, till only Kala Nag at the right of the line was left standing up; and he rocked slowly from side to side, his ears put forward to listen to the night wind as it blew very slowly across the hills. The air was full of all the night noises that, taken together, make one big silence – the click of one bamboo-stem against the other, the rustle of something alive in the undergrowth, the scratch and squawk of a half-waked bird (birds are awake in the night much more often than we imagine), and the fall of water ever so far away. Little Toomai slept for some time, and when he waked it was brilliant moonlight, and Kala Nag was still standing up with his ears cocked. Little Toomai turned, rustling in the fodder, and watched the curve of his big back against half the stars in heaven, and while he watched he heard, so far away that it sounded no more than a pinhole of noise pricked through the stillness, the 'hoot-toot' of a wild elephant. All the elephants in the lines jumped up as if they had been shot, and their grunts at last waked the sleeping mahouts, and they came out and drove in the picket-pegs with big mallets, and tightened this rope and knotted that till all was quiet. One new elephant had nearly grubbed up his picket, and Big Toomai took off Kala Nag's leg-chain and shackled that elephant fore-foot to hind-foot, but slipped a loop of grass-string round Kala Nag's leg, and told him to remember that he was tied fast. He knew that he and his father and his grandfather had done the very same thing hundreds of times before. Kala Nag did not answer to the order by gurgling, as he usually did. He stood still, looking out across the moonlight, his head a little raised and his ears spread like fans, up to the great folds of the Garo hills.

'Tend to him if he grows restless in the night,' said Big Toomai to Little Toomai, and he went into the hut and slept. Little Toomai was just going to sleep, too, when he heard the coir string snap with a little 'ting', and Kala Nag rolled out of his pickets as slowly and as silently as a cloud rolls out of the mouth of a valley. Little Toomai pattered after him, barefooted, down the road in the moonlight, calling under his breath, 'Kala Nag! Kala Nag! Take me with you, O Kala Nag!' The elephant turned without a sound, took three strides back to the boy in the moonlight, put down his trunk, swung him up to his neck, and almost before Little Toomai had settled his knees, slipped into the forest.

There was one blast of furious trumpeting from the lines, and then the silence shut down on everything, and Kala Nag began to move. Sometimes a tuft of high grass washed along his sides as a wave washes along the sides of a ship, and sometimes a cluster of wild-pepper vines would scrape along his back, or a bamboo would creak where his shoulder touched it; but between those times he moved absolutely without any sound, drifting through the thick Garo forest as though it had been smoke. He was going uphill, but though Little Toomai watched the stars in the rifts of the trees, he could not tell in what direction. Then Kala Nag reached the crest of the ascent and stopped for a minute, and Little Toomai could see the tops of the trees lying all speckled and furry under the moonlight for miles and miles, and the blue-white mist over the river in the hollow. Toomai leaned forward and looked, and he felt that the forest was awake below him – awake and alive and crowded. A big brown fruit-eating bat brushed past his ear; a porcupine's quills rattled in the thicket, and in the darkness between the tree-stems he heard a hog-bear[20] digging hard in the moist warm earth, and snuffing as it digged. Then the branches closed over his head again, and Kala Nag began to go down into the valley – not quietly this time, but as a runaway gun goes down a steep bank – in one rush. The huge limbs moved as steadily as pistons, eight feet to each stride, and the wrinkled skin of the elbow-points rustled. The undergrowth on either side of him ripped with a noise like torn canvas, and the saplings that he heaved away right and left with his shoulders sprang back again, and banged him on the flank, and great trails of creepers, all matted together, hung from his tusks as he threw his head from side to side and ploughed out his pathway. Then Little Toomai laid himself down close to the great neck lest a swinging bough should sweep him to the ground, and he wished that he were back in the lines again. The grass began to get squashy, and Kala Nag's feet sucked and squelched as he put them down, and the night mist at the bottom of the valley chilled Little Toomai. There was a splash and a trample, and the rush of running water, and Kala Nag strode through the bed of a river, feeling his way at each step. Above the noise of the water, as it swirled round the elephant's legs, Little Toomai could hear more splashing and some trumpeting both up-stream and down – great grunts and angry snortings, and all the mist about him seemed to be full of rolling wavy shadows. 'Ai!' he said, half aloud, his teeth chattering. 'The elephant-folk are out tonight. It *is* the dance, then!'

Kala Nag swashed out of the water, blew his trunk clear, and began another climb; but this time he was not alone, and he had not to make his path. That was made already, six feet wide, in front of him, where the bent jungle-grass was trying to recover itself and stand up. Many elephants must have gone that way only a few minutes before. Little Toomai looked back, and behind him a great wild tusker, with his little pig's eyes glowing like hot coals, was just lifting himself out of the misty river. Then the trees closed up again, and they went on and up, with trumpetings and crashings, and the sound of breaking branches on every side of them. At last Kala Nag stood still between two tree-trunks at the very top of the hill. They were part of a circle of trees that grew round an irregular space of some three or four acres, and in all that space, as Little Toomai could see, the ground had been trampled down as hard as a brick floor. Some trees grew in the centre of the clearing, but their bark was rubbed away, and the white wood beneath showed all shiny and polished in the patches of moonlight. There were creepers hanging from the upper branches, and the bells of the flowers of the creepers, great waxy white things like convolvuluses, hung down fast asleep; but within the limits of the clearing there was not a single blade of green – nothing but the trampled earth. The moonlight showed it all iron-gray, except where some elephants stood upon it, and their shadows were inky black. Little Toomai looked, holding his breath, with his eyes starting out of his head, and as he looked, more and more and more elephants swung out into the open from between the tree-trunks. Little Toomai could only count up to ten, and he counted again and again on his fingers till he lost count of the tens, and his head began to swim. Outside the clearing he could hear them crashing in the undergrowth as they worked their way up the hillside; but as soon as they were within the circle of the tree-trunks they moved like ghosts.

There were white-tusked wild males, with fallen leaves and nuts and twigs lying in the wrinkles of their necks and the folds of their ears; fat slow-footed she-elephants, with restless, little pinky-black calves only three or four feet high running under their stomachs; young elephants with their tusks just beginning to show, and very proud of them; lanky, scraggy old-maid elephants, with their hollow anxious faces, and trunks like rough bark; savage old bull elephants, scarred from shoulder to flank with great weals and cuts of bygone fights, and the caked dirt of their solitary mud-baths dropping from their shoulders; and there was one with a broken tusk and the marks of the full-stroke, the terrible drawing scrape, of a tiger's claws on his side. They were standing head to head, or walking to and fro across the ground in couples, or rocking and swaying all by themselves – scores and scores of elephants. Toomai knew that so long as he lay still on Kala Nag's neck nothing would happen to him; for even in the rush and scramble of a Keddah-drive a wild elephant does not reach up with his trunk and drag a man off the neck of a tame elephant; and these elephants were not thinking of men that night. Once they started and put their ears forward when they heard the chinking of a leg-iron in the forest, but it was Pudmini, Petersen Sahib's pet elephant, her chain snapped short off, grunting, snuffling up the hillside. She must have broken her pickets, and come straight from Petersen Sahib's camp; and Little Toomai saw another elephant, one that he did not know, with deep rope-galls on his back and breast. He, too, must have run away from some camp in the hills about.

At last there was no sound of any more elephants moving in the forest, and Kala Nag rolled out from his station between the trees and went into the middle of the crowd, clucking and gurgling, and all the elephants began to talk in their own tongue, and to move about. Still lying down, Little Toomai looked down upon scores and scores of broad backs, and wagging ears, and tossing trunks, and little rolling eyes. He heard the click of tusks as they crossed other tusks by accident, and the dry rustle of trunks twined together, and the chafing of enormous sides and shoulders in the crowd, and the incessant flick and *hissh* of the great tails. Then a cloud came over the moon, and he sat in black darkness; but the quiet, steady hustling and pushing and gurgling went on just the same. He knew that there were elephants all round Kala Nag, and that there was no chance of backing him out of the assembly; so he set his teeth and shivered. In a Keddah at least there was torch-light and shouting, but there he was all alone in the dark, and once a trunk came up and touched him on the knee. Then an elephant trumpeted, and they all took it up for five or ten terrible seconds. The dew from the trees above spattered down like rain on the unseen backs, and a dull booming noise began, not very loud at first, and Little Toomai could not tell what it was; but it grew and grew, and Kala Nag lifted up one fore foot and then the other, and brought them down on the ground – one-two, one-two, as steadily as trip-hammers. The elephants were stamping all together now, and it sounded like a war-drum beaten at the mouth of a cave. The dew fell from the trees till there was no more left to fall, and the booming went on, and the ground rocked and shivered, and Little Toomai put his hands up to his ears to shut out the sound. But it was all one gigantic jar that ran through him – this stamp of hundreds of heavy feet on the raw earth. Once or twice he could feel Kala Nag and all the others surge forward a few strides, and the thumping would change to the crushing sound of juicy green things being bruised, but in a minute or two the boom of feet on hard earth began again. A tree was creaking and groaning somewhere near him. He put out his arm and felt the bark, but Kala Nag moved forward, still tramping, and he could not tell where he was in the clearing. There was no sound from the elephants, except once, when two or three little calves squeaked together. Then he heard a thump and a shuffle, and the booming went on. It must have lasted fully two hours, and Little Toomai ached in every nerve; but he knew by the smell of the night air that the dawn was coming.

The morning broke in one sheet of pale yellow behind the green hills, and the booming stopped with the first ray, as though the light had been an order. Before Little Toomai had got the ringing out of his head, before even he had shifted his position, there was not an elephant in sight except Kala Nag, Pudmini, and the elephant with the rope-galls, and there was neither sign nor rustle nor whisper down the hillsides to show where the others had gone. Little Toomai stared again and again. The clearing, as he remembered it, had grown in the night. More trees stood in the middle of it, but the undergrowth

and the jungle-grass at the sides had been rolled back. Little
Toomai stared once more. Now he understood the trampling.
The elephants had stamped out more room – had stamped the
thick grass and juicy cane to trash, the trash into slivers, the
slivers into tiny fibres, and the fibres into hard earth.

'Wah!' said Little Toomai, and his eyes were very heavy.
'Kala Nag, my lord, let us keep by Pudmini and go to Petersen
Sahib's camp, or I shall drop from thy neck.'

The third elephant watched the two go away, snorted,
wheeled round, and took his own path. He may have belonged
to some little native king's establishment, fifty or sixty or a
hundred miles away.

Two hours later, as Petersen Sahib was eating early breakfast, his elephants, who had been double-chained that night,
began to trumpet, and Pudmini, mired to the shoulders, with
Kala Nag, very footsore, shambled into the camp. Little
Toomai's face was gray and pinched, and his hair was full of
leaves and drenched with dew; but he tried to salute Petersen
Sahib, and cried faintly: 'The dance – the elephant-dance! I
have seen it, and – I die!' As Kala Nag sat down, he slid off his
neck in a dead faint.

But, since native children have no nerves worth speaking of,
in two hours he was lying very contentedly in Petersen Sahib's
hammock with Petersen Sahib's shooting-coat under his head,
and a glass of warm milk, a little brandy, with a dash of quinine
inside of him, and while the old hairy, scarred hunters of the
jungles sat three-deep before him, looking at him as though he
were a spirit, he told his tale in short words, as a child will, and
wound up with:

'Now, if I lie in one word, send men to see, and they will find
that the elephant-folk have trampled down more room in their
dance-room, and they will find ten and ten, and many times
ten, tracks leading to that dance-room. They made more room
with their feet. I have seen it. Kala Nag took me, and I saw.
Also Kala Nag is very leg-weary!'

Little Toomai lay back and slept all through the long afternoon and into the twilight, and while he slept Petersen Sahib
and Machua Appa followed the track of the two elephants for

fifteen miles across the hills. Petersen Sahib had spent eighteen years in catching elephants, and he had only once before found such a dance-place. Machua Appa had no need to look twice at the clearing to see what had been done there, or to scratch with his toe in the packed, rammed earth.

'The child speaks truth,' said he. 'All this was done last night, and I have counted seventy tracks crossing the river. See, Sahib, where Pudmini's leg-iron cut the bark of that tree! Yes; she was there too.' They looked at one another and up and down, and they wondered; for the ways of elephants are beyond the wit of any man, black or white, to fathom.

'Forty years and five,' said Machua Appa, 'have I followed my lord the Elephant, but never have I heard that any child of man had seen what this child has seen. By all the Gods of the Hills, it is – what can we say?' and he shook his head.

When they got back to camp it was time for the evening meal. Petersen Sahib ate alone in his tent, but he gave orders that the camp should have two sheep and some fowls, as well as a double ration of flour and rice and salt, for he knew that there would be a feast. Big Toomai had come up hot-foot from the camp in the plains to search for his son and his elephant, and now that he had found them he looked at them as though he were afraid of them both. And there was a feast by the blazing camp-fires in front of the lines of picketed elephants, and Little Toomai was the hero of it all; and the big brown elephant-catchers, the trackers and drivers and ropers, and the men who know all the secrets of breaking the wildest elephants, passed him from one to the other, and they marked his forehead with blood from the breast of a newly killed jungle-cock, to show that he was a forester, initiated and free of all the jungles.

And at last, when the flames died down, and the red light of the logs made the elephants look as though they had been dipped in blood too, Machua Appa, the head of all the drivers of all the Keddahs – Machua Appa, Petersen Sahib's other self, who had never seen a made road in forty years: Machua Appa, who was so great that he had no other name than Machua Appa – leaped to his feet, with Little Toomai held high in the air above his head, and shouted: 'Listen, my brothers. Listen, too, you my lords in the lines there, for I, Machua Appa, am speaking! This little one shall no more be called Little Toomai, but Toomai of the Elephants, as his great-grandfather was called before him. What never man has seen he has seen through the long night, and the favour of the elephant-folk and of the Gods of the Jungles is with him. He shall become a great tracker; he shall become greater than I, even I, Machua Appa! He shall follow the new trail, and the stale trail, and the mixed trail, with a clear eye! He shall take no harm in the Keddah when he runs under their bellies to rope the wild tuskers; and if he slips before the feet of the charging bull-elephant, the bull-elephant shall know who he is and shall not crush him. *Aihai!* my lords in the chains' – he whirled up the line of pickets – 'here is the little one that has seen your dances in your hidden places – the sight that never man saw! Give him honour, my lords! *Salaam karo*, my children. Make your salute to Toomai of the Elephants! Gunga Pershad, ahaa! Hira Guj, Birchi Guj, Kuttar Guj,[21] ahaa! Pudmini – thou hast seen him at the dance, and thou too, Kala Nag, my pearl among elephants! – ahaa! Together! To Toomai of the Elephants. *Barrao!*'

And at that last wild yell the whole line flung up their trunks till the tips touched their foreheads, and broke out into the full salute – the crashing trumpet-peal that only the Viceroy of India hears, the Salaamut of the Keddah.

But it was all for the sake of Little Toomai, who had seen what never man had seen before – the dance of the elephants at night and alone in the heart of the Garo hills!

Shiv and the Grasshopper

The Song that Toomai's Mother sang to the Baby

Shiv, who poured the harvest and made the winds to blow,
Sitting at the doorways of a day of long ago,
Gave to each his portion, food and toil and fate,
From the King upon the *guddee* to the Beggar at the gate.
    All things made he – Shiva the Preserver.
    Mahadeo![1] Mahadeo! he made all –
    Thorn for the camel, fodder for the kine,
    And mother's heart for sleepy head, O little son of mine!

Wheat he gave to rich folk, millet to the poor,
Broken scraps for holy men that beg from door to door.
Cattle to the tiger, carrion to the kite,
And rags and bones to wicked wolves without the wall at night.
Naught he found too lofty, none he saw too low –
Parbati beside him watched them come and go,
Thought to cheat her husband, turning Shiv to jest,
Stole the little grasshopper and hid it in her breast!
    So she tricked him, Shiva the Preserver.
    Mahadeo! Mahadeo! turn and see.
    Tall are the camels, heavy are the kine,
    But this was Least of Little Things, O little son of mine!

When the dole was ended, laughingly she said,
'Master of a million mouths, is not one unfed?'
Laughing, Shiv made answer, 'All have had their part,
Even he the little one hidden 'neath thy heart.'
From her breast she plucked it, Parbati the thief,
Saw the Least of Little Things gnawed a new-grown leaf.
Saw and feared and wondered, making prayer to Shiv,
Who hath surely given meat to all that live.
    All things made he – Shiva the Preserver.
    Mahadeo! Mahadeo! he made all –
    Thorn for the camel, fodder for the kine,
    And mother's heart for sleepy head, O little son of mine!

SERVANTS OF
THE QUEEN

You can work it out by Fractions or by simple Rule of Three,[1]
But the way of Tweedle-dum is not the way of Tweedle-dee.[2]
You can twist it, you can turn it, you can plait it till you drop,
But the way of Pilly-Winky's *not* the way of Winkie-Pop![3]

It had been raining heavily for one whole month – raining on a camp of thirty thousand men and thousands of camels, elephants, horses, bullocks, and mules all gathered together at a place called Rawal Pindi,[4] to be reviewed by the Viceroy of India. He was receiving a visit from the Amir of Afghanistan – a wild king of a very wild country; and the Amir had brought with him for a bodyguard eight hundred men and horses who had never seen a camp or a locomotive before in their lives – savage men and savage horses from somewhere at the back of Central Asia. Every night a mob of these horses would be sure to break their heel-ropes and stampede up and down the camp through the mud in the dark, or the camels would break loose and run about and fall over the ropes of the tents,[5] and you can imagine how pleasant that was for men trying to go to sleep. My tent lay far away from the camel lines, and I thought it was safe; but one night a man popped his head in and shouted, 'Get out, quickly! They're coming! My tent's gone!'

I knew who 'they' were; so I put on my boots and waterproof and scuttled out into the slush. Little Vixen,[6] my fox-terrier, went out through the other side; and then there was a roaring and a grunting and bubbling, and I saw the tent cave in, as the pole snapped, and begin to dance about like a mad ghost. A camel had blundered into it, and wet and angry as I was, I could not help laughing. Then I ran on, because I did not know how many camels might have got loose, and before long I was out of sight of the camp, ploughing my way through the mud. At last I fell over the tail-end of a gun, and by that knew I was somewhere near the Artillery lines where the cannon were stacked at night. As I did not want to plowter[7] about any more in the drizzle and the dark, I put my waterproof over the muzzle of one gun, and made a sort of wigwam with two or three rammers that I found, and lay along the tail of another gun, wondering where Vixen had got to, and where I might be. Just as I was getting ready to go to sleep I heard a jingle of harness and a grunt, and a mule passed me shaking his wet ears. He belonged to a screw-gun battery, for I could hear the rattle of the straps and rings and chains and things on his saddle-pad. The screw-guns are tiny little cannon made in two pieces, that are screwed together when the time comes to use them. They are taken up mountains, anywhere that a mule can find a road, and they are very useful for fighting in rocky country. Behind the mule there was a camel, with his big soft feet squelching and slipping in the mud, and his neck bobbing to and fro like a strayed hen's. Luckily, I knew enough of beast-language – not wild-beast language, but camp-beast language, of course – from the natives to know what he was saying. He must have been the one that flopped into my tent, for he called to the mule, 'What shall I do? Where shall I go? I have fought with a white Thing that waved, and it took a stick and hit me on the neck.' (That was my broken tent-pole, and I was very glad to know it.) 'Shall we run on?'

'Oh, it was you,' said the mule, 'you and your friends, that have been disturbing the camp? All right. You'll be beaten for this in the morning; but I may as well give you something on account now.'

I heard the harness jingle as the mule backed and caught the camel two kicks in the ribs that rang like a drum. 'Another time,' he said, 'you'll know better than to run through a mule-battery at night, shouting "Thieves and fire!" Sit down, and keep your silly neck quiet.'

The camel doubled up camel-fashion, like a two-foot rule,

and sat down whimpering. There was a regular beat of hoofs in the darkness, and a big troop-horse cantered up as steadily as though he were on parade, jumped a gun-tail, and landed close to the mule.

'It's disgraceful,' he said, blowing out his nostrils. 'Those camels have racketed through our lines again – the third time this week. How's a horse to keep his condition if he isn't allowed to sleep? Who's here?'

'I'm the breech-piece mule of number two gun of the First Screw Battery,' said the mule, 'and the other's one of your friends. He's waked me up too. Who are you?'

'Number Fifteen, E troop, Ninth Lancers – Dick Cunliffe's horse. Stand over a little, there.'

'Oh, beg your pardon,' said the mule. 'It's too dark to see much. Aren't these camels too sickening for anything? I walked out of my lines to get a little peace and quiet here.'

'My lords,' said the camel humbly, 'we dreamed bad dreams in the night, and we were very much afraid. I am only a baggage-camel of the 39th Native Infantry, and I am not as brave as you are, my lords.'

'Then why didn't you stay[8] and carry baggage for the 39th Native Infantry, instead of running all round the camp?' said the mule.

'They were such very bad dreams,' said the camel. 'I am sorry. Listen! What is that? Shall we run on again?'

'Sit down,' said the mule, 'or you'll snap your long stick-legs between the guns.' He cocked one ear and listened. 'Bullocks!' he said. 'Gun-bullocks.[9] On my word, you and your friends have waked the camp very thoroughly. It takes a good deal of prodding to put up a gun-bullock.'

I heard a chain dragging along the ground, and a yoke of the great sulky white bullocks that drag the heavy siege-guns when the elephants won't go any nearer to the firing, came shouldering along together; and almost stepping on the chain was another battery mule, calling wildly for 'Billy'.

'That's one of our recruits,' said the old mule to the troop-horse. 'He's calling for me. Here, youngster, stop squealing; the dark never hurt anybody yet.'

The gun-bullocks lay down together and began chewing the cud, but the young mule huddled close to Billy.

'Things!' he said. 'Fearful and horrible Things, Billy! They came into our lines while we were asleep. D'you think they'll kill us?'

'I've a very great mind to give you a number one kicking,' said Billy. 'The idea of a fourteen-hand mule with your training disgracing the Battery before this gentleman!'

'Gently, gently!' said the troop-horse. 'Remember they are always like this to begin with. The first time I ever saw a man (it was in Australia when I was a three-year-old) I ran for half a day, and if I'd seen a camel, I should have been running still.'

Nearly all our horses for the English cavalry are brought to India from Australia, and are broken in by the troopers themselves.

'True enough,' said Billy. 'Stop shaking, youngster. The first time they put the full harness with all its chains on my back, I stood on my fore legs and kicked every bit of it off. I hadn't learned the *real* science of kicking then, but the battery said they had never seen anything like it.'

'But this wasn't harness or anything that jingled,' said the young mule. 'You know I don't mind that now, Billy. It was Things like trees, and they fell up and down the lines and bubbled; and my head-rope broke, and I couldn't find my driver, and I couldn't find you, Billy, so I ran off with – with these gentlemen.'

'H'm!' said Billy. 'As soon as I heard the camels were loose I came away on my own account.[10] When a battery – a screw-gun – mule calls gun-bullocks gentlemen, he must be very badly shaken up. Who are you fellows on the ground there?'

The gun-bullocks rolled their cuds, and answered both together: 'The seventh yoke of the first gun of the Big Gun Battery. We were asleep when the camels came, but when we were trampled on we got up and walked away. It is better to lie quiet in the mud than to be disturbed on good bedding. We told your friend here that there was nothing to be afraid of, but he knew so much that he thought otherwise. Wah!'

They went on chewing.

'That comes of being afraid,' said Billy. 'You get laughed at by gun-bullocks. I hope you like it, young 'un.'

The young mule's teeth snapped, and I heard him say something about not being afraid of any beefy old bullock in the world; but the bullocks only clicked their horns together and went on chewing.

'Now, don't be angry after you've been afraid. That's the worst kind of cowardice,' said the troop-horse. 'Anybody can be forgiven for being scared in the night, *I* think, if they see things they don't understand. We've broken out of our pickets, again and again, four hundred and fifty of us, just because a new recruit got to telling tales of whip-snakes at home in Australia till we were scared to death of the loose ends of our head-ropes.'

'That's all very well in camp,' said Billy; 'I'm not above stampeding myself, for the fun of the thing, when I haven't been out for a day or two; but what do you do on active service?'

'Oh, that's quite another set of new shoes,' said the troop-horse. 'Dick Cunliffe's on my back then, and drives his knees into me, and all I have to do is to watch where I am putting my feet, and to keep my hind legs well under me, and be bridle-wise.'

'What's bridle-wise?' said the young mule.

'By the Blue Gums of the Back Blocks,'[11] snorted the troop-horse, 'do you mean to say that you aren't taught to be bridle-wise in your business? How can you do anything, unless you can spin round at once when the rein is pressed on your neck? It means life or death to your man, and of course that's life and death to you. Get round with your hind legs under you the instant you feel the rein on your neck. If you haven't room to swing round, rear up a little and come round on your hind legs. That's being bridle-wise.'

'We aren't taught that way,' said Billy the mule stiffly. 'We're taught to obey the man at our head: step off when he says so, and step in when he says so. I suppose it comes to the same thing. Now, with all this fine fancy business and rearing, which must be very bad for your hocks, what do you *do*?'

'That depends,' said the troop-horse. 'Generally I have to go in among a lot of yelling, hairy men with knives – long shiny knives, worse than the farrier's knives – and I have to take care that Dick's boot is just touching the next man's boot without crushing it. I can see Dick's lance to the right of my right eye, and I know I'm safe. I shouldn't care to be the man or horse that stood up to Dick and me when we're in a hurry.'

'Don't the knives hurt?' said the young mule.

'Well, I got one cut across the chest once, but that wasn't Dick's fault—'

'A lot I should have cared whose fault it was, if it hurt!' said the young mule.

'You must,' said the troop-horse. 'If you don't trust your man, you may as well run away at once. That's what some of our horses do, and I don't blame them. As I was saying, it wasn't Dick's fault. The man was lying on the ground, and I stretched myself not to tread on him, and he slashed up at me. Next time I have to go over a man lying down I shall step on him – hard.'

'H'm!' said Billy; 'it sounds very foolish. Knives are dirty things at any time. The proper thing to do is to climb up a mountain with a well-balanced saddle, hang on by all four feet and your ears too, and creep and crawl and wriggle along, till you come out hundreds of feet above anyone else, on a ledge where's there just room enough for your hoofs. Then you stand still and keep quiet – never ask a man to hold your head, young 'un – keep quiet while the guns are being put together, and then you watch the little poppy shells drop down into the tree-tops ever so far below.'

'Don't you ever trip?' said the troop-horse.

'They say that when a mule trips you can split a hen's ear,' said Billy. 'Now and again *per-haps* a badly-packed saddle will upset a mule, but it's very seldom. I wish I could show you our business. It's beautiful. Why, it took me three years to find out what the men were driving at. The science of the thing is never to show up against the sky-line, because, if you do, you may get fired at. Remember that, young 'un. Always keep hidden as much as possible, even if you have to go a mile out of your way. I lead the battery when it comes to that sort of climbing.'

'Fired at without the chance of running into the people who are firing!' said the troop-horse, thinking hard. 'I couldn't stand that. I should want to charge – with Dick.'

'Oh no, you wouldn't; you know that as soon as the guns are in position *they'll* do all the charging. That's scientific and neat; but knives – pah!'

The baggage-camel had been bobbing his head to and fro for some time past, anxious to get a word in edgeways. Then I heard him say, as he cleared his throat, nervously:

'I – I – I have fought a little, but not in that climbing way or that running way.'

'No. Now you mention it,' said Billy, 'you don't look as though you were made for climbing or running – much. Well, how was it, old Hay-bales?'

'The proper way,' said the camel. 'We all sat down—'

'Oh, my Crupper and Breastplate!' said the troop-horse under his breath. 'Sat down!'

'We sat down – a hundred of us,' the camel went on, 'in a big square, and the men piled our kajawahs,[12] our packs and saddles, outside the square, and they fired over our backs, the men did, on all sides of the square.'

'What sort of men? Any men that came along?' said the troop-horse. 'They teach us in riding school to lie down and let our masters fire across us, but Dick Cunliffe is the only man I'd trust to do that. It tickles my girths, and, besides, I can't see with my head on the ground.'

'What does it matter who fires across you?' said the camel. 'There are plenty of men and plenty of other camels close by, and a great many clouds of smoke. I am not frightened then. I sit still and wait.'

'And yet,' said Billy, 'you dream bad dreams and upset the camp at night. Well! well! Before I'd lie down, not to speak of sitting down, and let a man fire across me, my heels and his head would have something to say to each other. Did you ever hear anything so awful as that?'

There was a long silence, and then one of the gun-bullocks lifted up his big head and said, 'This is very foolish indeed. There is only one way of fighting.'

'Oh, go on,' said Billy. '*Please* don't mind me. I suppose you fellows fight standing on your tails?'

'Only one way,' said the two together. (They must have been twins.) 'This is that way. To put all twenty yoke of us to the big gun as soon as Two Tails trumpets.' ('Two Tails' is camp-slang for the elephant.)

'What does Two Tails trumpet for?' said the young mule.

'To show that he is not going any nearer to the smoke on the other side. Two Tails is a great coward. Then we tug the big gun all together – *Heya – Hullah! Heeyah! Hullah! We* do not climb like cats nor run like calves. We go across the level plain, twenty yoke of us, till we are unyoked again, and we graze while the big guns talk across the plain to some town with mud walls, and pieces of the wall fall out, and the dust goes up as though many cattle were coming home.'

'Oh! And you choose that time for grazing?' said the young mule.

'That time or any other. Eating is always good. We eat till we are yoked up again and tug the gun back to where Two Tails is waiting for it. Sometimes there are big guns in the city that speak back, and some of us are killed, and then there is all the more grazing for those that are left. This is Fate – nothing but Fate. None the less, Two Tails is a great coward. That is the proper way to fight. We are brothers from Hapur.[13] Our father was a sacred bull of Shiva. We have spoken.'

'Well, I've certainly learned something tonight,' said the troop-horse. 'Do you gentlemen of the screw-gun battery feel inclined to eat when you are being fired at with big guns, and Two Tails is behind you?'

'About as much as we feel inclined to sit down and let men sprawl all over us, or run into people with knives. I never heard such stuff. A mountain ledge, a well-balanced load, a driver you can trust to let you pick your own way, and I'm your mule; but – the other things – No!' said Billy, with a stamp of his foot.

'Of course,' said the troop-horse, 'every one is not made in the same way, and I can quite see that your family, on your father's side, would fail to understand a great many things.'

'Never you mind my family on my father's side,' said Billy

angrily; for every mule hates to be reminded that his father was a donkey. 'My father was a Southern gentleman, and he could pull down and bite and kick into rags every horse he came across. Remember that, you big brown Brumby!'

Brumby means wild horse without any breeding. Imagine the feelings of Ormonde if a 'bus-horse called him a cocktail,[14] and you can imagine how the Australian horse felt. I saw the white of his eye glitter in the dark.

'See here, you son of an imported Malaga[15] jackass,' he said between his teeth, 'I'd have you know that I'm related on my mother's side to Carbine, winner of the Melbourne Cup,[16] and where I come from we aren't accustomed to being ridden over roughshod by any parrot-mouthed, pig-headed mule in a pop-gun pea-shooter battery. Are you ready?'

'On your hind legs!' squealed Billy. They both reared up facing each other, and I was expecting a furious fight, when a gurgly, rumbly voice called out of the darkness to the right – 'Children, what are you fighting about there? Be quiet.'

Both beasts dropped down with a snort of disgust, for neither horse nor mule can bear to listen to an elephant's voice.

'It's Two Tails!' said the troop-horse. 'I can't stand him. A tail at each end isn't fair!'

'My feelings exactly,' said Billy, crowding into the troop-horse for company. 'We're very alike in some things.'

'I suppose we've inherited them from our mothers,' said the troop-horse. 'It's not worth quarrelling about. Hi! Two Tails, are you tied up?'

'Yes,' said Two Tails, with a laugh all up his trunk. 'I'm picketed for the night. I've heard what you fellows have been saying. But don't be afraid. I'm not coming over.'

The bullocks and the camel said, half aloud: 'Afraid of Two Tails – what nonsense!' And the bullocks went on: 'We are sorry that you heard, but it is true. Two Tails, why are you afraid of the guns when they fire?'

'Well,' said Two Tails, rubbing one hind leg against the other, exactly like a little boy saying a poem,[17] 'I don't quite know whether you'd understand.'

'We don't, but we have to pull the guns,' said the bullocks.

'I know it, and I know you are a good deal braver than you think you are. But it's different with me. My battery captain called me a Pachydermatous Anachronism[18] the other day.'

'That's another way of fighting, I suppose?' said Billy, who was recovering his spirits.

'*You* don't know what that means, of course, but I do. It means betwixt and between, and that is just where I am. I can see inside my head what will happen when a shell bursts; and you bullocks can't.'

'I can,' said the troop-horse. 'At least a little bit. I try not to think about it.'

'I can see more than you, and I *do* think about it. I know there's a great deal of me to take care of, and I know that nobody knows how to cure me when I'm sick. All they can do is to stop my driver's pay till I get well, and I can't trust my driver.'[19]

'Ah!' said the troop-horse. 'That explains it. I can trust Dick.'

'You could put a whole regiment of Dicks on my back without making me feel any better. I know just enough to be uncomfortable, and not enough to go on in spite of it.'

'We do not understand,' said the bullocks.

'I know you don't. I'm not talking to you. You don't know what blood is.'

'We do,' said the bullocks. 'It is red stuff that soaks into the ground and smells.'

The troop-horse gave a kick and a bound and a snort.

'Don't talk of it,' he said. 'I can smell it now, just thinking of it. It makes me want to run – when I haven't Dick on my back.'

'But it is not here,' said the camel and the bullocks. 'Why are you so stupid?'

'It's vile stuff,' said Billy. 'I don't want to run, but I don't want to talk about it.'

'There you are!' said Two Tails, waving his tail to explain.

'Surely. Yes, we have been here all night,' said the bullocks.

Two Tails stamped his foot till the iron ring on it jingled. 'Oh, I'm not talking to *you*. You can't see inside your heads.'

'No. We see out of our four eyes,' said the bullocks. 'We see straight in front of us.'

'If I could do *that* and nothing else you wouldn't be needed to pull the big guns at all. If I was like my captain – he can see things inside his head before the firing begins, and he shakes all over, but he knows too much to run away – if I was like him I could pull the guns. But if I were as wise as all that I should never be here. I should be a king in the forest, as I used to be, sleeping half the day and bathing when I liked. I haven't had a good bath for a month.'

'That's all very fine,' said Billy; 'but giving a thing a long name doesn't make it any better.'

'H'sh!' said the troop-horse. 'I think I understand what Two Tails means.'

'You'll understand better in a minute,' said Two Tails angrily. 'Now you just explain to me why you don't like this!'

He began trumpeting furiously at the top of his trumpet.

'Stop that!' said Billy and the troop-horse together, and I could hear them stamp and shiver. An elephant's trumpeting is always nasty, especially on a dark night.

'I shan't stop,' said Two Tails. 'Won't you explain that, please? *Hhrrmph! Rrrt! Rrrmph! Rrrhha!*' Then he stopped suddenly, and I heard a little whimper in the dark, and knew that Vixen had found me at last. She knew as well as I did that if there is one thing in the world the elephant is more afraid of than another it is a little barking dog;[20] so she stopped to bully Two Tails in his pickets, and yapped round his big feet. Two Tails shuffled and squeaked. 'Go away, little dog!' he said. 'Don't snuff at my ankles, or I'll kick at you. Good little dog – nice little doggie, then! Go home, you yelping little beast! Oh, why doesn't some one take her away? She'll bite me in a minute.'

''Seems to me,' said Billy to the troop-horse, 'that our friend Two Tails is afraid of most things. Now, if I had a full meal for every dog I've kicked across the parade-ground I should be as fat as Two Tails nearly.'

I whistled, and Vixen ran up to me, muddy all over, and licked my nose, and told me a long tale about hunting for me all through the camp. I never let her know that I understood beast talk, or she would have taken all sorts of liberties. So I buttoned her into the breast of my overcoat, and Two Tails shuffled and stamped and growled to himself.

'Extraordinary! Most extraordinary!' he said. 'It runs in our family. Now, where has that nasty little beast gone to?'

I heard him feeling about with his trunk.

'We all seem to be affected in various ways,' he went on, blowing his nose. 'Now, you gentlemen were alarmed, I believe, when I trumpeted.'

'Not alarmed, exactly,' said the troop-horse, 'but it made me feel as though I had hornets where my saddle ought to be. Don't begin again.'

'I'm frightened of a little dog, and the camel here is frightened by bad dreams in the night.'

'It is very lucky for us that we haven't all got to fight in the same way,' said the troop-horse.

'What I want to know,' said the young mule, who had been quiet for a long time – 'what *I* want to know is, why we have to fight at all.'

'Because we're told to,' said the troop-horse, with a snort of contempt.

'Orders,' said Billy the mule; and his teeth snapped.

'*Hukm hai!*' (It is an order), said the camel with a gurgle; and Two Tails and the bullocks repeated, '*Hukm hai!*'

'Yes, but who gives the orders?' said the recruit-mule.

'The man who walks at your head – Or sits on your back – Or holds the nose-rope – Or twists your tail,' said Billy and the troop-horse and the camel and the bullocks one after the other.

'But who gives them the orders?'

'Now you want to know too much, young 'un,' said Billy, 'and that is one way of getting kicked. All you have to do is to obey the man at your head and ask no questions.'

'He's quite right,' said Two Tails. 'I can't always obey, because I'm betwixt and between; but Billy's right. Obey the man next to you who gives the order, or you'll stop all the battery, beside getting a thrashing.'

The gun-bullocks got up to go. 'Morning is coming,' they said. 'We will go back to our lines. It is true that we only see out of our eyes, and we are not very clever; but still, we are the only people to-night who have not been afraid. Good-night, you brave people.'

Nobody answered, and the troop-horse said, to change the conversation, 'Where's that little dog? A dog means a man somewhere about.'

'Here I am,' yapped Vixen, 'under the gun-tail with my man. You big, blundering beast of a camel you, you upset our tent. My man's very angry.'

'Phew!' said the bullocks. 'He must be white?'

'Of course he is,' said Vixen. 'Do you suppose I'm looked after by a black bullock-driver?'

'*Huah! Ouach! Ugh!*' said the bullocks. 'Let us get away quickly.'

They plunged forward in the mud, and managed somehow to run their yoke on the pole of an ammunition-waggon, where it jammed.

'Now you *have* done it,' said Billy calmly. 'Don't struggle. You're hung up till daylight. What on earth's the matter?'

The bullocks went off into the long hissing snorts that Indian cattle give, and pushed and crowded and slued[21] and stamped and slipped and nearly fell down in the mud, grunting savagely.

'You'll break your necks in a minute,' said the troop-horse. 'What's the matter with white men? I live with 'em.'

'They – eat – us! Pull!' said the near bullock: the yoke snapped with a twang, and they lumbered off together.

I never knew before what made Indian cattle so scared of Englishmen. We eat beef – a thing that no cattle-driver touches – and of course the cattle do not like it.

'May I be flogged with my own pad-chains! Who'd have thought of two big lumps like those losing their heads?' said Billy.

'Never mind. I'm going to look at this man. Most of the white men, I know, have things in their pockets,' said the troop-horse.

'I'll leave you, then. I can't say I'm over-fond of 'em myself. Besides, white men who haven't a place to sleep in are more than likely to be thieves, and I've a good deal of Government property on my back. Come along, young 'un, and we'll go back to our lines. Good-night, Australia! See you on parade

to-morrow, I suppose. Good-night, old Hay-bale! – try to control your feelings, won't you? Good-night, Two Tails! If you
pass us on the ground tomorrow, don't trumpet. It spoils our
formation.'

Billy the mule stumped off with the swaggering limp of an
old campaigner, as the troop-horse's head came nuzzling into
my breast, and I gave him biscuits; while Vixen, who is a most
conceited little dog, told him fibs about the scores of horses
that she and I kept.

'I'm coming to the parade to-morrow in my dog-cart,' she
said. 'Where will you be?'

'On the left hand of the second squadron. I set the time for
all my troop, little lady,' he said politely. 'Now I must go back
to Dick. My tail's all muddy, and he'll have two hours' hard
work dressing me for parade.'

The big parade of all the thirty thousand men was held that
afternoon, and Vixen and I had a good place close to the Viceroy and the Amir of Afghanistan, with his high big black hat of
astrachan wool and the great diamond star in the centre. The
first part of the review was all sunshine, and the regiments went
by in wave upon wave of legs all moving together, and guns all
in a line, till our eyes grew dizzy. Then the Cavalry came up, to
the beautiful cavalry canter of *Bonnie Dundee*,[22] and Vixen
cocked her ear where she sat on the dog-cart. The second
squadron of the Lancers shot by, and there was the troop-horse,
with his tail like spun silk, his head pulled into his breast, one
ear forward and one back, setting the time for all his squadron,
his legs going as smoothly as waltz-music. Then the big guns
came by, and I saw Two Tails and two other elephants harnessed in line to a forty-pounder siege-gun while twenty yoke
of oxen walked behind. The seventh pair had a new yoke, and
they looked rather stiff and tired. Last came the screw-guns,
and Billy the mule carried himself as though he commanded all
the troops, and his harness was oiled and polished till it winked.
I gave a cheer all by myself for Billy the mule, but he never
looked right or left.

The rain began to fall again, and for a while it was too misty
to see what the troops were doing. They had made a big

half-circle across the plain, and were spreading out into a line. That line grew and grew and grew till it was three-quarters of a mile long from wing to wing – one solid wall of men, horses, and guns. Then it came on straight towards the Viceroy and the Amir, and as it got nearer the ground began to shake, like the deck of a steamer when the engines are going fast.

Unless you have been there you cannot imagine what a frightening effect this steady come-down of troops has on the spectators, even when they know it is only a review. I looked at the Amir. Up till then he had not shown the shadow of a sign of astonishment or anything else; but now his eyes began to get bigger and bigger, and he picked up the reins on his horse's neck and looked behind him. For a minute it seemed as though he were going to draw his sword and slash his way out through the English men and women in the carriages at the back. Then the advance stopped dead, the ground stood still, the whole line saluted, and thirty bands began to play all together. That was the end of the review, and the regiments went off to their camps in the rain; and an infantry band struck up with –

> The animals went in two by two,
> Hurrah!
> The animals went in two by two,
> The elephant and the battery mu-
> l', and they all got into the Ark
> For to get out of the rain!

Then I heard an old grizzled, long-haired Central Asian chief, who had come down with the Amir, asking questions of a native officer.

'Now,' said he, 'in what manner was this wonderful thing done?'

And the officer answered, 'An order was given,[23] and they obeyed.'

'But are the beasts as wise as the men?' said the chief.

'They obey, as the men do. Mule, horse, elephant, or bullock, he obeys his driver, and the driver his sergeant, and the sergeant his lieutenant, and the lieutenant his captain, and the captain his major, and the major his colonel, and the colonel his brigadier commanding three regiments, and the brigadier the general, who obeys the Viceroy, who is the servant of the Empress. Thus it is done.'

'Would it were so in Afghanistan!' said the chief; 'for there we obey only our own wills.'

'And for that reason,' said the native officer, twirling his moustache, 'your Amir whom you do not obey must come here and take orders from our Viceroy.'

Parade-Song of the Camp-Animals

Elephants of the Gun-Team[1]

We lent to Alexander the strength of Hercules,
The wisdom of our foreheads, the cunning of our knees;
We bowed our necks to service: they ne'er were loosed again—
Make way there – way for the ten-foot teams
    Of the Forty-Pounder train!

Gun-Bullocks[2]

Those heroes in their harnesses avoid a cannon-ball,
And what they know of powder upsets them one and all;
Then *we* come into action and tug the guns again—
Make way there – way for the twenty yoke
    Of the Forty-Pounder train!

Cavalry Horses[3]

By the brand on my shoulder, the finest of tunes
Is played by the Lancers, Hussars, and Dragoons,
And it's sweeter than 'Stables' or 'Water' to me –
The Cavalry Canter of *Bonnie Dundee*!

Then feed us and break us and handle and groom,
And give us good riders and plenty of room,
And launch us in column of squadron and see
The Way of the War-horse to *Bonnie Dundee*!

Screw-Gun Mules[4]

As me and my companions were scrambling up a hill,
The path was lost in rolling stones but we went forward still,
For we can wriggle and climb, my lads, and turn up everywhere,
Oh, it's our delight on a mountain height, with a leg or two
    to spare!

Good luck to every sergeant, then, that lets us pick our road;
Bad luck to all the driver-men that cannot pack a load:
For we can wriggle and climb, my lads, and turn up everywhere,
Oh it's our delight on a mountain height with a leg or two
    to spare!

Commissariat Camels

We haven't a camelty tune of our own
To help us trollop along,
But every neck is a hair-trombone[5]
(*Rtt-ta-ta-ta!* is a hair-trombone!)
And this our marching-song:
Can't! Don't! Shan't! Won't!
Pass it along the line!
Somebody's pack has slid from his back,
'Wish it were only mine!
Somebody's load has tipped off in the road –
Cheer for a halt and a row!
Urrr! Yarrh! Grr! Arrh!
Somebody's catching it now!

All the Beasts Together

Children of the Camp are we,
Serving each in his degree;
Children of the yoke and goad,
Pack and harness, pad and load.
See our line across the plain,
Like a heel-rope bent again,
Reaching, writhing, rolling far,
Sweeping all away to war;
While the men that walk beside,
Dusty, silent, heavy-eyed,

Cannot tell why we or they
March and suffer day by day.
Children of the Camp are we,
Serving each in his degree;
Children of the yoke and goad,
Pack and harness, pad and load!

THE SECOND
JUNGLE BOOK

HOW FEAR CAME

The stream is shrunk – the pool is dry,
And we be comrades, thou and I;
With fevered jowl and dusty flank
Each jostling each along the bank;
And by one drouthy fear made still
Forgoing thought of quest or kill.
Now 'neath his dam the fawn may see,
The lean Pack-wolf as cowed as he,
And the tall buck, unflinching, note
The fangs that tore his father's throat.
The pools are shrunk – the streams are dry,
And we be playmates, thou and I,
Till yonder cloud – Good Hunting! – loose
The rain that breaks our Water Truce.

The Law of the Jungle – which is by far the oldest law in the world – has arranged for almost every kind of accident that may befall the Jungle People, till now its code is as perfect as time and custom can make it. If you have read the other stories about Mowgli, you will remember that he[1] spent a great part of his life in the Seeonee Wolf-Pack, learning the Law from Baloo the brown bear; and it was Baloo who told him, when the boy grew impatient at the constant orders, that the Law was like the Giant Creeper, because it dropped across everyone's back and no one could escape. 'When thou hast lived as long as I have, Little Brother, thou wilt see how all the Jungle obeys at least one Law. And that will be no pleasant sight,' said Baloo.

This talk went in at one ear and out at the other, for a boy who spends his life eating and sleeping does not worry about anything till it actually stares him in the face. But one year

Baloo's words came true, and Mowgli saw all the Jungle working under one Law.

It began when the winter Rains failed almost entirely, and Sahi, the Porcupine, meeting Mowgli in a bamboo thicket, told him that the wild yams were drying up. Now everybody knows that Sahi is ridiculously fastidious in his choice of food, and will eat nothing but the very best and ripest.[2] So Mowgli laughed and said, 'What is that to me?'

'Not much *now*,' said Sahi, rattling his quills in a stiff, uncomfortable way, 'but later we shall see. Is there any more diving into the deep rock-pool below the Bee-Rocks,[3] Little Brother?'

'No. The foolish water is going all away, and I do not wish to break my head,' said Mowgli, who was quite sure[4] he knew as much as any five of the Jungle People put together.

'That is thy loss. A small crack might let in some wisdom.' Sahi ducked quickly to prevent Mowgli from pulling his nose-bristles, and Mowgli told Baloo what Sahi had said. Baloo looked very grave, and mumbled half to himself: 'If I were alone I would change my hunting-grounds now, before the others began to think. And yet – hunting among strangers ends in fighting – and they might hurt my Man-cub.[5] We must wait and see how the *mohwa* blooms.'

That spring the *mohwa*[6] tree, that Baloo was so fond of, never flowered. The greeny, cream-coloured, waxy blossoms were heat-killed before they were born, and only a few bad-smelling petals came down when he stood on his hind legs and shook the tree. Then, inch by inch, the untempered heat crept into the heart of the Jungle, turning it yellow, brown, and at last black. The green growths in the sides of the ravines burned up to broken wires and curled films of dead stuff; the hidden pools sank down and caked over, keeping the last least footmark on their edges as if it had been cast in iron; the juicy-stemmed creepers fell away from the trees they clung to and died at their feet; the bamboos withered, clanking when the hot winds blew, and the moss peeled off the rocks deep in the Jungle, till they were as bare and as hot as the quivering blue boulders in the bed of the stream.

The birds and the monkey-people went north early in the year, for they knew what was coming; and the deer and the wild pig broke far away into the perished fields of the villages, dying sometimes before the eyes of men too weak to kill them. Chil, the Kite, stayed and grew fat, for there was a great deal of carrion, and evening after evening he brought the news to the beasts, too weak to force their way to fresh hunting-grounds, that the sun was killing the Jungle for three days' flight in every direction.

Mowgli, who had never known what real hunger meant, fell back on stale honey, three years old, scraped out of deserted rock-hives – honey black as a sloe, and dusty with dried sugar. He hunted, too, for deep-boring grubs under the bark of the trees, and robbed the wasps of their new broods. All the game in the Jungle was no more than skin and bone, and Bagheera could kill thrice in a night and hardly get a full meal. But the want of water was the worst, for though the Jungle People drink seldom they must drink deep.

And the heat went on and on, and sucked up all the moisture, till at last the main channel of the Waingunga was the only stream that carried a trickle of water between its dead banks; and when Hathi, the wild elephant, who lives for a hundred years and more, saw a long, lean blue ridge of rock show dry in the very centre of the stream, he knew that he was looking at the Peace Rock, and then and there he lifted up his trunk and proclaimed the Water Truce, as his father before him had proclaimed it fifty years ago. The deer, wild pig, and buffalo took up the cry hoarsely; and Chil, the Kite, flew in great circles far and wide, whistling and shrieking the warning.

By the Law of the Jungle it is death to kill at the drinking-places when once the Water Truce has been declared. The reason for this is that drinking comes before eating. Everyone in the Jungle can scramble along somehow when only game is scarce; but water is water, and when there is but one source of supply, all hunting stops while the Jungle People go there for their needs. In good seasons, when water was plentiful, those who came down to drink at the Waingunga – or anywhere else, for that matter – did so at the risk of their lives, and that risk made no small part of the fascination of the night's doings. To move down so cunningly that never a leaf stirred; to wade knee-deep in the roaring shallows that drown all noise from behind; to drink, looking backward over one shoulder, every muscle ready for the first desperate bound of keen terror; to roll on the sandy margin, and return, wet-muzzled and well plumped out, to the admiring herd, was a thing that all glossy-horned young bucks took a delight in, precisely because they knew that at any moment Bagheera or Shere Khan might leap upon them and bear them down. But now that life-and-death fun was ended, and the Jungle People came up, starved and weary, to the shrunken river – tiger, bear, deer, buffalo, and pig together – drank the fouled waters, and hung above them, too exhausted to move off.

The deer and pig had tramped all day in search of something better than dried bark and withered leaves. The buffaloes had found no wallows to be cool in, and no green crops to steal. The snakes had left the Jungle and come down to the river in the hope of catching a stray frog. They curled round wet stones, and never offered to strike when the snout of a rooting pig dislodged them. The river-turtles had long ago been killed by Bagheera, cleverest of hunters, and the fish had buried themselves deep in the cracked mud. Only the Peace Rock lay across the shallows like a long snake, and the little tired ripples hissed as they dried on its hot side.

It was here that Mowgli came nightly for the cool and the companionship. The most hungry of his enemies would hardly have cared for the boy then. His naked skin made him look more lean and wretched than any of his fellows. His hair was bleached to tow-colour by the sun; his ribs stood out like the ribs of a basket, and the lumps on his knees and elbows, where he was used to track on all fours, gave his shrunken limbs the look of knotted grass-stems. But his eye, under his matted forelock, was cool and quiet, for Bagheera, his adviser in this time of trouble, told him to move quietly, hunt slowly, and never, on any account, to lose his temper.

'It is an evil time,' said the Black Panther, one furnace-hot evening, 'but it will go if we can live till the end. Is thy stomach full, Man-cub?'

'There is stuff in my stomach, but I get no good of it. Think you, Bagheera, the Rains have forgotten us and will never come again?'

'Not I. We shall see the *mohwa* in blossom yet, and the little fawns all fat with new grass. Come down to the Peace Rock and hear the news. On my back, Little Brother.'

'This is no time to carry weight. I can still stand alone, but – indeed we be no fatted bullocks, we two.'

Bagheera looked along his ragged, dusty flank and whispered: 'Last night I killed a bullock under the yoke. So low was I brought that I think I should not have dared to spring if he had been loose. *Wou!*'

Mowgli laughed. 'Yes, we are great hunters now,' said he. 'I am very bold – to eat grubs,' and the two came down together through the crackling undergrowth to the river bank and the lace-work of shoals that ran out from it in every direction.

'The water cannot live long,' said Baloo, joining them. 'Look across! Yonder are trails like the roads of Man.'

On the level plain of the farther bank the stiff jungle-grass had died standing, and, dying, had mummied. The beaten tracks of the deer and the pig, all heading towards the river, had striped that colourless plain with dusty gullies driven through the ten-foot grass, and, early as it was, each long avenue was full of first-comers hastening to the water. You could hear the does and fawns coughing in the snuff-like dust.

Up-stream, at the bend of the sluggish pool round the Peace Rock, and Warden of the Water Truce, stood Hathi, the wild elephant, with his sons, gaunt and gray in the moonlight, rocking to and fro – always rocking. Below him a little were the vanguard of the deer; below these, again, the pig and the wild buffalo; and on the opposite bank, where the tall trees came down to the water's edge, was the place set apart for the Eaters of Flesh – the tiger, the wolves, the panther, the bear, and the others.

'We be under one Law, indeed,' said Bagheera, wading into the water and looking across at the lines of clicking horns and starting eyes where the deer and the pig pushed each other to and fro. 'Good hunting, all of you of my blood,' he added, lying down at full length, one flank thrust out of the shallows; and then, between his teeth, 'But for that which is the Law it would be *very* good hunting.'

The quick-spread ears of the deer caught the last sentence, and a frightened whisper ran along the ranks. 'The Truce! Remember the Truce!'

'Peace there, peace!' gurgled Hathi, the wild elephant. 'The Truce holds, Bagheera. This is no time to talk of hunting.'

'Who should know better than I?' Bagheera answered, rolling his yellow eyes up-stream. 'I am an eater of turtle – a fisher of frogs. *Ngaayah!* Would I could get good from chewing branches!'

'*We* wish so, very greatly,' bleated a young fawn, who had only been born that spring, and did not at all like it. Wretched as the Jungle People were, even Hathi could not help chuckling; while Mowgli, lying on his elbows in the warm water, laughed aloud, and beat up the foam with his feet.

'Well spoken, little bud-horn,' Bagheera purred. 'When the Truce ends that shall be remembered in thy favour,' and he looked keenly through the darkness to make sure of recognizing the fawn again.

Gradually the talk spread up and down the drinking-places. You could hear the scuffling, snorting pig asking for more room; the buffaloes grunting among themselves as they lurched out across the sandbars, and the deer telling pitiful stories of their long footsore searches in quest of food. Now and again they asked some question of the Eaters of Flesh across the river, but all the news was bad, and the roaring hot wind of the Jungle came and went, between the rocks and the rattling branches, and scattered twigs and dust on the water.

'The men-folk too, they die beside their ploughs,' said a young *sambhur*. 'I passed three between sunset and night. They lay still, and their bullocks with them. We also shall lie still in a little.'

'The river has fallen since last night,' said Baloo. 'O Hathi, hast thou ever seen the like of this drought?'

'It will pass, it will pass,' said Hathi, squirting water along his back and sides.

'We have one here that cannot endure long,' said Baloo; and he looked towards the boy he loved.

'I?' said Mowgli indignantly, sitting up in the water. 'I have no long fur to cover my bones, but – but if thy hide were pulled off, Baloo—'

Hathi shook all over at the idea, and Baloo said severely:

'Man-cub, that is not seemly to tell a Teacher of the Law. *Never* have I been seen without my hide.'

'Nay, I meant no harm, Baloo; but only that thou art, as it were, like the cocoanut in the husk, and I am the same cocoanut all naked. Now that brown husk of thine—' Mowgli was sitting cross-legged, and explaining things with his forefinger in his usual way, when Bagheera put out a paddy paw and pulled him over backwards into the water.

'Worse and worse,' said the Black Panther, as the boy rose spluttering. 'First, Baloo is to be skinned and now he is a cocoanut. Be careful that he does not do what the ripe cocoanuts do.'

'And what is that?' said Mowgli, off his guard for the minute, though that is one of the oldest catches in the Jungle.

'Break thy head,' said Bagheera quietly, pulling him under again.

'It is not good to make a jest of thy teacher,' said the Bear, when Mowgli had been ducked for the third time.

'Not good! What would ye have? That naked thing running to and fro makes a monkey-jest of those who have once been good hunters, and pulls the best of us by the whiskers for sport.' This was Shere Khan, the Lame Tiger, limping down to the water. He waited a little to enjoy the sensation he made among the deer on the opposite bank; then he dropped his square, frilled head and began to lap, growling: 'The Jungle has become a whelping-ground for naked cubs now. Look at me, Man-cub!'

Mowgli looked – stared, rather – as insolently as he knew how, and in a minute Shere Khan turned away uneasily. 'Man-cub this, and Man-cub that,' he rumbled, going on with his drink. 'The cub is neither man nor cub, or he would have been afraid. Next season I shall have to get his leave for a drink. *Aurgh!*'

'That may come, too,' said Bagheera, looking him steadily between the eyes. 'That may come, too . . . Faugh, Shere Khan! What new shame hast thou brought here?'

The Lame Tiger had dipped his chin and jowl in the water, and dark oily streaks were floating from it down-stream.

'Man!' said Shere Khan coolly, 'I killed an hour since.' He went on purring and growling to himself.

The line of beasts shook and wavered to and fro, and a whisper went up that grew to a cry: 'Man! Man! He has killed Man!' Then all looked towards Hathi, the wild elephant, but he seemed not to hear. Hathi never does anything till the time comes, and that is one of the reasons why he lives so long.

'At such a season as this to kill Man! Was there no other game afoot?' said Bagheera scornfully, drawing himself out of the tainted water, and shaking each paw, cat-fashion, as he did so.

'I killed for choice – not for food.' The horrified whisper began again, and Hathi's watchful little white eye cocked itself in Shere Khan's direction. 'For choice,' Shere Khan drawled. 'Now come I to drink and make me clean again. Is there any to forbid?'

Bagheera's back began to curve like a bamboo in a high wind, but Hathi lifted up his trunk and spoke quietly.

'Thy kill was from choice?' he asked; and when Hathi asks a question it is best to answer.

'Even so. It was my right and my Night. Thou knowest, O Hathi.' Shere Khan spoke almost courteously.

'Yea, I know,' Hathi answered; and, after a little silence, 'Hast thou drunk thy fill?'

'For to-night, yes.'

'Go, then. The river is to drink, and not to defile. None but the Lame Tiger would have boasted of his right at this season when – when we suffer together – Man and Jungle People alike. Clean or unclean, get to thy lair, Shere Khan!'

The last words rang out like silver trumpets, and Hathi's three sons rolled forward half a pace, though there was no need. Shere Khan slunk away, not daring to growl, for he knew – what everyone else knows – that when the last comes to the last Hathi is the Master of the Jungle.

'What is this right Shere Khan speaks of?' Mowgli whispered in Bagheera's ear. 'To kill Man is *always* shameful. The Law says so. And yet Hathi says—'

'Ask him. I do not know, Little Brother. Right or no right, if Hathi had not spoken I would have taught that lame butcher his lesson. To come to the Peace Rock fresh from a kill of Man – and to boast of it, is a jackal's trick. Besides, he tainted the good water.'

Mowgli waited for a minute to pick up his courage, because no one cared to address Hathi directly, and then he cried: 'What is Shere Khan's right, O Hathi?' Both banks echoed his words, for all the People of the Jungle are intensely curious, and they had just seen something that no one, except Baloo, who looked very thoughtful, seemed to understand.

'It is an old tale,' said Hathi; 'a tale older than the Jungle. Keep silence along the banks, and I will tell that tale.'

There was a minute or two of pushing and shouldering among the pigs and the buffalo, and then the leaders of the herds grunted, one after another, 'We wait,' and Hathi strode forward till he was almost knee-deep in the pool by the Peace Rock. Lean and wrinkled and yellow-tusked though he was, he looked what the Jungle held him to be[7] – their master.

'Ye know, children,' he began, 'that of all things ye most fear Man.' There was a mutter of agreement.

'This tale touches thee, Little Brother,' said Bagheera to Mowgli.

'I? I am of the Pack – a hunter of the Free People,' Mowgli answered. 'What have I to do with Man?'

'And ye do not know why ye fear Man?' Hathi went on. 'This is the reason. In the beginning of the Jungle, and none know when that was, we of the Jungle walked together, having no fear of one another. In those days there was no drought, and leaves and flowers and fruit grew on the same tree, and we ate nothing at all except leaves and flowers and grass and fruit and bark.'

'I am glad I was not born in those days,' said Bagheera. 'Bark is only good to sharpen claws.'

'And the Lord of the Jungle was Tha,[8] the First of the

Elephants. He drew the Jungle out of deep waters with his trunk, and where he made furrows in the ground with his tusks, there the rivers ran, and where he struck with his foot, there rose ponds of good water, and when he blew through his trunk thus – the trees fell. That was the manner in which the Jungle was made by Tha; and so the tale was told to me.'

'It has not lost fat in the telling,' Bagheera whispered, and Mowgli laughed behind his hand.

'In those days there was no corn or melons or pepper or sugar-cane, nor were there any little huts such as ye have all seen; and the Jungle People knew nothing of Man, but lived in the Jungle together, making one people. But presently they began to dispute over their food, though there was grazing enough for all. They were lazy. Each wished to eat where he lay, as sometimes we may do now when the Spring rains are good. Tha, the First of the Elephants, was busy making new jungles and leading the rivers in their beds. He could not walk everywhere, so he made the First of the Tigers the master and the judge of the Jungle, to whom the Jungle People should bring their disputes. In those days the First of the Tigers ate fruit and grass with the others. He was as large as I am, and he was very beautiful, in colour all over like the blossom of the yellow creeper. There was never stripe nor bar upon his hide in those good days when the Jungle was new. All the Jungle People came before him without fear, and his word was the Law of all the Jungle. We were then, remember ye, one people. Yet, upon a night, there was a dispute between two bucks – a grazing-quarrel such as ye now try out with the head and the forefeet – and it is said that as the two spoke together before the First of the Tigers lying among the flowers, a buck pushed him with his horns, and the First of the Tigers forgot that he was the master and judge of the Jungle, and, leaping upon that buck, broke his neck.

'Till that night never one of us had died, and the First of the Tigers, seeing what he had done, and being made foolish by the scent of the blood, ran away into the marshes of the North, and we of the Jungle, left without a judge, fell to fighting among ourselves. Tha heard the noise of it and came back; and some of us said this and some of us said that, but he saw the dead buck among the flowers, and asked who had killed, and we of the Jungle would not tell because the smell of the blood made us foolish, even as that same smell makes us foolish to-day.[9] We ran to and fro in circles, capering and crying out and shaking our heads. So therefore Tha gave an order to the trees that hang low, and to the trailing creepers of the Jungle, that they should mark the killer of the buck that he should know him again; and Tha said, "Who will now be Master of the Jungle People?" Then up leaped the Gray Ape who lives in the branches, and said, "I will now be Master of the Jungle." At this Tha laughed, and said, "So be it," and went away very angry.

'Children, ye know the Gray Ape. He was then as he is now. At the first he made a wise face for himself, but in a little while he began to scratch and to leap up and down, and when Tha returned he found the Gray Ape hanging, head down, from a bough, mocking those who stood below; and they mocked him again. And so there was no Law in the Jungle – only foolish talk and senseless words.

'Then Tha called us all together, and said: "The first of your masters has brought Death into the Jungle, and the second Shame. Now it is time there was a Law, and a Law that ye may not break. Now ye shall know Fear, and when ye have found him ye shall know that he is your master, and the rest shall follow." Then we of the Jungle said, "What is Fear?" And Tha said, "Seek till ye find." So we went up and down the Jungle seeking for Fear, and presently the buffaloes—'

'Ugh!' said Mysa,[10] the leader of the buffaloes, from their sandbank.

'Yes, Mysa, it was the buffaloes. They came back with the news that in a cave in the Jungle sat Fear, and that he had no hair, and went upon his hind legs. Then we of the Jungle followed the herd till we came to that cave, and Fear stood at the mouth of it, and he was, as the buffaloes had said, hairless, and he walked upon his hinder legs. When he saw us he cried out, and his voice filled us with the fear that we have now, and we ran away, tramping upon and tearing each other because we were afraid. That night, it was told to me, we of the Jungle did not lie down together as used to be our custom, but each tribe drew off by itself – the pig with the pig, the deer with the deer; horn to horn, hoof to hoof – like keeping to like, and so lay shaking in the Jungle.

'Only the First of the Tigers was not with us, for he was still hidden in the marshes of the North, and when word was brought to him of the Thing we had seen in the cave, he said: "I will go to this Thing and break his neck." So he ran all the night till he came to the cave, but the trees and the creepers on his path, remembering the order Tha had given, let down their branches and marked him as he ran, drawing their fingers across his back, his flank, his forehead and his jowl. Wherever they touched him there was a mark and a stripe upon his yellow hide. *And those stripes do his children wear to this day!* When he came to the cave, Fear, the Hairless One, put out his hand and called him "The Striped One that comes by night," and the First of the Tigers was afraid of the Hairless One, and ran back to the swamps howling.'

Mowgli chuckled quietly here, his chin in the water.

'So loud did he howl that Tha heard him and said, "What is the sorrow?" And the First of the Tigers, lifting up his muzzle to the new-made sky, which is now so old, said: "Give me back my power, O Tha. I am made ashamed before all the Jungle, and I have run away from an Hairless One, and he has called me a shameful name." "And why?" said Tha. "Because I am smeared with the mud of the marshes," said the First of the Tigers. "Swim, then, and roll on the wet grass, and if it be mud it will surely wash away," said Tha; and the First of the Tigers swam, and rolled, and rolled, till the Jungle ran round and round before his eyes, but not one little bar upon his hide was changed, and Tha, watching him, laughed. Then the First of the Tigers said, "What have I done that this comes to me?" Tha said, "Thou hast killed the buck, and thou hast let Death loose in the Jungle, and with Death has come Fear, so that the People of the Jungle are afraid one of the other as thou art afraid of the Hairless One." The First of the Tigers said, "They will never fear me, for I knew them since the beginning." Tha said, "Go and see." And the First of the Tigers ran to and fro, calling aloud to the deer and the pig and the *sambhur* and the porcupine and all the Jungle Peoples; but they all ran away from him who had been their Judge, because they were afraid.

'Then the First of the Tigers came back, his pride was broken in him, and, beating his head upon the ground, he tore up the earth with all his feet and said: "Remember that I was once the Master of the Jungle! Do not forget me, O Tha. Let my children remember that I was once without shame or fear!" And Tha said: "This much will I do, because thou and I together saw the Jungle made. For one night of each year it shall be as it was before the buck was killed – for thee and for thy children. In that one night, if ye meet the Hairless One – and his name is Man – ye shall not be afraid of him, but he shall be afraid of you as though ye were judges of the Jungle and masters of all things. Show him mercy in that night of his fear; for thou hast known what Fear is."

'Then the First of the Tigers answered, "I am content"; but when next he drank he saw the black stripes upon his flank and his side, and he remembered the name that the Hairless One had given him, and he was angry. For a year he lived in the marshes, waiting till Tha should keep his promise. And upon a night when the Jackal of the Moon (the Evening Star) stood clear of the Jungle, he felt that his Night was upon him, and he went to that cave to meet the Hairless One. Then it happened as Tha promised, for the Hairless One fell down before him and lay along the ground, and the First of the Tigers struck him and broke his back, for he thought that there was but one such a Thing in the Jungle, and that he had killed Fear. Then, nosing above the kill, he heard Tha coming down from the woods of the north, and presently the voice of the First of the Elephants, which is the voice that we hear now—'

The thunder was rolling up and down the dry, scarred hills, but it brought no rain – only heat-lightning that flickered behind the ridges – and Hathi went on: '*That* was the voice he heard, and it said: "Is this thy mercy?" The First of the Tigers licked his lips and said: "What matter? I have killed Fear." And Tha said: "O blind and foolish! Thou hast untied the feet of Death, and he will follow thy trail till thou diest. Thou hast taught Man to kill!"

'The First of the Tigers, standing stiffly to his kill, said: "He is as the buck was. There is no Fear. Now I will judge the Jungle Peoples once more."

'And Tha said: "Never again shall the Jungle Peoples come to thee. They shall never cross thy trail, nor sleep near thee, nor follow after thee, nor browse by thy lair. Only Fear shall follow thee, and with a blow that thou canst not see shall bid thee wait his pleasure. He shall make the ground to open under thy feet, and the creeper to twist about thy neck, and the tree-trunks to grow together about thee higher than thou canst leap, and at the last he shall take thy hide to wrap his cubs when they are cold. Thou hast shown him no mercy, and none will he show thee."

'The First of the Tigers was very bold, for his Night was still on him, and he said: "The Promise of Tha is the Promise of Tha. He will not take away my Night?" And Tha said: "Thy one Night is thine, as I have said, but there is a price to pay. Thou hast taught Man to kill, and he is no slow learner."

'The First of the Tigers said: "He is here under my foot, where his back is broken. Let the Jungle know that I have killed Fear."

'Then Tha laughed and said: "Thou hast killed one of many, but thou thyself shalt tell the Jungle – for thy Night is ended!"

'So the day came; and from the mouth of the cave went out another Hairless One, and he saw the kill in the path, and the First of the Tigers above it, and he took a pointed stick—'

'They throw a thing that cuts now,' said Sahi, rustling down the bank; for Sahi was considered uncommonly good eating by the Gonds – they called him Ho-Igoo[11] – and he knew something of the wicked little Gondee ax that whirls across a clearing like a dragon-fly.

'It was a pointed stick, such as they set in the foot of a pit-trap,' said Hathi; 'and throwing it, he struck the First of the Tigers deep in the flank. Thus it happened as Tha said, for the First of the Tigers ran howling up and down the Jungle till he tore out the stick, and all the Jungle knew that the Hairless One could strike from far off, and they feared more than before. So it came about that the First of the Tigers taught the Hairless One to kill – and ye know what harm that has since done to all our peoples – through the noose, and the pitfall, and the hidden trap, and the flying stick, and the stinging fly that comes out of white smoke (Hathi meant the rifle), and the Red Flower that drives us into the open. Yet for one night in the year the Hairless One fears the Tiger, as Tha promised, and never has the Tiger given him cause to be less afraid. Where he finds him, there he kills him, remembering how the First of the Tigers was made ashamed. For the rest, Fear walks up and down the Jungle by day and by night.'

'*Ahi! Aoo!*' said the deer, thinking of what it all meant to them.

'And only when there is one great Fear over all, as there is now, can we of the Jungle lay aside our little fears, and meet together in one place as we do now.'

'For one night only does Man fear the Tiger?' said Mowgli.

'For one night only,' said Hathi.

'But I – but we – but all the Jungle knows that Shere Khan kills Man twice and thrice in a moon.'

'Even so. *Then* he springs from behind and turns his head aside as he strikes, for he is full of fear. If Man looked at him he would run. But on his Night he goes openly down to the village. He walks between the houses and thrusts his head into the doorway, and the men fall on their faces, and there he does his kill. One kill in that Night.'

'Oh!' said Mowgli to himself, rolling over in the water. '*Now* I see why Shere Khan bade me look at him. He got no good of it, for he could not hold his eyes steady, and – and I certainly did not fall down at his feet. But then I am not a man; being of the Free People.'

'Umm!' said Bagheera deep in his furry throat. 'Does the Tiger know his Night?'

'Never till the Jackal of the Moon stands clear of the evening mist. Sometimes it falls in the dry summer and sometimes in the wet Rains – this one Night of the Tiger. But for the First of the Tigers this would never have been, nor would any of us have known fear.'

The deer grunted sorrowfully, and Bagheera's lips curled in a wicked smile. 'Do men know this – tale?' said he.

'None know it except the tigers, and we, the elephants – the Children of Tha. Now ye by the pools have heard it, and I have spoken.'

Hathi dipped his trunk into the water as a sign that he did not wish to talk.

'But – but – but,' said Mowgli, turning to Baloo, 'why did not the First of the Tigers continue to eat grass and leaves and trees? He did but break the buck's neck. He did not *eat*. What led him to the hot meat?'

'The trees and the creepers marked him, Little Brother, and made him the striped thing that we see. Never again would he eat their fruit; but from that day he revenged himself upon the deer, and the others, the Eaters of Grass,' said Baloo.

'Then *thou* knowest the tale. Heh? Why have I never heard?'

'Because the Jungle is full of such tales. If I made a beginning there would never be an end to them. Let go my ear, Little Brother.'

The Law of the Jungle

Just to give you an idea of the immense variety of the Jungle Law, I have translated into verse (Baloo always recited them in a sort of sing-song) a few of the laws that apply to the Wolves. There are, of course, hundreds and hundreds more, but these will serve as specimens of the simpler rulings.

Now this is the Law of the Jungle – as old and as true as
    the sky;
And the Wolf that shall keep it may prosper, but the Wolf that
    shall break it must die.
As the creeper that girdles the tree-trunk the Law runneth
    forward and back –
For the strength of the Pack is the Wolf, and the strength of
    the Wolf is the Pack.

Wash daily from nose-tip to tail-tip; drink deeply, but never
    too deep;
And remember the night is for hunting, and forget not the day
    is for sleep.

The Jackal may follow the Tiger, but, Cub, when thy whiskers
    are grown,
Remember the Wolf is a Hunter – go forth and get food of
    thine own.

Keep peace with the Lords of the Jungle – the Tiger, the
    Panther, and Bear.
And trouble not Hathi the Silent, and mock not the Boar in
    his lair.

When Pack meets with Pack in the Jungle, and neither will go
    from the trail,
Lie down till the leaders have spoken – it may be fair words
    shall prevail.

When ye fight with a Wolf of the Pack, ye must fight him
    alone and afar,
Lest others take part in the quarrel, and the Pack be diminished
    by war.

The Lair of the Wolf is his refuge, and where he has made him
    his home
Not even the Head Wolf may enter, not even the Council
    may come.

The Lair of the Wolf is his refuge, but where he has digged it
    too plain,
The Council shall send him a message, and so he shall change
    it again.

If ye kill before midnight, be silent, and wake not the woods
    with your bay,
Lest ye frighten the deer from the crop, and your brothers go
    empty away.

Ye may kill for yourselves, and your mates, and your cubs as
    they need, and ye can;
But kill not for pleasure of killing, and *seven times never
kill Man!*

If ye plunder his Kill from a weaker, devour not all in thy
    pride;
Pack-Right is the right of the meanest; so leave him the head
    and the hide.

The Kill of the Pack is the meat of the Pack. Ye must eat
    where it lies;
And no one may carry away of that meat to his lair, *or he dies.*

The Kill of the Wolf is the meat of the Wolf. He may do what
    he will;
But, till he has given permission, the Pack may not eat of
    that Kill.

Cub-Right is the right of the Yearling. From all of his Pack he
    may claim
Full-gorge when the killer has eaten; and none may refuse him
    the same.

Lair-Right is the right of the Mother. From all of her year she
    may claim
One haunch of each kill for her litter, and none may deny her
    the same.

Cave-Right is the right of the Father – to hunt by himself for
    his own:
He is freed of all calls to the Pack; he is judged by the Council
    alone.

Because of his age and his cunning, because of his gripe and
    his paw,
In all that the Law leaveth open, the word of your Head Wolf
    is Law.

Now these are the Laws of the Jungle, and many and mighty
    are they;
But the head and the hoof of the Law and the haunch and the
    hump is – Obey!

THE MIRACLE OF
PURUN BHAGAT

The night we felt the Earth would move
  We stole and plucked him by the hand,
Because we loved him with the love
  That knows but cannot understand.

And when the roaring hillside broke,
  And all our world fell down in rain,
We saved him, we the Little Folk;
  But lo! he will not come again!

Mourn now, we saved him for the sake
  Of such poor love as wild ones may.
Mourn ye! Our brother does not wake
  And his own kind drive us away!
                    Dirge of the Langurs[1]

There was once a man in India who was Prime Minister of one
of the semi-independent native States in the north-western part
of the country. He was a Brahmin, so high-caste that caste
ceased to have any particular meaning for him; and his father
had been an important official in the gay-coloured tag-rag and
bob-tail of an old-fashioned Hindoo Court. But as Purun Dass
grew up he realized that the ancient order[2] of things was changing, and that if anyone wished to get on[3] he must stand well
with the English, and imitate all the English believed to be good.
At the same time a native official must keep his own master's
favour. This was a difficult game, but the quiet, close-mouthed,
young Brahmin, helped by a good English education at a Bombay University, played it coolly, and rose, step by step, to be

Prime Minister of the kingdom.[4] That is to say, he held more real power than his master, the Maharajah.

When the old king – who was suspicious of the English, their railways and telegraphs – died, Purun Dass stood high with his young successor, who had been tutored by an Englishman; and between them, though he always took care that his master should have the credit, they established schools for little girls, made roads, and started State dispensaries and shows of agricultural implements, and published a yearly blue-book on the 'Moral and Material Progress of the State', and the Foreign Office and the Government of India were delighted. Very few native States take up English progress without reservations, for they will not believe, as Purun Dass showed he did, that what is good for the Englishman must be twice as good for the Asiatic. The Prime Minister became the honoured friend of Viceroys and Governors, and Lieutenant-Governors, and medical missionaries, and common missionaries, and hard-riding English officers who came to shoot in the State preserves, as well as of whole hosts of tourists who travelled up and down India in the cold weather, showing how things ought to be managed. In his spare time he would endow scholarships for the study of medicine and manufactures on strictly English lines, and write letters to the *Pioneer*,[5] the greatest Indian daily paper, explaining his master's aims and objects.

At last he went to England on a visit, and had to pay enormous sums to the priests when he came back; for even so high-caste a Brahmin as Purun Dass lost caste by crossing the black sea. In London he met and talked with everyone worth knowing – men whose names go all over the world – and saw a great deal more than he said. He was given honorary degrees by learned universities, and he made speeches and talked of Hindu social reform to English ladies in evening dress, till all London cried, 'This is the most fascinating man we have ever met at dinner since cloths were first laid!'

When he returned to India there was a blaze of glory, for the Viceroy himself made a special visit to confer upon the Maharajah the Grand Cross of the Star of India[6] – all diamonds and ribbons and enamel; and at the same ceremony, while the cannon boomed, Purun Dass was made a Knight Commander of the Order of the Indian Empire;[7] so that his name stood Sir Purun Dass, K.C.I.E.[8]

That evening at dinner in the big Viceregal tent he stood up with the badge and the collar of the Order on his breast, and replying to the toast of his master's health, made a speech that few Englishmen could have surpassed.

Next month, when the city had returned to its sun-baked quiet, he did a thing no Englishman would have dreamed of doing, for, so far as the world's affairs went, he died. The jeweled order of his knighthood returned to the Indian Government, and a new Prime Minister was appointed to the charge of affairs, and a great game of General Post[9] began in all the subordinate appointments. The priests knew what had happened and the people guessed; but India is the one place in the world where a man can do as he pleases and nobody asks why; and the fact that Dewan[10] Sir Purun Dass, K.C.I.E., had resigned position, palace, and power, and taken up the begging-bowl and ochre-coloured dress of a Sunnyasi or holy man, was considered nothing extraordinary. He had been, as the Old Law recommends, twenty years a youth, twenty years a fighter – though he had never carried a weapon in his life – and twenty years head of a household. He had used his wealth and his power for what he knew both to be worth; he had taken honour when it came his way; he had seen men and cities far and near, and men and cities had stood up and honoured him. Now he would let these things go, as a man drops the cloak he needs no longer.

Behind him, as he walked through the city gates, an antelope skin and brass-handled crutch under his arm, and a begging-bowl of polished brown *coco-de-mer*[11] in his hand, barefoot, alone, with eyes cast on the ground – behind him they were firing salutes from the bastions in honour of his happy successor. Purun Dass nodded. All that life was ended; and he bore it no more ill-will or good-will than a man bears to a colourless dream of the night. He was a Sunnyasi – a houseless, wandering mendicant, depending on his neighbours for his daily bread; and so long as there is a morsel to divide in India neither priest nor beggar starves. He had never in his life tasted meat, and very seldom eaten even fish. A five-pound-note would have covered his personal expenses for food through any one of the many years in which he had been absolute master of millions of money. Even when he was being lionized in London he had held before him his dream of peace and quiet – the long, white, dusty Indian road, printed all over with bare feet, the incessant, slow-moving traffic, and the sharp-smelling wood-smoke curling up under the fig-trees in the twilight, where the wayfarers sat at their evening meal.

When the time came to make that dream true the Prime Minister took the proper steps, and in three days you might more easily have found a bubble in the trough of the long Atlantic seas than Purun Dass among the roving, gathering, separating millions of India.

At night his antelope skin was spread where the darkness overtook him – sometimes in a Sunnyasi monastery by the roadside; sometimes by a mud pillar shrine of Kala Pir, where the Jogis,[12] who are another misty division of holy men, would receive him as they do those who know what castes and divisions are worth; sometimes on the outskirts of a little Hindu village, where the children would steal up with the food their parents had prepared; and sometimes on the pitch of the bare grazing-grounds where the flame of his stick fire waked the drowsy camels. It was all one to Purun Dass – or Purun Bhagat, as he called himself now. Earth, people, and food were all one. But, unconsciously, his feet drew him away northward and eastward; from the south to Rohtak; from Rohtak to Kurnool; from Kurnool to ruined Samanah,[13] and then up-stream along the dried bed of the Gugger river[14] that fills only when the rain falls in the hills, till, one day, he saw the far line of the great Himalayas.

Then Purun Bhagat smiled, for he remembered that his mother was of Rajput Brahmin birth, from Kulu[15] way – a Hill-woman, always homesick for the snows – and that the least touch of Hill blood draws a man in the end back to where he belongs.

'Yonder,' said Purun Bhagat, breasting the lower slopes of

the Sewaliks,[16] where the cacti stand up like seven-branched candlesticks, 'yonder I shall sit down and get knowledge'; and the cool wind of the Himalayas whistled about his ears as he trod the road that led to Simla.[17]

The last time he had come that way it had been in state, with a clattering cavalry escort, to visit the gentlest and most affable of Viceroys; and the two had talked for an hour together about mutual friends in London, and what the Indian common folk really thought of things. This time Purun Bhagat paid no calls, but leaned on the rail of the Mall, watching the glorious view of the Plains spread out forty miles below, till a native Mohammedan policeman told him he was obstructing traffic; and Purun Bhagat salaamed[18] reverently to the Law, because he knew the value of it, and was seeking for a Law of his own. Then he moved on, and slept that night in an empty hut at Chota Simla,[19] which looks like the very last end of the earth, but it was only the beginning of his journey. He followed the Himalaya–Thibet road, the little ten-foot track that is blasted out of solid rock, or strutted out on timbers over gulfs a thousand feet deep; that dips into warm, wet, shut-in valleys, and climbs across bare, grassy hill-shoulders where the sun strikes like a burning-glass; or turns through dripping, dark forests where the tree-ferns dress the trunks from head to heel, and the pheasant calls to his mate. And he met Thibetan herdsmen with their dogs and flocks of sheep, each sheep with a little bag of borax[20] on his back, and wandering wood-cutters, and cloaked and blanketed Lamas from Thibet, coming into India on pilgrimage, and envoys of little solitary Hill-states, posting furiously on ring-straked and piebald ponies, or the cavalcade of a Rajah paying a visit; or else for a long, clear day he would see nothing more than a black bear grunting and rooting down below in the valley. When he first started, the roar of the world he had left still rang in his ears, as the roar of a tunnel rings a little after the train has passed through; but when he had put the Mutteeanee Pass[21] behind him that was all done, and Purun Bhagat was alone with himself, walking, wondering, and thinking, his eyes on the ground, and his thoughts with the clouds.

One evening he crossed the highest pass he had met till

then – it had been a two days' climb – and came out on a line of snow-peaks that belted all the horizon – mountains from fifteen to twenty thousand feet high, looking almost near enough to hit with a stone, though they were fifty or sixty miles away. The pass was crowned with dense, dark forest – deodar, walnut, wild cherry, wild olive, and wild pear, but mostly deodar, which is the Himalayan cedar; and under the shadow of the deodars stood a deserted shrine to Kali – who is Durga, who is Sitala,[22] who is sometimes worshipped against the smallpox.

Purun Dass swept the stone floor clean, smiled at the grinning statue, made himself a little mud fireplace at the back of the shrine, spread his antelope skin on a bed of fresh pine needles, tucked his *bairagi* – his brass-handled crutch – under his armpit, and sat down to rest.

Immediately below him the hillside fell away, clean and cleared for fifteen hundred feet, to where a little village of stone-walled houses, with roofs of beaten earth, clung to the steep tilt. All round it tiny terraced fields lay out like aprons of patchwork on the knees of the mountain, and cows no bigger than beetles grazed between the smooth stone circles of the threshing-floors. Looking across the valley the eye was deceived by the size of things, and could not at first realize that what seemed to be low scrub, on the opposite mountain-flank, was in truth a forest of hundred-foot pines. Purun Bhagat saw an eagle swoop across the enormous hollow,[23] but the great bird dwindled to a dot ere it was half-way over. A few bands of scattered clouds strung up and down the valley, catching on a shoulder of the hills, or rising up and dying out when they were level with the head of the pass. And 'Here shall I find peace,' said Purun Bhagat.

Now, a Hill-man makes nothing of a few hundred feet up or down, and as soon as the villagers saw the smoke in the deserted shrine, the village priest climbed up the terraced hillside to welcome the stranger.

When he met Purun Bhagat's eyes – the eyes of a man used to control thousands – he bowed to the earth, took the begging-bowl without a word, and returned to the village, saying, 'We have at last a holy man. Never have I seen such a man.

He is of the plains – but pale coloured – a Brahmin of the Brahmins.' Then all the housewives of the village said, 'Think you he will stay with us?' and each did her best to cook the most savoury meal for the Bhagat. Hill-food is very simple, but with buckwheat and Indian corn, and rice and red pepper, and little fish out of the stream in the little valley, and honey from the flue-like hives built in the stone walls, and dried apricots, and turmeric, and wild ginger, and bannocks[24] of flour, a devout woman can make good things; and it was a full bowl that the priest carried to the Bhagat. Was he going to stay? asked the priest. Would he need a *chela* – a disciple – to beg for him? Had he a blanket against the cold weather? Was the food good?

Purun Bhagat ate, and thanked the giver. It was in his mind to stay. That was sufficient, said the priest. Let the begging-bowl be placed outside the shrine, in the hollow made by those two twisted roots, and daily should the Bhagat be fed; for the village felt honoured that such a man – he looked timidly into the Bhagat's face – should tarry among them.

That day saw the end of Purun Bhagat's wanderings. He had come to the place appointed for him – the silence and the space. After this, time stopped, and he, sitting at the mouth of the shrine, could not tell whether he were alive or dead; a man with control of his limbs, or a part of the hills, and the clouds, and the shifting rain, and sunlight. He would repeat a Name softly to himself a hundred hundred times, till, at each repetition, he seemed to move more and more out of his body, sweeping up to the doors of some tremendous discovery; but, just as the door was opening, his body would drag him back, and, with grief, he felt he was locked up again in the flesh and bones of Purun Bhagat.

Every morning the filled begging-bowl was laid silently in the crotch of the roots outside the shrine. Sometimes the priest brought it; sometimes a Ladakhi[25] trader, lodging in the village, and anxious to get merit, trudged up the path; but, more often, it was the woman who had cooked the meal overnight; and she would murmur, hardly above her breath: 'Speak for me before the gods, Bhagat. Speak for such an one, the wife of so-and so!' Now and then some bold child would be allowed the honour, and Purun Bhagat would hear him drop the bowl and run as fast as his little legs could carry him, but the Bhagat never came down to the village. It was laid out like a map at his feet. He could see the evening gatherings held on the circle of the threshing-floors, because that was the only level ground; could see the wonderful unnamed green of the young rice, the indigo blues of the Indian corn; the dock-like patches of buckwheat, and, in its season, the red bloom of the amaranth, whose tiny seeds, being neither grain nor pulse, make a food that can be lawfully eaten by Hindus in time of fasts.

When the year turned, the roofs of the huts were all little squares of purest gold, for it was on the roofs that they laid out their cobs of corn to dry. Hiving and harvest, rice-sowing and husking, passed before his eyes, all embroidered down there on the many-sided fields,[26] and he thought of them all, and wondered what they all led to at the long last.

Even in populated India a man cannot a day sit still before the wild things run over him as though he were a rock; and in that wilderness very soon the wild things, who knew Kali's Shrine well, came back to look at the intruder. The *langurs*, the big gray-whiskered monkeys of the Himalayas, were, naturally, the first, for they are alive with curiosity; and when they had upset the begging-bowl, and rolled it round the floor, and tried their teeth on the brass-handled crutch, and made faces at the antelope skin, they decided that the human being who sat so still was harmless. At evening, they would leap down from the pines, and beg with their hands for things to eat, and then swing off in graceful curves. They liked the warmth of the fire, too, and huddled round it till Purun Bhagat had to push them aside to throw on more fuel; and in the morning, as often as not, he would find a furry ape sharing his blanket. All day long, one or other of the tribe would sit by his side, staring out at the snows, crooning and looking unspeakably wise and sorrowful.

After the monkeys came the *barasingh*,[27] that big deer which is like our red deer, but stronger. He wished to rub off the velvet of his horns against the cold stones of Kali's statue, and stamped his feet when he saw the man at the shrine. But Purun Bhagat never moved, and, little by little, the royal stag edged up and nuzzled his shoulder. Purun Bhagat slid one cool hand along the hot antlers, and the touch soothed the fretted beast, who bowed his head, and Purun Bhagat very softly rubbed and ravelled off the velvet. Afterwards, the *barasingh* brought his doe and fawn – gentle things that mumbled on the holy man's blanket – or would come alone at night, his eyes green in the fire-flicker, to take his share of fresh walnuts. At last, the musk-deer, the shyest and almost the smallest of the deerlets, came, too, her big, rabbity ears erect; even brindled, silent *mushick-nabha*[28] must needs find out what the light in the shrine meant, and drop her moose-like nose into Purun Bhagat's lap, coming and going with the shadows of the fire. Purun Bhagat called them all 'my brothers', and his low call of '*Bhai! Bhai!*'[29] would draw them from the forest at noon if they were within earshot. The Himalayan black bear, moody and suspicious – Sona,[30] who has the V-shaped white mark under his chin – passed that way more than once; and since the Bhagat showed no fear, Sona showed no anger, but watched him, and came closer, and begged a share of the caresses, and a dole of bread or wild berries. Often, in the still dawns, when the Bhagat would climb to the very crest of the notched pass to watch the red day walking along the peaks of the snows, he would find Sona shuffling and grunting at his heels, thrusting a curious forepaw under fallen trunks, and bringing it away with a *whoof* of impatience; or his early steps would wake Sona where he lay curled up, and the great brute, rising erect, would think to fight, till he heard the Bhagat's voice and knew his best friend.

Nearly all hermits and holy men who live apart from the big cities have the reputation of being able to work miracles with the wild things, but all the miracle lies in keeping still, in never making a hasty movement, and, for a long time, at least, in never looking directly at a visitor. The villagers saw the outlines of the *barasingh* stalking like a shadow through the dark forest behind the shrine; saw the *minaul*, the Himalayan pheasant, blazing in her best colours before Kali's statue; and the *langurs* on their haunches, inside, playing with the walnut shells. Some of the children, too, had heard Sona singing to himself, bear-fashion, behind the fallen rocks, and the Bhagat's reputation as miracle-worker stood firm.

Yet nothing was further from his mind than miracles. He believed that all things were one big Miracle, and when a man knows that much he knows something to go upon. He knew for a certainty that there was nothing great and nothing little in this world; and day and night he strove to think out his way into the heart of things, back to the place whence his soul had come.

So thinking, his untrimmed hair fell down about his shoulders, the stone slab at the side of the antelope-skin was dented into a little hole by the foot of his brass-handled crutch, and the place between the tree-trunks, where the begging-bowl rested day after day, sunk and wore into a hollow almost as smooth as the brown shell itself; and each beast knew his exact place at the fire. The fields changed their colours with the seasons; the threshing-floors filled and emptied, and filled again and again; and again and again, when winter came, the *langurs* frisked among the branches feathered with light snow, till the mother-monkeys brought their sad-eyed little babies up from the warmer valleys with the spring. There were few changes in the village. The priest was older, and many of the little children who used to come with the begging-dish sent their own children now; and when you asked of the villagers how long their holy man had lived in Kali's Shrine at the head of the pass, they answered, 'Always.'

Then came such summer rains as had not been known in the Hills for many seasons. Through three good months the valley was wrapped in cloud and soaking mist – steady, unrelenting downfall, breaking off into thunder-shower after thunder-shower. Kali's Shrine stood above the clouds, for the most part, and there was a whole month in which the Bhagat never caught a glimpse of his village. It was packed away under a white floor of cloud that swayed and shifted and rolled on itself and bulged upward, but never broke from its piers – the streaming flanks of the valley.

All the time he heard nothing but the sound of a million little waters, overhead from the trees, and underfoot along the ground, soaking through the pine-needles, dripping from the tongues of draggled fern, and spouting in newly-torn muddy channels down the slopes. Then the sun came out, and drew forth the good incense of the deodars and the rhododendrons, and that far-off, clean smell the Hill People call 'the smell of the snows'. The hot sunshine lasted for a week, and then the rains gathered together for their last downpour, and the water fell in sheets that flayed off the skin of the ground and leaped back in mud. Purun Bhagat heaped his fire high that night, for he was sure his brothers would need warmth; but never a beast came to the shrine, though he called and called till he dropped asleep, wondering what had happened in the woods.

It was in the black heart of the night, the rain drumming like a thousand drums, that he was roused by a plucking at his blanket, and, stretching out, felt the little hand of a *langur*. 'It is better here than in the trees,' he said sleepily, loosening a fold of blanket; 'take it and be warm.' The monkey caught his hand and pulled hard. 'Is it food, then?' said Purun Bhagat. 'Wait a while, and I will prepare some.' As he kneeled to throw fuel on the fire the *langur* ran to the door of the shrine, crooned, and ran back again, plucking at the man's knee.

'What is it? What is thy trouble, Brother?' said Purun Bhagat, for the *langur*'s eyes were full of things that he could not tell. 'Unless one of thy caste be in a trap – and none set traps here – I will not go into that weather. Look, Brother, even the *barasingh* comes for shelter.'

The deer's antlers clashed as he strode into the shrine, clashed against the grinning statue of Kali. He lowered them in Purun Bhagat's direction and stamped uneasily, hissing through his half-shut nostrils.

'Hai! Hai! Hai!' said the Bhagat, snapping his fingers. 'Is *this* payment for a night's lodging?' But the deer pushed him towards the door, and as he did so Purun Bhagat heard the sound of something opening with a sigh, and saw two slabs of the floor draw away from each other, while the sticky earth below smacked its lips.

'Now I see,' said Purun Bhagat. 'No blame to my brothers that they did not sit by the fire tonight. The mountain is falling. And yet – why should I go?' His eye fell on the empty begging-bowl, and his face changed. 'They have given me good food daily since – since I came, and, if I am not swift, tomorrow there will not be one mouth in the valley. Indeed, I must go and warn them below. Back there, Brother! Let me get to the fire.'

The *barasingh* backed unwillingly as Purun Bhagat drove a torch deep into the flame, twirling it till it was well lit. 'Ah! ye came to warn me,' he said, rising. 'Better than that we shall do, better than that. Out, now, and lend me thy neck, Brother, for I have but two feet.'

He clutched the bristling withers of the *barasingh* with his right hand, held the torch away with his left, and stepped out of the shrine into the desperate night. There was no breath of wind, but the rain nearly drowned the torch as the great deer hurried down the slope, sliding on his haunches. As soon as they were clear of the forest more of the Bhagat's brothers joined them. He heard, though he could not see, the *langurs* pressing about him, and behind them the *uhh! uhh!* of Sona. The rain matted his long white hair into ropes; the water splashed beneath his bare feet, and his yellow robe clung to his frail old body, but he stepped down steadily, leaning against the *barasingh*. He was no longer a holy man, but Sir Purun Dass, K.C.I.E., Prime Minister of no small State, a man accustomed to command, going out to save life. Down the steep plashy path they poured all together, the Bhagat and his brothers, down and down till the deer clicked and stumbled on the wall of a threshing-floor, and snorted because he smelt Man. Now they were at the head of the one crooked village street, and the Bhagat beat with his crutch at the barred windows of the blacksmith's house as his torch blazed up in the shelter of the eaves. 'Up and out!' cried Purun Bhagat; and he did not know his own voice, for it was years since he had spoken aloud to a man. 'The hill falls! The hill is falling! Up and out, oh, you within!'

'It is our Bhagat,' said the blacksmith's wife. 'He stands among his beasts. Gather the little ones and give the call.'

It ran from house to house, while the beasts, cramped in the narrow way, surged and huddled round the Bhagat, and Sona puffed impatiently.

The people hurried into the street – they were no more than seventy souls all told – and in the glare of their torches they saw their Bhagat holding back the terrified *barasingh*, while the monkeys plucked piteously at his skirts, and Sona sat on his haunches and roared.

'Across the valley and up the next hill!' shouted Purun Bhagat. 'Leave none behind! We follow!'

Then the people ran as only Hill-folk can run, for they knew that in a landslide you must climb for the highest ground across the valley. They fled, splashing through the little river at the bottom, and panted up the terraced fields on the far side, while the Bhagat and his brethren followed. Up and up the opposite mountain they climbed, calling to each other by name – the roll-call of the village – and at their heels toiled the big *barasingh*, weighted by the failing strength of Purun Bhagat. At last the deer stopped in the shadow of a deep pine-wood, five hundred feet up the hillside. His instinct, that had warned him of the coming slide, told him he would be safe here.

Purun Bhagat dropped fainting by his side, for the chill of the rain and that fierce climb were killing him; but first he called to the scattered torches ahead, 'Stay and count your numbers'; then, whispering to the deer as he saw the lights gather in a cluster: 'Stay with me, Brother. Stay – till – I – go!'

There was a sigh in the air that grew to a mutter, and a mutter that grew to a roar, and a roar that passed all sense of hearing, and the hillside on which the villagers stood was hit in the darkness, and rocked to the blow. Then a note as steady, deep, and true as the deep C of the organ drowned everything for perhaps five minutes, while the very roots of the pines quivered to it. It died away, and the sound of the rain falling on miles of hard ground and grass changed to the muffled drums of water on soft earth. That told its own tale.

Never a villager – not even the priest – was bold enough to speak to the Bhagat who had saved their lives. They crouched under the pines and waited till the day. When it came they looked across the valley, and saw that what had been forest, and terraced field, and track-threaded grazing-ground was one raw, red, fan-shaped smear, with a few trees flung head-down on the scarp. That red ran high up the hill of their refuge, damming back the little river, which had begun to spread into a

brick-coloured lake. Of the village, of the road to the shrine, of
the shrine itself, and the forest behind, there was no trace. For
one mile in width and two thousand feet in sheer depth the
mountain-side had come away bodily, planed clean from head
to heel.

And the villagers, one by one, crept through the wood to
pray before their Bhagat. They saw the *barasingh* standing over
him, who fled when they came near, and they heard the *langurs*
wailing in the branches, and Sona moaning up the hill; but
their Bhagat was dead, sitting cross-legged, his back against a
tree, his crutch under his armpit, and his face turned to the
north-east.

The priest said: 'Behold a miracle after a miracle, for in this
very attitude must all Sunnyasis be buried! Therefore, where he
now is we will build the temple to our holy man.'

They built the temple before a year was ended, a little stone
and earth shrine, and they called the hill the Bhagat's Hill, and
they worship there with lights and flowers and offerings to this
day. But they do not know that the saint of their worship is the
late Sir Purun Dass, K.C.I.E., D.C.L.,[31] Ph.D., etc., once Prime
Minister of the progressive and enlightened State of Mohiniwala,[32] and honorary or corresponding member of more
learned and scientific societies than will ever do any good in
this world or the next.

A Song of Kabir

Oh, light was the world that he weighed in his hands!
Oh, heavy the tale of his fiefs and his lands!
He has gone from the *guddee*[1] and put on the shroud,
And departed in guise of *bairagi*[2] avowed!

Now the white road to Delhi is mat for his feet,
The *sal* and the *kikar*[3] must guard him from heat;
His home is the camp, and the waste, and the crowd –
He is seeking the Way, a *bairagi* avowed!

He has looked upon Man and his eyeballs are clear
(There was One; there is One, and but One, saith Kabir);
The Red Mist of Doing is thinned to a cloud –
He has taken the Path, a *bairagi* avowed!

To learn and discern of his brother the clod,
Of his brother the brute, and his brother the God,
He has gone from the council and put on the shroud
('Can ye hear?' saith Kabir), a *bairagi* avowed!

LETTING IN THE JUNGLE

Veil them, cover them, wall them round,
  Blossom and creeper and weed;
Let us forget the sight and the sound,
  And the smell and the touch of the breed!

Fat black ash by the altar-stone
  Here is the white-foot rain!
And the does bring forth in the fields unsown,
  And none may affright them again;
And the blind walls crumble, unknown, o'erthrown,
  And none may inhabit again!

You will remember, if you have read the tales in the first Jungle Book,[1] that after Mowgli had pinned Shere Khan's hide to the Council Rock, he told as many as were left of the Seeonee Pack that henceforward he would hunt in the Jungle alone; and the four children of Mother and Father Wolf said that they would hunt with him. But it is not easy to change all one's life at once – particularly in the Jungle. The first thing Mowgli did, when the disorderly Pack had slunk off, was to go to the home-cave, and sleep for a day and a night. Then he told Mother Wolf and Father Wolf as much as they could understand of his adventures among men; and when he made the morning sun flicker up and down the blade of his skinning-knife – the same he had skinned Shere Khan with – they said he had learned something. Then Akela and Gray Brother had to explain their share of the great buffalo-drive in the ravine, and Baloo toiled up the hill to hear all about it, and Bagheera scratched himself all over with pure delight at the way in which Mowgli had managed his war.

It was long after sunrise, but no one dreamed of going to

sleep, and from time to time, Mother Wolf would throw up her head, and sniff a deep snuff of satisfaction as the wind brought her the smell of the tiger-skin on the Council Rock.

'But for Akela and Gray Brother here,' Mowgli said, at the end, 'I could have done nothing. Oh, mother, mother! if thou hadst seen the blue herd-bulls pour down the ravine, or hurry through the gates when the Man-Pack flung stones at me!'

'I am glad I did not see that last,' said Mother Wolf, stiffly. 'It is not *my* custom to suffer my cubs to be driven to and fro like jackals! *I* would have taken a price from the Man-Pack; but I would have spared the woman who gave thee the milk. Yes, I would have spared her alone.'

'Peace, peace, Raksha!' said Father Wolf, lazily. 'Our Frog has come back again – so wise that his own father must lick his feet; and what is a cut, more or less, on the head? Leave Man alone.' Baloo and Bagheera both echoed: 'Leave Man alone.'[2]

Mowgli, his head on Mother Wolf's side, smiled contentedly, and said that, for his own part, he never wished to see, or hear, or smell Man again.

'But what,' said Akela, cocking one ear, 'but what if men do not leave thee alone, Little Brother?'

'We be *five*,' said Gray Brother, looking round at the company, and snapping his jaws on the last word.

'We also might attend to that hunting,' said Bagheera, with a little *switch-switch* of his tail, looking at Baloo. 'But why think of Man[3] now, Akela?'

'For this reason,' the Lone Wolf answered. 'When that yellow thief's hide was hung up on the rock, I went back along our trail to the village, stepping in my tracks, turning aside, and lying down, to make a mixed trail in case any should follow us. But when I had fouled the trail so that I myself hardly knew it again, Mang, the Bat, came hawking between the trees, and hung up above me. Said Mang, "The village of the Man-Pack, where they cast out the Man-cub, hums like a hornet's nest."'

'It was a big stone that I threw,' chuckled Mowgli, who had often amused himself by throwing ripe paw-paws into a hornet's nest, and racing to the nearest pool before the hornets caught him.

'I asked of Mang what he had seen. He said that the Red Flower blossomed at the gate of the village, and men sat about it carrying guns. Now *I* know, for I have good cause' – Akela looked here at the old dry scars on his flank and side – 'that men do not carry guns for pleasure. Presently, Little Brother, a man with a gun follows our trail – if, indeed, he be not already on it.'

'But why should he? Men have cast me out. What more do they need?' said Mowgli angrily.

'Thou art a man, Little Brother,' Akela returned. 'It is not for us, the Free Hunters, to tell thee what thy brethren do, or why.'

He had just time to snatch up his paw as the skinning-knife cut deep into the ground below. Mowgli struck quicker than an average human eye could follow, but Akela was a wolf; and even a dog, who is very far removed from the wild wolf, his ancestor, can be waked out of deep sleep by a cart-wheel touching his flank, and can spring away unharmed before that wheel comes on.

'Another time,' Mowgli said, quietly, returning the knife to its sheath, 'speak of the Man-Pack and of Mowgli in *two* breaths – not one.'

'Phff! That is a sharp tooth,' said Akela, snuffing at the blade's cut in the earth, 'but living with the Man-Pack has spoiled thine eye, Little Brother. I could have killed a buck while thou wast striking.'

Bagheera sprang to his feet, thrust up his head as far as he could, sniffed, and stiffened through every curve in his body. Gray Brother followed his example quickly, keeping a little to his left to get the wind that was blowing from the right, while Akela bounded fifty yards up-wind, and, half-crouching, stiffened too. Mowgli looked on enviously. He could smell things as very few human beings could, but he had never reached the hair-trigger-like sensitiveness of a Jungle nose; and his three months in the smoky village had put him back sadly. However, he dampened his finger, rubbed it on his nose, and stood erect to catch the upper scent, which, though the faintest, is the truest.

'Man!' Akela growled, dropping on his haunches.

'Buldeo!' said Mowgli, sitting down. 'He follows our trail, and yonder is the sunlight on his gun. Look!'

It was no more than a splash of sunlight, for a fraction of a second, on the brass clamps of the old Tower musket, but nothing in the Jungle winks with just that flash, except when the clouds race over the sky. Then a piece of mica, or a little pool, or even a highly-polished leaf will flash like a heliograph.[4] But that day was cloudless and still.

'I knew men would follow,' said Akela, triumphantly. 'Not for nothing have I led the Pack!'

Mowgli's four wolves said nothing, but ran downhill on their bellies, melting into the thorn and under-brush.[5]

'Whither go ye, and without word?' Mowgli called.

'H'sh! We roll his skull here before mid-day!' Gray Brother answered.

'Back! Back and wait! Man does not eat Man!' Mowgli shrieked.

'Who was a wolf but now? Who drove the knife at me for thinking he might be a Man?'[6] said Akela, as the Four turned back sullenly and dropped to heel.

'Am I to give reason for all I choose to do?' said Mowgli, furiously.

'That is Man! There speaks Man!' Bagheera muttered under his whiskers. 'Even so did men talk round the King's cages at Oodeypore. We of the Jungle know that Man is wisest of all. If we trusted our ears we should know that of all things he is most foolish.' Raising his voice, he added, 'The Man-cub is right in this. Men hunt in packs. To kill one, unless we know what the others will do, is bad hunting. Come, let us see what this Man means towards us.'

'We will not come,' Gray Brother growled. 'Hunt alone, Little Brother. We know our own minds! The skull would have been ready to bring by now.'

Mowgli had been looking from one to the other of his friends, his chest heaving and his eyes full of tears. He strode forward, and, dropping on one knee, said: 'Do I not know my mind? Look at me!'

They looked uneasily, and when their eyes wandered, he called them back again and again, till their hair stood up all over their bodies, and they trembled in every limb, while Mowgli stared and stared.

'Now,' said he, 'of us five, which is leader?'

'Thou art leader, Little Brother,' said Gray Brother, and he licked Mowgli's foot.

'Follow, then,' said Mowgli, and the four followed at his heels with their tails between their legs.

'This comes of living with the Man-Pack,' said Bagheera, slipping down after them. 'There is more in the Jungle now than Jungle Law, Baloo.'

The old bear said nothing, but he thought many things.

Mowgli cut across noiselessly through the Jungle, at right angles to Buldeo's path, till, parting the undergrowth, he saw the old man, his musket on his shoulder, running up the two days' old trail[7] at a dog-trot.

You will remember that Mowgli had left the village with the heavy weight of Shere Khan's raw hide on his shoulders, while Akela and Gray Brother trotted behind, so that the trail was very clearly marked. Presently Buldeo came to where Akela, as you know, had gone back and mixed it all up. Then he sat down, and coughed and grunted, and made little casts round and about into the Jungle to pick it up again, and all the time he could have thrown a stone over those who were watching him. No one can be so silent as a wolf when he does not care to be heard; and Mowgli, though the wolves thought he moved very clumsily, could come and go like a shadow. They ringed the old man as a school of porpoises ring a steamer at full speed, and as they ringed him they talked unconcernedly, for their speech began below the lowest end of the scale that untaught human beings can hear. (The other end is bounded by the high squeak of Mang, the Bat, which very many people cannot catch at all. From that note all the bird and bat and insect talk takes on.)

'This is better than any kill,' said Gray Brother, as Buldeo stooped and peered and puffed. 'He looks like a lost pig in the Jungles by the river. What does he say?' Buldeo was muttering savagely.

Mowgli translated. 'He says that packs of wolves must have danced round me. He says that he never saw such a trail in his life. He says he is tired.'

'He will be rested before he picks it up again,' said Bagheera coolly, as he slipped round a tree-trunk, in the game of blindman's-buff that they were playing. 'Now, what does the lean thing do?'

'Eat or blow smoke out of his mouth. Men always play with their mouths,' said Mowgli; and the silent trailers saw the old man fill and light, and puff at a water-pipe, and they took good note of the smell of the tobacco, so as to be sure of Buldeo in the darkest night, if necessary.

Then a little knot of charcoal-burners came down the path, and naturally halted to speak to Buldeo, whose fame as a hunter reached for at least twenty miles round. They all sat down and smoked, and Bagheera and the others came up and watched while Buldeo began to tell the story of Mowgli, the Devil-child, from one end to another, with additions and inventions. How he himself had really killed Shere Khan; and how Mowgli had turned himself into a wolf, and fought with him all the afternoon, and changed into a boy again and bewitched Buldeo's rifle, so that the bullet turned the corner, when he pointed it at Mowgli, and killed one of Buldeo's own buffaloes; and how the village, knowing him to be the bravest hunter in Seeonee, had sent him out to kill this Devil-child. But meantime the village had got hold of Messua and her husband, who were undoubtedly the father and mother of this Devil-child, and had barricaded them in their own hut, and presently would torture them to make them confess they were witch and wizard, and then they would be burned to death.

'When?' said the charcoal-burners, because they would very much like to be present at the ceremony.

Buldeo said that nothing would be done till he returned, because the village wished him to kill the Jungle Boy first. After that they would dispose of Messua and her husband, and divide their land and buffaloes among the village. Messua's husband had some remarkably fine buffaloes, too. It was an excellent thing to destroy wizards, Buldeo thought; and people who entertained Wolf-children out of the Jungle were clearly the worst kind of witches.

But, said the charcoal-burners, what would happen if the English heard of it? The English, they had been told, were a perfectly mad people, who would not let honest farmers kill witches in peace.

Why, said Buldeo, the head-man of the village would report that Messua and her husband had died of snake-bite. That was all arranged, and the only thing now was to kill the Wolf-child. They did not happen to have seen anything of such a creature?

The charcoal-burners looked round cautiously, and thanked their stars they had not; but they had no doubt that so brave a man as Buldeo would find him if anyone could. The sun was getting rather low, and they had an idea that they would push on to Buldeo's village and see the wicked witch. Buldeo said that, though it was his duty to kill the Devil-child, he could not think of letting a party of unarmed men go through the Jungle, which might reveal the Wolf-demon at any minute, without his escort. He, therefore, would accompany them, and if the sorcerer's child appeared – well, he would show them how the best hunter in Seeonee dealt with such things. The Brahmin, he said, had given him a charm against the creature that made everything perfectly safe.

'What says he? What says he? What says he?' the wolves repeated every few minutes; and Mowgli translated until he came to the witch part of the story, which was a little beyond him, and then he said that the man and woman who had been so kind to him were trapped.

'Do men trap men?' said Gray Brother.[8]

'So he says. I cannot understand the talk. They are all mad together. What have Messua and her man to do with me that they should be put in a trap; and what is all this talk about the Red Flower? I must look to this. Whatever they would do to Messua they will not do till Buldeo returns. And so—' Mowgli thought hard, with his fingers playing round the haft of his skinning-knife, while Buldeo and the charcoal-burners went off very valiantly in single file.

'I go hot-foot back to the Man-Pack,' Mowgli said at last.

'And those?' said Gray Brother, looking hungrily after the brown backs of the charcoal-burners.

'Sing them home,' said Mowgli with a grin; 'I do not wish them to be at the village gate till it is dark. Can ye hold them?'

Gray Brother bared his white teeth in contempt. 'We can

head them round and round in circles like tethered goats – if I know Man.'

'That I do not need. Sing to them a little lest they be lonely on the road, and, Gray Brother, the song need not be of the sweetest. Go with them, Bagheera, and help make that song. When night is laid down, meet me by the village – Gray Brother knows the place.'

'It is no light hunting to track for a Man-cub. When shall I sleep?' said Bagheera, yawning, though his eyes showed he was delighted with the amusement. 'Me to sing to naked men! But let us try.'

He lowered his head so that the sound would travel, and cried a long, long 'Good hunting' – a midnight call in the afternoon, which was quite awful enough to begin with. Mowgli heard it rumble, and rise, and fall, and die off in a creepy sort of whine behind him, and laughed to himself as he ran through the Jungle. He could see the charcoal-burners huddled in a knot; old Buldeo's gun-barrel waving, like a banana-leaf, to every point of the compass at once. Then Gray Brother gave the *Ya-la-hi! Yalaha!* call for the buck-driving, when the Pack drives the Nilghai,[9] the big blue cow, before them, and it seemed to come from the very ends of the earth, nearer, and nearer, and nearer, till it ended in a shriek snapped off short. The other three answered, till even Mowgli could have vowed that the Full Pack was in full cry, and then they all broke into the magnificent Morning-song in the Jungle, with every turn, and flourish, and grace-note, that a deep-mouthed wolf of the Pack knows. This is a rough rendering of the song, but you must imagine what it sounds like when it breaks the afternoon hush of the Jungle:

> One moment past our bodies cast
>   No shadow on the plain;
> Now clear and black they stride our track,
>   And we run home again.
> In morning-hush, each rock and bush
>   Stands hard, and high, and raw:
> Then give the Call: '*Good rest to all*
>   *That keep the Jungle Law!*'

Now horn and pelt our peoples melt
  In covert to abide;
Now crouched and still, to cave and hill
  Our Jungle Barons glide.
Now, stark and plain, Man's oxen strain,
  That draw the new-yoked plough;
Now stripped and dread the dawn is red
  Above the lit *talao*.[10]

Ho! Get to lair! The sun's aflare
  Behind the breathing grass:
And creaking through the young bamboo
  The warning whispers pass.
By day made strange, the woods we range
  With blinking eyes we scan;
While down the skies the wild duck cries:
  '*The Day – the Day to Man!*'

The dew is dried that drenched our hide,
  Or washed about our way;
And where we drank, the puddled bank
  Is crisping into clay.
The traitor Dark gives up each mark
  Of stretched or hooded claw;
Then hear the Call: '*Good rest to all
  That keep the Jungle Law!*'

But no translation can give the effect of it, or the yelping scorn the Four threw into every word of it, as they heard the trees crash when the men hastily climbed up into the branches, and Buldeo began repeating incantations and charms. Then they laid down and slept, for like all who live by their own exertions, they were of a methodical cast of mind; and no one can work well without sleep.

Meantime, Mowgli was putting the miles behind him, nine to the hour, swinging on, delighted to find himself so fit after all his cramped months among men. The one idea in his head was to get Messua and her husband out of the trap, whatever it

was, for he had a natural mistrust of traps. Later on, he promised himself, he would begin to pay his debts to the village at
large.

It was at twilight when he saw the well-remembered
grazing-grounds, and the *dhâk*-tree where Gray Brother had
waited for him on the morning that he killed Shere Khan.
Angry as he was at the whole breed and community of Man,
something jumped up in his throat and made him catch his
breath when he looked at the village roofs. He noticed that
everyone had come in from the fields unusually early, and that,
instead of getting to their evening cooking, they gathered in a
crowd under the village tree, and chattered, and shouted.

'Men must always be making traps for men, or they are not
content,' said Mowgli. 'Two nights ago[11] it was Mowgli – but
that night seems many Rains old. Tonight it is Messua and her
man. Tomorrow, and for very many nights after, it will be
Mowgli's turn again.'

He crept along outside the wall till he came to Messua's hut,
and looked through the window into the room. There lay Messua, gagged, and bound hand and foot, breathing hard, and
groaning; her husband was tied to the gaily painted bedstead.
The door of the hut that opened into the street was shut fast,
and three or four people were sitting with their backs to it.

Mowgli knew the manners and customs of the villagers very
fairly. He argued that so long as they could eat, and talk, and
smoke, they would not do anything else; but as soon as they
had fed they would begin to be dangerous. Buldeo would be
coming in before long, and if his escort had done its duty
Buldeo would have a very interesting tale to tell. So he went in
through the window, and, stooping over the man and the
woman, cut their thongs, pulling out the gags, and looked
round the hut for some milk.

Messua was half wild with pain and fear (she had been
beaten and stoned all the morning), and Mowgli put his hand
over her mouth just in time to stop a scream. Her husband was
only bewildered and angry, and sat picking dust and things out
of his torn beard.

'I knew – I knew he would come,' Messua sobbed at last.

'Now do I *know* that he is my son'; and she caught Mowgli to her heart. Up to that time Mowgli had been perfectly steady, but here he began to tremble all over, and that surprised him immensely.

'Why are these thongs? Why have they tied thee?' he asked, after a pause.

'To be put to the death for making a son of thee – what else?' said the man, sullenly. 'Look! I bleed.'

Messua said nothing, but it was at *her* wounds that Mowgli looked, and they heard him grit his teeth when he saw the blood.

'Whose work is this?' said he. 'There is a price to pay.'

'The work of all the village. I was too rich. I had too many cattle. *Therefore* she and I are witches, because we gave thee shelter.'

'I do not understand. Let Messua tell the tale.'

'I gave thee milk, Nathoo; dost thou remember?' Messua said, timidly. 'Because thou wast my son, whom the tiger took, and because I loved thee very dearly. They said that I was thy mother, the mother of a devil, and therefore worthy of death.'

'And what is a devil?' said Mowgli. 'Death I have seen.'

The man looked up gloomily under his eyebrows, but Messua laughed. 'See!' she said to her husband, 'I knew – I said that he was no sorcerer! He is my son – my son!'

'Son or sorcerer, what good will that do us?' the man answered. 'We be as dead already.'

'Yonder is the road through the Jungle' – Mowgli pointed through the window. 'Your hands and feet are free. Go now.'

'We do not know the Jungle, my son, as – as thou knowest,' Messua began. 'I do not think that I could walk far.'

'And the men and women would be upon our backs and drag us here again,' said the husband.

'H'm!' said Mowgli, and he tickled the palm of his hand with the tip of his skinning-knife; 'I have no wish to do harm to anyone of this village – *yet*. But I do not think they will stay thee. In a little while they will have much to think upon. Ah!' he lifted his head and listened to shouting and trampling outside. 'So they have let Buldeo come home at last?'

'He was sent out this morning to kill thee,' Messua cried. 'Didst thou meet him?'

'Yes – we – I met him. He has a tale to tell; and while he is telling it there is time to do much. But first I will learn what they mean. Think where ye would go, and tell me when I come back.'

He bounded through the window and ran along again outside the wall of the village till he came within earshot of the crowd round the peepul tree. Buldeo was lying on the ground, coughing and groaning, and everyone was asking him questions. His hair had fallen about his shoulders; his hands and legs were skinned from climbing up trees, and he could hardly speak, but he felt the importance of his position keenly. From time to time he said something about devils and singing devils, and magic enchantment, just to give the crowd a taste of what was coming. Then he called for water.

'Bah!' said Mowgli. 'Chatter – chatter! Talk, talk! Men are blood-brothers of the *Bandar-log*. Now he must wash his mouth with water; now he must blow smoke; and when all that is done he has still his story to tell. They are very wise people – men. They will leave no one to guard Messua till their ears are stuffed with Buldeo's tales. And – I grow as lazy as they!'

He shook himself and glided back to the hut. Just as he was at the window he felt a touch on his foot.

'Mother,' said he, for he knew that tongue well, 'what dost *thou* here?'

'I heard my children singing through the woods, and I followed the one I loved best. Little Frog, I have a desire to see that woman who gave thee milk,' said Mother Wolf, all wet with the dew.

'They have bound and mean to kill her. I have cut those ties, and she goes with her man through the Jungle.'

'I also will follow. I am old, but not yet toothless.' Mother Wolf reared herself up on end, and looked through the window into the dark of the hut.

In a minute she dropped noiselessly, and all she said was: 'I gave thee thy first milk; but Bagheera speaks truth: Man goes to Man at the last.'

'Maybe,' said Mowgli, with a very unpleasant look on his face; 'but tonight I am very far from that trail. Wait here, but do not let her see.'

'*Thou* wast never afraid of *me*, Little Frog,' said Mother Wolf, backing into the high grass, and blotting herself out, as she knew how.

'And now,' said Mowgli, cheerfully, as he swung into the hut again, 'they are all sitting round Buldeo, who is saying that which did not happen. When his talk is finished, they say they will assuredly come here with the Red – with fire and burn you both. And then?'

'I have spoken to my man,' said Messua. 'Kanhiwara[12] is thirty miles from here, but at Kanhiwara we may find the English—'

'And what Pack are they?' said Mowgli.

'I do not know. They be white, and it is said that they govern all the land, and do not suffer people to burn or beat each other without witnesses. If we can get thither tonight we live. Otherwise we die.'

'Live then. No man passes the gates tonight. But what does *he* do?' Messua's husband was on his hands and knees digging up the earth in one corner of the hut.

'It is his little money,' said Messua. 'We can take nothing else.'

'Ah, yes. The stuff that passes from hand to hand and never grows warmer. Do they need it outside this place also?' said Mowgli.

The man stared angrily. 'He is a fool, and no devil,' he muttered. 'With the money I can buy a horse. We are too bruised to walk far, and the village will follow us in an hour.'

'I say they will *not* follow till I choose, but a horse is well thought of, for Messua is tired.' Her husband stood up and knotted the last of the rupees into his waist-cloth. Mowgli helped Messua through the window, and the cool night air revived her, but the Jungle in the starlight looked very dark and terrible.

'Ye know the trail to Kanhiwara?' Mowgli whispered.

They nodded.

'Good. Remember, now, not to be afraid. And there is no

need to go quickly. Only – only there may be some small singing in the Jungle behind you and before.'

'Think you we would have risked a night in the Jungle through anything less than the fear of burning? It is better to be killed by beasts than by men,' said Messua's husband; but Messua looked at Mowgli and smiled.

'I say,' Mowgli went on, just as though he were Baloo repeating an old Jungle Law for the hundredth time to an inattentive cub, 'I say that not a tooth in the Jungle is bared against you; not a foot in the Jungle is lifted against you. Neither man nor beast shall stay you till you come within eye-shot of Kanhiwara. There will be a watch about you.' He turned quickly to Messua, saying, '*He* does not believe, but thou wilt believe?'

'Ay, surely, my son. Man, ghost, or wolf of the Jungle, I believe.'

'*He* will be afraid when he hears my people singing. Thou wilt know and understand. Go now, and slowly, for there is no need of any haste. The gates are shut.'

Messua flung herself sobbing at Mowgli's feet, but he lifted her very quickly with a shiver. Then she hung about his neck and called him every name of blessing she could think of, but her husband looked enviously across his fields, and said: '*If we reach Kanhiwara, and I get the ear of the English, I will bring such a lawsuit against the Brahmin and old Buldeo and the others as shall eat this village to the bone. They shall pay me twice over for my crops untilled and my buffaloes unfed. I will have a great justice.*'

Mowgli laughed. 'I do not know what justice is, but – come thou back next Rains and see what is left.'

They went off toward the Jungle, and Mother Wolf leaped from her place of hiding.

'Follow!' said Mowgli; 'and look to it that all the Jungle knows these two are safe. Give tongue a little. I would call Bagheera.'

The long, low howl rose and fell, and Mowgli saw Messua's husband flinch and turn, half minded to run back to the hut.

'Go on,' Mowgli shouted, cheerfully. 'I said there might be singing. That call will follow up to Kanhiwara. It is the Favour of the Jungle.'

Messua urged her husband forward, and the darkness shut down on them and Mother Wolf as Bagheera rose up almost under Mowgli's feet, trembling with delight of the night that drives the Jungle People wild.

'I am ashamed of thy brethren,' he said, purring.

'What? Did they not sing sweetly to Buldeo?' said Mowgli.

'Too well! Too well! They made even *me* forget my pride, and, by the Broken Lock that freed me, I went singing through the Jungle as though I were out wooing in the spring! Didst thou not hear us?'

'I had other game afoot. Ask Buldeo if he liked the song. But where are the Four? I do not wish one of the Man-Pack to leave the gates tonight.'

'What need of the Four, then?' said Bagheera, shifting from foot to foot, his eyes ablaze, and purring louder than ever. 'I can hold them, Little Brother. Is it killing at last? The singing and the sight of the men climbing up the trees have made me very ready. Who is Man that we should care for him – the naked brown digger, the hairless and toothless, the eater of earth?[13] I have followed him all day – at noon – in the white sunlight. I herded him as the wolves herd buck. I am Bagheera! Bagheera! Bagheera! As I dance with my shadow so I danced with those men. Look!' The great panther leaped as a kitten leaps at a dead leaf whirling overhead, struck left and right into the empty air, that sung under the strokes, landed noiselessly, and leaped again and again, while the half purr, half growl gathered head as steam rumbles in a boiler. 'I am Bagheera – in the Jungle – in the night, and my strength is in me. Who shall stay my stroke? Man-cub, with one blow of my paw I could beat thy head flat as a dead frog in the summer!'

'Strike, then!' said Mowgli, in the dialect of the village, *not* the talk of the Jungle; and the human words brought Bagheera to a full stop, flung back on his haunches that quivered under him, his head just at the level of Mowgli's. Once more Mowgli stared, as he had stared at the rebellious cubs, full into the beryl-green eyes, till the red glare behind their green went out like the light of a lighthouse shut off twenty miles across the sea; till the eyes dropped, and the big head with them – dropped lower and lower, and the red rasp of a tongue grated on Mowgli's instep.

'Brother – Brother – Brother!' the boy whispered, stroking steadily and lightly from the neck along the heaving back: 'Be still, be still! It is the fault of the night, and no fault of thine.'

'It was the smells of the night,' said Bagheera, penitently. 'This air cries aloud to me. But how dost *thou* know?'

Of course the air round an Indian village is full of all kinds of smells, and to any creature who does nearly all his thinking through his nose, smells are as maddening as music and drugs are to human beings. Mowgli gentled the panther for a few minutes longer, and he lay down like a cat before a fire, his paws tucked under his breast, and his eyes half shut.

'Thou art of the Jungle and *not* of the Jungle,' he said at last. 'And I am only a black panther. But I love thee, Little Brother.'

'They are very long at their talk under the tree,' Mowgli said, without noticing the last sentence. 'Buldeo must have told many tales. They should come soon to drag the woman and her man out of the trap and put them into the Red Flower. They will find that trap sprung. Ho! Ho!'

'Nay, listen,' said Bagheera. 'The fever is out of my blood now. Let them find *me* there! Few would leave their houses after meeting me. It is not the first time I have been in a cage; and I do not think they will tie *me* with cords.'

'Be wise, then,' said Mowgli, laughing; for he was beginning to feel as reckless as the panther, who had glided into the hut.

'Pah!' Bagheera puffed; 'This place is rank with Man, but here is just such a bed as they gave me to lie upon in the King's cages at Oodeypore. Now I lie down.' Mowgli heard the strings of the cot crack under the great brute's weight. 'By the Broken Lock that freed me, they will think they have caught big game! Come and sit beside me, Little Brother; we will give them "good hunting" together!'

'No; I have another thought in my stomach. The Man-Pack shall not know what share I have in the sport. Make thine own hunt. I do not wish to see them.'

'Be it so,' said Bagheera. 'Now they come!'

The conference under the peepul-tree had been growing

noisier and noisier, at the far end of the village. It broke in wild yells, and a rush up the street of men and women, waving clubs and bamboos and sickles and knives. Buldeo and the Brahmin were at the head of it, but the mob was close at their heels, and they cried, 'The witch and the wizard! Let us see if hot coins will make them confess! Burn the hut over their heads! We will teach them to shelter Wolf-devils! Nay, beat them first! Torches! More torches! Buldeo, heat the gun-barrel!'

Here was some little difficulty with the catch of the door. It had been very firmly fastened, but the crowd tore it away bodily, and the light of the torches streamed into the room where, stretched at full length on the bed, his paws crossed and lightly hung down over one end, black as the Pit and terrible as a demon, was Bagheera. There was one half-minute of desperate silence, as the front ranks of the crowd clawed and tore their way back from the threshold, and in that minute Bagheera raised his head and yawned – elaborately, carefully, and ostentatiously – as he would yawn when he wished to insult an equal. The fringed lips drew back and up; the red tongue curled; the lower jaw dropped and dropped till you could see half-way down the hot gullet; and the gigantic dog-teeth stood clear to the pit of the gums till they rang together, upper and under, with the snick of steel-faced wards shooting home round the edges of a safe. Next minute the street was empty; Bagheera had leaped back through the window, and stood at Mowgli's side, while a yelling, screaming torrent scrambled and tumbled one over another in their panic haste to get to their huts.

'They will not stir till the day comes,' said Bagheera, quietly. 'And now?'

The silence of the afternoon sleep seemed to have overtaken the village, but, as they listened, they could hear the sound of heavy grain-boxes being dragged over earthen floors and pushed against doors. Bagheera was quite right; the village would not stir till daylight. Mowgli sat still and thought, and his face grew darker and darker.

'What have I done?' said Bagheera, at last, fawning.

'Nothing but great good. Watch them now till the day. I sleep.' Mowgli ran off into the Jungle, and dropped[14] across a rock, and slept and slept the day round, and the night back again.

When he waked, Bagheera was at his side, and there lay a newly-killed buck at his feet. Bagheera watched curiously while Mowgli went to work with his skinning-knife, ate and drank, and turned over with his chin in his hands.

'The man and thy woman[15] came safe within eye-shot of Kanhiwara,' Bagheera said. 'Thy mother[16] sent the word back by Chil. They found a horse before midnight of the night they were freed, and went very quickly. Is not that well?'

'That is well,' said Mowgli.

'And thy Man-Pack in the village did not stir till the sun was high this morning. Then they ate their food and ran back quickly to their houses.'

'Did they, by chance, see thee?'

'It may have been. I was rolling in the dust before the gate at dawn, and I may have made also some small song to myself. Now, Little Brother, there is nothing more to do. Come hunting with me and Baloo. He has new hives that he wishes to show, and we all desire thee back again as of old. Take off that look which makes even *me* afraid. The man and woman will not be put into the Red Flower, and all goes well in the Jungle. Is it not true? Let us forget the Man-Pack.'

'They shall be forgotten – in a little while. Where does Hathi feed tonight?'

'Where he chooses. Who can answer for the Silent One? But why? What is there Hathi can do which we cannot?'

'Bid him and his three sons come here to me.'

'But, indeed, and truly, Little Brother, it is not – it is not seemly to say "Come", and "Go", to Hathi. Remember, he is the Master of the Jungle, and before the Man-Pack changed the look on thy face, he taught thee a Master-word[17] of the Jungle.'

'That is all one. I have a Master-word for him now. Bid him come to Mowgli, the Frog, and if he does not hear at first, bid him come because of the Sack of the Fields of Bhurtpore.'[18]

'The Sack of the Fields of Bhurtpore,' Bagheera repeated two or three times to make sure. 'I go. Hathi can but be angry at the worst, and I would give a moon's hunting to hear a Master-word that compels the Silent One.'

He went away, leaving Mowgli stabbing furiously with his skinning-knife into the earth. Mowgli had never seen human blood in his life before till he had seen, and – what meant much more to him – smelled Messua's blood on the thongs that bound her. And Messua had been kind to him, and, so far as he knew anything about love, he loved Messua as completely as he hated the rest of mankind. But deeply as he loathed them, their talk, their cruelty and their cowardice, not for anything the Jungle had to offer could he bring himself to take a human life, and have that terrible scent of blood back again in his nostrils. His plan was simpler but much more thorough; and he laughed to himself when he thought that it was one of old Buldeo's tales told under the peepul-tree in the evening that had put the idea into his head.

'It *was* a Master-word,' Bagheera whispered in his ear. 'They were feeding by the river, and they obeyed as though they were bullocks. Look, where they come now!'

Hathi and his three sons had appeared in their usual way, without a sound. The mud of the river was still fresh on their flanks, and Hathi was thoughtfully chewing the green stem of a young plantain-tree that he had gouged up with his tusks. But every line in his vast body showed to Bagheera, who could see things when he came across them, that it was not the Master of the Jungle speaking to a Man-cub, but one who was afraid coming before one who was not. His three sons rolled side by side, behind their father.

Mowgli hardly lifted his head as Hathi gave him 'Good hunting'. He kept him swinging and rocking, and shifting from one foot to another, for a long time before he spoke, and when he opened his mouth it was to Bagheera, not to the elephants.

'I will tell a tale that was told to me by the hunter ye hunted today,' said Mowgli. 'It concerns an elephant, old and wise, who fell into a trap, and the sharpened stake in the pit[19] scarred him from a little above his heel to the crest of his shoulder, leaving a white mark.' Mowgli threw out his hand, and as Hathi wheeled the moonlight showed a long white scar on his slaty side, as though he had been struck with a red-hot whip. 'Men came to take him from the trap,' Mowgli continued, 'but he broke his ropes, for he was strong, and he went away till his wound was healed. Then came he, angry, by night to the fields of those hunters. And I remember now that he had three sons. These things happened many, many Rains ago, and very far away – among the fields of Bhurtpore. What came to those fields at the next reaping, Hathi?'

'They were reaped by me and by my three sons,' said Hathi.

'And to the ploughing that follows the reaping?' said Mowgli.

'There was no ploughing,' said Hathi.

'And to the men that live by the green crops on the ground?' said Mowgli.

'They went away.'

'And to the huts in which the men slept?' said Mowgli.

'We tore the roofs to pieces, and the Jungle swallowed up the walls,' said Hathi.

'And what more, besides?' said Mowgli.

'As much good ground as I can walk over in two nights from the east to the west, and from the north to the south as much as I can walk over in three nights, the Jungle took. We let in the Jungle upon five villages; and in those villages, and in their lands, the grazing-ground and the soft crop-grounds, there is not one man today who gets his food from the ground. That was the Sack of the Fields of Bhurtpore, which I and my three sons did; and now I ask, Man-cub, how the news of it came to thee?' said Hathi.

'A man told me; and now I see even Buldeo can speak truth. It was well done, Hathi with the white mark; but the second time it shall be done better, for the reason that there is a man to direct. Thou knowest the village of the Man-Pack that cast me out? They are idle, senseless, and cruel; they play with their mouths, and they do not kill the weaker for food, but for sport. When they are full-fed they would throw their own breed into the Red Flower. This I have seen. It is not well that they should live here any more. I hate them!'

'Kill, then,' said the youngest of Hathi's three sons, picking up a tuft of grass, dusting it against his fore-legs, and throwing it away, while his little red eyes glanced furtively from side to side.

'What good are white bones to me?' Mowgli answered furiously. 'Am I the cub of a wolf to play in the sun with a raw head? I have killed Shere Khan, and his hide rots on the Council Rock; but – but I do not know whither Shere Khan is gone, and my stomach is still empty. Now I will take that which I can see and touch. Let in the Jungle upon that village, Hathi!'

Bagheera shivered, and cowered down. He could understand, if the worst came to the worst, a quick rush down the village street, and a right and left blow into a crowd, or a crafty killing of men as they ploughed in the twilight, but this scheme for deliberately blotting out an entire village from the eyes of man and beast frightened him. Now he saw why Mowgli had sent for Hathi. No one but the long-lived elephant could plan and carry through such a war.

'Let them run as the men ran from the fields of Bhurtpore, till we have the rain-water for the only plough, and the noise of the rain on the thick leaves for the pattering of their spindles – till Bagheera and I lair in the house of the Brahmin, and the buck drink at the tank behind the temple! Let in the Jungle, Hathi!'

'But I – but we have no quarrel with them, and it needs the red rage of great pain ere we tear down the places where men sleep,' said Hathi, rocking doubtfully.

'Are ye the only eaters of grass in the Jungle? Drive in your peoples. Let the deer and the pig and the nilghai look to it. Ye need never show a hand's-breadth of hide till the fields are naked. Let in the Jungle, Hathi!'

'There will be no killing? My tusks were red at the Sack of the Fields of Bhurtpore, and I would not wake that smell again.'

'Nor I. I do not wish even their bones to lie on our clean earth. Let them go find a fresh lair. They cannot stay here! I have seen and smelt the blood of the woman that gave me food – the woman whom they would have killed but for me. Only the smell of the new grass on their door-steps can take away that smell. It burns in my mouth. Let in the Jungle, Hathi!'

'Ah!' said Hathi. 'So did the scar of the stake burn on my hide till we watched their villages die under in the spring growth. Now I see. Thy war shall be our war. We will let in the Jungle.'

Mowgli had hardly time to catch his breath – he was shaking all over with rage and hate – before the place where the elephants had stood was empty, and Bagheera was looking at him with terror.

'By the Broken Lock that freed me!' said the Black Panther at last. 'Art *thou* the naked thing I spoke for in the Pack when all was young? Master of the Jungle, when my strength goes, speak for me – speak for Baloo – speak for us all! We are cubs before thee! Snapped twigs under foot! Fawns that have lost their doe!'

The idea of Bagheera being a stray fawn upset Mowgli altogether, and he laughed and caught his breath, and sobbed and laughed again, till he had to jump into a pool to make himself stop. Then he swam round and round, ducking in and out of the bars of the moonlight like the frog, his namesake.

By this time Hathi and his three sons had turned, each to one point of the compass, and were striding silently down the valleys a mile away. They went on and on for two days' march – that is to say, a long sixty miles – through the Jungle; while every step they took, and every wave of their trunks, was known and noted and talked over by Mang and Chil and the Monkey People and all the birds. Then they began to feed, and fed quietly for a week or so. Hathi and his sons are like Kaa the Rock Python. They never hurry till they have to.

At the end of that time – and none knew who had started it – a rumour went through the Jungle that there was better food and water to be found in such and such a valley. The pig – who, of course, will go to the ends of the earth for a full meal – moved first by companies, scuffling over the rocks, and the deer followed, with the little wild foxes that live on the dead and dying of the herds; and the heavy-shouldered nilghai moved parallel with the deer, and the wild buffaloes of the swamps came after the nilghai. The least little thing would have turned the scattered, straggling droves that grazed and

sauntered and drank and grazed again; but whenever there was
an alarm someone would rise up and soothe them. At one time
it would be Sahi[20] the Porcupine, full of news of good feed just
a little farther on; at another Mang would cry cheerily and flap
down a glade to show it was all empty; or Baloo, his mouth full
of roots, would shamble alongside a wavering line and half
frighten, half romp it clumsily back to the proper road. Very
many creatures broke back or ran away or lost interest, but
very many were left to go forward. At the end of another ten
days or so the situation was this. The deer and the pig and the
nilghai were milling round and round in a circle of eight or ten
miles' radius, while the Eaters of Flesh skirmished round its
edge. And the centre of that circle was the village, and round
the village the crops were ripening, and in the crops sat men on
what they call *machans* – platforms like pigeon-perches, made
of sticks at the top of four poles – to scare away birds and other
stealers. Then the deer were coaxed no more. The Eaters of
Flesh were close behind them, and forced them forward and
inward.

It was a dark night when Hathi and his three sons slipped
down from the Jungle, and broke off the poles of the *machans*
with their trunks, and they fell as a snapped stalk of hemlock in
bloom falls, and the men that tumbled from them heard the deep
gurgling of the elephants in their ears. Then the vanguard of
the bewildered armies of the deer broke down and flooded into
the village grazing-grounds and the ploughed fields; and the
sharp-hoofed, rooting wild pig came with them, and what the
deer left the pig spoiled, and from time to time an alarm of
wolves would shake the herds, and they would rush to and fro
desperately, treading down the young barley, and cutting flat the
banks of the irrigating channels. Before the dawn broke the pressure on the outside of the circle gave way at one point. The Eaters
of Flesh had fallen back and left an open path to the south, and
drove upon drove of buck fled along it. Others, who were bolder,
lay up in the thickets to finish their meal next night.

But the work was practically done. When the villagers
looked in the morning they saw their crops were lost. That
meant death if they did not get away, for they lived year in and

year out as near to starvation as the Jungle was near to them. When the buffaloes were sent to graze the hungry brutes found that the deer had cleared the grazing-grounds, and so wandered into the Jungle and drifted off with their wild mates;[21] and when twilight fell the three or four ponies that belonged to the village lay in their stables with their heads beaten in. Only Bagheera could have given those strokes, and only Bagheera would have thought of insolently dragging the last carcase to the open street.

The villagers had no heart to make fires in the fields that night, so Hathi and his three sons went gleaning among what was left; and where Hathi gleans there is no need to follow. The men decided to live on their stored seed-corn until the rains had fallen, and then to take work as servants till they could catch up with the lost year; but as the grain-dealer was thinking of his well-filled crates of corn, and the prices he would levy at the sale of it, Hathi's sharp tusks were picking out the corner of his mud-house, and smashing up the big wicker-chest, leeped[22] with cow-dung, where the precious stuff lay.

When that last loss was discovered, it was the Brahmin's turn to speak. He had prayed to his own Gods without answer. It might be, he said, that, unconsciously, the village had offended some one of the Gods of the Jungle, for, beyond doubt, the Jungle was against them. So they sent for the head man of the nearest tribe of wandering Gonds – little, wise, and very black hunters, living in the deep Jungle, whose fathers came of the oldest race in India – the aboriginal owners of the land. They made the Gond welcome with what they had, and he stood on one leg, his bow in his hand, and two or three poisoned arrows stuck through his top-knot, looking half afraid and half contemptuously at the anxious villagers and their ruined fields. They wished to know whether his Gods – the Old Gods – were angry with them, and what sacrifices should be offered. The Gond said nothing, but picked up a trail of the Karela,[23] the vine that bears the bitter wild gourd, and laced it to and fro across the temple door in the face of the staring red Hindu image. Then he pushed with his hand in the open air along the road to Kanhiwara, and went back to his Jungle, and watched the Jungle people drifting through it. He knew that when the Jungle moves only white men can hope to turn it aside.

There was no need to ask his meaning. The wild gourd would grow where they had worshipped their God, and the sooner they saved themselves the better.

But it is hard to tear a village from its moorings. They stayed on as long as any summer food was left to them, and they tried to gather nuts in the Jungle, but shadows with glaring eyes watched them, and rolled before them even at midday, and when they ran back afraid to their walls, on the tree trunks they had passed not five minutes before the bark would be striped and chiselled with the stroke of some great taloned paw. The more they kept to their village, the bolder grew the wild things that gambolled and bellowed on the grazing-grounds by the Waingunga. They had no heart[24] to patch and plaster the rear walls of the empty byres that backed on to the Jungle; the wild pig trampled them down, and the knotty-rooted vines hurried after and threw their elbows over the new-won ground, and the coarse grass bristled behind the vines.[25] The unmarried men ran away first, and carried the news far and near that the village was doomed. Who could fight, they said, against the Jungle, or the Gods of the Jungle, when the very village cobra had left his hole in the platform under the peepul? So their little commerce with the outside world shrunk as the trodden paths across the open grew fewer and fainter. And the nightly trumpetings of Hathi and his three sons ceased to trouble them; they had no more to go.[26] The crop on the ground and the seed in the ground had been taken. The outlying fields were already losing their shape, and it was time to throw themselves on the charity of the English at Kanhiwara.

Native fashion, they delayed their departure from one day to another till the first Rains caught them and the unmended roofs let in a flood, and the grazing-ground stood ankle deep, and all green things came on with a rush after the heat of the summer. Then they waded out – men, women, and children – through the blinding hot rain of the morning, but turned naturally for one farewell look at their homes.

They heard, as the last burdened family filed through the

gate, a crash of falling beams and thatch behind the walls. They saw a shiny, snaky black trunk lifted for an instant, scattering sodden thatch. It disappeared, and there was another crash, followed by a squeal. Hathi had been plucking off the roofs of the huts as you pluck water-lilies, and a rebounding beam had pricked him. He needed only this to unchain his full strength, for of all things in the Jungle the wild elephant enraged is the most wantonly destructive. He kicked backward at a mud wall that crumbled at the stroke, and, crumbling, melted to yellow mud under the torrents of rain. Then he wheeled and squealed, and tore through the narrow streets, leaning against the huts right and left, shivering the crazy doors, and crumpling up the eaves; while his three sons raged behind as they had raged at the Sack of the Fields of Bhurtpore.

'The Jungle will swallow these shells,' said a quiet voice in the wreckage. 'It is the outer walls that must lie down,' and Mowgli, with the rain sluicing over his bare shoulders and arms, leaped back from a wall that was settling like a tired buffalo.

'All in good time,' panted Hathi. 'Oh, but my tusks were red at Bhurtpore! To the outer wall, children! With the head! Together! Now!'

The four pushed side by side; the outer wall bulged, split, and fell, and the villagers, dumb with horror, saw the savage, clay-streaked heads of the wreckers in the ragged gap. Then they fled, houseless and foodless, down the valley, as their village, shredded and tossed and trampled, melted behind them.

A month later the place was a dimpled mound, covered with soft, green young stuff; and by the end of the Rains there was the roaring Jungle in full blast on the spot that had been under plough not six months before.

Mowgli's Song Against People

I will let loose against you the fleet-footed vines –
I will call in the Jungle to stamp out your lines!
　　The roofs shall fade before it,
　　　The house-beams shall fall,
　　And the *Karela*, the bitter *Karela*,
　　　Shall cover it all!

In the gates of these your councils my people shall sing,
In the doors of these your garners the Bat-folk shall cling;
　　And the snake shall be your watchman,
　　　By a hearthstone unswept;
　　For the *Karela*, the bitter *Karela*,
　　　Shall fruit where ye slept!

Ye shall not see my strikers; ye shall hear them and guess;
By night, before the moon-rise, I will send for my cess,[1]
　　And the wolf shall be your herdsman
　　　By a landmark removed,
　　For the *Karela*, the bitter *Karela*,
　　　Shall seed where ye loved!

I will reap your fields before you at the hands of a host;
Ye shall glean behind my reapers for the bread that is lost;
　　And the deer shall be your oxen
　　　By a headland untilled,
　　For the *Karela*, the bitter *Karela*,
　　　Shall leaf where ye build!

I have untied against you the club-footed vines,
I have sent in the Jungle to swamp out your lines.
　　The trees – the trees are on you!
　　　The house-beams shall fall,
　　And the *Karela*, the bitter *Karela*,
　　　Shall cover you all!

THE UNDERTAKERS

When ye say to Tabaqui, 'My Brother!' when ye call the
   Hyena to meat,
Ye may cry the Full Truce with Jacala[1] – the Belly that runs
   on four feet.

Jungle Law

'Respect the Aged!'

It was a thick voice – a muddy voice that would have made
you shudder – a voice like something soft breaking in two.
There was a quaver in it, a croak and a whine.

'*Respect the aged! O companions of the River – respect the
aged!*'

Nothing could be seen on the broad reach of the river except
a little fleet of square-sailed, wooden-pinned barges, loaded
with building-stone, that had just come under the railway
bridge,[2] and were driving down-stream. They put their clumsy
helms over to avoid the sand-bar made by the scour of the
bridge-piers, and as they passed, three abreast, the horrible
voice began again:

'*O Brahmins of the River – respect the aged and infirm!*'

A boatman turned where he sat on the gunwale, lifted up his
hand, said something that was not a blessing, and the boats
creaked on through the twilight. The broad Indian river, that
looked more like a chain of little lakes than a stream, was as
smooth as glass, reflecting the sandy-red sky in mid-channel,
but splashed with patches of yellow and dusky purple near and
under the low banks. Little creeks ran into it in the wet season,
but now their dry mouths hung clear above water-line. On the
left shore, almost under the railway bridge, stood a mud-and-
brick and thatch-and-stick village, whose main street, full of
cattle going back to their byres, ran straight to the river, and

ended in a sort of rude brick pier-head, where people who wanted to wash could wade in step by step. That was the Ghaut of the village of Mugger-Ghaut.[3]

Night was falling fast over the fields of lentils and rice and cotton in the low-lying grounds yearly flooded by the river; over the reeds that fringed the elbow of the bend, and the tangled jungle of the grazing-grounds behind the still reeds. The parrots and crows, who had been chattering and shouting over their evening drink, had flown inland to roost, crossing the out-going battalions of the flying-foxes;[4] and cloud upon cloud of water-birds came whistling and 'honking' to the cover of the reed-beds. There were geese, barrel-headed and black-backed, teal, widgeon, mallard and sheldrake, with curlews, and here and there a flamingo.

A lumbering Adjutant-crane[5] brought up the rear, flying as though each slow stroke would be his last.

'Respect the aged! Brahmins of the River – respect the aged!'

The Adjutant half turned his head, sheered a little in the direction of the voice, and landed stiffly on the sand-bar below the bridge. Then you saw what a ruffianly brute he really was. His back-view was immensely respectable, for he stood nearly six feet high, and looked rather like a very proper bald-headed parson. In front it was different, for his Ally Sloper-like[6] head and neck had not a feather to them, and there was a horrible raw-skin pouch on his neck under his chin – a hold-all for the things his pick-axe beak might steal. His legs were long and thin and skinny, but he moved them delicately, and looked at them with pride as he preened down his ashy-gray tail-feathers, glanced over the smooth of his shoulder, and stiffened into 'Stand at attention.'

A mangy little Jackal, who had been yapping hungrily on a low bluff, cocked up his ears and tail, and scuttered across the shallows to join the Adjutant.

He was the lowest of his caste – not that the best of jackals are good for much, but this one was peculiarly low, being half a beggar, half a criminal – a cleaner-up of village rubbish-heaps, desperately timid or wildly bold, everlastingly hungry, and full of cunning that never did him any good.

'Ugh!' he said, shaking himself dolefully as he landed. 'May the red mange destroy the dogs of this village! I have three bites for each flea upon me, and all because I looked – only looked, mark you – at an old shoe in a cow-byre. Can I eat mud?' He scratched himself under his left ear.

'I heard,' said the Adjutant, in a voice like a blunt saw going through a thick board – 'I *heard* there was a new-born puppy in that same shoe.'

'To hear is one thing; to know is another,' said the Jackal, who had a very fair knowledge of proverbs, picked up by listening to men round the village fires of an evening.

'Quite true. So, to make sure, I took care of that puppy while the dogs were busy elsewhere.'

'They were *very* busy,' said the Jackal. 'Well, I must not go to the village hunting for scraps yet awhile. And so there truly was a blind puppy in that shoe?'

'It is here,' said the Adjutant, squinting over his beak at his full pouch. 'A small thing, but acceptable now that charity is dead in the world.'

'Ahai! The world is iron in these days,' wailed the Jackal. Then his restless eye caught the least possible ripple on the water, and he went on quickly: 'Life is hard for us all, and I doubt not that even our excellent master, the Pride of the Ghaut and the Envy of the River—'

'A liar, a flatterer, and a Jackal were all hatched out of one egg,' said the Adjutant to nobody in particular; for he was rather a fine sort of a liar on his own account when he took the trouble.

'Yes, the Envy of the River,' the Jackal repeated, raising his voice. 'Even he, I doubt not, finds that since the bridge has been built good food is more scarce. But on the other hand, though I would by no means say this to his noble face, he is so wise and so virtuous – as I, alas! am not—'

'When the Jackal says that he is gray, how black must the Jackal be!' muttered the Adjutant. He could not see what was coming.

'That *his* food never fails, and in consequence—'

There was a soft grating sound as though a boat had just touched in shoal water. The Jackal spun round quickly and faced (it is always best to face) the creature he had been talking about. It was a twenty-four-foot crocodile, cased in what looked like treble-riveted boiler-plate, studded and keeled and crested; the yellow points of his upper teeth just overhanging his beautifully fluted lower jaw. It was the blunt-nosed Mugger of Mugger-Ghaut, older than any man in the village, who had given his name to the village; the demon of the ford before the railway bridge came – murderer, man-eater, and local fetish in one. He lay with his chin in the shallows, keeping his place by an almost invisible rippling of his tail, and well the Jackal knew that one stroke of that same tail in the water could carry the Mugger up the bank with the rush of a steam-engine.

'Auspiciously met, Protector of the Poor!' he fawned, backing at every word. 'A delectable voice was heard, and we came in the hopes of sweet conversation. My tailless presumption, while waiting here, led me, indeed, to speak of thee. It is my hope that nothing was overheard.'

Now the Jackal had spoken just to be listened to, for he knew flattery was the best way of getting things to eat, and the Mugger knew that the Jackal had spoken for this end, and the Jackal knew that the Mugger knew, and the Mugger knew that the Jackal knew that the Mugger knew; and so they were all very contented together.

The old brute pushed and panted and grunted up the bank, mumbling, 'Respect the aged and infirm!' and all the time his little eyes burned like coals under the heavy horny eyelids on the top of his triangular head, as he shoved his bloated barrel-body along between his crutched legs. Then he settled down, and accustomed as the Jackal was to his ways, he could not help starting, for the hundredth time, when he saw how exactly the Mugger imitated a log adrift on the bar. He had even taken pains to lie at the exact angle a naturally stranded log would make with the water, having regard to the current of the season at the time and place. All this was only a matter of habit, of course, because the Mugger had come ashore for pleasure; but a crocodile is never quite full, and if the Jackal had been deceived by the likeness he would not have lived to philosophize over it.

'My child, I heard nothing,' said the Mugger, shutting one eye. 'The water was in my ears, and also I was faint with hunger. Since the railway bridge was built my people at my village have ceased to love me; and that is breaking my heart.'

'Ah, shame!' said the Jackal. 'So noble a heart, too! But men are all alike to my mind.'

'Nay, there are very great differences indeed,' the Mugger answered, gently. 'Some are as lean as boat-poles. Others again are fat as young ja— dogs. Never would I causelessly revile men. They are of all fashions, but the long years have shown me that, one with another, they are very good. Men, women, and children – I have no fault to find with them. And remember, child, he who rebukes the world is rebuked by the world.'

'Flattery is worse than an empty tin can in the belly. But that which we have just heard is wisdom,' said the Adjutant, bringing down one foot.

'Consider, though, their ingratitude to this excellent one,' began the Jackal, tenderly.

'Nay, nay, not ingratitude!' the Mugger said. 'They do not think for others; that is all. But I have noticed, lying at my station below the ford, that the stairs of the new bridge are cruelly hard to climb, both for old people and young children. The old, indeed, are not so worthy of consideration, but I am grieved – I am truly grieved – on account of the small fat children. Still, I think, in a little while, when the newness of the bridge has worn away, we shall see my people's bare brown legs bravely splashing through the ford as before. Then the old Mugger will be honoured again.'

'But surely I saw marigold wreaths floating off the edge of the Ghaut only this noon,' said the Adjutant. Marigold wreaths are a sign of reverence all India over.

'An error – an error. It was the wife of the sweetmeat-seller. She loses her eyesight year by year, and cannot tell a log from me – the Mugger of the Ghaut! I saw the mistake when she threw the garland, for I was lying at the very foot of the Ghaut, and had she taken another step I might have shown her some little difference. Yet she meant well, and we must consider the spirit of the offering.'

'What profit are marigold wreaths when one is on the rubbish-heap?' said the Jackal, hunting for fleas, but keeping one wary eye on his Protector of the Poor.

'True, but they have not yet begun to make the rubbish-heap that shall carry me. Five times have I seen the river draw back from the village and make new land at the foot of the street. Five times have I seen the village rebuilt on the banks, and I shall see it built yet times five more. I am no faithless, fish-hunting Gavial,[7] I, at Kasi today and Prayag to-morrow,[8] as the saying is, but the true and constant watcher of the ford. It is not for nothing, child, that the village bears my name, and "he who watches long," as the saying is, "shall at last have his reward."'

'*I* have watched long – very long – nearly all my life, and my reward has been bites and blows,' said the Jackal.

'Ho! ho! ho!' roared the Adjutant.

> 'In August was the Jackal born;
> The Rains fell in September;
> "Now such a fearful flood as this,"
> Said he, "I can't remember!"'[9]

There is one very unpleasant peculiarity about the Adjutant. At uncertain times he suffers from acute attacks of the fidgets or cramp in his legs, and though he is more virtuous to behold than any of the cranes, who are all immensely respectable, he flies off into wild, cripple-stilt war-dances,[10] half-opening his wings and bobbing his bald head up and down; while for reasons best known to himself he is very careful to time his worst attacks with his nastiest remarks. At the last word of his song he came to attention again, ten times adjutaunter than before.

The Jackal winced, though he was full three seasons old, but one cannot resent an insult from a person with a beak a yard long, and the power of driving it like a javelin. The Adjutant was a most notorious coward, but the Jackal was worse.

'We must live before we can learn,' said the Mugger, 'and there is this to say: Little jackals are very common, child, but such a mugger as I am is not common. For all that, I am not proud, since pride is destruction; but take notice, it is Fate, and against his Fate no one who swims or walks or runs should say anything at all. I am well contented with Fate. With good luck, a keen eye, and the custom of considering whether a creek or a backwater has an outlet to it ere you ascend, much may be done.'

'Once I heard that even the Protector of the Poor made a mistake,' said the Jackal viciously.

'True; but there my Fate helped me. It was before I had come to my full growth – before the last famine but three (by the Right and Left of Gunga!¹¹ how full the streams used to be in those days!). Yes, I was young and unthinking, and when the flood came, who was so pleased as I? A little made me very happy then. The village was deep in flood, and I swam above the Ghaut and went far inland, up to the rice-fields, and they were deep in good mud. I remember also a pair of bracelets (glass they were, and troubled me not a little) that I found that evening. Yes, glass bracelets; and, if my memory serves me well, a shoe. I should have shaken off both shoes, but I was hungry. I learned better later. Yes. And so I fed and rested me; but when I was ready to go to the river again the flood had fallen, and I walked through the mud of the main street. Who but I? Came out all my people, priests and women and children, and I looked upon them with benevolence. The mud is not a good place to fight in. Said a boatman, "Get axes and kill him, for he is the Mugger of the ford." "Not so," said the Brahman.¹² "Look, he is driving the flood before him! He is the godling of the village." Then they threw many flowers at me, and by happy thought one led a goat across the road.'

'How good – how very good is goat!' said the Jackal.

'Hairy – too hairy, and when found in the water more than likely to hide a cross-shaped hook. But that goat I accepted, and went down to the Ghaut in great honour. Later, my Fate sent me the boatman who had desired to cut off my tail with an axe. His boat grounded upon an old shoal which you would not remember.'

'We are not *all* jackals here,' said the Adjutant. 'Was it the shoal made where the stone-boats sank in the year of the great drouth – a long shoal that lasted three floods?'

'There were two,' said the Mugger; 'an upper and a lower shoal.'

'Ay, I forgot. A channel divided them, and later dried up again,' said the Adjutant, who prided himself on his memory.

'On the lower shoal, children, my well-wisher's craft grounded. He was sleeping in the bows, and, half awake, leaped over to his waist – no, it was no more than to his knees – to push off. His empty boat went on and touched again below the next reach, as the river ran then. I followed, because I knew men would come out to drag it ashore.'

'And did they do so?' said the Jackal, a little awe-stricken. This was hunting on a scale that impressed him.

'There and lower down they did. I went no farther, but that gave me three in one day – well-fed *manjis* (boatmen) all, and, except in the case of the last (then I was careless), never a cry to warn those on the bank.'

'Ah, noble sport! But what cleverness and great judgment it requires!' said the Jackal.

'Not cleverness, child, but thought. A little thought in life is like salt upon rice, as the boatmen say, and I have thought deeply always. The Gavial, my cousin, the fish-eater, has told me how hard it is for him to follow his fish, and how one fish differs from the other, and how he must know them all, both together and apart. I say that is wisdom; but, on the other hand, my cousin, the Gavial, lives among his people. *My* people do not swim in companies, with their mouths out of the water, as Rewa does; nor do they constantly rise to the surface of the water, and turn over on their sides, like Mohoo and little Chapta; nor do they gather in shoals after flood, like Batchua and Chilwa.'[13]

'All are very good eating,' said the Adjutant, clattering his beak.

'So my cousin says, and makes a great to-do over hunting them, but they do not climb the banks to escape his sharp nose. *My* people are otherwise. Their life is on the land, in the houses, among the cattle. I must know what they do, and what they are about to do, and, adding the tail to the trunk, as the saying is, I make up the whole elephant. Is there a green branch and an iron ring hanging over a doorway? The old Mugger knows that a boy has been born in that house, and must some day come down to the Ghaut to play. Is a maiden to be married? The old Mugger knows, for he sees the men carry gifts back and forth; and she, too, comes down to the Ghaut to bathe before her wedding, and – he is there. Has the river changed its channel, and made new land where there was only sand before? The Mugger knows.'

'Now, of what use is that knowledge?' said the Jackal. 'The river has shifted even in my little life.' Indian rivers are nearly always moving about in their beds, and will shift, sometimes, as much as two or three miles in a season, drowning the fields on one bank, and spreading good silt on the other.

'There is no knowledge so useful,' said the Mugger, 'for new land means new quarrels. The Mugger knows. Oho! the Mugger knows. As soon as the water has drained off, he creeps up the little creeks that men think would not hide a dog, and there he waits. Presently comes a farmer saying he will plant cucumbers here, and melons there, in the new land that the river has given him. He feels the good mud with his bare toes. Anon comes another, saying he will put onions, and carrots, and sugar-cane in such and such places. They meet as boats adrift meet, and each rolls his eye at the other under the big blue turban. The old Mugger sees and hears. Each calls the other "Brother", and they go to mark out the boundaries of the new land. The Mugger hurries with them from point to point, shuffling very low through the mud. Now they begin to quarrel! Now they say hot words! Now they pull turbans! Now they lift up their *lathis* (clubs), and at last one falls backward into the mud, and the other runs away. When he comes back the dispute is settled, as the iron-bound bamboo of the loser witnesses. Yet they are not grateful to the Mugger. No, they cry "Murder!" and their families fight with sticks, twenty a-side. My people are good people – upland Jats – Malwais of the Bêt.[14] They do not give blows for sport, and, when the fight is done, the old Mugger waits far down the river, out of sight of the village, behind the *kikar*-scrub[15] yonder. Then come they down, my broad-shouldered Jats – eight or nine together under the stars, bearing the dead man upon a bed. They are old men with

gray beards, and voices as deep as mine. They light a little fire –
ah! how well I know that fire! – and they drink tobacco, and
they nod their heads together forward in a ring, or sideways
toward the dead man upon the bank. They say the English Law
will come with a rope for this matter, and that such a man's
family will be ashamed, because such a man must be hanged
in the great square of the jail. Then say the friends of the
dead, "Let him hang!" and the talk is all to do over again –
once, twice, twenty times in the long night. Then says one, at
last, "The fight was a fair fight. Let us take blood-money, a
little more than is offered by the slayer, and we will say no
more about it." Then do they haggle over the blood-money, for
the dead was a strong man, leaving many sons. Yet before
amratvela (sunrise) they put the fire to him a little, as the custom is, and the dead man comes to me, and *he* says no more
about it. Aha! my children, the Mugger knows – the Mugger
knows – and my Malwah Jats are a good people!'

'They are too close – too narrow in the hand for my crop,'
croaked the Adjutant. 'They waste not the polish on the cow's
horn, as the saying is; and, again, who can glean after a
Malwai?'

'Ah, I – glean – *them*,' said the Mugger.

'Now, in Calcutta of the South, in the old days,' the Adjutant went on, 'everything was thrown into the streets, and we
picked and chose. Those were dainty seasons. But today they
keep their streets as clean as the outside of an egg, and my
people fly away. To be clean is one thing; to dust, sweep, and
sprinkle seven times a day wearies the very Gods themselves.'

'There was a down-country jackal had it from a brother,
who told me, that in Calcutta of the South all the jackals were
as fat as otters in the Rains,' said the Jackal, his mouth water-
ing at the bare thought of it.

'Ah, but the white-faces are there – the English – and they
bring dogs from somewhere down the river, in boats – big fat
dogs – to keep these same jackals lean,' said the Adjutant.

'They are, then, as hard-hearted as these people? I might
have known. Neither earth, sky, nor water shows charity to a
jackal. I saw the tents of a white-face last season, after the

Rains, and also I took a new yellow bridle to eat. The white-faces do not dress their leather in the proper way. It made me very sick.'

'That was better than my case,' said the Adjutant. 'When I was in my third season, a young and a bold bird, I went down to the river where the big boats come in. The boats of the English are thrice as big as this village.'

'He has been as far as Delhi, and says all the people there walk on their heads,' muttered the Jackal. The Mugger opened his left eye, and looked keenly at the Adjutant.

'It is true,' the big bird insisted. 'A liar only lies when he hopes to be believed. No one who had not seen those boats *could* believe this truth.'

'*That* is more reasonable,' said the Mugger. 'And then?'

'From the insides of this boat they were taking out great pieces of white stuff, which, in a little while, turned to water. Much split off, and fell about on the shore, and the rest they swiftly put into a house with thick walls. But a boatman, who laughed, took a piece no larger than a small dog, and threw it to me. I – all my people – swallow without reflection, and that piece I swallowed as is our custom. Immediately I was afflicted with an excessive cold, which, beginning in my crop, ran down to the extreme end of my toes, and deprived me even of speech, while the boatmen laughed at me. Never have I felt such cold. I danced in my grief and amazement till I could recover my breath, and then I danced and cried out against the falseness of this world; and the boatmen derided me till they fell down. The chief wonder of the matter, setting aside that marvellous cold-ness, was that there was nothing at all in my crop when I had finished my lamentings!'

The Adjutant had done his very best to describe his feelings after swallowing a seven-pound lump of Wenham Lake ice, off an American ice-ship, in the days before Calcutta made her ice by machinery;[16] but as he did not know what ice was, and as the Mugger and the Jackal knew rather less, the tale missed fire.

'Anything,' said the Mugger, shutting his left eye again – '*anything* is possible that comes out of a boat thrice the size of Mugger-Ghaut. My village is not a small one.'

There was a whistle overhead on the bridge, and the Delhi Mail slid across, all the carriages gleaming with light, and the shadows faithfully following along the river. It clanked away into the dark again; but the Mugger and the Jackal were so well used to it that they never turned their heads.

'Is that anything less wonderful than a boat thrice the size of Mugger-Ghaut?' said the bird, looking up.

'I saw that built, child. Stone by stone I saw the bridge-piers rise, and when the men fell off (they were wondrous sure-footed for the most part – but *when* they fell) I was ready. After the first pier was made they never thought to look down the stream for the body to burn. There, again, I saved much trouble. There was nothing strange in the building of the bridge,' said the Mugger.

'But that which goes across, pulling the roofed carts, *that* is strange,' the Adjutant repeated.

'It is, past any doubt, a new breed of bullock. Some day it will not be able to keep its foothold up yonder, and will fall as the men did. The old Mugger will then be ready.'

The Jackal looked at the Adjutant, and the Adjutant looked at the Jackal. If there was one thing they were more certain of than another, it was that the engine was everything in the wide world except a bullock. The Jackal had watched it time and again from the aloe hedges at the side of the line, and the Adjutant had seen engines since the first engine ran in India. But the Mugger had only looked up at the thing from below, where the brass dome seemed rather like a bullock's hump.

'M— yes, a new kind of bullock,' the Mugger repeated ponderously, to make himself quite sure in his own mind; and 'Certainly it is a bullock,' said the Jackal.

'And again it might be—' began the Mugger pettishly.

'Certainly – most certainly,' said the Jackal, without waiting for the other to finish.

'What?' said the Mugger angrily, for he could feel that the others knew more than he did. 'What might it be? *I* never finished my words. You said it was a bullock.'

'It is anything the Protector of the Poor pleases. I am *his* servant – not the servant of the thing that crosses the river.'

'Whatever it is, it is white-face work,' said the Adjutant; 'and for my own part, I would not lie out upon a place so near to it as this bar.'

'You do not know the English as I do,' said the Mugger. 'There was a white-face here when the bridge was built, and he would take a boat in the evenings and shuffle with his feet on the bottom-boards, and whisper: "Is he here? Is he there? Bring me my gun." I could hear him before I could see him – each sound that he made – creaking and puffing and rattling his gun, up and down the river. As surely as I had picked up one of his workmen, and thus saved great charges in wood for the burning, so surely would he come down to the Ghaut, and shout in a loud voice that he would hunt me, and rid the river of me – the Mugger of Mugger-Ghaut! *Me!* Children, I have swum under the bottom of his boat for hour after hour, and heard him fire his gun at logs; and when I was well sure he was wearied, I have risen by his side and snapped my jaws in his face. When the bridge was finished he went away. All the English hunt in that fashion; except when they are hunted.'

'Who hunts the white-faces?' yapped the Jackal, excitedly.

'No one now, but I have hunted them in my time.'[17]

'I remember a little of that Hunting. I was young then,' said the Adjutant, clattering his beak significantly.

'I was well established here. My village was being built for the third time, as I remember, when my cousin, the Gavial, brought me word of rich waters above Benares. At first I would not go, for my cousin, who is a fish-eater, does not always know the good from the bad; but I heard my people talking in the evenings, and what they said made me certain.'

'And what did they say?' the Jackal asked.

'They said enough to make me, the Mugger of Mugger-Ghaut, leave water and take to my feet. I went by night, using the littlest streams as they served me; but it was the beginning of the hot weather and all streams were low. I crossed dusty roads; I went through tall grass; I climbed hills in the moonlight. Even rocks did I climb, children – consider this well! I crossed the tail of Sirhind, the waterless,[18] before I could find the set of the little rivers that flow Gungaward. I was a month's journey from my own people and the banks that I knew. That was very marvellous!'

'What food on the way?' said the Jackal, who kept his soul in his little stomach, and was not a bit impressed by the Mugger's land travels.

'That which I could find – *cousin*,' said the Mugger slowly, dragging each word.

Now you do not call a man a cousin in India unless you think you can establish some kind of blood-relationship; and as it is only in old fairy-tales that the Mugger ever marries a jackal, the Jackal knew for what reason he had been suddenly lifted into the Mugger's family circle.[19] If they had been alone he would not have cared, but the Adjutant's eyes twinkled with mirth at the ugly jest.

'Assuredly, Father, I might have known,' said the Jackal. A Mugger does not care to be called a father of jackals, and the Mugger of Mugger-Ghaut said as much – and a great deal more which there is no use in repeating here.

'The Protector of the Poor has claimed kinship. How can I remember the precise degree? Moreover, we eat the same food. He has said it,' was the Jackal's reply.

That made matters rather worse, for what the Jackal hinted at was that the Mugger must have eaten his food on that land-march fresh, and fresh every day, instead of keeping it by him till it was in a fit and proper condition, as every self-respecting mugger and most wild beasts do when they can. Indeed, one of the worst terms of contempt along the river-bed is 'eater of fresh meat'. It is nearly as bad as calling a man a cannibal.

'That food was eaten thirty seasons ago,' said the Adjutant, quietly. 'If we talk for thirty seasons more it will never come back. Tell us, now, what happened when the good waters were reached after thy most wonderful land-journey. If we listened to the howling of every jackal the business of the town would stop, as the saying is.'

The Mugger must have been grateful for the interruption, because he went on, with a rush:

'By the Right and Left of Gunga! when I came there never did I see such waters!'

'Were they better, then, than the big flood of last season?' said the Jackal.

'Better! That flood was no more than comes every five years – a handful of drowned strangers, some chickens, and a dead bullock in muddy water with cross-currents. But the season I think of, the river was low, smooth, and even, and, as the Gavial had warned me, the dead English came down, touching each other. I got my girth in that season – my girth and my depth. From Agra, by Etawah and the broad waters by Allahabad—'[20]

'Oh, the eddy that set under the walls of the fort at Allahabad!' said the Adjutant. 'They came in there like widgeon to the reeds, and round and round they swung – thus!'

He went off into his horrible dance again, while the Jackal looked on enviously. He naturally could not remember the terrible year of the Mutiny they were talking about. The Mugger continued:

'Yes, by Allahabad one lay still in the slack-water and let twenty go by to pick one; and, above all, the English were not cumbered with jewelry and nose-rings and anklets as my women are nowadays. To delight in ornaments is to end with a rope for necklace, as the saying is. All the muggers of all the rivers grew fat then, but it was my Fate to be fatter than them all. The news was that the English were being hunted into the rivers, and by the Right and Left of Gunga, we believed it was true! So far as I went south I believed it to be true, and I went down-stream beyond Monghyr and the tombs that look over the river.'

'I know that place,' said the Adjutant. 'Since those days Monghyr is a lost city. Very few live there now.'

'Thereafter I worked up-stream very slowly and lazily, and a little above Monghyr there came down a boatful of white-faces – alive! They were, as I remember, women, lying under a cloth spread over sticks, and crying aloud. There was never a gun fired at us watchers of the fords in those days. All the guns were busy elsewhere. We could hear them day and night inland, coming and going as the wind shifted. I rose up full before the boat, because I had never seen white-faces alive, though I knew them well – otherwise. A naked white child kneeled by the side of the boat, and stooping over, must needs try to trail his hands in the river. It is a pretty thing to see how a child loves running water. I had fed that day, but there was a little unfilled space within me. Still, it was for sport and not for food that I rose at the child's hands. They were so clear a mark that I did not even look when I closed; but they were so small that though my jaws rang true – I am sure of that – the child drew them up swiftly, unhurt. They must have passed between tooth and tooth – those small white hands. I should have caught him cross-wise at the elbows; but, as I said, it was only for sport and desire to see new things that I rose at all. They cried out one after another in the boat, and presently I rose again to watch them. The boat was too heavy to push over. They were only women, but he who trusts a woman will walk on duckweed in a pool, as the saying is: and by the Right and Left of Gunga! that is truth.'

'Once a woman gave me some dried skin from a fish,' said the Jackal. 'I had hoped to get her baby, but horse-food is better than the kick of a horse, as the saying is. What did thy woman do?'

'She fired at me with a short gun of a kind I have never seen before or since. Five times, one after another' (the Mugger must have met with an old-fashioned revolver); 'and I stayed open-mouthed and gaping, my head in the smoke. Never did I see such a thing. Five times, as swiftly as I wave my tail – thus!'

The Jackal, who had been growing more and more interested in the story, had just time to leap back as the huge tail swung by like a scythe.

'Not before the fifth shot,' said the Mugger, as though he had never dreamed of stunning one of his listeners – 'not before the fifth shot did I sink, and I rose in time to hear a boatman telling all those white women that I was most certainly dead. One bullet had gone under a neck-plate of mine. I know not if it is there still, for the reason I cannot turn my head. Look and see, child. It will show that my tale is true.'

'I?' said the Jackal. 'Shall an eater of old shoes, a bone-cracker, presume to doubt the word of the Envy of the River?

May my tail be bitten off by blind puppies if the shadow of such a thought has crossed my humble mind. The Protector of the Poor has condescended to inform me, his slave, that once in his life he has been wounded by a woman. That is sufficient, and I will tell the tale to all my children, asking for no proof.'

'Over-much civility is sometimes no better than over-much discourtesy; for, as the saying is, one can choke a guest with curds. I do *not* desire that any children of thine should know that the Mugger of Mugger-Ghaut took his only wound from a woman. They will have much else to think of if they get their meat as miserably as does their father.'

'It is forgotten long ago! It was never said! There never was a white woman! There was no boat! Nothing whatever happened at all.'

The Jackal waved his brush to show how completely everything was wiped out of his memory, and sat down with an air.

'Indeed, very many things happened,' said the Mugger, beaten in his second attempt that night to get the better of his friend. (Neither bore malice, however. Eat and be eaten was fair law along the river, and the Jackal came in for his share of plunder when the Mugger had finished a meal.) 'I left that boat and went up-stream, and, when I had reached Arrah[21] and the back-waters behind it, there were no more dead English. The river was empty for a while. Then came one or two dead, in red coats, not English,[22] but of one kind all – Hindus and Purbeeahs[23] – then five and six abreast, and at last, from Arrah to the North beyond Agra, it was as though whole villages had walked into the water. They came out of little creeks one after another, as the logs come down in the Rains. When the river rose they rose also in companies from the shoals they had rested upon; and the falling flood dragged them with it across the fields and through the Jungle by the long hair. All night, too, going North, I heard the guns, and by day the shod feet of men crossing fords, and that noise which a heavy cart-wheel makes on sand under water; and every ripple brought more dead. At last even I was afraid, for I said: "If this thing happens to men, how shall the Mugger of Mugger-Ghaut escape?" There were boats, too, that came up behind me without sails, burning continually, as the cotton-boats sometimes burn, but never sinking.'

'Ah!' said the Adjutant. 'Boats like those come to Calcutta of the South. They are tall and black, they beat up the water behind them with a tail, and they—'

'Are thrice as big as my village. *My* boats were low and white; they beat up the water on either side of them, and were no larger than the boats of one who speaks truth should be. They made me very afraid, and I left water and went back to this my river, hiding by day and walking by night, when I could not find little streams to help me. I came to my village again, but I did not hope to see any of my people there. Yet they were ploughing and sowing and reaping, and going to and fro in their fields as quietly as their own cattle.'

'Was there still good food in the river?' said the Jackal.

'More than I had any desire for. Even I – and I do not eat mud – even *I* was tired, and, as I remember, a little frightened of this constant coming down of the silent ones. I heard my people say in my village that all the English were dead; but those that came, face down, with the current were *not* English, as my people saw. Then my people said that it was best to say nothing at all, but to pay the tax and plough the land. After a long time the river cleared, and those that came down it had been clearly drowned by the floods, as I could well see; and, though it was not so easy then to get food, I was heartily glad. A little killing here and there is no bad thing – but even the Mugger is sometimes satisfied, as the saying is.'

'Mavellous! Most truly marvellous!' said the Jackal. 'I am become fat through merely hearing about so much good eating. And afterward what, if it be permitted to ask, did the Protector of the Poor do?'

'I said to myself – and by the Right and Left of Gunga! I locked my jaws on that vow – I said I would never go roving any more. So I lived by the Ghaut, very close to my own people, and I watched over them year after year; and they loved me so much that they threw marigold wreaths at my head whenever they saw it lift. Yes, and my Fate has been very kind to me, and all the River is good enough to respect my poor and infirm presence; only—'

'No one is all happy from his beak to his tail,' said the Adjutant, sympathetically. 'What does the Mugger of Mugger-Ghaut need more?'

'That little white child which I did not get,' said the Mugger, with a deep sigh. 'He was very small, but I have not forgotten. I am aged now, but before I die it is my desire to try one new thing. It is true they are a heavy-footed, noisy, and foolish people, and the sport would be small, but I remember the old days above Benares, and, if the child lives, he will remember still. It may be he goes up and down the bank of some river telling how he once passed his hands between the teeth of the Mugger of Mugger-Ghaut, and lived to make a tale of it. My Fate has been very kind, but that plagues me sometimes in my dreams – the thought of the little white child in the bows of that boat.' He yawned, and closed his jaws. 'And now I will rest and think. Keep silent, my children, and respect the aged.'

He turned stiffly, and shuffled to the top of the sand-bar, while the Jackal drew back with the Adjutant to the shelter of a tree stranded on the end nearest the railway bridge.

'That was a pleasant and profitable life,' he grinned, looking up inquiringly at the bird who towered above him. 'And not once, mark you, did he think fit to tell me where a morsel might have been left along the banks. Yet I have told *him* a hundred times of good things wallowing down-stream. How true is the saying, "All the world forgets the Jackal and the barber when the news has been told!" Now he is going to sleep! *Arrah!*'

'How can a Jackal hunt with a Mugger?' said the Adjutant, coolly. 'Big thief and little thief; it is easy to say who gets the pickings.'

The Jackal turned, whining impatiently, and was going to curl himself up under the tree-trunk, when suddenly he cowered, and looked up through the draggled branches at the bridge almost above his head.

'What now?' said the Adjutant, opening one wing uneasily.

'Wait till we see. The wind blows from us to them, but they are not looking for us – those two men.'

'Men, is it? My office protects me. All India knows I am holy.' The Adjutant, being a first-class scavenger, is allowed to go where he pleases, and so this one never flinched.

'I am not worth a blow from anything better than an old shoe,' said the Jackal, and listened again. 'Hark to that foot-fall!' he went on. 'That was no country leather, but the shod foot of a white-face. Listen again! Iron hits iron up there! It is a gun! Friend, those heavy-footed, foolish English are coming to speak with the Mugger.'

'Warn him, then. He was called Protector of the Poor by someone not unlike a starving Jackal but a little time ago.'

'Let my cousin protect his own hide. He has told me again and again there is nothing to fear from the white-faces. They must be white-faces. Not a villager of Mugger-Ghaut would dare to come after him. See, I said it was a gun! Now, with good luck, we shall feed before daylight. He cannot hear well out of water, and – this time it is not a woman!'

A shiny barrel glittered for a minute in the moonlight on the girders. The Mugger was lying on the sand-bar as still as his own shadow, his forefeet spread out a little, his head dropped between them, snoring like a – mugger.

A voice on the bridge whispered: 'It's an odd shot – straight down almost – but as safe as houses. Better try behind the neck. Golly! what a brute! The villagers will be wild if he's shot, though. He's the *deota* (godling) of these parts.'

'I don't care a rap,' another voice answered. 'He took about fifteen of my best coolies while the bridge was building, and it's time he was put an end to. I've been after him in a boat for weeks. Stand by with the Martini[24] as soon as I've given him both barrels of this.'

'Mind the kick, then. A double four-bore's no joke.'

'That's for him to decide. Here goes!'

There was a roar like the sound of a small cannon (the biggest sort of elephant-rifle is not very different from some artillery), and a double streak of flame, followed by the sting-ing crack of a Martini, whose long bullet makes nothing of a crocodile's plates. But the explosive bullets did the work. One of them struck just behind the Mugger's neck, a hand's breadth to the left of the backbone, while the other burst a little lower down, at the beginning of the tail. In ninety-nine cases out of a hundred a mortally-wounded crocodile can scramble off for deep water and get away; but the Mugger of Mugger-Ghaut was literally broken into three pieces. He hardly moved his head before the life went out of him, and he lay as flat as the Jackal.

'Thunder and lightning! Lightning and thunder!' said that miserable little beast. 'Has the thing that pulls the covered carts over the bridge tumbled at last?'

'It is no more than a gun,' said the Adjutant, though his very tail-feathers quivered. 'Nothing more than a gun. He is certainly dead. Here come the white-faces.'

The two Englishmen had hurried down from the bridge and across to the sand-bar, where they stood admiring the length of the Mugger. Then a native with an axe cut off the big head, and four men dragged it across the spit.

'The last time that I had my hand in a Mugger's mouth,' said one of the Englishmen, stooping down (he was the man who had built the bridge),[25] 'it was when I was about five years old – coming down the river by boat to Monghyr. I was a Mutiny baby, as they call it. Poor mother was in the boat, too, and she often told me how she fired dad's old pistol at the beast's head.'

'Well, you've certainly had your revenge on the chief of the clan – even if the gun has made your nose bleed. Hi, you boatmen! Haul that head up the bank, and we'll boil it for the skull. The skin's too knocked about to keep. Come along to bed now. This was worth sitting up all night for, wasn't it?'

Curiously enough, the Jackal and the Adjutant made the very same remark not three minutes after the men had left.

A Ripple Song

Once a ripple came to land
   In the golden sunset burning –
Lapped against a maiden's hand,
   By the ford returning.

Dainty foot and gentle breast –
Safe across[1] be glad and rest.
'Maiden, wait,' the ripple saith;
'Wait awhile, for I am Death!'

'Where my lover calls I go –
   Shame it were to treat him coldly –
'Twas a fish that circled so,
   Turning over boldly.'

Dainty foot and tender heart,
Wait the loaded ferry-cart.
'Wait, ah, wait!' the ripple saith;
'Maiden, wait, for I am Death!'

'When my lover calls I haste –
   Dame Disdain was never wedded!'
Ripple-ripple round her waist,
   Clear the current eddied.

Foolish heart and faithful hand,
Little feet that touched no land.
Far away the ripple fled,
Ripple – ripple – running red!

THE KING'S ANKUS

These are the Four that are never content: that have never
   been filled since the Dews began –
Jacala's mouth, and the glut of the Kite, and the hands of the
   Ape and the Eyes of Man.

Jungle Saying[1]

Kaa, the big rock-python, had changed his skin for perhaps the
two hundredth time[2] since his birth; and Mowgli, who never
forgot that he owed his life to Kaa for a night's work at Cold
Lairs,[3] which you may perhaps remember, went to congratulate
him. Skin-changing always makes a snake moody and depressed
till the new skin begins to shine and look beautiful. Kaa never
made sport of Mowgli any more, but accepted him, as the other
Jungle People did, for the Master of the Jungle, and brought
him all the news that a python of his size would naturally hear.
What Kaa did not know about the Middle Jungle, as they call
it – the life that runs close to the earth or under it, the boulder,
burrow, and the tree-bole life – might have been written upon
the smallest of his scales.

That afternoon Mowgli was sitting in the circle of Kaa's
great coils, fingering the flaked and broken old skin that lay all
looped and twisted among the rocks just as Kaa had left it. Kaa
had very courteously packed himself under Mowgli's broad,
bare shoulders, so that the boy was really resting in a living
arm-chair.

'Even to the scales of the eyes it is perfect,' said Mowgli,
under his breath, playing with the old skin. 'Strange to see the
covering of one's own head at one's own feet.'

'Ay, but I lack feet,' said Kaa; 'and since this is the custom of
all my people, I do not find it strange. Does thy skin never feel
old and harsh?'

'Then go I and wash, Flathead; but, it is true, in the great heats I have wished I could slough my skin without pain, and run skinless.'

'I wash, and *also* I take off my skin. How looks the new coat?'

Mowgli ran his hand down the diagonal checkerings of the immense back. 'The Turtle is harder-backed, but not so gay,' he said judgmatically. 'The Frog, my name-bearer, is more gay, but not so hard. It is very beautiful to see – like the mottling in the mouth of a lily.'

'It needs water. A new skin never comes to full colour before the first bath. Let us go bathe.'

'I will carry thee,' said Mowgli; and he stooped down, laughing, to lift the middle section of Kaa's great body, just where the barrel was thickest. A man might just as well have tried to heave up a two-foot water-main; and Kaa lay still, puffing with quiet amusement. Then their regular evening game began – the Boy in the flush of his great strength, and the Python in his sumptuous new skin, standing up one against the other for a wrestling match – a trial of eye and strength. Of course, Kaa could have crushed a dozen Mowglis had he let himself go; but he played carefully, and never loosed one-tenth of his power. Ever since Mowgli was strong enough to endure a little rough handling, Kaa had taught him this game, and it suppled his limbs as nothing else could. Sometimes Mowgli would stand lapped almost to his throat in Kaa's shifting coils, striving to get one arm free and catch him by the throat. Then Kaa would give way limply, and Mowgli, with both quick-moving feet, would try to cramp the purchase of that huge tail as it flung backward feeling for a rock or a stump. They would rock to and fro, head to head, each waiting for his chance, till the beautiful, statue-like group melted in a whirl of black-and-yellow coils and struggling legs and arms, to rise up again and again. 'Now! now! now!' said Kaa, making feints with his head that even Mowgli's quick hand could not turn aside. 'Look! I touch thee here, Little Brother! Here, and here! Are thy hands numb? Here again!'

The game always ended in one way – with a straight, driving

blow of the head that knocked the boy over and over. Mowgli could never learn the guard for that lightning lunge, and, as Kaa said, there was not the least use in trying.

'Good hunting!' Kaa grunted at last; and Mowgli, as usual, was shot away half a dozen yards, gasping and laughing. He rose with his fingers full of grass, and followed Kaa to the wise snake's pet bathing-place – a deep, pitchy-black pool surrounded with rocks, and made interesting by sunken tree-stumps. The boy slipped in, Jungle-fashion, without a sound, and dived across; rose, too, without a sound, and turned on his back, his arms behind his head, watching the moon rising above the rocks, and breaking up her reflection in the water with his toes. Kaa's diamond-shaped head cut the pool like a razor, and came out to rest on Mowgli's shoulder. They lay still, soaking luxuriously in the cool water.

'It is *very* good,' said Mowgli at last, sleepily. 'Now, in the Man-Pack, at this hour, as I remember, they laid them down upon hard pieces of wood in the inside of a mud-trap, and, having carefully shut out all the clean winds, drew foul cloth over their heavy heads, and made evil songs through their noses. It is better in the Jungle.'

A hurrying cobra slipped down over a rock and drank, gave them 'Good hunting!' and went away.

'Sssh!' said Kaa, as though he had suddenly remembered something. 'So the Jungle gives thee all that thou hast ever desired, Little Brother?'

'Not all,' said Mowgli, laughing; 'else there would be a new and strong Shere Khan to kill once a moon. *Now*, I could kill with my own hands, asking no help of buffaloes. And also I have wished the sun to shine in the middle of the Rains, and the Rains to cover the sun in the deep of summer; and also I have never gone empty but I wished that I had killed a goat; and also I have never killed a goat but I wished it had been buck; nor buck but I wished it had been nilghai. But thus do we feel, all of us.'

'Thou hast no other desire?' the big snake demanded.

'What more can I wish? I have the Jungle, and the Favour of the Jungle! Is there more between sunrise and sunset?'

'Now, the Cobra said—' Kaa began.

'What cobra? He that went away just now said nothing. He was hunting.'

'It was another.'

'Hast thou many dealings with the Poison People? I give them their own path. They carry death in the fore-tooth, and that is not good – for they are so small. But what hood is this thou hast spoken with?'

Kaa rolled slowly in the water like a steamer in a beam sea. 'Three or four moons since,' said he, 'I hunted in Cold Lairs, which place, may be, thou hast not forgotten. And the thing I hunted fled shrieking past the tanks and to that house whose side I once broke for thy sake, and ran into the ground.'

'But the people of Cold Lairs do not live in burrows.' Mowgli knew that Kaa was talking of the Monkey People.

'This thing was not living, but seeking to live,' Kaa replied, with a quiver of his tongue. 'He ran into a burrow that led very far. I followed, and having killed, I slept. When I waked I went forward.'

'Under earth?'

'Even so. Coming at last upon a White Hood (a white cobra), who spoke of things beyond my knowledge, and showed me many things I had never before seen.'

'New game? Was it good hunting?' Mowgli turned quickly on his side.

'It was no game, and would have broken all my teeth; but the White Hood said that a man – he spoke as one that knew the breed – that a man would give the hot breath under his ribs for only the sight of those things.'

'We will look,' said Mowgli. 'I now remember that I was once a man.'

'Slowly – slowly. It was haste killed the Yellow Snake that ate the sun. We two spoke together under the earth, and I spoke of thee, naming thee as a man. Said the White Hood (and he is indeed as old as the Jungle): "It is long since I have seen a man. Let him come, and he shall see all these things, for the least of which very many men would die." '

'That *must* be new game. And yet the Poison People do not tell us when game is afoot. They are unfriendly folk.'

'It is *not* game. It is – it is – I cannot say what it is.'

'We will go there. I have never seen a White Hood, and I wish to see the other things. Did he kill them?'

'They are all dead things. He says he is the keeper of them all.'

'Ah! As a wolf stands above meat he has taken to his own lair. Let us go.'

Mowgli swam to bank, rolled in the grass to dry himself, and the two set off for Cold Lairs, the deserted city of which you may have heard.[3] Mowgli was not in the least afraid of the Monkey People in those days, but the Monkey People had the liveliest horror of Mowgli. Their tribes, however, were raiding in the Jungle, and so Cold Lairs stood empty and silent in the moonlight. Kaa led up to the ruins of the queen's pavilion that stood on the terrace, slipped over the rubbish, and dived down the half-choked staircase that went underground from the centre of the pavilion. Mowgli gave the Snake-call – 'We be of one blood, ye and I' – and followed on his hands and knees. They crawled a long distance down a sloping passage that turned and twisted several times, and at last came to where the root of some great tree, growing thirty feet overhead, had forced out a solid stone in the wall. They crept through the gap, and found themselves in a large vault, whose domed roof had been also broken away by tree-roots so that a few streaks of light dropped down into the darkness.

'A safe lair,' said Mowgli, rising to his firm feet, 'but over-far to visit daily. And now what do we see?'

'Am I nothing?' said a voice in the middle of the vault; and Mowgli saw something white move, till, little by little, there stood up the hugest cobra he had ever set eyes on – a creature nearly eight feet long, and bleached by being in darkness to an old ivory-white. Even the spectacle marks of his spread hood had faded to a faint yellow. His eyes were as red as rubies, and altogether he was most wonderful to see.

'Good hunting!' said Mowgli, who carried his manners with his knife, and that never left him.

'What of the city?' said the White Cobra, without answering the greeting. 'What of the great, the walled city – the city of an hundred elephants and twenty thousand horses, and cattle past counting – the city of the King of Twenty Kings? I grow deaf here, and it is long since I heard the war-gongs.'

'The Jungle is above our heads,' said Mowgli. 'I know only Hathi and his sons among elephants. Bagheera has slain all the horses in one village, and – what is a King?'

'I told thee,' said Kaa softly to the Cobra – 'I told thee, four moons ago, that thy city was not.'

'The city – the great city of the forest whose gates are guarded by the King's towers – can never pass. They built it before my father's father came from the egg, and it shall endure when my sons' sons are as white as I. Salomdhi, son of Chandrabija, son of Viyeja, son of Yegasuri, built it in the days of Bappa Rawal.[4] Whose cattle are *ye*?'

'It is a lost trail,' said Mowgli, turning to Kaa. 'I know not his talk.'

'Nor I. He is very old. Father of Cobras, there is only the Jungle here, as it has been since the beginning.'

'Then who is *he*,' said the White Cobra, 'sitting down before me, unafraid, knowing not the name of the King, talking our talk through a man's lips? Who is he with the knife and the snake's tongue?'

'Mowgli they call me,' was the answer. 'I am of the Jungle. The Wolves are my people, and Kaa here is my brother. Father of Cobras, who art thou?'

'I am the Warden of the King's Treasure. Kurrun Raja built the stone above me, in the days when my skin was dark, that I might teach death to those who came to steal. Then they let down the treasure through the stone, and I heard the song of the Brahmins my masters.'

'Umm!' said Mowgli to himself. 'I have dealt with one Brahmin already, in the Man-Pack, and – I know what I know. Evil comes here in a little.'

'Five times since my wardship has the stone been lifted, but always to let down more, and never to take away. There are no riches like these riches – the treasures of an hundred kings. But it is long and long since the stone was last moved, and I think that my city has forgotten.'

'There is no city. Look up. Yonder are the roots of the great trees tearing the stones apart. Trees and men do not grow together,' Kaa insisted.

'Twice and thrice have men found their way here,' the White Cobra answered savagely; 'but they never spoke till I came upon them groping in the dark, and then they cried only a little time. But *ye* come with lies, Man and Snake both, and would have me believe that my city is not, and that my wardship ends. Little do men change in the years. But *I* change never! Till the stone is lifted, and the Brahmins come down singing the songs that I know, and feed me with warm milk, and take me to the light again, I – I – *I*, and no other, am the Warden of the King's Treasure! The city is dead, ye say, and here are the roots of the trees? Stoop down, then, and take what ye will. Earth has no treasure like these. Man with the snake's tongue, if thou canst go alive by the way that thou hast entered at, the lesser kings will be thy servants!'

'Again the trail is lost,' said Mowgli, coolly. 'Can any jackal have burrowed so deep and bitten this great White Hood? He is surely mad. Father of Cobras, I see nothing here to take away.'

'By the Gods of the Sun and Moon, it is the madness of death upon the boy!' hissed the cobra. 'Before thine eyes close I will allow thee this favour. Look thou, and see what man has never seen before!'

'They do not well in the Jungle who speak to Mowgli of favours,' said the boy, between his teeth; 'but the dark changes all, as I know. I will look, if that please thee.'

He stared with puckered-up eyes round the vault, and then lifted up from the floor a handful of something that glittered.

'Oho!' said he, 'this is like the stuff they play with in the Man-Pack: only this is yellow and the other was brown.'

He let the gold pieces fall, and moved forward. The floor of the vault was buried some five or six feet deep in coined gold and silver that had burst from the sacks it had been originally stored in, and, in the long years, the metal had packed and settled as sand packs at low tide. On it and in it, and rising through it, as wrecks lift through the sand, were jewelled elephant-howdahs[5] of embossed silver, studded with plates of hammered gold, and adorned with carbuncles and turquoises. There were palanquins and litters for carrying queens, framed and braced with silver and enamel, with jade-handled poles and amber curtain-rings; there were golden candlesticks hung with pierced emeralds that quivered on the branches; there were studded images, five feet high, of forgotten gods, silver with jewelled eyes; there were coats of mail, gold inlaid on steel, and fringed with rotted and blackened seed-pearls; there were helmets, crested and beaded with pigeon's-blood rubies; there were shields of lacquer, of tortoise-shell and rhinoceros-hide, strapped and bossed with red gold and set with emeralds at the edge; there were sheaves of diamond-hilted swords, daggers, and hunting-knives; there were golden sacrificial bowls and ladles, and portable altars of a shape that never sees the light of day; there were jade cups and bracelets; there were incense-burners, combs, and pots for perfume, henna, and eye-powder, all in embossed gold; there were nose-rings, armlets, headbands, finger-rings, and girdles past any counting; there were belts seven fingers broad, of square-cut diamonds and rubies, and wooden boxes, trebly clamped with iron, from which the wood had fallen away in powder, showing the pile of uncut star-sapphires, opals, cat's-eyes, sapphires, rubies, diamonds, emeralds, and garnets within.

The White Cobra was right. No mere money would begin to pay the value of this treasure, the sifted pickings of centuries of war, plunder, trade, and taxation. The coins alone were priceless, leaving out of count all the precious stones; and the dead weight of the gold and silver alone might be two or three hundred tons. Every native ruler in India today, however poor, has a hoard to which he is always adding; and, though once in a long while some enlightened prince may send off forty or fifty bullock-cart loads of silver to be exchanged for Government securities, the bulk of them keep their treasure and the knowledge of it very closely to themselves.

But Mowgli naturally did not understand what these things meant. The knives interested him a little, but they did not balance as well as his own, and so he dropped them. At last he found something really fascinating laid on the front of a how-dah half buried in the coins. It was a two-foot ankus, or elephant-goad – something like a small boat-hook. The top was one round shining ruby, and eight inches of the handle below it were studded with rough turquoises close together, giving a most satisfactory grip. Below them was a rim of jade with a flower-pattern running round it – only the leaves were emeralds, and the blossoms were rubies sunk in the cool, green stone. The rest of the handle was a shaft of pure ivory, while the point – the spike and hook – was gold-inlaid steel with pictures of elephant-catching: and the pictures attracted Mowgli, who saw that they had something to do with his friend Hathi.

The White Cobra had been following him closely.

'Is it not worth dying to behold?' he said. 'Have I not done thee a great favour?'

'I do not understand,' said Mowgli. 'The things are hard and cold, and by no means good to eat. But this' – he lifted the ankus – 'I desire to take away, that I may see it in the sun. Thou sayest they are all thine. Wilt thou give it to me, and I will bring thee frogs to eat?'

The White Cobra fairly shook with evil delight. 'Assuredly I will give it,' he said. 'All that is here I will give thee – till thou goest away.'

'But I go now. This place is dark and cold, and I wish to take the thorn-pointed thing to the Jungle.'

'Look by thy foot! What is that there?'

Mowgli picked up something white and smooth. 'It is the bone of a man's head,' he said quietly. 'And here are two more.'

'They came to take the treasure away many years ago. I spoke to them in the dark, and they lay still.'

'But what do I need of this that is called treasure? If thou wilt give me the ankus to take away, it is good hunting. If not, it is good hunting none the less. I do not fight with the Poison People, and I was also taught the Master-word of thy tribe.'

'There is but one Master-word here. It is mine!'

Kaa flung himself forward with blazing eyes. 'Who bade me bring the Man?' he hissed.

'I surely,' the old Cobra lisped. 'It is long since I have seen Man, and this Man speaks our tongue.'

'But there was no talk of killing. How can I go to the Jungle and say that I have led him to his death?' said Kaa.

'I talk not of killing till the time. And as to thy going or not going, there is the hole in the wall. Peace, now, thou fat monkey-killer! I have but to touch thy neck, and the Jungle will know thee no longer. Never Man came here that went away with the breath under his ribs. I am the Warden of the Treasure of the King's City!'

'But, thou white worm of the dark, I tell thee there is neither king nor city! The Jungle is all about us!' cried Kaa.

'There is still the Treasure. But this can be done. Wait a while, Kaa of the Rocks, and see the boy run. There is room for great sport here. Life is good. Run to and fro a while, and make sport, boy!'

Mowgli put his hand on Kaa's head quietly.

'The white thing has dealt with men of the Man-Pack until now. He does not know me,' he whispered. 'He has asked for this hunting. Let him have it.' Mowgli had been standing with the ankus held point down. He flung it from him quickly, and it dropped crossways just behind the great snake's hood, pinning him to the floor. In a flash, Kaa's weight was upon the writhing body, paralysing it from hood to tail. The red eyes burned, and the six spare inches of the head struck furiously right and left.

'Kill!' said Kaa, as Mowgli's hand went to his knife.

'No,' he said, as he drew the blade; 'I will never kill again save for food. But look you, Kaa!' He caught the snake behind the hood, forced the mouth open with the blade of the knife, and showed the terrible poison-fangs of the upper jaw lying black and withered in the gum. The White Cobra had outlived his poison, as a snake will. '*Thuu*'[6] ('It is dried up'),* said Mowgli; and motioning Kaa away, he picked up the ankus, setting the White Cobra free.

'The King's Treasure needs a new Warden,' he said gravely.

---

* Literally, a rotted out tree-stump.

'Thuu, thou hast not done well. Run to and fro and make sport, Thuu!'

'I am shamed. Kill me!' hissed the White Cobra.

'There has been too much talk of killing. We will go now. I take the thorn-pointed thing, Thuu, because I have fought and worsted thee.'

'See, then, that the thing does not kill thee at last. It is Death! Remember, it is Death! There is enough in that thing to kill the men of all my city. Not long wilt thou hold it, Jungle Man, nor he who takes it from thee. They will kill, and kill, and kill for its sake! My strength is dried up, but the ankus will do my work. It is Death! It is Death! It is Death!'

Mowgli crawled out through the hole into the passage again, and the last that he saw was the White Cobra striking furiously with his harmless fangs at the stolid golden faces of the gods that lay on the floor, and hissing, 'It is Death!'

They were glad to get to the light of day once more; and when they were back in their own Jungle and Mowgli made the ankus glitter in the morning light, he was almost as pleased as though he had found a bunch of new flowers to stick in his hair.

'This is brighter than Bagheera's eyes,' he said delightedly, as he twirled the ruby. 'I will show it to him; but what did the Thuu mean when he talked of death?'

'I cannot say. I am sorrowful to my tail's tail that he felt not thy knife. There is always evil at Cold Lairs – above ground and below. But now I am hungry. Dost thou hunt with me this dawn?' said Kaa.

'No; Bagheera must see this thing. Good hunting!' Mowgli danced off, flourishing the great ankus, and stopping from time to time to admire it, till he came to that part of the Jungle Bagheera chiefly used, and found him drinking after a heavy kill. Mowgli told him all his adventures from beginning to end, and Bagheera sniffed at the ankus between whiles. When Mowgli came to the White Cobra's last words, Bagheera purred approvingly.

'Then the White Hood spoke the thing which is?' Mowgli asked quickly.

'I was born in the King's cages at Oodeypore, and it is in my stomach that I know some little of Man. Very many men would kill thrice in a night for the sake of that one red stone alone.'

'But the stone makes it heavy to the hand. My little bright knife is better; and – see! the red stone is not good to eat. Then *why* would they kill?'

'Mowgli, go thou and sleep. Thou hast lived among men, and—'

'I remember. Men kill because they are not hunting; – for idleness and pleasure. Wake again, Bagheera. For what use was this thorn-pointed thing made?'

Bagheera half opened his eyes – he was very sleepy – with a malicious twinkle.

'It was made by men to thrust into the head of the Sons of Hathi, so that the blood should pour out. I have seen the like in the streets of Oodeypore, before our cages. That thing has tasted the blood of many such as Hathi.'

'But why do they thrust into the heads of elephants?'

'To teach them Man's Law. Having neither claws nor teeth, men make these things – and worse.'

'Always more blood when I come near, even to the things the Man-Pack have made!' said Mowgli disgustedly. He was a little tired of the weight of the ankus. 'If I had known this, I would not have taken it. First it was Messua's blood on the thongs, and now it is Hathi's. I will use it no more. Look!'

The ankus flew sparkling, and buried itself point down fifty yards away,[7] between the trees. 'So my hands are clean of Death,' said Mowgli, rubbing his hands on the fresh, moist earth. 'The Thuu said Death would follow me. He is old and white and mad.'

'White or black, or death or life, *I* am going to sleep, Little Brother. I cannot hunt all night and howl all day, as do some folk.'

Bagheera went off to a hunting-lair that he knew, about two miles off. Mowgli made an easy way for himself up a convenient tree, knotted three or four creepers together, and in less time than it takes to tell was swinging in a hammock fifty feet above ground. Though he had no positive objection to strong daylight, Mowgli followed the custom of his friends, and used it as little as he could. When he waked among the very loud-voiced peoples that live in the trees, it was twilight once more, and he had been dreaming of the beautiful pebbles he had thrown away.

'At least I will look at the thing again,' he said, and slid down a creeper to the earth; but Bagheera was before him. Mowgli could hear him snuffing in the half light.

'Where is the thorn-pointed thing?' cried Mowgli.

'A man has taken it. Here is his trail.'

'Now we shall see whether the Thuu spoke truth. If the pointed thing is Death, that man will die. Let us follow.'

'Kill first,' said Bagheera. 'An empty stomach makes a careless eye. Men go very slowly, and the Jungle is wet enough to hold the lightest mark.'

They killed as soon as they could, but it was nearly three hours before they finished their meat and drink and buckled down to the trail. The Jungle People know that nothing makes up for being hurried over your meals.

'Think you the pointed thing will turn in the man's hand and kill him?' Mowgli asked. 'The Thuu said it was Death.'

'We shall see when we find,' said Bagheera, trotting with his head low. 'It is single-foot' (he meant that there was only one man), 'and the weight of the thing has pressed his heel far into the ground.'

'Hai! This is as clear as summer lightning,' Mowgli answered; and they fell into the quick, choppy trail-trot in and out through the checkers of the moonlight, following the marks of those two bare feet.

'Now he runs swiftly,' said Mowgli. 'The toes are spread apart.' They went on over some wet ground. 'Now why does he turn aside here?'

'Wait!' said Bagheera, and flung himself forward with one superb bound as far as ever he could. The first thing to do when a trail ceases to explain itself is to cast forward without leaving your own confusing foot-marks on the ground. Bagheera turned as he landed, and faced Mowgli, crying, 'Here comes another trail to meet him. It is a smaller foot, this second trail, and the toes turn inward.'

Then Mowgli ran up and looked. 'It is the foot of a Gond hunter,' he said. 'Look! Here he dragged his bow on the grass. That is why the first trail turned aside so quickly. Big Foot hid from Little Foot.'

'That is true,' said Bagheera. 'Now, lest by crossing each other's tracks we foul the signs, let each take one trail. I am Big Foot, Little Brother, and thou art Little Foot, the Gond.'

Bagheera leaped back to the original trail, leaving Mowgli stooping above the curious in-toed track of the wild little man of the woods.

'Now,' said Bagheera, moving step by step along the chain of footprints, 'I, Big Foot, turn aside here. Now I hide me behind a rock and stand still, not daring to shift my feet. Cry thy trail, Little Brother.'

'Now, I, Little Foot, come to the rock,' said Mowgli, running up his trail. 'Now sit I down under the rock, leaning upon my right hand, and resting my bow between my toes. I wait long, for the mark of my feet is deep here.'

'I also,' said Bagheera, hidden behind the rock. 'I wait, resting the end of the thorn-pointed thing upon a stone. It slips, for here is a scratch upon the stone. Cry thy trail, Little Brother.'

'One, two twigs and a big branch are broken here,' said Mowgli, in an undertone. 'Now, how shall I cry *that*? Ah! It is plain now. I, Little Foot, go away making noises and tramplings so that Big Foot may hear me.' He moved away from the rock pace by pace among the trees, his voice rising in the distance as he approached a little cascade. 'I – go – far – away – to – where – the – noise – of – falling – water – covers – my – noise; and – here – I – wait. Cry thy trail, Bagheera, Big Foot!'

The panther had been casting in every direction to see how Big Foot's trail led away from behind the rock. Then he gave tongue.

'I come from behind the rock upon my knees, dragging the thorn-pointed thing. Seeing no one, I run. I, Big Foot, run swiftly. The trail is clear. Let each follow his own. I run!'

Bagheera swept on along the clearly-marked trail, and Mowgli followed the steps of the Gond. For a time there was silence in the Jungle.

'Where art thou, Little Foot?' cried Bagheera. Mowgli's voice answered him not fifty yards to the right.

'Um!' said the panther, with a deep cough. 'The two run side by side, drawing nearer!'

They raced on another half mile, always keeping about the same distance, till Mowgli, whose head was not so close to the ground as Bagheera's, cried: 'They have met. Good hunting – look! Here stood Little Foot, with his knee on a rock – and yonder is Big Foot.'

Not ten yards in front of them, stretched across a pile of broken rocks, lay the body of a villager of the district, a lean, small-feathered Gond arrow through his back and breast.

'Was the Thuu so old and so mad, Little Brother?' said Bagheera, gently. 'Here is one death, at least.'

'Follow on. But where is the drinker of elephant's blood – the red-eyed thorn?'

'Little Foot has it – perhaps. It is single-foot again now.'

The single trail of a light man who had been running quickly and bearing a burden on his left shoulder, held on round a long, low spur of dried grass, where each footfall seemed to the sharp eyes of the trackers marked in hot iron.

Neither spoke till the trail ran up to the ashes of a camp-fire hidden in a ravine.

'Again!' said Bagheera, checking as though he had been turned into stone.

The body of a little wizened Gond lay with its feet in the ashes, and Bagheera looked inquiringly at Mowgli.

'That was done with a bamboo,' said the boy, after one glance. 'I have used such a thing among the buffaloes when I served the Man-Pack. The Father of Cobras – I am sorrowful that I made a jest of him – knew the breed well, as I might have known. Said I not that men kill for idleness?'

'Indeed, they killed for the sake of red and blue stones,' Bagheera answered. 'Remember, *I* was in the King's cages at Oodeypore.'

'One, two, three, four tracks,' said Mowgli, stooping over the ashes. 'Four tracks of men with shod feet. They do not go so quickly as Gonds. Now, what evil had the little woodman done to them? See, they talked together, all five, standing up, before they killed him. Bagheera, let us go back. My stomach is heavy in me, and yet it dances up and down like an oriole's nest at the end of a branch.'

'It is no good hunting to leave game afoot. Follow!' said the panther. 'Those eight shod feet have not gone far.'

No more was said for fully an hour, as they took up the broad trail of the four men with shod feet.

It was clear, hot daylight now, and Bagheera said, 'I smell smoke.'

'Men are always more ready to eat than to run,' Mowgli answered, trotting in and out between the low scrub bushes of the new Jungle they were exploring. Bagheera, a little to his left, made an indescribable noise in his throat.

'Here is one that is done with feeding,' said he. A tumbled bundle of gay-coloured clothes lay under a bush, and round it was some spilt flour.

'That was done by the bamboo again,' said Mowgli. 'See! That white dust is what men eat. They have taken the kill from this one – he carried their food – and given him for a kill to Chil, the Kite.'

'It is the third,' said Bagheera.

'I will go with new, big frogs to the Father of Cobras, and feed him fat,' said Mowgli to himself. 'This drinker of elephant's blood is Death himself – but still I do not understand!'

'Follow!' said Bagheera.

They had not gone half a mile farther when they heard Ko, the Crow, singing a death-song in the top of a tamarisk under whose shade three men were lying. A half-dead fire smoked in the centre of the circle, beneath an iron plate which held a blackened and burned cake of unleavened bread. Close to the fire, and blazing in the sunshine, lay the ruby-and-turquoise ankus.

'The thing works quickly; all ends here,' said Bagheera. 'How did *these* die, Mowgli? There is no mark nor rub on any one.'

A Jungle-dweller gets to learn by experience as much as many doctors know of poisonous plants and berries. Mowgli

sniffed the smoke that came up from the fire, broke off a morsel of the blackened bread, tasted it, and spat it out again.

'Apple of Death,' he coughed. 'The first must have made it
ready in the food for *these*, who killed him, having first killed
the Gond.'

'Good hunting, indeed! The kills follow close,' said Bagheera.

'Apple of Death' is what the Jungle call thorn-apple or dhat-
ura, the readiest poison in all India.

'What now?' said the panther. 'Must thou and I kill each
other for yonder red-eyed slayer?'

'Can it speak?' said Mowgli in a whisper. 'Did I do it a
wrong when I threw it away? Between us two it can do no
wrong, for we do not desire what men desire. If it be left here,
it will assuredly continue to kill men one after another as fast
as nuts fall in a high wind. I have no love to men, but even I
would not have them die six in a night.'

'What matter? They are only men. They killed one another
and were well pleased,' said Bagheera. 'That first little woodman hunted well.'

'They are cubs none the less; and a cub will drown himself
to bite the moon's light on the water. The fault was mine,' said
Mowgli, who spoke as though he knew all about everything. 'I
will never again bring into the Jungle strange things – not
though they be as beautiful as flowers. This' – he handled the
ankus gingerly – 'goes back to the Father of Cobras. But first
we must sleep, and we cannot sleep near these sleepers. Also we
must bury *him*, lest he run away and kill another six. Dig me a
hole under that tree.'

'But, Little Brother,' said Bagheera, moving off to the spot,
'I tell thee it is no fault of the blood-drinker. The trouble is
with men.'

'All one,' said Mowgli. 'Dig the hole deep. When we wake
I will take him up and carry him back.'

Two nights later, as the White Cobra sat mourning in the darkness of the vault, ashamed, and robbed, and alone, the turquoise
ankus whirled through the hole in the wall, and clashed on the
floor of golden coins.

'Father of Cobras,' said Mowgli (he was careful to keep the other side of the wall), 'get thee a young and ripe one of thine own people to help thee guard the King's Treasure, so that no man may come away alive any more.'

'Ah-ha! It returns, then. I said the thing was Death. How comes it that thou art still alive?' the old Cobra mumbled, twining lovingly round the ankus-haft.

'By the Bull that bought me, I do not know! That thing has killed six times in a night. Let him go out no more.'

The Song of the Little Hunter

Ere Mor the Peacock flutters, ere the Monkey-People cry,
  Ere Chil the Kite swoops down a furlong sheer,
Through the Jungle very softly flits a shadow and a sigh –
  He is Fear, O Little Hunter, he is Fear!
Very softly down the glade runs a waiting, watching shade,
  And the whisper spreads and widens far and near;
And the sweat is on thy brow, for he passes even now –
  He is Fear, O Little Hunter, he is Fear!

Ere the moon has climbed the mountain, ere the rocks are
      ribbed with light,
  When the downward-dipping tails are dank and drear,
Comes a breathing hard behind thee, *snuffle-snuffle* through
      the night –
  It is Fear, O Little Hunter, it is Fear!
On thy knees and draw the bow; bid the shrilling arrow go;
  In the empty mocking thicket plunge the spear;
But thy hands are loosed and weak, and the blood has left thy
      cheek –
  It is Fear, O Little Hunter, it is Fear!

When the heat-cloud sucks the tempest, when the slivered
      pine trees fall,
  When the blinding, blaring rain-squalls lash and veer;
Through the trumpets of the thunder rings a voice more loud
      than all –
  It is Fear, O Little Hunter, it is Fear!
Now the spates are banked and deep; now the footless
      boulders leap;
  Now the lightning shows each littlest leaf-rib clear,
But thy throat is shut and dried, and thy heart against thy side
  Hammers: Fear, O Little Hunter – this is Fear!

QUIQUERN

The People of the Eastern Ice, they are melting like the snow –
They beg for coffee and sugar; they go where the white men go.
The People of the Western Ice, they learn to steal and fight:
They sell their furs to the trading-post: they sell their soul to the white.

The People of the southern Ice, they trade with the whaler's crew;
Their women have many ribbons, but their tents are torn and few.
But the People of the Elder Ice, beyond the white man's ken –
Their spears are made of the narwhal[1] horn, and they are the last of
    the Men.

Translation

'He has opened his eyes. Look!'

'Put him in the skin again. He will be a strong dog. On the fourth month we will name him.'

'For whom?' said Amoraq.

Kadlu's eye rolled round the skin-lined snow-house till it came to fourteen year old Kotuko sitting on the sleeping-bench, making a button out of walrus ivory. 'Name him for me,' said Kotuko, with a grin. 'I shall need him one day.'

Kadlu grinned back till his eyes were almost buried in the fat of his flat cheeks, and nodded to Amoraq, while the puppy's fierce mother whined to see her baby wriggling far from reach in the little sealskin pouch hung above the warmth of the blubber-lamp.[2] Kotuko went on with his carving, and Kadlu threw a rolled bundle of leather dog-harnesses into a tiny little room that opened from one side of the house, slipped off his heavy deerskin hunting-suit, put it into a whalebone net that hung above another lamp, and dropped down on the sleeping-bench to whittle at a piece of frozen seal-meat till Amoraq, his wife, should bring the regular dinner of boiled meat and blood-soup. He had been out since early dawn at the seal-holes eight miles away, and had come home with three big seal. Half way down the long low snow passage or tunnel that led to the inner door of the house you could hear snappings and yelpings, as the dogs of his sleigh-team, released from the day's work, scuffled for warm places.

When the yelpings grew too loud Kotuko lazily rolled off the sleeping-bench and picked up a whip with an eighteen-inch handle of springy whalebone, and twenty-five feet of heavy plaited thong. He dived into the passage, where it sounded as though all the dogs were eating him alive; but that was no more than their regular grace before meals. When he crawled out at the far end, half a dozen furry heads followed him with their eyes as he went to a sort of gallows of whale jawbones, from which the dog's meat was hung; split off the frozen stuff in big lumps with a broad-headed spear; and waited, his whip in one hand and the meat in the other. Each beast was called by name – the weakest first, and woe betide any dog that moved out of his turn, for the tapering lash would shoot out like thonged lightning and flick away an inch or so of hair and hide. Each beast simply growled, snapped once, choked over his portion, and hurried back to the passage, while the boy stood up on the snow under the blazing Northern Lights[3] and dealt out justice. The last to be served was the big black leader of the team, who kept order when the dogs were harnessed, and to him Kotuko gave a double allowance of meat as well as an extra crack of the whip.

'Ah!' said Kotuko, coiling up the lash, 'I have a little one over the lamp that will make a great many howlings. *Sarpok!* Get in!'

He crawled back over the huddled dogs, dusted the dry snow from his furs with the whalebone beater that Amoraq kept by the door, tapped the skin-lined roof of the house to shake off any icicles that might have fallen from the dome of snow above, and curled up on the bench. The dogs in the passage snored and whined in their sleep, the boy-baby in Amoraq's deep fur hood kicked and choked and gurgled, and the mother of the newly-named puppy lay at Kotuko's side, her eyes fixed on the bundle of sealskin, warm and safe above the broad yellow flame of the lamp.

And all this happened far away to the north, beyond Labrador; beyond Hudson's Strait where the great tides throw the ice about – north of Melville Peninsula – north even of the narrow Fury and Hecla Straits – on the north shore of Baffin Land where Bylot's Island stands above the ice of Lancaster Sound like a pudding-bowl wrong side up. North of Lancaster Sound there is little we know anything about, except North Devon and Ellesmere Land;[4] but even there live a few scattered people, next door, as it were, to the very Pole.

Kadlu was an Inuit – what you call an Esquimau[5] – and his tribe, some thirty persons, all told, belonged to the Tununirmiut[6] – 'the country lying at the back of something'. On the maps that desolate coast is written Navy Board Inlet,[7] but the Inuit name is best because that country lies at the very back of everything in the world. For nine months of the year there is only ice and snow and gale after gale; with a cold no one can realize who has never seen the thermometer go down even to zero. For six months of those nine it is dark, and that is what makes it so horrible. In the three months of summer it only freezes every other day and every night, and then the snow begins to weep away from the southerly slopes, and a few ground-willows put out their woolly buds, a tiny stonecrop or so makes believe to blossom; beaches of fine gravel and rounded stones run down to the open sea, and polished boulders and streaked rocks lift up above the granulated snow. But all that goes in a few weeks, and the wild winter locks down again on the land; while at sea the ice tears up and down the offing, jamming and ramming, and splitting and hitting, and pounding and grounding till it all freezes together, ten feet thick, from the shore outward to deep water.

In the winter Kadlu would follow the seal to the edge of this land-ice and spear them as they came up to breathe at their blow holes. The seal must have open sea-water to live and catch fish in, and the ice would sometimes run eighty miles without a break from the nearest land. In the spring he and his people retreated from the thawing ice to the rocky mainland, where they put up tents of skins and snared the sea-birds, or speared the young seal basking on the beaches. Later, they would go south into Baffin Land after the reindeer and to get their year's store of salmon from the hundreds of streams and lakes of the interior; coming back north in September or October for the musk-ox[8] hunting and the regular winter sealery. This travelling was done with dog-sleighs, twenty and thirty miles a day, or sometimes down the coast in big skin 'woman-boats',[9] when the dogs and the babies lay among the feet of the rowers, and the women sang songs as they glided from cape to cape over the glassy, cold waters. All the luxuries that the Tununirmiut knew came from the south – drift-wood for sleigh-runners, rod-iron for harpoon-tips, steel knives, tin kettles that cooked food much better than the old soapstone affairs,[10] flint and steel, and even matches, coloured ribbons for the women's hair, little cheap mirrors and red cloth for the edging of deerskin dress-jackets. Kadlu traded the rich, creamy, twisted narwhal horn and musk-ox teeth (these are just as valuable as pearls[11]) to the Southern Inuit, and they in turn traded with the whalers and the missionary posts of Exeter and Cumberland Sounds;[12] and so the chain went on till a kettle picked up by a ship's cook in the Bhendy Bazaar[13] might end its days over a blubber lamp somewhere on the cool side of the Arctic Circle.

Kadlu being a good hunter was rich in iron harpoons, snow-knives, bird-darts and all the other things that make life easy up there in the great cold, and he was the head of his tribe, or, as they say, 'the man who knows all about it by practice'.[14] This did not give him any authority, except now and then he could advise his friends to change their hunting-grounds; but Kotuko used it to domineer a little, in the lazy fat Inuit fashion, over the other boys when they came out at night to play ball in the moonlight, or to sing The Child's Song to the Aurora Borealis.

But at fourteen an Inuit feels himself a man, and Kotuko was tired of making snares for wild-fowl and kit-foxes,[15] and very tired of helping the women to chew seal- and deer-skins (that supples them as nothing else can) the long day through while the men were out hunting. He wanted to go into the *quaggi*, the Singing-House, when the hunters gathered there for their mysteries, and the *angekok*, the sorcerer, frightened them into the most delightful fits after the lamps were put out, and you could hear the Spirit of the Reindeer stamping on the roof, and when a spear was thrust out into the open black night it came back covered with hot blood. He wanted to throw his big boots into the net with the tired air of the head of a family, and to gamble with the hunters when they dropped in of an evening and played a sort of home-made roulette with a tin pot and a nail. There were hundreds of things that he wanted to do, but the grown men laughed at him and said, 'Wait till you have been in the buckle,[16] Kotuko. Hunting is not *all* catching.'

Now that his father had named a puppy for him things looked brighter. An Inuit does not waste a good dog on his son till the boy knows something of dog-driving; and Kotuko was more than sure that he knew more than everything.

If the puppy had not had an iron constitution he would have died from over-stuffing and over-handling. Kotuko made him a tiny harness with a trace to it, and hauled him all over the house-floor shouting: 'Aua! Ja aua!' (Go to the right). 'Choia-choi, Ja choiachoi!' (Go to the left). 'Ohaha!' (Stop). The puppy did not like it at all, but being fished for in this way was pure happiness beside being put to the sleigh for the first time. He just sat down on the snow and played with the seal-hide trace that ran from his harness to the *pitu*, the big thong in the bows of the sleigh. Then the team started and the puppy found the heavy ten-foot sleigh running up his back and dragging him along the snow, while Kotuko laughed till the tears ran down his face. There followed days and days of the cruel whip that hisses like the wind over ice, and his companions all bit him because he did not know his work, and the harness chafed him, and he was not allowed to sleep with Kotuko any more, but had to take the coldest place in the passage. It was a sad time for the puppy.

The boy learned, too, as fast as the dog; though a dog-sleigh is a heart-breaking thing to manage. Each beast is harnessed – the weakest nearest to the driver – by his own separate trace,[17] which runs under his left fore-leg to the main thong, where it is fastened by a sort of button and loop which can be slipped by a turn of the wrist, thus freeing one dog at a time. This is very necessary, because young dogs often get the trace between their hind legs, where it cuts to the bone. And they one and all *will* go visiting their friends as they run, jumping in and out among the traces. Then they fight, and the result is more mixed than a wet fishing-line next morning. A great deal of trouble can be avoided by scientific use of the whip. Every Inuit boy prides himself as being a master of the long lash; but it is easy to flick at a mark on the ground and difficult to lean forward and catch a shirking dog just behind the shoulders when the sleigh is going at full speed. If you call one dog's name for 'visiting' and accidentally lash another the two will fight it out at once, and stop all the others. Again, if you travel with a companion and begin to talk, or by yourself and sing, the dogs will halt, turn round, and sit down and hear what you have to say. Kotuko was run away from once or twice through forgetting to block the sleigh when he stopped; and he broke many lashings and ruined a few thongs ere he could be trusted with a full team of eight and the light sleigh. Then he felt himself a person of consequence, and on smooth black ice, with a bold heart and a quick elbow, he smoked along over the levels as fast as a pack in full cry. He would go ten miles to the seal-holes, and when he was on the hunting-grounds he would twitch a trace loose from the *pitu* and free the big black leader, who was then the cleverest dog in the team. As soon as the dog had scented a breathing-hole Kotuko would reverse the sleigh, driving a couple of sawed-off antlers that stuck up like perambulator handles deep into the snow, so that the team could not get away. Then he would crawl forward inch by inch and wait till the seal came up to breathe. Then he would stab down swiftly with his spear and running line, and presently would haul his seal on to the lip of the ice while the black leader came up and helped to pull the carcass across the ice to the sleigh. That was the time when the harnessed dogs yelled and foamed with excitement, and Kotuko laid the long lash like a red-hot bar across all their faces till the carcass froze stiff. Going home was the heavy work. The loaded sleigh had to be humoured among the rough ice, and the dogs sat down and looked hungrily at the seal instead of pulling. At last they would strike the well-worn sleigh-road to the village, and toodle-ki-yi[18] along the ringing ice, heads down and tails up, while Kotuko struck up the 'Angutivun tai-na tau-na-ne taina' (The Song of the Returning Hunter),[19] and voices hailed him from house to house under all that dim, star-litten sky.

When Kotuko, the dog, came to his full growth, he enjoyed himself too. He fought his way up the team steadily, fight after fight, till one fine evening over their food he tackled the big black leader (Kotuko, the boy, saw fair play) and made second dog of him, as they say. So he was promoted to the long thong of the leading dog, running five feet in advance of all the others: it was his bounden duty to stop all fighting, in harness or out of it, and he wore a collar of copper wire, very thick and heavy. On special occasions he was fed with cooked food inside the house, and sometimes was allowed to sleep on the bench with Kotuko. He was a good seal-dog, and would keep a musk-ox at bay by running round him and snapping at his heels. He would even – and this for a sleigh-dog is the last proof of bravery – he would even stand up to the gaunt Arctic wolf, whom all dogs of the north, as a rule, fear beyond anything that walks the snow. He and his master – they did not count the team of ordinary dogs as company – hunted together, day after day and night after night – fur-wrapped boy and savage, long-haired, narrow-eyed, white-fanged, yellow brute. All an Inuit has to do is to get food and skins for himself and his family. The women-folk make the skins into clothing, and occasionally help in trapping small game; but the bulk of the food – and they eat enormously – must be found by the men. If the supply fails there is no one up there to buy or beg or borrow from. The people must die.

An Inuit does not think of these chances till he is forced to. Kadlu, Kotuko, Amoraq, and the boy baby who kicked about the fur hood and chewed pieces of blubber all day, were as happy together as any family in the world. They came of a very gentle race – an Inuit seldom loses his temper, and almost never strikes a child – who did not know exactly what telling a real

lie meant; still less how to steal. They were content to spear
their living out of the heart of the bitter, hopeless cold; to smile
oily smiles, and tell queer ghost and fairy-tales of evenings; and
eat till they could eat no more, and sing the endless woman's
song: 'Amna aya, aya amna, ah! ah!'[20] through the long lamp-
lighted days as they mended their clothes and hunting gear.

But one terrible winter everything betrayed them. The Tununirmiut returned from the yearly salmon fishing and made their
houses on the fresh ice to the north of Bylot's Island ready to go
after the seal as soon as the sea froze. But it was an early and
savage autumn. All through September there were continuous
gales that broke up the smooth seal ice where it was only four
or five feet thick and forced it inland, and piled a great barrier
some twenty miles broad of lumped and ragged and needly ice,
over which it was impossible to draw the sleighs. The edge of
the floe off which the seal were used to fish in winter lay perhaps twenty miles beyond this barrier and out of reach of the
Tununirmiut. Even so, they might have managed to scrape
through the winter on their stock of frozen salmon and stored
blubber and what the traps gave them, but in December one of
their hunters came across a *tupik*, a skin-tent, of three women
and a girl nearly dead, whose men had come down from the far
north and been crushed in their little skin hunting-boats while
they were out after the long-horned narwhal. Kadlu, of course,
could only distribute the women among the huts of the winter
village, for no Inuit dare refuse a meal to a stranger. He never
knows when his own turn may come to beg. Amoraq took the
girl, who was about fourteen, into her own house as a sort of
servant. From the cut of her sharp-pointed hood, and the long
diamond pattern of her white deer-skin leggings, they supposed
she came from Ellesmere Land. She had never seen tin
cooking-pots or wooden-shod sleighs before; but Kotuko the
boy and Kotuko the dog were rather fond of her.

Then all the foxes went south, and even the wolverine,[21] that
growling, blunt-headed little thief of the snow, did not take the
trouble to follow the line of empty traps that Kotuko set. The
tribe lost a couple of their best hunters, who were badly crippled
in a fight with a musk-ox, and this threw more work on the

others. Kotuko went out, day after day, with a light hunting-sleigh and six or seven of the strongest dogs, looking till his eyes ached for some patch of clear ice where a seal might, perhaps, have scratched a breathing-hole. Kotuko, the dog, ranged far and wide, and in the dead stillness of the ice-fields Kotuko, the boy, could hear his half-choked whine of excitement, above a seal-hole three miles away, as plainly as though he were at his elbow. When the dog found a hole the boy would build himself a little low snow wall to keep off the worst of the bitter wind, and there he would wait ten, twelve, twenty hours for the seal to come up to breathe, his eyes glued to the tiny mark he had made above the hole to guide the downward thrust of his harpoon, a little sealskin mat under his feet, and his legs tied together in the *tutareang*[22] – the buckle that the old hunters had talked about. This helps to keep a man's legs from twitching as he waits and waits and waits for the quick-eared seal to rise. Though there is no excitement in it, you can easily believe that the sitting still in the buckle with the thermometer perhaps forty degrees below zero is the hardest work an Inuit knows. When a seal was caught, Kotuko, the dog, would bound forward, his trace trailing behind him, and help to pull the body to the sleigh where the tired and hungry dogs lay sullenly under the lee of the broken ice.

A seal did not go very far, for each mouth in the little village had a right to be filled, and neither bone, hide, nor sinew was wasted. The dog's meat was taken for human use, and Amoraq fed the team with pieces of old summer skin-tents raked out from under the sleeping-bench, and they howled and howled again; and waked to howl hungrily. One could tell by the lamps in the huts that famine was near. In good seasons, when blubber was plentiful, the light in the boat-shaped bowls would be two feet high – cheerful, oily, and yellow. Now it was a bare six inches: Amoraq carefully pricked down the moss wick when an unwatched flame brightened for a moment, and the eyes of all the family followed her hand. The horror of famine up there in the great cold is not so much dying as dying in the dark. All the Inuit dread the dark that presses on them without a break for six months in each year; and when the lamps are low in the houses the minds of people begin to be shaken and confused.

But worse was to come.

The underfed dogs snapped and growled in the passages, glaring at the cold stars and snuffing into the bitter wind night after night. When they stopped howling the silence fell down again as solid and as heavy as a snowdrift against a door, and men could hear the beating of their blood in the thin passages of the ear and the thumping of their own hearts that sounded as loud as the noise of sorcerers' drums beaten across the snow. One night Kotuko the dog, who had been unusually sullen in harness, leaped up and pushed his head against Kotuko's knee. Kotuko patted him, but the dog still pushed blindly forward, fawning. Then Kadlu waked and gripped the heavy wolf-like head and stared into the glassy eyes. The dog whimpered as though he were afraid, and shivered between Kadlu's knees. The hair rose about his neck and he growled as though a stranger were at the door; then he barked joyously and rolled on the ground and bit at Kotuko's boot like a puppy.

'What is it?' said Kotuko, for he was beginning to be afraid.

'The sickness,' Kadlu answered. 'It is the dog-sickness.' Kotuko the dog lifted his nose and howled and howled again.

'I have not seen this before. What will he do?' said Kotuko.

Kadlu shrugged one shoulder a little and crossed the hut for his short stabbing-harpoon. The big dog looked at him, howled again, and slunk away down the passage, while the other dogs drew aside right and left to give him ample room. When he was out on the snow he barked furiously, as though on the trail of a musk-ox, and, barking and leaping and frisking, passed out of sight. His trouble was not hydrophobia[23] but simple plain madness. The cold and the hunger, and above all the dark, had turned his head: and when the terrible dog-sickness once shows itself in a team it spreads like wild-fire. Next hunting day another dog sickened, and was killed then and there by Kotuko as he bit and struggled among the traces. Then the black second-dog who had been the leader in the old days suddenly gave tongue on an imaginary reindeer track, and when they slipped him from the *pitu* he flew at the throat of an ice-cliff, and ran away as his leader had done, his harness on his back. After that no one would take the dogs out again. They needed them for something else, and the dogs knew it; and though they were tied down and fed by hand their eyes were full of despair and fear. To make things worse the old women began to tell ghost-tales, and to say that they had met the spirits of the dead hunters lost that autumn who prophesied all sorts of horrible things.

Kotuko grieved more for the loss of his dog than anything else, for though an Inuit eats enormously he also knows how to starve. But the hunger, the darkness, the cold, and the exposure told on his strength, and he began to hear voices inside his head, and to see people, who were not there, out of the tail of his eye. One night – he had unbuckled himself after ten hours waiting above a 'blind' seal-hole, and was staggering back to the village faint and dizzy – he halted to lean his back against a boulder, which happened to be supported like a rocking-stone on a single jutting point of ice. His weight disturbed the balance of the thing, it rolled over ponderously, and as Kotuko sprang aside to avoid it, slid after him squeaking and hissing on the ice-slope.

That was enough for Kotuko. He had been brought up to believe that every rock and boulder had its owner (its *inua*), who was generally a one-eyed kind of a Woman-Thing called a *tornaq*, and that when a *tornaq* meant to help a man she rolled after him inside her stone house, and asked him whether he would take her for a guardian spirit. (In summer thaws the ice-propped rocks and boulders roll and slip all over the face of the land, so you can easily see how the idea of live stones arose.) Kotuko heard the blood beating in his ears as he had heard it all day, and he thought that was the *tornaq* of the stone speaking to him. Before he reached home he was quite certain that he had held a long conversation with her, and as all his people believed that this was quite possible no one contradicted him.

'She said to me: "I jump down, I jump down from my place on the snow,"' cried Kotuko with hollow eyes, leaning forward in the half-lighted hut. 'She said, "I will be a guide." She says, "I will guide you to good seal-holes." Tomorrow I go out and the *tornaq* will guide me.'

Then the *angekok*, the village sorcerer, came in and Kotuko told him the tale a second time. It lost nothing in the telling.

'Follow the *tornait* (the spirits of the stones) and they will bring us food again,' said the *angekok*.

Now the girl from the north had been lying near the lamp, eating very little and saying less for days past, but when Amoraq and Kadlu next morning packed and lashed a little hand-sleigh for Kotuko, and loaded it with his hunting gear and as much blubber and frozen seal-meat as they could spare, she took the pulling-rope, and stepped out boldly at the boy's side.

'Your house is my house,' she said, as the little bone-shod sleigh squeaked and bumped behind them in the awful Arctic night.

'My house is your house,' said Kotuko, 'but *I* think that we shall both go to Sedna together.'

Now Sedna is the Mistress of the Underworld, and the Inuit believe that everyone who dies must spend a year in her horrible country before going to Quadliparmiut, the Happy Place, where it never freezes and fat reindeer trot up when you call.

Through the village people were shouting: 'The *tornait* have spoken to Kotuko. They will show him open ice. He will bring us the seal again.' Their voices were soon swallowed up by the cold empty dark, and Kotuko and the girl shouldered close together as they strained on the pulling-rope or humoured the sleigh through the ice, in the direction of the Polar Sea. Kotuko insisted that the *tornaq* of the stone had told him to go north, and so north they went under Tuktuqdjung the Reindeer – those stars that we call the Great Bear.[24]

No European could have made five miles a day over the ice-rubbish and the sharp-edged drifts; but those two knew exactly the turn of the wrist that coaxes a sleigh round a hummock, the jerk that neatly lifts it out of an ice-crack, and the exact strength that goes to the few quiet strokes of the spear-head that make a path possible when everything looks hopeless.

The girl said nothing, but bowed her head, and the long wolverine-fur fringe of her ermine hood blew across her broad, dark face. The sky above them was an intense velvety black, changing to bands of Indian red on the horizon, where the great stars burned like street-lamps. From time to time a green-ish wave of the Northern Lights would roll across the hollow of the high heavens, flick like a flag and disappear; or a meteor would crackle from darkness to darkness trailing a shower of sparks behind. Then they could see the ridged and furrowed surface of the floe all tipped and laced with strange colours – red, copper, and bluish; but in the ordinary starlight everything turned to one frost-bitten gray. The floe, as you will remember, had been battered and tormented by the autumn gales till it was one frozen earthquake. There were gullies and ravines; and holes like gravel-pits cut in ice, lumps and scattered pieces frozen down to the original floor of the floe; blotches of old black ice that had been thrust under the floe in some gale, and heaved up again; roundish boulders of ice; saw-like edges of ice carved by the snow that flies before the wind and sunk pits where thirty or forty acres lay five or six feet below the level of the rest of the field. From a little distance you might have taken the lumps for seal, or walrus, overturned sleighs or men on a hunting expedition, or even the great Ten-legged White Spirit-Bear[25] himself, but in spite of these fantastic shapes, all on the very edge of starting into life, there was neither sound nor the least faint echo of sound. And through this silence and through this waste where the sudden lights flapped and went out again, the sleigh and the two that pulled it crawled like things in a nightmare – a nightmare of the end of the world at the end of the world.

When they were tired Kotuko would make what the hunters call a 'half-house', a very small snow hut, into which they would huddle with the travelling lamp, and try to thaw out the frozen seal-meat. When they had slept, the march began again – thirty miles a day to get five miles[26] northward. The girl was always very silent, but Kotuko muttered to himself and broke out into songs he had learned in the Singing-House – summer songs, and reindeer and salmon songs – all horribly out of place at that season. He would declare that he heard the *tornaq* growling to him, and would run wildly up a hummock tossing his arms and speaking in loud threatening tones. To tell the truth, Kotuko was very nearly crazy for the time being; but the girl was sure that he was being guided by his guardian spirit, and that everything would come right. She was not surprised, therefore, when at the end of the fourth march, Kotuko, whose eyes were burning like fire-balls in his head, told her that his *tornaq* was following them across the snow in the shape of a two-headed dog. The girl looked where Kotuko pointed, and some Thing seemed to slip into a ravine. It was certainly not human, but everybody knew that the *tornait* preferred to appear in the shape of bear and seal and such like.

It might have been the Ten-legged White Spirit-Bear himself, or it might have been anything, for Kotuko and the girl were so starved that their eyes were untrustworthy. They had trapped nothing and seen no trace of game since they had left the village; their food would not hold out for another week, and there was a gale coming. A Polar storm will blow for ten days without a break, and all that while it is certain death to be abroad. Kotuko laid up a snow-house large enough to take in the hand-sleigh (it is never wise to be separated from your meat), and while he was shaping the last irregular block of ice that makes the keystone of the roof he saw a Thing looking at him from a little cliff of ice half a mile away. The air was hazy, and the Thing seemed to be forty feet long and ten feet high, with twenty feet of tail and a shape that quivered all along the out-lines.[27] The girl saw it too, but instead of crying aloud with terror, said quietly: 'That is Quiquern. What comes after?'

'He will speak to me,' said Kotuko, but the snow-knife trembled in his hand as he spoke, because however much a man may believe that he is a friend of strange and ugly spirits he sel-dom likes to be taken quite at his word. Quiquern, too, is the phantom of a gigantic toothless dog without any hair, who is supposed to live in the far north, and to wander about the country just before things are going to happen. They may be pleasant or unpleasant things, but not even the sorcerers care to speak about Quiquern. He makes the dogs go mad. Like the Spirit Bear he has several extra pairs of legs – six or eight – and this Thing jumping up and down in the haze had more legs than any real dog needed.

Kotuko and the girl huddled into their hut quickly. Of course if Quiquern had wanted them he could have torn it to pieces above their heads, but the sense of a foot-thick snow wall between themselves and the wicked dark was great comfort. The gale broke with a shriek of wind like the shriek of a train, and for three days and three nights it held, never varying one point and never lulling even for a minute. They fed the stone lamp between their knees and nibbled at the half-warm seal meat, and watched the black soot gather on the roof for seventy-two long hours. The girl counted up the food in the sleigh; there was not more than two days' supply, and Kotuko looked over the iron heads and the deer-sinew fastenings of his harpoon and his seal-lance and his bird-dart. There was nothing else to do.

'We shall go to Sedna soon – very soon,' the girl whispered. 'In three days we shall lie down and go. Will your *tornaq* do nothing? Sing her an *angekok*'s song to make her come here.'

He began to sing in the high-pitched howl of the magic songs, and the gale went down slowly. In the middle of his song the girl started, laid her mittened hand and then her head to the ice floor of the hut. Kotuko followed her example, and the two kneeled staring into each other's eyes, and listening with every nerve. He ripped a thin sliver of whale-bone from the rim of a bird snare that lay on the sleigh, and after straightening set it upright in a little hole in the ice, firming it down with his mitten. It was almost as delicately adjusted as a compass needle, and now, instead of listening, they watched. The thin rod quivered a little – the least little jar in the world – then vibrated steadily for a few seconds, came to rest and vibrated again, this time nodding to another point of the compass.

'Too soon!' said Kotuko. 'Some big floe has broken far away outside.'

The girl pointed at the rod and shook her head. 'It is the big breaking,' she said. 'Listen to the ground-ice. It knocks.'

When they kneeled this time they heard the most curious muffled grunts, and knockings apparently under their feet. Sometimes it sounded as though a blind puppy were squeaking above the lamp; then as if a stone were being ground on hard ice; and again, like muffled blows on a drum; but all dragged out and made small, as though they had travelled through a little horn a weary distance away.

'We shall not go to Sedna lying down,' said Kotuko. 'It is the breaking. The *tornaq* has cheated us. We shall die.'

All this may sound absurd enough, but the two were face to face with a very real danger. The three days' gale had driven the deep water of Baffin's Bay[28] southerly, and piled it on to the edge of the far reaching land-ice that stretches from Bylot's Island to the west. Also, the strong current which sets east out of Lancaster Sound carried with it mile upon mile of what they call pack-ice – rough ice that has not frozen into fields; and this pack was bombarding the floe at the same time that the swell and heave of the storm-worked sea was weakening and undermining it. What Kotuko and the girl had been listening to were the faint echoes of that fight thirty or forty miles away, and the tell-tale little rod quivered to the shock of it.

Now, as the Inuit say, when the ice once wakes after its long winter sleep there is no knowing what may happen, for solid floe-ice changes shape almost as quickly as a cloud. The gale was evidently a spring gale sent out of time and anything was possible.

Yet the two were happier in their minds than before. If the floe broke up there would be no more waiting and suffering. Spirits, goblins, and witch-people were moving about on the racking ice, and they might find themselves stepping into Sedna's country side by side with all sorts of wild Things, the flush of excitement still on them. When they left the hut after the gale, the noise on the horizon was steadily growing, and the tough ice moaned and buzzed all round them.

'It is still waiting,' said Kotuko.

On the top of a hummock sat or crouched the eight-legged Thing that they had seen three days before – and it howled horribly.

'Let us follow,' said the girl. 'It may know some way that does not lead to Sedna,' but she reeled from weakness as she took the pulling-rope. The Thing moved off slowly and clumsily across the ridges, heading always toward the westward and the land, and they followed while the growling thunder at the edge of the floe rolled nearer and nearer. The floe's lip was split and cracked in every direction for three or four miles inland, and great pans of ten-foot-thick ice, from a few yards to twenty acres square, were jolting and ducking and surging into one another and into the yet unbroken floe as the heavy swell took and shook and spouted between them. This battering-ram-ice was, so to speak, the first army that the sea was flinging against the floe. The incessant crash and jar of these cakes almost drowned the ripping sound of sheets of pack-ice driven bodily under the floe as cards are hastily pushed under a table-cloth. Where the water was shallow these sheets would be piled one atop of the other till the bottommost touched mud fifty feet down and the discoloured sea banked behind the muddy ice till the increasing pressure drove all forward again. In addition to the floe and the pack-ice, the gale and the currents were bringing down true bergs, sailing mountains of ice, snapped off from the Greenland side of things[29] or the north shore of Melville Bay.[30] They pounded in solemnly, the waves breaking white round them, and advanced on the floe like an old-time fleet under full sail. But a berg that seemed ready to carry the world before it would ground helplessly,[31] reel over, and wallow in a lather of foam and mud, and flying frozen spray, while a much smaller and lower one would rip and ride into the flat floe, flinging tons of rubbish[32] on either side, and cutting a track a mile long before it was stopped. Some fell like swords, shearing a raw-edged canal, and others splintered into a shower of blocks, weighing scores of tons apiece, that whirled and skirled among the hummocks. Others, again, rose up bodily out of the water when they shoaled, twisted as though in pain, and fell solidly on their sides, while the sea threshed over their shoulders. This trampling and crowding and bending and buckling and arching of the ice into every possible shape was going on as far as the eye could reach all along the north line of the floe. From where Kotuko and the girl were, the confusion looked no more than an uneasy rippling crawling movement under the horizon, but it came towards them each moment, and they could hear far away to landward a heavy booming, as it might have been the boom of artillery through a fog. That showed that the floe was being jammed home against the iron cliffs of Bylot's Island, the land to the southward, behind them.

'This has never been before,' said Kotuko, staring stupidly. 'This is not the time. How can the floe break *now*?'

'Follow *that*!' the girl cried, pointing to the Thing half-limping, half-running distractedly before them. They followed, tugging the hand-sleigh, while nearer and nearer came the roaring march of the ice. At last the fields round them cracked and starred in every direction, and the cracks opened and snapped like the teeth of wolves. But where the Thing rested, on a mound of old and scattered ice-blocks some fifty feet high, there was no motion. Kotuko leaped forward wildly, dragged the girl after him, and crawled to the bottom of the mound. The talking of the ice grew louder and louder round them, but the mound stayed fast, and as the girl looked at him he threw his right elbow upwards and outwards, making the Inuit sign for land in the shape of an island. And land it was that the eight-legged limping Thing had led them to – some granite-tipped, sand-beached islet off the coast, shod and sheathed and masked with ice so that no man could have told it from the floe, but at the bottom solid earth, and not shifting ice. The smashing and rebound of the floes as they grounded and splintered marked the borders of it, and a friendly shoal ran out to the northward, turning aside the rush of the heaviest ice exactly as a ploughshare turns over loam. There was a danger, of course, that some heavily-squeezed ice-field might shoot up the beach and plane off the top of the islet bodily, but that did not trouble Kotuko and the girl, when they made their snow-house and began to eat, and heard the ice hammer and skid along the beach. The Thing had disappeared, and Kotuko was talking excitedly about his power over spirits as he crouched round the lamp. In the middle of his wild sayings the girl began to laugh and rock herself backwards and forwards.

Behind her shoulder, crawling into the hut crawl by crawl, there were two heads, one yellow and one black, that belonged to two of the most sorrowful and ashamed dogs that ever you saw. Kotuko the dog was one and the black leader was the other. Both were now fat, well-looking, and quite restored to their proper minds; but coupled to each other in an extraordinary fashion. When the black leader ran off, you remember, his harness was still on him. He must have met Kotuko the dog and played or fought with him, for his shoulder-loop had caught in the plaited copper wire of Kotuko's collar, and had drawn tight, so that neither dog could get at the trace to gnaw it apart, but each was fastened sidelong to his neighbour's neck. That, with the freedom of hunting on their own account, must have helped to cure their madness. They were very sober.

The girl pushed the two shame-faced creatures towards Kotuko, and, sobbing with laughter, cried, 'That is Quiquern, who led us to safe ground. Look at his eight legs and double head!'

Kotuko cut them free, and they fell into his arms, yellow and black together, trying to explain how they had got their senses back again. Kotuko ran a hand down their ribs, which were round and well clothed. 'They have found food,' he said, with a grin. 'I do not think we shall go to Sedna so soon. My *tornaq* sent these. The sickness has left them.'

As soon as they had greeted Kotuko these two, who had been forced to sleep and eat and hunt together for the past few weeks, flew at each other's throat, and there was a beautiful battle in the snow-house. 'Empty dogs do not fight,' Kotuko said. 'They have found the seal. Let us sleep. We shall find food.'

When they waked there was open water on the north beach of the island, and all the loosened ice had been driven landward. The first sound of the surf is one of the most delightful that the Inuit can hear, for it means that Spring is on the road. Kotuko and the girl took hold of hands and smiled: the clear full roar of the surge among the ice reminded them of salmon and reindeer time and the smell of blossoming ground-willows. Even as they looked the sea began to skim over between the floating cakes of ice, so intense was the cold, but on the horizon there was a vast red glare, and that was the light of the sunken sun. It was more like hearing him yawn in his sleep than seeing him rise, and the glare lasted for only a few minutes, but it marked the turn of the year. Nothing, they felt, could alter that.

Kotuko found the dogs fighting outside over a fresh-killed seal who was following the fish that a gale always disturbs. He was the first of some twenty or thirty seal that landed on the island in the course of the day, and, till the sea froze hard, there were hundreds of keen black heads rejoicing in the shallow free water and floating about with the floating ice.

It was good to eat seal-liver again; to fill the lamps recklessly with blubber and watch the flame blaze three feet in the air; but as soon as the new sea-ice bore, Kotuko and the girl loaded the hand-sleigh and made the two dogs pull as they had never pulled in their lives, for they feared what might have happened in their village. The weather was as pitiless as ever; but it is easier to draw a sleigh loaded with good food than to hunt starving. They left five-and-twenty seal carcasses buried in the ice of the beach all ready for use and hurried back to their people. The dogs showed them the way as soon as Kotuko told them what was expected, and though there was no sign of a landmark, in two days they were giving tongue outside Kadlu's village. Only three dogs answered them; the others had been eaten, and the houses were nearly dark.[33] But when Kotuko shouted, 'Ojo!' (boiled meat) weak voices answered, and when he called the roll-call of the village name by name, very distinctly, there were no gaps in it.

An hour later the lamps blazed in Kadlu's house, snow-water was heating, the pots were beginning to simmer, and the snow was dripping from the roof as Amoraq made ready a meal for all the village, and the boy-baby chewed at a strip of rich nutty blubber, and the hunters slowly and methodically filled themselves to the very brim with seal-meat. Kotuko and the girl told their tale. The two dogs sat between them, and whenever their names came in they cocked an ear apiece and looked most thoroughly ashamed of themselves. A dog who has once gone mad and recovered, the Inuit say, is safe against all further attacks.

'So the *tornaq* did not forget us,' said Kotuko. 'The storm blew; the ice broke, and the seal swam in behind the fish that were frightened by the storm. Now the new seal-holes are not two days' distant. Let the good hunters go to-morrow and bring back the seal I have speared – twenty-five seal buried in the ice. When we have eaten those we will all follow the seal on the floe.'

'What do *you* do?' said the village sorcerer, in the same sort
of voice as he used to Kadlu, richest of the Tununirmiut.

Kotuko looked at the girl from the North and said quietly:
'*We* build a house.' He pointed to the north-west side of Kadlu's house, for that is the side on which the married son or
daughter always lives.

The girl turned her hands, palm upward, with a little despairing shake of her head. She was a foreigner, picked up
starving, and she could bring nothing to house-keeping.

Amoraq jumped from the bench where she sat and began to
sweep things into the girl's lap – stone lamps, iron skin-scrapers,
tin kettles, deer-skins embroidered with musk-ox teeth, and
real canvas-needles such as sailors use – the finest dowry ever
given on the far edge of the Arctic circle, and the girl from the
North bowed her head down to the very floor.

'Also these!' said Kotuko laughing and signing to the dogs,
who thrust their cold muzzles into the girl's face.

'Ah,' said the *angekok*, with an important cough, as though he
had been thinking it all over. 'As soon as Kotuko left the village I
went to the Singing-House and sang magic. I sang all the long
nights and called upon the Spirit of the Reindeer. *My* singing
made the gale blow that broke the ice and drew the two dogs
towards Kotuko when the ice would have crushed his bones. *My*
song drew the seal in behind the broken ice. My body lay still in
the *quaggi*, but my spirit ran about on the ice and guided Kotuko
and the dogs in all the things they did. *I* did it.'

Everybody was full and sleepy, so no one contradicted; and
the *angekok* helped himself to yet another lump of boiled meat
and lay down to sleep with the others, in the warm, well-lighted,
oil-smelling home.

Now Kotuko, who drew very well in the Inuit style, scratched
pictures of all these adventures on a long flat piece of ivory
with a hole at one end. When he and the girl went north to
Ellesmere Land in the year of the Wonderful Open Winter, he
left the picture-story with Kadlu, who lost it in the shingle
when his dog-sleigh broke down one summer on the beach of
Lake Netilling at Nikosiring,[34] and there a Lake Inuit found it

next spring and sold it to a man at Imigen[35] who was inter-
preter on a Cumberland Sound whaler, and he sold it to Hans
Olsen, who was afterwards a quartermaster on board a big
steamer that took tourists to the North Cape in Norway. When
the tourist season was over the steamer ran between London
and Australia, stopping at Ceylon, and there Olsen sold the
ivory to a Cingalese[36] jeweller for two imitation sapphires. I
found it under some rubbish in a house at Colombo, and have
translated it from one end to the other.

Angutivun Tina

This is a very free translation of the Song of the Returning Hunter,[1] as the men used to sing it after seal-spearing. The Inuit always repeat things over and over again.

Our gloves are stiff with the frozen blood,
  Our furs with the drifted snow,
As we come in with the seal – the seal!
  In from the edge of the floe.

Au jana! Aua! Oha! Haq!
  And the yelping dog-teams go,
And the long whips crack, and the men come back,
  Back from the edge of the floe!

We tracked the seal to his secret place,
  We heard him scratch below,
We made our mark, and we watched beside,
  Out on the edge of the floe.

We raised our lance when he rose to breathe,
  We drove it downward – so!
And we played him thus, and we killed him thus,
  Out on the edge of the floe.

Our gloves are glued with the frozen blood,
  Our eyes with the drifting snow;
But we come back to our wives again,
  Back from the edge of the floe!

Au jana! Aua! Oha! Haq!
  And the yelping dog-teams go,
And the wives can hear their men come back,
  Back from the edge of the floe.

RED DOG

For our white and our excellent nights – for the nights of swift
    running,
Fair ranging, far-seeing, good hunting, sure cunning!
For the smells of the dawning, untainted, ere dew has departed!
For the rush through the mist, and the quarry blind-started!
For the cry of our mates when the *sambhur* has wheeled and is
    standing at bay,
  For the risk and the riot of night!
  For the sleep at the lair-mouth by day –
    It is met, and we go to the fight.
        Bay! O Bay!

It was after the letting in of the Jungle that the pleasantest part of Mowgli's life began. He had the good conscience that comes from paying a just debt;[1] and all the Jungle was his friend, for all the Jungle was afraid[2] of him. The things that he did and saw and heard when he was wandering from one people to another, with or without his four companions, would make many, many stories, each as long as this one. So you will never be told how he met and escaped from the Mad Elephant of Mandla,[3] who killed two-and-twenty bullocks drawing eleven carts of coined silver to the Government Treasury, and scattered the shiny rupees in the dust; how he fought Jacala, the Crocodile, all one long night in the Marshes of the North, and broke his skinning-knife on the brute's back-plates; how he found a new and longer knife round the neck of a man who had been killed by a wild boar, and how he tracked that boar and killed him as a fair price for the knife; how he was caught up in the Great Famine[4] by the moving of the deer, and nearly crushed to death in the swaying hot herds; how he saved Hathi the Silent from being caught in a pit[5] with a stake at the bottom, and how next day he himself fell into a very cunning leopard-trap, and how Hathi broke the thick wooden bars to pieces about him; how he milked the wild buffaloes in the swamp, and how—

But we must tell one tale at a time. Father and Mother Wolf died, and Mowgli rolled a big boulder against the mouth of the cave and cried the Death Song over them, and Baloo grew very old and stiff, and even Bagheera, whose nerves were steel and whose muscles were iron, seemed slower at the kill. Akela turned from gray to milky white with pure age; his ribs stuck out, and he walked as though he had been made of wood, and Mowgli killed for him. But the young wolves, the children of the disbanded Seeonee Pack, throve and increased, and when there were some forty of them, masterless,[6] clean-footed five-year-olds, Akela told them that they ought to gather themselves together and follow the Law, and run under one head, as befitted the Free People.

This was not a matter in which Mowgli gave advice, for, as he said, he had eaten sour fruit, and he knew the tree it hung from; but when Phao, son of Phaona[7] (his father was the Gray Tracker in the days of Akela's headship), fought his way to the leadership of the Pack according to the Jungle Law, and when the old calls and the old songs began to ring under the stars once more, Mowgli came to the Council Rock for memory's sake. If he chose to speak the Pack waited till he had finished, and he sat at Akela's side on the rock above Phao. Those were the days of good hunting and good sleeping. No stranger cared to break into the jungles that belonged to Mowgli's people, as they called the Pack, and the young wolves grew fat and strong, and there were many cubs to bring to the Looking-over. Mowgli always attended a Looking-over, for he remembered the night when a black panther brought a naked brown baby into the pack, and the long call, 'Look, look well, O Wolves,' made his heart flutter with strange feelings.[8] Otherwise, he would be far away in the jungle; tasting, touching, seeing, and feeling new things.

One twilight when he was trotting leisurely across the ranges to give Akela the half of a buck that he had killed, while his

four wolves were jogging behind him, sparring a little and tumbling one over another for joy of being alive, he heard a cry
that he had not heard since the bad days of Shere Khan. It was
what they call in the Jungle the *Pheeal*,[9] a kind of shriek that
the jackal gives when he is hunting behind a tiger, or when
there is some big killing afoot. If you can imagine a mixture of
hate, triumph, fear, and despair, with a kind of leer running
through it, you will get some notion of the *Pheeal* that rose and
sank and wavered and quavered far away across the Waingunga. The Four began to bristle and growl. Mowgli's hand
went to his knife and he too checked as though he had been
turned into stone.[10]

'There is no Striped One would dare kill here,' he said, at last.

'That is not the cry of the Forerunner,' said Gray Brother. 'It
is some great killing. Listen!'

It broke out again, half sobbing and half chuckling, just as
though the jackal had soft human lips. Then Mowgli drew
deep breath, and ran to the Council Rock, overtaking on his
way hurrying wolves of the Pack. Phao and Akela were on the
Rock together, and below them, every nerve strained, sat the
others. The mothers and the cubs were cantering to their lairs;
for when the *Pheeal* cries it is no time for weak things to be
abroad.

They could hear nothing except the Waingunga gurgling in
the dark and the evening winds among the tree-tops, till suddenly across the river a wolf called. It was no wolf of the Pack,
for those were all at the Rock. The note changed to a long despairing bay;[11] and 'Dhole!'[12] it said, 'Dhole! Dhole! Dhole!' In
a few minutes they heard tired feet on the rocks, and a gaunt,
dripping wolf, streaked with red on his flanks, his right
fore-paw useless, and his jaws white with foam, flung himself
into the circle and lay gasping at Mowgli's feet.

'Good hunting! Under whose headship?' said Phao gravely.

'Good hunting! Won-tolla[13] am I,' was the answer. He meant
that he was a solitary wolf, fending for himself, his mate, and
his cubs in some lonely lair. Won-tolla means an outlier – one
who lies out from any pack. When he panted they could see his
heart shake him backwards and forwards.

'What moves?' said Phao, for that is the question all the Jungle asks after the *Pheeal*.

'The dhole, the dhole of the Dekkan[14] – Red Dog, the Killer! They came north from the south saying the Dekkan was empty and killing out by the way. When this moon was new there were four to me – my mate and three cubs. She would teach them to kill on the grass plains, hiding to drive the buck, as we do who are of the open. At midnight I heard them together full tongue on the trail. At the dawn-wind I found them stiff in the grass – four, Free People, four when this moon was new! Then sought I my Blood-Right and found the dhole.'

'How many?' said Mowgli: the Pack growled deep in their throats.

'I do not know. Three of them will kill no more, but at the last they drove me like the buck; on three legs they drove me. Look, Free People!'

He thrust out his mangled fore-foot, all dark with dried blood. There were cruel bites low down on his side, and his throat was torn and worried.

'Eat,' said Akela, rising up from the meat Mowgli had brought him; the outlier flung himself on it famishing.

'This shall be no loss,' he said humbly when he had taken off the edge of his hunger. 'Give me a little strength, Free People, and I also will kill! My lair is empty that was full when this moon was new, and the Blood Debt is not all paid.'

Phao heard his teeth crack on a haunch-bone and grunted approvingly.

'We shall need those jaws,' said he. 'Were their cubs with the dhole?'

'Nay, nay. Red hunters all: grown dogs of their pack, heavy and strong.'[15]

That meant that the dhole, the red hunting-dog of the Dekkan, was moving to fight, and the wolves knew well that even the tiger will surrender a new kill to the dhole. They drive straight through the Jungle, and what they meet they pull down and tear to pieces. Though they are not as big nor half as cunning as the wolf, they are very strong and very numerous. The dhole, for instance, do not begin to call themselves a pack till they are a hundred strong, whereas forty wolves make a very fair pack. Mowgli's wanderings had taken him to the edge of the high grassy downs of the Dekkan, and he had often seen the fearless dholes sleeping and playing and scratching themselves among the little hollows and tussocks that they use for lairs. He despised and hated them because they did not smell like the Free People, because they did not live in caves, and above all, because they had hair between their toes while he and his friends were clean-footed. But he knew, for Hathi had told him, what a terrible thing a dhole hunting pack was. Hathi himself moves aside from their line, and until they are all killed, or till game is scarce, they go forward killing as they go.

Akela knew something of the dholes, too; he said to Mowgli quietly: 'It is better to die in the Full Pack than leaderless and alone. It is good hunting, and – my last. But, as men live, thou hast very many more nights and days, Little Brother. Go north and lie down, and if any wolf live after the dhole has gone by he shall bring thee word of the fight.'

'Ah,' said Mowgli, quite gravely, 'must I go to the marshes and catch little fish and sleep in a tree, or must I ask help of the *bandar-log* and eat nuts while the pack fights below?'

'It is to the death,' said Akela. 'Thou hast never met the dhole – the Red Killer. Even the Striped One—'

'Aowa! Aowa!' said Mowgli pettingly. 'I have killed one striped ape.[16] Listen now: There was a wolf, my father, and there was a wolf, my mother, and there was an old gray wolf (not too wise: he is white now) was my father and my mother. Therefore I—' he raised his voice, 'I say that when the dhole come, and if the dhole come, Mowgli and the Free People are of one skin for that hunting; and I say, by the Bull that bought me, by the bull Bagheera paid for me in the old days which ye of the Pack do not remember, *I* say, that the Trees and the River may hear and hold fast if I forget; *I* say that this my knife shall be as a tooth to the Pack – and I do not think it is so blunt. This is my Word which has gone from me.'

'Thou dost not know the dhole, man with a wolf's tongue,' Won-tolla cried. 'I look only to clear my blood debt against them ere they have me in many pieces. They move slowly, killing out as they go, but in two days a little strength will come back to me and I turn again for my blood debt. But for *ye*, Free People, my counsel is that ye go north and eat but little for a while till the dhole are gone. There is no sleep[17] in this hunting.'

'Hear the Outlier!' said Mowgli with a laugh. 'Free People, we must go north and eat lizards and rats from the bank, lest by chance we meet the dhole. He must kill out our hunting grounds while we lie hid in the north till it please him to give us our own again. He is a dog – and the pup of a dog – red, yellow-bellied, lairless, and haired between every toe! He counts his cubs six and eight at the litter, as though he were Chikai, the little leaping rat.[18] Surely we must run away, Free People, and beg leave of the peoples of the north for the offal of dead cattle! Ye know the saying: "North are the vermin; South are the lice." *We* are the Jungle. Choose ye, O choose. It is good hunting! For the Pack – for the Full Pack – for the lair and the litter; for the in-kill and the out-kill; for the mate that drives the doe and the little, little cub within the cave, it is met – it is met – it is met!'

The Pack answered with one deep crashing bark that sounded in the night like a tree falling. 'It is met,' they cried.

'Stay with these,' said Mowgli to his Four. 'We shall need every tooth. Phao and Akela must make ready the battle. I go to count the dogs.'

'It is death!' Won-tolla cried, half-rising. 'What can such an hairless one do against the Red Dog? Even the Striped One, remember—'

'Thou art indeed an outlier,' Mowgli called back, 'but we will speak when the dholes are dead. Good hunting all!'

He hurried off into the darkness wild with excitement, hardly looking where he set foot, and the natural consequence was that he tripped full length over Kaa's great coils where the python lay watching a deer-path near the river.

'Kssha!' said Kaa angrily. 'Is this jungle work to stamp and tramp and undo a night's hunting – when the game are moving so well, too?'

'The fault was mine,' said Mowgli, picking himself up. 'Indeed I was seeking thee, Flathead, but each time we meet thou art longer and broader by the length of my arm. There is none like thee in the Jungle, wise, old, strong, and most beautiful Kaa.'

'Now whither does *this* trail lead?' Kaa's voice was gentler. 'Not a moon since there was a Manling with a knife threw stones at my head and called me bad little tree-cat names because I lay asleep in the open.'

'Ay, and turned every driven deer to all the winds, and Mowgli was hunting, and this same Flathead was too deaf to hear his whistle and leave the deer-roads free,' Mowgli answered composedly, sitting down among the painted coils.

'Now this same Manling comes with soft, tickling words to this same Flathead, telling him that he is wise, and strong, and beautiful, and this same old Flathead believes and coils a place, thus, for this same stone-throwing Manling and . . . Art thou at ease now? Could Bagheera give thee so good a resting-place?'

Kaa had, as usual, made a sort of soft half-hammock of himself under Mowgli's weight. The boy reached out in the darkness and gathered in the supple cable-like neck till Kaa's head rested on his shoulder, and then he told him all that had happened in the jungle that night.

'Wise I may be,' said Kaa at the end, 'but deaf I surely am. Else I should have heard the *Pheeal*. Small wonder the eaters-of-grass are uneasy. How many be the dhole?'

'I have not seen yet. I came hot foot to thee. Thou art older than Hathi. But, oh, Kaa,' – here Mowgli wriggled with joy, 'it will be good hunting! Few of us will see another moon.'

'Dost *thou* strike in this? Remember thou art a man; and remember what pack cast thee out. Let the wolf look to the dog. *Thou* art a man.'

'Last year's nuts are this year's black earth,' said Mowgli. 'It is true that I am a man, but it is in my stomach that this night I have said that I am a wolf. I called the River and the Trees to remember. I am of the Free People, Kaa, till the dhole has gone by.'

'Free People,' Kaa grunted. 'Free thieves! And thou hast tied thyself into the Death-knot for the sake of the memory of dead wolves! This is no good hunting.'

'It is my Word which I have spoken. The Trees know, the River knows. Till the dhole have gone by my Word comes not back to me.'

'Ngssh! That changes all trails. I had thought to take thee away with me to the northern marshes, but the Word – even the Word of a little, naked, hairless Manling – is the Word. Now I, Kaa, say—'

'Think well, Flathead, lest thou tie thyself into the Death-knot also. I need no Word from thee, for well I know—'

'Be it so, then,' said Kaa. 'I will give no Word; but what is in thy stomach to do when the dhole come?'

'They must swim the Waingunga. I thought to meet them with my knife in the shallows, the Pack behind me; and so stabbing and thrusting we might turn them down stream, or cool their throats a little.'

'The dhole do not turn and their throats are hot,' said Kaa. 'There will be neither Manling nor wolf-cub when that hunting is done, but only dry bones.'

'Alala! If we die we die. It will be most good hunting. But my stomach is young, and I have not seen many Rains. I am not wise nor strong. Hast thou a better plan, Kaa?'

'I have seen a hundred and a hundred Rains. Ere Hathi cast his milk-tushes[19] my trail was big in the dust. By the First Egg, I am older than many trees, and I have seen all that the Jungle has done.'

'But *this* is new hunting,' said Mowgli. 'Never before has the dhole crossed our trail.'

'What is has been. What will be is no more than a forgotten year striking backwards. Be still while I count those my years.'

For a long hour Mowgli lay back among the coils, playing with his knife, while Kaa, his head motionless on the ground, thought of all that he had seen and known since the day he came from the egg. The light seemed to go out of his eyes and leave them like stale opals, and now and again he made little stiff passes with his head to right and left, as though he were hunting in his sleep. Mowgli dozed quietly, for he knew that there is nothing like sleep before hunting, and he was trained to take it at any hour of the day or night.

Then he felt Kaa grow bigger and broader below him as the huge python puffed himself out, hissing with the noise of a sword drawn from a steel scabbard.

'I have seen all the dead seasons,' Kaa said at last, 'and the great trees and the old elephants and the rocks that were bare and sharp-pointed ere the moss grew. Art *thou* still alive, Manling?'

'It is only a little after moonrise,'[20] said Mowgli. 'I do not understand—'

'Hssh! I am again Kaa. I knew it was but a little time. Now we will go to the river, and I will show thee what is to be done against the dhole.'

He turned, straight as an arrow, for the main stream of the Waingunga, plunging in a little above the pool that hid the Peace Rock, Mowgli at his side.

'Nay, do not swim. I go swiftly. My back, Little Brother.'

Mowgli tucked his left arm round Kaa's neck, dropped his right close to his body and straightened his feet. Then Kaa breasted the current as he alone could, and the ripple of the checked water stood up in a frill round Mowgli's neck and his feet were waved to and fro in the eddy under the python's lashing sides. A mile or so above the Peace Rock the Waingunga narrows between a gorge of marble rocks from eighty to a hundred feet high, and the current runs like a mill-race between and over all manner of ugly stones. But Mowgli did not trouble his head about the water: no water in the world could have given him a moment's fear. He was looking at the gorge on either side and sniffing uneasily, for there was a sweetish-sourish smell in the air, very like the smell of a big ant-hill on a hot day. Instinctively he lowered himself in the water, only raising his head to breathe, and Kaa came to anchor with a double twist of his tail round a sunken rock, holding Mowgli in the hollow of a coil, while the water raced by.

'This is the Place of Death,' said the boy. 'Why do we come here?'

'They sleep,' said Kaa. 'Hathi will not turn aside for the Striped One. Yet Hathi and the Striped One together turn aside for the dhole, and the dhole they say turns aside for nothing.

And yet for whom do the Little People of the Rocks turn aside? Tell me, Master of the Jungle, who is the Master of the Jungle?'

'These,' Mowgli whispered. 'It is the Place of Death. Let us go.'

'Nay, look well, for they are asleep. It is as it was when I was not the length of thy arm.'

The split and weatherworn rocks of the gorge of the Waingunga had been used since the beginning of the Jungle by the Little People of the Rocks[21] – the busy, furious, black, wild bees of India; and, as Mowgli knew well, all trails turned off half a mile away from their country. For centuries the Little People had hived and swarmed from cleft to cleft and swarmed again, staining the white marble with stale honey, and made their combs tall and deep and black in the dark of the inner caves, and neither man nor beast nor fire nor water had ever touched them. The length of the gorge on both sides was hung as it were with black shimmery velvet curtains, and Mowgli sank as he looked, for those were the clotted millions of the sleeping bees. There were other lumps and festoons and things like decayed tree-trunks studded on the face of the rock – the old combs of past years, or new cities built in the shadow of the windless gorge – and huge masses of spongy, rotten trash had rolled down and stuck among the trees and creepers that clung to the rock-face. As he listened he heard more than once the rustle and slide of a honey-loaded comb turning over or falling away somewhere in the dark galleries; then a booming of angry wings and the sullen drip, drip, drip, of the wasted honey, guttering along till it lipped over some ledge in the open and sluggishly trickled down on the twigs. There was a tiny little beach, not five feet broad, on one side of the river, and that was piled high with the rubbish of uncounted years. There lay dead bees, drones, sweepings, stale combs, and wings of marauding moths and beetles that had strayed in after honey, all tumbled in smooth piles of the finest black dust. The mere sharp smell of it was enough to frighten anything that had no wings, and knew what the Little People were.

Kaa moved up stream again till he came to a sandy bar at the head of the gorge.

'Here is this season's kill,' said he. 'Look!'

On the bank lay the skeletons of a couple of young deer and a buffalo. Mowgli could see that no wolf nor jackal had touched the bones, which were laid out naturally.

'They came beyond the line, they did not know,'[22] murmured Mowgli, 'and the Little People killed them. Let us go ere they awake.'

'They do not wake till the dawn,' said Kaa. 'Now I will tell thee. A hunted buck from the south, many, many Rains ago, came hither from the south, not knowing the jungle, a pack on his trail. Being made blind by fear he leaped from above, the pack running by sight, for they were hot and blind on the trail. The sun was high, and the Little People were many and very angry. Many, too, were those of the pack who leaped into the Waingunga, but they were dead ere they took water. Those who did not leap died also in the rocks above. But the buck lived.'

'How?'

'Because he came first, running for his life, leaping ere the Little People were aware, and was in the river when they gathered to kill. The pack, following, was altogether lost under the weight of the Little People, who had been roused by the feet of that buck.'[23]

'The buck lived?' Mowgli repeated slowly.

'At least he did not die *then*, though none waited his coming down with a strong body to hold him safe against the water, as a certain old, fat, deaf, yellow Flathead would wait for a Manling – yea, though there were all the dholes of the Dekkan on his trail. What is in thy stomach?'

Kaa's head lay on Mowgli's wet shoulder, and his tongue quivered by the boy's ear. There was a long silence before Mowgli whispered:[24]

'It is to pull the very whiskers of Death, but – Kaa, thou art, indeed, the wisest of all the Jungle.'

'So many have said. Look now, if the dholes follow thee—'

'As surely they will follow. Ho! ho! I have many little thorns under my tongue to prick into their hides.'

'If they follow thee hot and blind, looking only at thy shoulders, those who do not die up above will take water either here or lower down, for the Little People will rise up and cover them. Now the Waingunga is hungry water, and they will have no Kaa to hold them, but will go down, such as live, to the shallows by the Seeonee lairs, and there thy Pack may meet them by the throat.'

'Ahai! Eowawa! Better could not be till the Rains fall in the dry season. There is now only the little matter of the run and the leap. I will make me known to the dholes, so that they shall follow me very closely.'

'Hast thou seen the rocks above thee? From the landward side?'

'Indeed no. That I had forgotten.'

'Go look. It is all rotten ground, cut and full of holes. One of thy clumsy feet set down without seeing would end the hunt. See, I leave thee here, and for thy sake only I will carry word to the Pack that they may know where to look for the dhole. For myself, I am not of one skin with *any* wolf.'

When Kaa disliked an acquaintance he could be more unpleasant than any of the Jungle people, except perhaps Bagheera. He swam down stream, and opposite the Rock he came on Phao and Akela listening to the night noises.

'Hssh! dogs,' he said cheerfully. 'The dhole will come down stream. If ye be not afraid ye can kill them in the shallows.'

'When come they?' said Phao. 'And where is my man-cub?' said Akela.

'They come when they come,' said Kaa. 'Wait and see. As for *thy* man-cub, from whom thou hast taken his Word and so laid him open to Death, *thy* man-cub is with *me*, and if he be not already dead the fault is none of thine, bleached dog! Wait here for the dhole, and be glad that the man-cub and I strike on thy side.'

Kaa flashed up stream again and moored himself in the middle of the gorge, looking upwards at the line of the cliff. Presently he saw Mowgli's head move against the stars: then there was a whizz in the air, the keen clean *schloop* of a body falling feet first; next minute the boy was at rest again in the loop of Kaa's body.

'It is no leap by night,' said Mowgli quietly. 'I have jumped twice as far for sport; but that is an evil place above – low bushes and gullies that go down deep – all full of the Little People. I have put big stones one above the other by the side of three gullies. These I shall throw down with my feet in running, and the Little People will rise up behind me angry.'

'That is man's cunning,' said Kaa. 'Thou art wise, but the Little People are always angry.'

'Nay, at twilight all wings near and far rest for awhile. I will play with the dhole at twilight, for the dhole hunts best by day. He follows now Won-tolla's blood-trail.'

'Chil does not leave a dead ox, nor the dhole a blood-trail,' said Kaa.

'Then I will make him a new blood-trail – of his own blood if I can, and give him dirt to eat. Thou wilt stay here, Kaa, till I come with my dholes?'

'Ay, but what if they kill thee in the Jungle or the Little People kill thee before thou canst leap down to the river?'

'When to-morrow comes we will kill to-morrow,' said Mowgli, quoting a Jungle saying; and again, 'When I am dead it is time to sing the Death Song. Good hunting, Kaa.'

He loosed his arm from the python's neck and went down the gorge like a log in a freshet, paddling towards the far bank, where he found slack water, and laughing aloud from sheer happiness. There was nothing Mowgli liked better than, as he himself said, 'to pull the whiskers of Death' and make the Jungle feel that he was their overlord. He had often, with Baloo's help, robbed bees' nests in single trees, and he knew that the Little People disliked the smell of wild garlic. So he gathered a small bundle of it, tied it up with a bark string, and then followed Won-tolla's blood-trail as it ran southerly from the lairs, for some five miles, looking at the trees with his head on one side and chuckling as he looked.

'Mowgli the Frog have I been,' said he to himself, 'Mowgli the Wolf have I said that I am. Now Mowgli the Ape must I be before I am Mowgli the Buck. At the end I shall be Mowgli the Man. Ho!' and he slid his thumb along the eighteen-inch blade of his knife.

Won-tolla's trail, all rank with dark blood-spots, ran under a forest of thick trees that grew close together and stretched

away north-eastward, gradually growing thinner and thinner
to within two miles of the Bee Rocks. From the last tree to the
low scrub of the Bee Rocks was open country, where there was
hardly cover enough to hide a wolf. Mowgli trotted along
under the trees, judging distances between branch and branch,
occasionally climbing up a trunk and taking a trial leap from
one tree to another, till he came to the open ground, which he
studied very carefully for an hour. Then he turned, picked up
Won-tolla's trail where he had left it, settled himself in a tree
with an outrunning branch some eight feet from the ground,
hung his bunch of garlic in a safe crotch, and sat still, sharpening his knife on the sole of his foot.[25]

A little before midday when the sun was very warm, he
heard the patter of feet and smelt the abominable smell of the
dhole pack as they trotted steadily and pitilessly along
Won-tolla's trail. Seen from above the red dhole does not look
half the size of a wolf, but Mowgli knew how strong his feet
and jaws were. He watched the sharp bay head of the leader
snuffing along the trail and gave him 'Good hunting!'

The brute looked up and his companions halted behind him,
scores and scores of red dogs with low-hung tails, heavy shoulders, weak quarters, and bloody mouths. The dholes are a very
silent people as a rule, and they have no manners even in their
own Dekkan. Fully two hundred must have gathered below
him, but he could see that the leaders sniffed hungrily on
Won-tolla's trail, and tried to drag the pack forward. That
would never do, or they would be at the lairs in broad daylight,
and Mowgli meant to hold them under his tree till twilight.

'By whose leave do ye come here?' said Mowgli.

'All jungles are our jungle,' was the reply, and the dhole that
gave it bared his white teeth. Mowgli looked down with a smile
and imitated perfectly the sharp chitter-chatter of Chikai, the
leaping rat of the Dekkan, meaning the dholes to understand
that he considered them no better than Chikai. The pack closed
up round the tree trunk and the leader bayed savagely, calling
Mowgli a tree-ape. For an answer Mowgli stretched down one
naked leg and wriggled his bare toes just above the leader's
head. That was enough, and more than enough, to wake the

pack to stupid rage. Those who have hair between their toes do not care to be reminded of it. Mowgli caught his foot away as the leader leaped and said sweetly: 'Dog, red dog! Go back to the Dekkan and eat lizards. Go to Chikai thy brother, dog, dog, red, red dog! There is hair between every toe!' He twiddled his toes a second time.

'Come down ere we starve thee out, hairless ape,' yelled the pack, and this was exactly what Mowgli wanted. He laid himself down along the branch, his cheek to the bark, his right arm free, and for some five minutes he told the pack what he thought and knew about them, their manners, their customs, their mates, and their puppies. There is no speech in the world so rancorous and so stinging as the language the Jungle People use to show scorn and contempt. When you come to think of it you will see how this must be so. As Mowgli told Kaa, he had many little thorns under his tongue, and slowly and deliberately he drove the dholes from silence to growls, from growls to yells, and from yells to hoarse slavery ravings. They tried to answer his taunts, but a cub might as well have tried to answer Kaa in a rage, and all the while Mowgli's right hand lay crooked at his side, ready for action, his feet locked round the branch. The big bay leader had leaped many times into the air, but Mowgli dared not risk a false blow. At last, made furious beyond his natural strength, he bounded up seven or eight feet clear of the ground. Then Mowgli's hand shot out like the head of a tree-snake, and gripped him by the scruff of his neck, and the branch shook with the jar as his weight fell back, and Mowgli was almost wrenched on to the ground. But he never loosed his grip, and inch by inch he hauled the beast, hanging like a drowned jackal, up on the branch. With his left hand he reached for his knife and cut off the red, bushy tail, flinging the dhole back to earth again. That was all he needed. The dhole would not go forward on Won-tolla's trail now till they had killed Mowgli, or Mowgli had killed them. He saw them settle down in circles with a quiver of the haunches that meant revenge to the death,[26] and so he climbed to a higher crotch, settled his back comfortably and went to sleep.

After three or four hours he waked and counted the pack.

They were all there, silent, husky, and dry, with eyes of steel. The sun was beginning to sink. In half an hour the Little People of the Rocks would be ending their labours, and, as you know, the dhole does not fight well in the twilight.

'I did not need such faithful watchers,' he said, standing up on a branch, 'but I will remember this. Ye be true dholes, but to my thinking too much of one kind. For that reason I do not give the big lizard-eater his tail again. Art thou not pleased, Red Dog?'

'I myself will tear out thy stomach,' yelled the leader, biting the foot of the tree.

'Nay, but consider, wise rat of Dekkan. There will now be many litters of little tailless red dogs, yea, with raw red stumps that sting when the sand is hot. Go home, Red Dog, and cry that an ape has done this. Ye will not go? Come then with me, and I will make ye very wise.'

He moved monkey-fashion[27] into the next tree, and so on into the next and the next, the pack following with lifted hungry heads. Now and then he would pretend to fall, and the pack would tumble one over the other in their haste to be in at the death. It was a curious sight – the boy with the knife that shone in the low sunlight as it sifted through the upper branches, and the silent pack with their red coats all aflame huddling and following below. When he came to the last tree he took the garlic and rubbed himself all over carefully, and the dholes yelled with scorn. 'Ape with a wolf's tongue, dost thou think to cover thy scent?' they said. 'We will follow to the death.'

'Take thy tail,' said Mowgli, flinging it back along the course he had taken. The pack naturally rushed back a little when they smelt the blood.[28] 'And follow now – to the death!'

He had slipped down the tree trunk, and headed like the wind in bare feet for the Bee Rocks, before the dholes saw what he would do.

They gave one deep howl and settled down to the long lobbing canter that can, at the last, run down anything that lives. Mowgli knew their pack pace to be much slower than that of the wolves, or he would never have risked a two-mile run in full sight. They were sure that the boy was theirs at last, and he was sure that he had them to play with as he pleased. All his trouble was to keep them sufficiently hot behind him to prevent them turning off too soon. He ran cleanly, evenly, and springily; the tailless leader not five yards behind him; and the pack stringing out[29] over perhaps a quarter of a mile of ground, crazy and blind with the rage of slaughter. So he kept his distance by ear, reserving his last effort for the rush across the Bee Rocks.

The Little People had gone to sleep in the early twilight, for it was not the season of late blossoming flowers;[30] but as Mowgli's first footfalls rang hollow on the hollow ground he heard a sound as though all the earth were humming. Then he ran as he had never run in his life before, spurned aside one – two – three of the piles of stones into the dark sweet-smelling gullies; heard a roar like the roar of the sea in a cave, saw with the tail of his eye the air grow dark behind him, saw the current of the Waingunga far below, and a flat, diamond-shaped head in the water; leaped outward with all his strength, the tailless dhole snapping at his shoulder in mid-air, and dropped feet first to the safety of the river, breathless and triumphant. There was not a sting on his body, for the smell of the garlic had checked the Little People for just the few seconds that carried him across the rocks. When he rose Kaa's coils were steadying him and things were bounding over the edge of the cliff – great lumps, it seemed, of clustered bees falling like plummets; and as each lump touched water the bees flew upward and the body of a dhole whirled down stream. Overhead they could hear furious short yells that were drowned in a roar like thunder – the roar of the wings of the Little People of the Rocks. Some of the dholes, too, had fallen into the gullies that communicated with the underground caves, and there choked, and fought, and snapped among the tumbled honeycombs, and at last, borne up dead on the heaving waves of bees beneath them, shot out of some hole in the river face, to roll over on the black rubbish heaps. There were dholes who had leaped short into the trees on the cliffs, and the bees blotted out their shapes; but the greater number of them, maddened by the stings, had flung themselves into the river; and, as Kaa said, the Waingunga was hungry water.

Kaa held Mowgli fast till the boy had recovered his breath.

'We may not stay here,' he said. 'The Little People are roused indeed. Come!'

Swimming low and diving as often as he could, Mowgli went down the river with the knife in his hand.

'Slowly, slowly!' said Kaa. 'One tooth does not kill a hundred unless it be a cobra's, and many of the dholes took water swiftly when they saw the Little People rise. *They* are unhurt.'[31]

'The more work for my knife, then. Phai! How the Little People follow.' Mowgli sank again. The face of the water was blanketed with wild bees buzzing sullenly and stinging all they found.

'Nothing was ever yet lost by silence,' said Kaa – no sting could penetrate his scales – 'and thou hast all the long night for the hunting. Hear them howl!'

Nearly half the pack had seen the trap their fellows rushed into, and, turning sharp aside, had flung themselves into the water where the gorge broke down in steep banks. Their cries of rage and their threats against the 'tree-ape' who had brought them to their shame mixed with the yells and growls of those who had been punished by the Little People. To remain ashore was death, and every dhole knew it. The pack was swept along the current, down and down to the rocks[32] of the Peace Pool, but even there the angry Little People followed and forced them to the water again. Mowgli could hear the voice of the tailless leader bidding his people hold on and kill out every wolf in Seeonee. But he did not waste his time in listening.

'One kills in the dark behind us!' snapped a dhole. 'Here is tainted water!'

Mowgli had dived forward like an otter, twitched a struggling dhole under water before he could open his mouth, and dark, oily rings rose in the Peace Pool as the body plopped up, turning on its side. The dholes tried to turn, but the current forced them by, and the Little People darted at their heads and ears, and they could hear the challenge of the Seeonee Pack growing louder and deeper in the gathering darkness ahead. Again Mowgli dived, and again a dhole went under and rose dead, and again the clamour broke out at the rear of the pack, some howling that it was best to go ashore, others calling on their leader to lead them back to the Dekkan, and others bidding Mowgli show himself and be killed.

'They come to the fight with two stomachs and many voices,' said Kaa. 'The rest is with thy brethren below yonder. The Little People go back to sleep, and I will turn also. I do not help wolves.'[33]

A wolf came running along the bank on three legs, leaping up and down, laying his head sideways close to the ground, hunching his back, and breaking a couple of feet into the air, as though he were playing with his cubs. It was Won-tolla, the Outlier, and he said never a word, but continued his horrible sport beside the dholes. They had been long in the water now, and were swimming laboriously, their coats drenched and heavy, and their bushy tails dragging like sponges, so tired and shaken that they, too, were silent, watching the pair of blazing eyes that moved abreast of them.

'This is no good hunting,' said one at last.

'Good hunting!' said Mowgli as he rose boldly at the brute's side and sent the long knife home behind the shoulder, pushing hard to avoid the dying snap.

'Art thou there, man-cub?' said Won-tolla, from the bank.

'Ask of the dead, Outlier,' Mowgli replied. 'Have none come down stream? I have filled these dogs' mouths with dirt; I have tricked them in the broad daylight, and their leader lacks his tail, but here be some few for thee still. Whither shall I drive them?'

'I will wait,' said Won-tolla. 'The long night is before me, and I shall see well.'[34]

Nearer and nearer came the bay of the Seeonee wolves. 'For the Pack, for the full Pack it is met!' and a bend in the river drove the dholes forward among the sands and shoals opposite the Seeonee lairs.

Then they saw their mistake. They should have landed half a mile higher up and rushed the wolves on dry ground. Now it was too late. The bank was lined with burning eyes, and except for the horrible *Pheeal* cry that had never stopped since sundown there was no sound in the jungle. It seemed as though

Won-tolla was fawning on them to come ashore; and 'Turn and take hold!' said the leader of the dholes. The entire pack flung themselves at the shore, threshing and squattering through the shoal water till the face of the Waingunga was all white and torn, and the great ripples went from side to side like bow-waves from a boat. Mowgli followed the rush, stabbing and slicing as the dholes, huddled together, rushed up the river-beach in a wave.

Then the long fight began, heaving and straining and splitting and scattering and narrowing and broadening along the red wet sands, and over and between the tangled tree-roots, and through and among the bushes, and in and out of the grass clumps, for even now the dholes were two to one. But they met wolves fighting for all that made the pack, and not only the short, deep-chested white-tusked hunters of the pack, but the wild-eyed lahinis[35] – the she-wolves of the lair, as the saying is – fighting for their litters, with here and there a yearling wolf, his first coat still half woolly, tugging and grappling by their sides. A wolf, you must know, flies at the throat or snaps at the flank, while a dhole by preference bites low,[36] so when the dholes were struggling out of the water and had to raise their heads the odds were with the wolves; on dry land the wolves suffered, but in the water or on land Mowgli's knife came and went the same.[37] The Four had worked their way to his aid.[38] Gray Brother, crouched between the boy's knees, protected his stomach, while the others guarded his back and either side, or stood over him when the shock of a leaping, yelling dhole who had thrown himself on the steady blade bore him down. For the rest, it was one tangled confusion – a locked and swaying mob that moved from right to left and from left to right along the bank, and also ground round and round slowly on its own centre. Here would be a heaving mound, like a water-blister in a whirlpool, which would break like a water-blister, and throw up four or five mangled dogs, each striving to get back to the centre; here would be a single wolf borne down by two or three dholes dragging them forward, and sinking the while; here a yearling cub would be held up by the pressure round him, though he had been killed early in the fight, while his mother, crazed with dumb rage, rolled over snapping and passing on; and in the middle of the thickest fight, perhaps, one wolf and one dhole, forgetting everything else, would be manoeuvring for first hold till they were swept away by a rush of yelling fighters. Once Mowgli passed Akela, a dhole on either flank, and his all but toothless jaws closed over the loins of a third; and once he saw Phao, his teeth set in the throat of a dhole, tugging the unwilling beast forward till the yearlings could finish him. But the bulk of the fight was blind flurry and smother in the dark; hit, trip, and tumble, yelp, groan and worry-worry-worry round him and behind him and above him.

As the night wore on the quick giddy-go-round motion increased. The dholes were wearied and afraid[39] to attack the stronger wolves, though they did not yet dare to run[40] away; but Mowgli felt that the end was coming soon, and contented himself with striking to cripple. The yearlings were growing bolder; there was time to breathe; and now the mere flicker of the knife would sometimes turn a dhole aside.[41]

'The meat is very near the bone,' Gray Brother gasped. He was bleeding from a score of flesh-wounds.

'But the bone is yet to be cracked,' said Mowgli. 'Aowawa! *Thus* do we do in the Jungle!' The red blade ran like a flame along the side of a dhole whose hind-quarters were hidden by the weight of a clinging wolf.

'My kill!' snorted the wolf through his wrinkled nostrils. 'Leave him to me!'

'Is thy stomach *still* empty, Outlier?' said Mowgli. Won-tolla was fearfully punished, but his grip had paralysed the dhole, who could not turn round and reach him.

'By the Bull that bought me,' Mowgli cried, with a bitter laugh, 'it is the tailless one!' And indeed it was the big bay-coloured leader.

'It is not wise to kill cubs and lahinis,' Mowgli went on philosophically, wiping the blood out of his eyes, 'unless one also kills the lair-father, and it is in my stomach that this lair-father kills thee.'[42]

A dhole leaped to his leader's aid, but before his teeth had found Won-tolla's flank, Mowgli's knife was in his chest, and Gray Brother took what was left.

'And thus do we do in the Jungle,' said Mowgli.

Won-tolla said not a word, only his jaws were closing and closing on the backbone as life ebbed. The dhole shuddered, his head dropped and he lay still, and Won-tolla dropped above him.

'Huh! The Blood Debt is paid,' said Mowgli. 'Sing the song, Won-tolla.'

'He hunts no more,' said Gray Brother, 'and Akela too is silent, this long time.'

'The bone is cracked!' thundered Phao, son of Phaona. 'They go! Kill, kill out, O hunters of the Free People!'

Dhole after dhole was slinking away from those dark and bloody sands to the river, to the thick jungle, up stream or down stream as he saw the road clear.

'The debt! The debt!' shouted Mowgli. 'Pay the debt! They have slain the Lone Wolf! Let not a dog go!'

He was flying to the river, knife in hand, to check any dhole who dared to take water, when, from under a mound of nine dead, rose Akela's head and fore-quarters, and Mowgli dropped on his knees beside the Lone Wolf.

'Said I not it would be my last fight?' Akela gasped. 'It is good hunting. And thou, Little Brother?'

'I live, having killed many.'

'Even so. I die, and I would – I would die by thee, Little Brother.'

Mowgli took the terrible scarred head on his knees, and put his arms round the torn neck.

'It is long since the old days of Shere Khan and a man-cub that rolled naked in the dust,' coughed Akela.

'Nay, nay, I am a wolf. I am of one skin with the Free People,' Mowgli cried. 'It is no will of mine that I am a man.'

'Thou art a man, Little Brother, wolfling of my watching. Thou art all a man, or else the Pack had fled before the dhole. My life I owe to thee, and today thou hast saved the Pack even as once I saved thee. Hast thou forgotten? All debts are paid now. Go to thine own people. I tell thee again, eye of my eye, this hunting is ended. Go to thine own people.'

'I will never go. I will hunt alone in the Jungle. I have said it.'

'After the summer come the rains, and after the rains comes the spring. Go back before thou art driven.'

'Who will drive me?'

'Mowgli will drive Mowgli. Go back to thy people. Go to man.'

'When Mowgli drives Mowgli I will go,' Mowgli answered.

'There is no more for thee,'[43] said Akela. 'Now I would speak to my kind.[44] Little Brother, canst thou raise me to my feet? I also am a leader of the Free People.'

Very carefully and gently Mowgli raised[45] Akela to his feet, both arms round him, and the Lone Wolf drew a deep breath and began the Death Song that a leader of the Pack should sing when he dies. It gathered strength as he went on, lifting and lifting and ringing far across the river, till it came to the last 'Good hunting!' and Akela shook himself clear of Mowgli for an instant, and leaping into the air, fell backwards dead upon his last and most terrible kill.

Mowgli sat with his head on his knees, careless of anything else, while the last of the dying dholes[46] were being overtaken and run down by the merciless lahinis. Little by little the cries died away, and the wolves came back limping as their wounds stiffened to take stock of the dead. Fifteen of the pack, as well as half a dozen lahinis, were dead by the river, and of the others not one was unmarked. Mowgli sat through it all till the cold daybreak, when Phao's wet red muzzle was dropped in his hand, and Mowgli drew back to show the gaunt body of Akela.

'Good hunting!' said Phao, as though Akela were still alive, and then over his bitten shoulder to the others: 'Howl, dogs! A wolf has died to-night!'

But of all the pack of two hundred fighting dholes, Red Dogs of the Dekkan, whose boast is that no living thing in the Jungle dare stand before them,[47] not one returned to the Dekkan to carry that news.

Chil's Song

This is the song that Chil sang as the kites dropped down
one after another to the river-bed, when the great fight
was finished. Chil is good friends with everybody, but he
is a cold-blooded kind of creature at heart, because he
knows that almost everybody in the Jungle comes to him
in the long-run.

These were my companions going forth by night,
              (*Chil!*[1] *Look you, for Chil!*)
Now come I to whistle them the ending of the fight.
              (*Chil! Vanguards of Chil!*)
Word they gave me overhead of quarry newly slain,
Word I gave them underfoot of buck upon the plain.
Here's an end of every trail – they shall not speak again!

They that gave the hunting-cry – they that followed fast –
              (*Chil! Look you, for Chil!*)
They that bade the *sambhur* wheel, and pinned him as he
   passed
              (*Chil! Vanguards of Chil!*)
They that lagged behind the scent – they that ran before,
They that shunned the level horn – they that overbore,
Here's an end of every trail – they shall not follow more.

These were my companions. Pity 't was they died!
              (*Chil! Look you, for Chil!*)
Now come I to comfort them that knew them in their pride.
              (*Chil! Vanguards of Chil!*)
Tattered flank and sunken eye, open mouth and red,
Locked and lank and lone they lie, the dead upon their dead.
Here's an end of every trail – and here my hosts are fed!

THE SPRING RUNNING

Man goes to Man! Cry the challenge through the Jungle!
   He that was our Brother goes away.
Hear, now, and judge, O ye People of the Jungle,
   Answer, who shall turn him – who shall stay?

Man goes to Man! He is weeping in the Jungle:
   He that was our Brother sorrows sore!
Man goes to Man! (Oh, we loved him in the Jungle!)
   To the Man-trail where we may not follow more.

The second year after the great fight with Red Dog and the
death of Akela, Mowgli must have been nearly seventeen years
old. He looked older, for hard exercise, the best of good eating,
and baths whenever he felt in the least hot or dusty had given
him strength and growth far beyond his age. He could swing by
one hand from a top branch for half an hour at a time, when he
had occasion to look along the tree-roads. He could stop a
young buck in mid-gallop and throw him sideways by the head.
He could even jerk over the big blue wild boars that lived in the
Marshes of the North. The Jungle People, who used to fear him
for his wits, feared him now for his mere strength, and when he
moved quietly on his own affairs the whisper of his coming
cleared the wood paths. And yet the look in his eyes was always
gentle. Even when he fought his eyes never blazed as Bagheera's
did. They only grew more and more interested and excited, and
that was one of the things that Bagheera himself did not
understand.

He asked Mowgli about it, and the boy laughed and said,
'When I miss the kill I am angry. When I must go empty for two
days I am very angry. Do not my eyes talk then?'

'The mouth is hungry,'[1] said Bagheera, 'but the eyes say

nothing. Hunting, eating, or swimming, it is all one – like a stone in wet or dry weather.' Mowgli looked at him lazily from under his long eye-lashes, and, as usual, the panther's head dropped. Bagheera knew his master.

They were lying out far up the side of a hill overlooking the Waingunga, and the morning mists lay below them in bands of white and green. As the sun rose they changed into bubbling seas of red and gold, churned off, and let the low rays stripe the dried grass on which Mowgli and Bagheera were resting. It was the end of the cold weather, the leaves and the trees looked worn and faded, and there was a dry ticking rustle when the wind blew. A little leaf tap-tap-tapped furiously against a twig as a single leaf caught in a current will. It roused Bagheera, for he snuffed the morning air with a deep hollow cough, threw himself on his back and struck with his fore paws at the nodding leaf above.

'The year turns,' he said. 'The Jungle goes forward. The Time of New Talk is near. That leaf knows. It is very good.'

'The grass is dry,' Mowgli answered, pulling up a tuft. 'Even Eye-of-the-Spring (that is a little trumpet-shaped waxy red flower that runs in and out among the grasses) – even Eye-of-the-Spring is shut and . . . Bagheera, *is* it well for the Black Panther so to lie on his back and beat with his paws in the air as though he were the tree-cat?'

'Aowh!' said Bagheera. He seemed to be thinking of other things.

'I say, *is* it well for the Black Panther so to mouth and cough and howl and roll. Remember, we be the Masters of the Jungle, thou and I.'

'Indeed, yes; I hear, Man-cub.' Bagheera rolled over hurriedly and sat up, the dust on his ragged black flanks. (He was just casting his winter coat.) 'We be surely the Masters of the Jungle! Who is so strong as Mowgli? Who so wise?' There was a curious drawl in the voice that made Mowgli turn to see whether by any chance the Black Panther were making fun of him, for the Jungle is full of words that sound like one thing but mean another. 'I said we be beyond question the Masters of the Jungle,' Bagheera repeated. 'Have I done wrong? I did not know that the Man-cub no longer lay upon the ground. Does he fly, then?'

Mowgli sat with his elbows on his knees looking out across the valley at the daylight. Somewhere down in the woods below a bird was trying over in a husky, reedy voice the first few notes of his spring song. It was no more than a shadow of the full-throated tumbling call he would be crying later, but Bagheera heard it.

'I said the Time of New Talk was near,' growled the Panther, switching his tail.

'I hear,' Mowgli answered. 'Bagheera, why dost thou shake all over? The sun is warm.'

'That is Ferao,[2] the scarlet woodpecker,' said Bagheera. '*He* has not forgotten. Now I too must remember my song,' and he began purring and crooning to himself, harking back dissatisfied again and again.

'There is no game afoot,' said Mowgli, lazily.

'Little Brother, are *both* thine ears stopped? That is no killing-word but my song that I make ready against the need.'[3]

'I had forgotten. I shall know when the Time of New Talk is here, because then thou and the others run away and leave me single-foot.' Mowgli spoke rather savagely.

'But, indeed, Little Brother,' Bagheera began, 'we do not always—'

'I say ye do,' said Mowgli, shooting out his fore-finger angrily. 'Ye *do* run away, and I, who am the Master of the Jungle, must needs walk single-foot. How was it last season, when I would gather sugar-cane from the fields of a Man-Pack? I sent a runner – I sent thee! – to Hathi bidding him to come upon such a night and pluck the sweet grass for me with his trunk.'

'He came only two nights later,' said Bagheera, cowering a little, 'and of that long sweet grass that pleased thee so, he gathered more than any Man-cub could eat in all the nights of the Rains. His was no fault of mine.'

'He did not come upon the night when I sent him the word. No, he was trumpeting and running and roaring through valleys in the moonlight. His trail was like the trail of three elephants, for he would not hide among the trees. He danced in the moonlight before the houses of the Man-Pack. I saw him, and yet he would not come to me; and *I* am the Master of the Jungle!'

'It was the Time of New Talk,' said the Panther, always very humble. 'Perhaps, Little Brother, thou didst not that time call him by a Master-word? Listen to Ferao!'[4]

Mowgli's bad temper seemed to have boiled itself away. He lay back with his head on his arms, his eyes shut. 'I do not know – nor do I care,' he said sleepily. 'Let us sleep, Bagheera. My stomach is heavy in me. Make me a rest for my head.'

The Panther lay down again with a sigh, because he could hear Ferao practising and repractising his song against the spring-time of New Talk, as they say.

In an Indian Jungle the seasons slide one into the other almost without division. There seem to be only two – the wet and the dry, but if you look closely below the torrents of rain and the clouds of char and dust you will find all four going round in their regular order. Spring is the most wonderful, because she has not to cover a clean bare field with new leaves and flowers, but to drive before her and to put away the hanging-on, over-surviving raffle of half-green things which the gentle winter has suffered to live, and to make the partly dressed, stale earth feel new and young once more. And this she does so well that there is no spring in the world like the Jungle spring.

There is one day when all things are tired, and the very smells as they drift on the heavy air are old and used. One cannot explain, but it feels so. Then there is another day – to the eye nothing whatever has changed – when all the smells are new and delightful and the whiskers of the Jungle People quiver to their roots, and the winter hair comes away from their sides in long draggled locks. Then, perhaps, a little rain falls, and all the trees and the bushes and the bamboos and the mosses and the juicy-leaved plants wake with a noise of growing that you can almost hear, and under this noise runs, day and night, a deep hum. *That* is the noise of the Spring – a vibrating boom which is neither bees nor falling water nor the wind in the tree-tops, but the purring of the warm, happy world.

Up to this year Mowgli had always delighted in the turn of the seasons. It was he who generally saw the first Eye-of-the-Spring deep down among the grasses, and the first bank of spring clouds which are like nothing else in the Jungle. His voice could be heard in all sorts of wet star-lighted blossoming places, helping the big frogs through their choruses, or mocking the little upside down owls that hoot through the white nights. Like all his people, spring was the season he chose for his flittings – moving for mere joy of rushing through the warm air, thirty, forty, or fifty miles between twilight and the morning star, and coming back panting and laughing and wreathed with strange flowers. The Four did not follow him on these wild ringings of the Jungle, but went off to sing songs with other wolves. The Jungle People are very busy in the spring, and Mowgli could hear them grunting and screaming and whistling according to their kind. Their voices then are different from their voices at other times of the year, and that is one of the reasons why spring is called the Time of New Talk.

But that spring, as he told Bagheera, his stomach was new in him. Ever since the bamboo shoots turned spotty-brown he had been looking forward to the morning when the smells should change. But when that morning came, and Mor, the peacock, blazing in bronze and blue and gold, cried it aloud all along the misty woods, and Mowgli opened his mouth to send on the cry, the words choked between his teeth, and a feeling came over him that began at his toes and ended in his hair – a feeling of pure unhappiness, and he looked himself over to be sure that he had not trodden on a thorn. Mor cried the new smells, the other birds took it over, and from the rocks by the Waingunga he heard Bagheera's hoarse scream – something between the scream of an eagle and the neighing of a horse. There was a yelling and scattering of *bandar-log* in the new-budding branches above, and there stood Mowgli, his chest, filled to answer Mor, sinking in little gasps as the breath was driven out of it by this unhappiness.

He stared, but he could see no more than the mocking *bandar-log* scudding through the trees, and Mor, his tail spread in full splendour, dancing on the slopes below.

'The smells have changed,' screamed Mor. 'Good hunting, Little Brother! Where is thy answer?'

'Little Brother, good hunting!' whistled Chil the Kite and his mate swooping down together. The two baffed under Mowgli's nose so close that a pinch of downy white feathers brushed out.

A light spring rain – elephant-rain they call it – drove across the Jungle in a belt half a mile wide, left the new leaves wet and nodding behind, and died out in a double rainbow and a light roll of thunder. The spring-hum broke out for a minute and was silent, but all the Jungle folk seemed to be giving tongue at once. All except Mowgli.

'I have eaten good food,' he said to himself. 'I have drunk good water. Nor does my throat burn and grow small, as it did when I bit the blue-spotted root that Oo the turtle said was clean food. But my stomach is heavy, and I have, for no cause, given very bad talk to Bagheera and others, people of the Jungle and my people. Now, too, I am hot and now I am cold, and now I am neither hot nor cold, but angry with that which I cannot see. Huhu! It is time to make a running! To-night I will cross the ranges; yes, I will make a spring running to the Marshes of the North and back again. I have hunted too easily too long. The Four shall come with me, for they grow as fat as white grubs.'

He called, but never one of the Four answered. They were far beyond earshot, singing over the spring songs – the Moon and Sambhur Songs – with the wolves of the Pack, for in the spring-time the Jungle people make little difference between the day and the night. He gave the sharp barking note, but his only answer was the mocking *maiou* of the little spotted tree-cat winding in and out among the branches for early birds' nests. At this he shook all over with rage and half drew his knife. Then he became very haughty, though there was no one to see him, and stalked severely down the hillside, chin up and eyebrows down. But never a single one of his people asked him a question, for they were all too busy with their own affairs.

'Yes,' said Mowgli to himself, though in his heart he knew that he had no reason. 'Let the Red Dhole come from the Dekkan or the Red Flower dance among the bamboos, and all the Jungle runs whining to Mowgli calling him great elephant-names. But now, because Eye-of-the-Spring is red; and Mor, forsooth, must show his naked legs in some spring-dance, the Jungle goes mad as Tabaqui ... By the Bull that bought me, am I the Master of the Jungle or am I not? Be silent! What do ye here?'

A couple of young wolves of the pack were cantering down a path looking for open ground in which to fight. (You will remember that the law of the jungle forbids fighting where the pack can see.) Their neck-bristles were as stiff as wire, and they bayed furiously, crouching for the first grapple. Mowgli leaped forward, caught one outstretched throat in either hand, expecting to fling the creatures backwards, as he had often done in games or Pack hunts. But he had never before interfered with a spring fight. The two leaped forward and dashed him aside to the earth, and without word to waste rolled over and over close locked.

Mowgli was on his feet almost before he fell, his knife and his white teeth were bared, and at that minute he would have killed both for no reason but that they were fighting when he wished them to be quiet, although every wolf has full right under the law to fight. He danced round them with lowered shoulders and quivering hand ready to send in a double blow when the first flurry of the scuffle should be over, but while he waited the strength seemed to go out of his body, the knife point lowered, and he sheathed the knife and watched.

'I have eaten poison,' he said at last. 'Since I broke up the council with the Red Flower – since I killed Shere Khan none of the pack could fling me aside. And these be only tail-wolves in the pack, little hunters. My strength is gone from me, and presently I shall die. Oh, Mowgli, why dost thou not kill them both?'

The fight went on till one wolf ran away, and Mowgli was left alone on the torn and bloody ground looking now at his knife, and now at his legs and arms, while the feeling of unhappiness he had never known before covered him as water covers a log.

He killed early that evening and ate but little, so as to be in good fettle for his spring running, and he ate alone because all the Jungle People were away singing or fighting. It was a perfect white night, as they call it. All green things seemed to have made a month's growth since the morning. The branch that was yellow-leaved the day before dripped sap when Mowgli broke it. The mosses curled deep and warm over his feet, the young grass had no cutting edges, and all the voices of the jungle boomed like one deep harp-string touched by the moon – the full moon of New Talk, who splashed her light full on rock and pool, slipped it between trunk and creeper, and sifted it through the million leaves. Unhappy as he was,[5] Mowgli sang aloud with pure delight as he settled into his stride. It was more like flying than anything else, for he had chosen the long downward slope that leads to the Northern Marshes through the heart of the main jungle, where the springy ground deadened the fall of his feet. A man-taught man would have picked his way with many stumbles through the cheating moonlight, but Mowgli's muscles, trained by years of experience, bore him up as though he were a feather. When a rotten log or a hidden stone turned under his foot he saved himself, never checking his pace, without effort and without thought. When he tired of ground-going he threw up his hands monkey-fashion to the nearest creeper, and seemed to float rather than to climb up into the thin branches, whence he would follow a tree-road till his mood changed, and he shot downwards in a long leafy curve to the levels again. There were still hot hollows surrounded by wet rocks where he could hardly breathe for the heavy scents of the night-flowers, and the bloom along the creeper-buds; dark avenues where the moonlight lay in belts as regular as chequered marbles in a church aisle; thickets where the wet young growth stood breast-high about him and threw its arms round his waist; and hill tops crowned with broken rock, where he leaped from stone to stone above the lairs of the frightened little foxes. He would hear, very faint and far off, the *chug-drug* of a boar sharpening his tusks on a bole; and later would come across the great brute all alone, scribing and rending the red bark of a tree, his mouth dripping with foam and his eyes blazing like fire. Or he would turn aside to the sound of clashing horns and hissing grunts and dash past a couple of furious sambhur, staggering to and fro with lowered heads, striped with blood that shows black in the moonlight. Or at some rushing ford he would hear Jacala the crocodile bellowing like a bull; or disturb a knot of the Poison People; but before they could strike he would be away and across the glistening shingle, and deep into the Jungle again.

So he ran, sometimes shouting, sometimes singing to himself, the happiest thing in all the Jungle that night, till the smell of the flowers warned him that he was near the Marshes, and those lay far beyond his furthest hunting-grounds.

Here, again, a man-trained man would have sunk over head in three strides, but Mowgli's feet had eyes in them and they passed him from tussock to tussock and clump to quaking clump without asking help from the eyes in his head. He headed out to the middle of the swamp, disturbing the duck as he ran, and sat down on a moss-coated tree-trunk lapped in the black water. The marsh was awake all round him, for in the spring the Bird People sleep very lightly, and companies of them were coming or going the night through. But no one took any notice of Mowgli sitting among the tall reeds humming songs without words and looking at the soles of his hard brown feet in case of neglected thorns. All his unhappiness seemed to have been left behind in his own Jungle, and he was just beginning a song when it came back again – ten times worse than before. To make all worse the moon was setting.

This time Mowgli was frightened. 'It is here also!' he said half aloud. 'It has followed me,' and he looked over his shoulder to see whether the It were not standing behind him. 'There is no one here.' The night noises in the marsh went on, but never bird or beast spoke to him, and the new feeling of misery grew.

'I have eaten poison,' he said, in an awe-stricken voice. 'It must be that carelessly I have eaten poison, and my strength is going from me. I was afraid – and yet it was not *I* that was afraid – Mowgli was afraid when the two wolves fought. Akela, or even Phao, would have silenced them; yet Mowgli was afraid. That is sure sign I have eaten poison . . . But what do they care in the Jungle? They sing and howl and fight, and run in companies under the moon, and I – *Hai mai!*[6] – I am dying in the marshes, of that poison which I have eaten.' He was so sorry for himself that he nearly wept. 'And after,' he went on, 'they will find me lying in the black water. Nay, I will go back to my own Jungle and I will die upon the Council Rock, and Bagheera whom I love, if he is not screaming in the valley, Bagheera, perhaps, may watch by what is left for a little, lest Chil use me as he used Akela.'

A large warm tear splashed down on his knee, and, miserable as he was, Mowgli felt happy that he was so miserable, if you can understand that upside-down sort of happiness. 'As Chil the Kite used Akela,' he repeated, 'on the night I saved the Pack from Red Dog.' He was quiet for a little, thinking of the last words of the Lone Wolf, which you, of course, remember. 'Now Akela said to me many foolish things before he died, for when we die our stomachs change. He said . . . None the less, I *am* of the Jungle!'

In his excitement, as he remembered the fight on Waingunga bank, he shouted the last words aloud, and a wild buffalo-cow among the reeds sprang to her knees, snorting, 'Man!'

'Uhh!' said Mysa, the wild buffalo (Mowgli could hear him turn in his wallow), '*that* is no man. It is only the hairless wolf of the Seeonee Pack. On such nights runs he to and fro.'

'Uhh!' said the cow, dropping her head again to graze, 'I thought it was man.'

'I say no. Oh, Mowgli, is it danger?' lowed Mysa.

'Oh, Mowgli, is it danger?' the boy called back mockingly. 'That is all Mysa thinks for: is it danger? But for Mowgli, who goes to and fro in the Jungle by night watching, what care ye?'

'How loud he cries!' said the cow.

'Thus do they cry,' Mysa answered contemptuously, 'who having torn the grass up know not how to eat it.'

'For less than this,' Mowgli groaned to himself, 'for less than this even last Rains I had pricked Mysa out of his wallow and ridden him through the swamp on a rush halter.' He stretched his hand to break one of the feathery reeds, but drew it back with a sigh. Mysa went on steadily chewing the cud and the long grass ripped where the cow grazed. 'I will not die *here*,' he said angrily. 'Mysa, who is of one blood with Jacala and the pig, would mock me. Let us go beyond the swamp, and see what comes. Never have I run such a spring-running – hot and cold together. Up, Mowgli!'

He could not resist the temptation of stealing across the reeds to Mysa and pricking him with the point of his knife. The great dripping bull broke out of his wallow like a shell exploding, while Mowgli laughed till he sat down.

'Say now that the hairless wolf of the Seeonee Pack once herded thee, Mysa,' he called.

'Wolf! *Thou?*' the bull snorted, stamping in the mud. 'All the Jungle knows thou wast a herder of tame cattle – such a man's brat as shouts in the dust by the crops yonder. *Thou* of the Jungle! What hunter would have crawled like a snake among the leeches, and for a muddy jest – a jackal's jest – have shamed me before my cow? Come to firm ground, and I will – I will' . . . Mysa frothed at the mouth, for he has nearly the worst temper of anyone in the Jungle.

Mowgli watched him puff and blow with eyes that never changed. When he could make himself heard through the spattering mud-shower, he said: 'what Man-Pack lair here by the marshes, Mysa? This is new Jungle to me.'

'Go north, then,' roared the angry bull, for Mowgli had pricked him rather sharply. 'It was a naked cow-herd's jest. Go and tell them at the village at the foot of the marsh.'

'The Man-Pack do not love jungle-tales, nor do I think, Mysa, that a scratch more or less on thy hide is any matter for a council. But I will go and look at this village. Yes, I will go. Softly now! It is not every night that the Master of the Jungle comes to herd thee.'

He stepped out to the shivering ground on the edge of the marsh, well knowing that Mysa would never charge over it, and laughed, as he ran, to think of the bull's anger.

'My strength is not altogether gone,' he said. 'It may be the poison is not to the bone. There is a star sitting low yonder.' He looked at it steadily between half-shut hands. 'By the Bull that bought me, it is the Red Flower – the Red Flower that I lay beside before – before I came even to the first Seeonee Pack! Now that I have seen I will finish the running.'

The marsh ended in a broad plain where a light twinkled. It was a long time since Mowgli had concerned himself with the doings of men, but this night the glimmer of the Red Flower drew him forward as if it had been new game.[7]

'I will look,' said he, 'and I will see[8] how far the Man-Pack has changed.'

Forgetting that he was no longer in his own Jungle where he could do what he pleased, he trod carelessly through the dew-loaded grasses till he came to the hut where the light stood. Three or four yelping dogs gave tongue, for he was on the outskirts of a village.

'Ho!' said Mowgli, sitting down noiselessly, after sending back a deep wolf-growl that silenced the curs. 'What comes will come. Mowgli, what hast thou to do any more with the lairs of the Man-Pack?' He rubbed his mouth, remembering where a stone had struck it years ago when the other Man-Pack had cast him out.

The door of the hut opened and a woman stood peering out into the darkness. A child cried, and the woman said over her shoulder, 'Sleep. It was but a jackal that waked the dogs. In a little time morning comes.'

Mowgli in the grass began to shake as though he had the fever. He knew that voice well, but to make sure he cried softly, surprised to find how man's talk came back, 'Messua! O Messua!'

'Who calls?' said the woman, a quiver in her voice.

'Hast thou forgotten?' said Mowgli: his throat was dry as he spoke.

'If it be *thou*, what name did I give thee? Say!' She had half-shut the door, and her hand was clutching at her breast.

'Nathoo! Ohé Nathoo!' said Mowgli, for, as you know, that was the name Messua gave him when he first came to the Man-Pack.

'Come, my son,' she called, and Mowgli stepped into the light, and looked full at Messua, the woman who had been good to him, and whose life he had saved from the Man-Pack so long before. She was older, and her hair was gray, but her eyes and her voice had not changed. Woman-like, she expected to find Mowgli where she had left him, and her eyes travelled upwards in a puzzled fashion from his chest to his head, that touched the top of the door.

'My son,' she stammered, and then sinking to his feet: 'but it is no longer my son. It is a Godling of the woods! Ahai!'

As he stood in the red light of the oil-lamp, strong, tall, and beautiful, his long black hair sweeping over his shoulders, the knife swinging at his neck, and his head crowned with a wreath of white jasmine, he might easily have been mistaken for some wild god of a jungle legend. The child half asleep on a cot sprang up and shrieked aloud with terror. Messua turned to soothe him while Mowgli stood still, looking in at the water-jars and cooking-pots, the grain-bin and all the other human belongings that he found himself remembering so well.

'What wilt thou eat or drink?' Messua murmured. 'This is all thine. We owe our lives to thee. But art thou him I called Nathoo, or a Godling, indeed?'

'I am Nathoo,' said Mowgli, 'I am very far from my own place. I saw this light and came hither. I did not know thou wast here.'

'After we came to Kanhiwara,' Messua said timidly, 'the English would have helped us against those villagers that sought to burn us. Rememberest thou?'

'Indeed, I have not forgotten.'

'But when the English Law was made ready we went to the village of those evil people and it was no more to be found.'

'That also I remember,' said Mowgli, with a quiver of the nostril.

'My man, therefore, took service in the fields, and at last, for indeed he was a strong man, we held a little land here. It is not so rich as the old village, but we do not need much – we two.'

'Where is he – the man that dug in the dirt when he was afraid on that night?'

'He is dead – a year.'

'And he?' Mowgli pointed to the child.

'My son that was born two Rains ago. If thou art a Godling

give him the Favour of the Jungle that he may be safe among thy – thy people as we were safe on that night.'

She lifted up the child, who, forgetting his fright, reached out to play with the knife that hung on Mowgli's chest, and Mowgli put the little fingers aside very carefully.

'And if thou art Nathoo whom the tigers carried away,' Messua went on, choking, 'he is then thy younger brother. Give him an elder brother's blessing.'

'*Hai mai!* What do I know of the thing called a blessing? I am neither a Godling nor his brother, and – O mother, mother, my heart is heavy in me.' He shivered as he set down the child.

'Like enough,' said Messua, bustling among the cooking-pots. 'This comes of running about the marshes by night. Beyond question, a fever has soaked thee to the marrow.' Mowgli smiled a little at the idea of anything in the Jungle hurting him. 'I will make a fire and thou shalt drink warm milk. Put away the jasmine wreath, the smell is heavy in so small a place.'

Mowgli sat down, muttering, his face in his hands. All manner of strange feelings were running over him, exactly as though he had been poisoned, and he felt dizzy and a little sick. He drank the warm milk in long gulps, Messua patting him on the shoulder from time to time, not quite sure whether he were her son Nathoo of the long ago days or some wonderful Jungle being, but glad to feel that he was at least flesh and blood.

'Son,' she said at last – her eyes were full of pride – 'have any told thee that thou art beautiful beyond all men?'

'Hah?' said Mowgli, for of course he had never heard anything of the kind. Messua laughed softly and happily. The look in his face was enough for her.

'I am the first, then? It is right, though it comes seldom, that a mother should tell her son these good things. Thou art very beautiful. Never have I looked upon such a man.'

Mowgli twisted his head and tried to see over his own hard shoulder, and Messua laughed again so long that Mowgli, not knowing why, was forced to laugh with her, and the child ran from one to the other laughing too.

'Nay, thou must not mock thy brother,' said Messua catching him to her breast. 'When thou art one-half as fair we will marry thee to the youngest daughter of a king and thou shalt ride great elephants.'

Mowgli could not understand one word in three of the talk here; the warm milk was taking effect on him after his forty-mile run; so he curled up and in a minute was deep asleep, and Messua put the hair back from his eyes, threw a cloth over him and was happy. Jungle fashion, he slept out the rest of that night and all the next day, for his instincts, which never wholly slept, warned him there was nothing to fear. He waked at last with a bound that shook the hut, for the cloth over his face made him dream of traps; and there he stood, his hand on his knife, the sleep all heavy in his rolling eyes, ready for any fight.

Messua laughed and set the evening meal before him. There were only a few coarse cakes baked over the smoky fire, some rice, and a lump of sour preserved tamarinds – just enough to go on with till he could get to his evening kill. The smell of the dew in the marshes made him hungry and restless. He wanted to finish his spring running, but the child insisted on sitting in his arms, and Messua would have it that his long blue-black hair must be combed out. So she sang as she combed, foolish little baby songs, now calling Mowgli her son, and now begging him to give some of his jungle-power to the child. The hut door was closed, but Mowgli heard a sound he knew well, and saw Messua's jaw drop with horror as a great gray paw came under the bottom of the door, and Gray Brother outside whined a muffled and penitent whine of anxiety and fear.

'Out and wait. Ye would not come when I called,' said Mowgli in Jungle-talk, never turning his head; and the great gray paw disappeared.

'Do not – do not bring thy – thy servants with thee,' said Messua. 'I – we have always lived at peace with the Jungle.'

'It is peace,' said Mowgli rising. 'Think of that night on the road to Kanhiwara. There were scores of such folk before thee and behind thee. But I see that even in springtime the Jungle people do not always forget. Mother, I go.'

Messua drew aside humbly – he was indeed a wood-god, she

thought – but as his hand was on the door the mother in her made her throw her arms round Mowgli's neck again and again.

'Come back!' she whispered. 'Son or no son, come back, for I love thee – and look, he too grieves.'

The child was crying because the man with the shiny knife was going away.

'Come back again,' Messua repeated. 'By night or by day this door is never shut to thee.'

Mowgli's throat worked as though the cords in it were being pulled, and his voice seemed to be dragged from it as he answered, 'I will surely come back.'

'And now,' he said, as he put aside the head of the fawning wolf on the threshold, 'I have a little cry against thee, Gray Brother. Why came ye not, all Four, when I called so long ago?'

'So long ago? It was but last night. I – we – were singing in the Jungle, the new songs, for this is the Time of New Talk. Rememberest thou?'

'Truly, truly.'

'And as soon as the songs were sung,' Gray Brother went on earnestly, 'I followed thy trail. I ran from all the others and followed hot-foot. But, O Little Brother, what has *thou* done – eating and sleeping with the Man-Pack?'

'If ye had come when I called this had never been,' said Mowgli, running much faster.

'And now what is to be?' said Gray Brother.

Mowgli was going to answer when a girl in a white cloth came down some path that led from the outskirts of the village. Gray Brother dropped out of sight at once and Mowgli backed noiselessly into a field of high springing crops. He could almost have touched her with his hand when the warm green stalks closed before his face and he disappeared like a ghost. The girl screamed, for she thought she had seen a spirit, and then she gave a deep sigh. Mowgli parted the stalks with his hands and watched her till she was out of sight.

'And now I do not know,' he said, sighing in his turn. '*Why* did ye not come when I called?'

'We follow thee – we follow thee,' Gray Brother mumbled,

licking at Mowgli's heel. 'We follow thee always except in the Time of the New Talk.'

'And would ye follow me to the Man-Pack?' Mowgli whispered.

'Did I not follow thee on the night that our old Pack cast thee out? Who waked thee lying among the crops?'

'Ay, but again?'

'Have I not followed thee to-night?'

'Ay, but again and again, and it may be again, Gray Brother?'

Gray Brother was silent. When he spoke he growled to himself, 'The Black One spoke truth.'

'And he said?'

'Man goes to Man at the last. Raksha our mother said—'

'So also said Akela on the night of Red Dog,' Mowgli muttered.

'So also said Kaa, who is wiser than us all.'

'What dost thou say, Gray Brother?'

'They cast thee out once, with bad talk. They cut thy mouth with stones. They sent Buldeo to slay thee. They would have thrown thee into the Red Flower. Thou, and not I, hast said that they are evil and senseless. Thou and not I – I follow my own people – didst let in the Jungle upon them. Thou and not I didst make song against them more bitter even than our song against Red Dog.'

'I ask thee what *thou* sayest?'

They were talking as they ran. Gray Brother cantered on awhile without replying, and then he said between bound and bound as it were – 'Man-cub – Master of the Jungle – Son of Raksha – Lair-brother to me – though I forget for a little while in the spring, thy trail is my trail, thy lair is my lair, thy kill is my kill, and thy death-fight is my death-fight. I speak for the Three. But what wilt thou say to the Jungle?'

'That is well thought. Between the sight and the kill it is not good to wait. Go before and cry them all to the Council Rock, and I will tell them what is in my stomach. But they may not come – in the Time of the New Talk they may forget me.'

'Hast thou then forgotten nothing?' snapped Gray Brother

over his shoulder, as he laid himself down to gallop, and Mowgli followed, thinking.

At any other season his news would have called all the Jungle together with bristling necks, but now they were busy hunting and fighting and killing and singing. From one to another Gray Brother ran, crying, 'The Master of the Jungle goes back to Man. Come to the Council Rock!' And the happy, eager people only answered, 'He will return in the summer heats. The Rains will drive him to lair. Run and sing with us, Gray Brother.'

'But the Master of the Jungle goes back to Man,' Gray Brother would repeat.

'Eee – Yowa? Is the Time of New Talk any less good for that?' they would reply. So when Mowgli, heavy-hearted, came up through the well-remembered rocks to the place where he had been brought into the Pack, he found only the Four, Baloo, who was nearly blind with age, and the heavy, cold-blooded Kaa, coiled round Akela's empty seat.

'Thy trail ends here, then, Manling?' said Kaa, as Mowgli threw himself down, his face in his hands. 'Cry thy cry. We be of one blood, thou and I – Man and Snake together.'

'Why was I not torn in two by Red Dog?'[9] the boy moaned. 'My strength is gone from me, and it is not the poison. By night and by day I hear a double step upon my trail. When I turn my head it is as though one had hidden himself from me that instant. I go to look behind the trees and he is not there. I call and none cry again, but it is as though one listened and kept back the answer. I lie down, but I do not rest. I run the spring-running, but I am not made still. I bathe, but I am not made cool. The kill sickens me, but I have no heart to fight except I kill. The Red Flower is in my body, my bones are water – and – I know not what I know.'

'What need of talk?' said Baloo, slowly, turning his head to where Mowgli lay. 'Akela by the river said it, that Mowgli should drive Mowgli back to the Man-Pack. I said it. But who listens now to Baloo? Bagheera – where is Bagheera this night? – he knows also. It is the Law.'

'When we met at Cold Lairs, Manling, I knew it,' said Kaa, turning a little in his mighty coils. 'Man goes to Man at the last, though the Jungle does not cast him out.'

The Four looked at one another and at Mowgli, puzzled but obedient.

'The Jungle does not cast me out, then?' Mowgli stammered.

Gray Brother and the Three growled furiously, beginning, 'So long as we live none shall dare—' But Baloo checked them.

'I taught thee the Law. It is for me to speak,' he said, 'and though I cannot now see the rocks before me, I see far. Little Frog, take thine own trail; make thy lair with thine own blood and pack and people; but when there is need of foot or tooth or eye or a word carried swiftly by night, remember, Master of the Jungle, the Jungle is thine at call.'

'The Middle Jungle is thine also,' said Kaa. 'I speak for no small people.'

'*Hai mai*, my brothers,' cried Mowgli, throwing up his arms with a sob. 'I know not what I know, I would not go, but I am drawn by both feet. How shall I leave these nights?'

'Nay, look up, Little Brother,' Baloo repeated. 'There is no shame in this hunting. When the honey is eaten we leave the empty hive.'

'Having cast the skin,' said Kaa, 'we may not creep into it afresh. It is the Law.'

'Listen, dearest of all to me,' said Baloo. 'There is neither word nor will here to hold thee back. Look up! Who may question the Master of the Jungle? I saw thee playing among the white pebbles yonder when thou wast a little frog; and Bagheera, that bought thee for the price of a young bull newly killed, saw thee also. Of that Looking Over we two only remain, for Raksha, thy lair-mother, is dead with thy lair-father; the old Wolf-Pack is long since dead; thou knowest whither Shere Khan went, and Akela died among the dholes, where but for thy wisdom and strength the second Seeonee Pack would also have died. There remain nothing but old bones. It is no longer the Man-cub that asks leave of his Pack, but the Master of the Jungle that changes his trail. Who shall question Man in his ways?'

'But Bagheera and the Bull that bought me,' said Mowgli. 'I would not—'

His words were cut short by a roar and a crash in the thicket below, and Bagheera, light, strong, and terrible as always, stood before him.

'*Therefore*,' he said, stretching out a dripping right paw, 'I did not come. It was a long hunt, but he lies dead in the bushes now – a bull in his second year – the Bull that frees thee, Little Brother. All debts are paid now. For the rest, my word is Baloo's word.' He licked Mowgli's foot. 'Remember Bagheera loved thee,' he cried and bounded away. At the foot of the hill he cried again long and loud, 'Good hunting on a new trail, Master of the Jungle! Remember Bagheera loved thee.'

'Thou hast heard,' said Baloo. 'There is no more. Go now; but first come to me. O wise Little Frog, come to me!'

'It is hard to cast the skin,'[10] said Kaa, as Mowgli sobbed and sobbed with his head on the blind bear's side and his arms round his neck, while Baloo tried feebly to lick his feet.

'The stars are thin,' said Gray Brother snuffing at the dawn-wind. 'Where shall we lair to-day? for, from now we follow new trails.'

And this is the last of the Mowgli stories.[11]

The Outsong

This is the song that Mowgli heard behind him in the
Jungle till he came to Messua's door again.

Baloo

For the sake of him who showed
One wise Frog the Jungle-Road,
Keep the Law the Man-Pack make –
For thy blind old Baloo's sake!
Clean or tainted, hot or stale,
Hold it as it were the trail,
Through the day and through the night,
Questing neither left nor right.
For the sake of him who loves
Thee beyond all else that moves,
When thy Pack would make thee pain,
Say 'Tabaqui sings again.'
When thy Pack would work thee ill,
Say: 'Shere Khan is yet to kill.'
When the knife is drawn to slay,
Keep the Law and go thy way.
(Root and honey, palm and spathe,[1]
Guard a cub from harm and scathe.)
Wood and Water, Wind and Tree,
Jungle-Favour go with thee!

Kaa

Anger is the egg of Fear –
Only lidless eyes are clear.
Cobra-poison none may leech;
Even so with Cobra-speech.
Open talk shall call to thee
Strength whose mate is Courtesy.

Send no lunge beyond thy length;
Lend no rotten bough thy strength.
Gauge thy gape with buck or goat,
Lest thine eye should choke thy throat.
After gorging, wouldst thou sleep?
Look thy den is hid and deep,
Lest a wrong, by thee forgot,
Draw thy killer to the spot.
East and West and North and South,
Wash thy skin and close thy mouth.
(Pit and rift and blue pool-brim
Middle-Jungle follow him!)
Wood and Water, Wind and Tree,
Jungle-Favour go with thee!

Bagheera

In the cage my life began;
Well I know the ways of Man.[2]
By the Broken Lock that freed –
Man-cub, 'ware the Man-cub's breed!
Scenting-dew or starlight pale,
Choose no idle tree-cat trail.
Pack or council, hunt or den,
Cry no truce with Jackal-Men.
Feed them silence when they say:
'Come with us an easy way.'
Feed them silence when they seek
Help of thine to hurt the weak.
Make no *bandar*'s boast of skill;
Hold thy peace above the kill.
Let nor call nor song nor sign
Turn thee from thy hunting-line.
(Morning mist or twilight clear
Serve him, Wardens of the Deer!)
Wood and Water, Wind and Tree,
Jungle-Favour go with thee!

The Three

On the trail that thou must tread
To the threshold of our dread,
Where the Flower blossoms red;
Through the nights when thou shalt lie
'Prisoned from our Mother-sky,
Hearing us, thy loves, go by;
In the dawns, when thou shalt wake
To the toil thou canst not break,
Heartsick for the Jungle's sake;
Wood and Water, Wind and Tree,
Jungle-Favour go with thee!

Appendix

IN THE RUKH

The Only Son lay down again and dreamed that he dreamed a dream.
The last ash dropped from the dying fire with the click of a falling spark,
And the Only Son woke up again and called across the dark: –
'Now, was I born of womankind and laid in a mother's breast?
For I have dreamed of a shaggy hide whereon I went to rest.
And was I born of womankind and laid on a father's arm?
For I have dreamed of long white teeth that guarded me from harm.
Oh, was I born of womankind and did I play alone?
For I have dreamed of playmates twain that bit me to the bone.
And did I break the barley bread and steep it in the tyre?[1]
For I have dreamed of a youngling kid new riven from the byre.
An hour it lacks and an hour it lacks to the rising of the moon,
But I can see the black roof-beams as plain as it were noon!
'Tis a league and a league to the Lena Falls where the trooping sambhur go,
But I can hear the little fawn that bleats behind the doe!
'Tis a league and a league to the Lena Falls where the crop and the upland meet,
But I can smell the warm wet wind that whispers through the wheat!'

The Only Son

Of the wheels of public service which turn under the Indian Government, there is none more important than the Department of Woods and Forests. The reboisement[2] of all India is in its hands; or will be when Government has the money to spend. Its servants wrestle with wandering sand-torrents and shifting dunes: wattling them at the sides, damming them in front, and pegging them down atop with coarse grass and spindling pine[3] after the rules of Nancy.[4] They are responsible for all the timber in the State forests of the Himalayas, as well as for the denuded hillsides that the monsoons wash into dry gullies and aching ravines; each cut a mouth crying aloud what carelessness can do. They experiment with battalions of foreign trees, and coax the blue gum[5] to take root and, perhaps, dry up the Canal fever. In the Plains the chief part of their duty is to see that the belt fire-lines in the forest reserves are kept clean, so that when drought comes and the cattle starve, they may throw the reserve open to the villager's herds and allow the man himself to gather sticks. They poll and lop[6] for the stacked railway-fuel along the lines that burn no coal; they calculate the profit of their plantations to five points of decimals; they are the doctors and midwives of the huge teak forests of Upper Burma, the rubber of the Eastern Jungles, and the gall-nuts of the South; and they are always hampered by lack of funds. But since a Forest Officer's business takes him far from the beaten roads and the regular Stations, he learns to grow wise in more than wood-lore alone; to know the people and the polity of the jungle; meeting tiger, bear, leopard, wild-dog, and all the deer, not once or twice after days of beating, but again and again in the execution of his duty. He spends much time in saddle or under canvas – the friend of newly-planted trees, the associate of uncouth rangers and hairy trackers – till the woods, that show his care, in turn set their mark upon him, and he ceases to sing the naughty French songs he learned at Nancy, and grows silent with the silent things of the underbrush.

Gisborne of the Woods and Forests had spent four years in the Service. At first he loved it without comprehension, because it led him into the open on horseback and gave him authority. Then he hated it furiously, and would have given a year's pay for one month of such society as India affords. That crisis over, the forests took him back again, and he was content to serve them, to deepen and widen his fire-lines, to watch the green mist of his new plantation against the older foliage, to dredge out the choked stream, and to follow and strengthen the last struggle of the forest where it broke down and died among the long pig-grass. On some still day that grass would be burned off, and a hundred beasts that had their homes there would rush out before the pale flames at high noon. Later, the forest would creep forward over the blackened ground in orderly lines of saplings, and Gisborne, watching, would be well pleased. His bungalow, a thatched white-walled cottage of two rooms, was set at one end of the great *rukh* and overlooking it. He made no pretence at keeping a garden, for the *rukh* swept up to his door, curled over in a thicket of bamboo, and he rode from his veranda into its heart without the need of any carriage-drive.

Abdul Gafur, his fat Mohammedan butler, fed him when he was at home, and spent the rest of the time gossiping with the little band of native servants whose huts lay behind the bungalow. There were two grooms, a cook, a water-carrier, and a sweeper, and that was all. Gisborne cleaned his own guns and kept no dog. Dogs scared the game, and it pleased the man to be able to say where the subjects of his king-dom would drink at moonrise, eat before dawn, and lie up in the day's heat. The rangers and Forest-guards lived in little huts far away in the *rukh*, only appearing when one of them had been injured by a falling tree or a wild beast. Thus Gisborne was alone.

In spring the *rukh* put out few new leaves, but lay dry and still untouched by the finger of the year, waiting for rain. Only there was then more calling and roaring in the dark on a quiet night; the tumult of a battle-royal among the tigers, the bellowing of arrogant buck, or the steady wood-chopping of an old boar sharpening his tushes against a bole. Then Gisborne laid aside his little-used gun altogether, for it was to him a sin to kill. In summer, through the furious May heats, the *rukh* reeled in the haze, and Gisborne watched for the first sign of curling smoke that should betray a forest fire. Then came the Rains with a roar, and the *rukh* was blotted out in fetch after fetch of warm mist, and the broad leaves drummed the night through under the big drops; and there was a noise of running water, and of juicy green stuff crackling where the wind struck it, and the lightning wove patterns behind the dense matting of the foliage, till the sun broke loose again and the *rukh* stood with hot flanks smoking to the newly-washed sky. Then the heat and the dry cold subdued everything to tiger-colour again. So Gisborne learned to know his *rukh* and was very happy. His pay came month by month, but he had very little need for money. The currency notes accumulated in the drawer where he kept his home-letters and the recapping-machine.[7] If he drew anything, it was to make a purchase from the Calcutta Botanical Gar-dens,[8] or to pay a ranger's widow a sum that the Government of India would never have sanctioned for her man's death.

Payment was good, but vengeance was also necessary, and he took that when he could. One night of many nights a runner, breathless and gasping, came to him with the news that a Forest-guard lay dead by the Kanye stream, the side of his head smashed in as though it had been an egg-shell. Gisborne went out at dawn to look for the mur-derer. It is only travellers, and now and then young soldiers, who are known to the world as great hunters. The Forest Officers take their *shikar*[9] as part of the day's work, and no one hears of it. Gisborne went on foot to the place of the kill: the widow was wailing over the corpse as it lay on a bedstead, while two or three men were looking at footprints on the moist ground. 'That is the Red One,' said a man. 'I knew he would turn to man in time, but surely there is game enough even for him. This must have been done for devilry.'[10]

'The Red One lies up in the rocks at the back of the *sal* trees,'[11] said Gisborne. He knew the tiger under suspicion.

'Not now, Sahib, not now. He will be raging and ranging to and fro. Remember that the first kill is a triple kill always. Our blood makes them mad. He may be behind us even as we speak.'

'He may have gone to the next hut,' said another 'It is only four *koss*.[12] Wallah, who is this?'

Gisborne turned with the others. A man was walking down the dried bed of the stream, naked except for the loin-cloth, but crowned with a wreath of the tasselled blossoms of the white convolvulus-creeper. So noiselessly did he move over the little pebbles that even Gisborne, used to the soft-footedness of trackers, started.

'The tiger that killed,' he began, without any salute, 'has gone to drink, and now he is asleep under a rock beyond that hill.' His voice was clear and bell-like, utterly different from the usual whine of the native, and his face as he lifted it in the sunshine might have been that of an angel strayed among the woods. The widow ceased wailing above the corpse and looked round-eyed at the stranger, returning to her duty with double strength.

'Shall I show the Sahib?' he said simply.

'If thou art sure—' Gisborne began.

'Sure indeed. I saw him only an hour ago – the dog. It is before his time to eat man's flesh. He has yet a dozen sound teeth in his evil head.'

The men kneeling above the footprints slunk off quietly, for fear that Gisborne should ask them to go with him, and the young man laughed a little to himself.

'Come, Sahib,' he cried, and turned on his heel, walking before his companion.

'Not so fast. I cannot keep that pace,' said the white man. 'Halt there. Thy face is new to me.'

'That may be. I am but newly come into this forest.'

'From what village?'

'I am without a village. I came from over there.' He flung out his arm towards the north.

'A gipsy then?'

'No, Sahib. I am a man without caste, and for matter of that without a father.'

'What do men call thee?'

'Mowgli, Sahib. And what is the Sahib's name?'

'I am the warden of this *rukh* – Gisborne is my name.'

'How? Do they number the trees and the blades of grass here?'

'Even so; lest such gipsy fellows as thou set them afire.'

'I! I would not hurt the Jungle for any gift. That is my home.'

He turned to Gisborne with a smile that was irresistible, and held up a warning hand.

'Now, Sahib, we must go a little quietly. There is no need to wake the dog, though he sleeps heavily enough. Perhaps it were better if I went forward alone and drove him down wind to the Sahib.'

'Allah! Since when have tigers been driven to and fro like cattle by naked men?' said Gisborne, aghast at the man's audacity.

He laughed again softly. 'Nay, then, come along with me and shoot him in thine own way with the big English rifle.'

Gisborne stepped in his guide's track, twisted, crawled, and clomb[13] and stooped and suffered through all the many agonies of a jungle-stalk. He was purple and dripping with sweat when Mowgli at the last bade him raise his head and peer over a blue baked rock near a tiny hill pool. By the waterside lay the tiger extended and at ease, lazily licking clean again an enormous elbow and fore-paw. He was old, yellow-toothed, and not a little mangy,[14] but in that setting and sunshine, imposing enough.

Gisborne had no false ideas of sport where the maneater was concerned. This thing was vermin, to be killed as speedily as possible. He waited to recover his breath, rested the rifle on the rock and whistled. The brute's head turned slowly not twenty feet from the rifle-mouth, and Gisborne planted his shots, business-like, one behind the shoulder and the other a little below the eye. At that range the heavy bones were no guard against the rending bullets.

'Well, the skin was not worth keeping at any rate,' said he, as the smoke cleared away and the beast lay kicking and gasping in the last agony.

'A dog's death for a dog,' said Mowgli quietly. 'Indeed there is nothing in that carrion worth taking away.'

'The whiskers. Dost thou not take the whiskers?' said Gisborne, who knew how the Forest rangers valued such things.

'I? Am I a lousy *shikari*[15] of the jungle to paddle with a tiger's muzzle? Let him lie. Here come his friends already.'

A dropping kite whistled shrilly overhead, as Gisborne snapped out the empty shells and wiped his face.

'And if thou art not a *shikari*, where didst thou learn thy knowledge of the tiger-folk?' said he. 'No tracker could have done better.'

'I hate all tigers,' said Mowgli curtly. 'Let the Sahib give me his gun to carry. It is a very fine one. And where does the Sahib go now?'

'To my house.'

'May I come? I have never yet looked withinsides a white man's house.'

Gisborne returned to his bungalow, Mowgli striding noiselessly before him, his brown skin glistening in the sunlight.

He stared curiously at the veranda and the two chairs there, fingered the split bamboo shade curtains with suspicion, and entered, looking always behind him. Gisborne loosed a curtain to keep out the sun. It dropped with a clatter, but almost before it touched the flagging of the veranda Mowgli had leaped clear, and was standing with heaving chest in the open.

'It is a trap!' he said quickly.

Gisborne laughed. 'White men do not trap men. Indeed thou art altogether of the jungle.'

'I see,' said Mowgli, 'it has neither catch nor fall. I – never beheld these things till to-day.'

He came in on tiptoe and stared with large eyes at the furniture of the two rooms. Abdul Gafur, who was laying lunch, looked at him with deep disgust.

'So much trouble to eat, and so much trouble to lie down after you have eaten!' said Mowgli with a grin. 'We do better in the jungle. It is very wonderful. There are very many rich things here. Is the Sahib not afraid that he may be robbed? I have never seen such wonderful things.' He was staring at a dusty Benares brass plate on a rickety bracket.

'Only a thief from the jungle would rob here,' said Abdul Gafur, setting down a plate with a clatter. Mowgli opened his eyes wide and stared at the white-bearded Mohammedan.

'In my country when goats bleat very loud we cut their throats,' he returned cheerfully. 'But have no fear, thou. I am going.'

He turned and disappeared into the *rukh*. Gisborne looked after him with a laugh that ended in a little sigh. There was not much outside his regular work to interest the Forest Officer, and this son of the forest, who seemed to know tigers as other people know dogs, would have been a diversion.

'He's a most wonderful chap,' thought Gisborne; 'he's like the illustrations in the Classical Dictionary. I wish I could have made him a gun-boy. There's no fun in *shikaring* alone, and this fellow would have been a perfect *shikari*. I wonder what in the world he is.'

That evening he sat on the veranda under the stars, smoking as he wondered. A puff of smoke curled from the pipe-bowl. As it cleared he was aware of Mowgli sitting with arms crossed on the veranda edge. A ghost could not have drifted up more noiselessly. Gisborne started and let the pipe drop.

'There is no man to talk to out there in the *rukh*,' said Mowgli. 'I came here, therefore.' He picked up the pipe and returned it to Gisborne.

'Oh,' said Gisborne, and after a long pause, 'What news is there in the *rukh*? Hast thou found another tiger?'

'The nilghai are changing their feeding-ground against the new moon, as is their custom. The pig are feeding near the Kanye river now, because they will not feed with the nilghai; and one of their sows has been killed by a leopard in the long grass at the water-head. I do not know any more.'

'And how didst thou know all these things?' said Gisborne, leaning forward and looking at the eyes that glittered in the starlight.

'How should I not know? The nilghai has his custom and his use, and a child knows that pig will not feed with him.'

'I do not know this,' said Gisborne.

'Tck! Tck! And thou art in charge – so the men of the huts tell me – in charge of all this *rukh*?' He laughed to himself.

'It is well enough to talk and to tell child's tales,' Gisborne retorted, nettled at the chuckle. 'To say that this and that goes on in the *rukh*. No man can deny thee.'

'As for the sow's carcass, I will show thee her bones to-morrow,' Mowgli returned, absolutely unmoved. 'Touching the matter of the nilghai, if the Sahib will sit here very still I will drive one nilghai up to this place, and by listening to the sounds carefully, the Sahib can tell whence that nilghai has been driven.'

'Mowgli, the jungle has made thee mad,' said Gisborne. 'Who can drive nilghai?'

'Still! – Sit still, then. I go.'

'Gad, the man's a ghost!' said Gisborne; for Mowgli had faded out into the darkness and there was no sound of feet. The *rukh* lay out in great velvety folds in the uncertain shimmer of the star-dust – so still that the least little wandering wind among the tree-tops came up as the sigh of a child sleeping equably. Abdul Gafur in the cook-house was clicking plates together.

'Be still there!' shouted Gisborne, and composed himself to listen as a man can who is used to the stillness of the *rukh*. It had been his custom, to preserve his self-respect in his isolation, to dress for dinner each night, and the stiff white shirt-front creaked with his regular breathing till he shifted a little sideways. Then the tobacco of a somewhat foul pipe began to purr, and he threw the pipe from him. Now, except for the night-breath in the *rukh*, everything was dumb.

From an inconceivable distance, and drawled through immeasurable darkness, came the faint, faint echo of a wolf's howl. Then silence again for, it seemed, long hours. At last, when his legs below the knees had lost all feeling, Gisborne heard something that might have been a crash far off through the undergrowth. He doubted till it was repeated again and yet again.

'That's from the west,' he muttered; 'there's something on foot there.' The noise increased – crash on crash, plunge on plunge – with the thick grunting of a hotly pressed nilghai, flying in panic terror and taking no heed to his course.

A shadow blundered out from between the tree-trunks, wheeled back, turned again grunting, and with a clatter on the bare ground dashed up almost within reach of his hand. It was a bull nilghai, dripping with dew – his withers hung with a torn trail of creeper, his eyes shining in the light from the house. The creature checked at sight of the man, and fled along the edge of the *rukh* till he melted in the darkness. The first idea in Gisborne's bewildered mind was the indecency of thus dragging out for inspection the big Blue Bull of the *rukh* – the putting him through his paces in the night which should have been his own.

Then said a smooth voice at his ear as he stood staring: –

'He came from the water-head where he was leading the herd. From the west he came. Does the Sahib believe now, or shall I bring up the herd to be counted? The Sahib is in charge of this *rukh*.'

Mowgli had reseated himself on the veranda, breathing a little quickly. Gisborne looked at him with open mouth. 'How was that accomplished?' he said.

'The Sahib saw. The bull was driven – driven as a buffalo is. Ho! ho! He will have a fine tale to tell when he returns to the herd.'

'That is a new trick to me. Canst thou run as swiftly as the nilghai, then?'

'The Sahib has seen. If the Sahib needs more knowledge at any time of the movings of the game, I, Mowgli, am here. This is a good *rukh*. I shall stay in it.'

'Stay, then, and if thou hast need of a meal at any time my servants shall give thee one.'

'Yes, indeed. I am fond of cooked food,' Mowgli answered quickly. 'No man may say that I do not eat boiled and roast as much as any other man. I will come for that meal. Now, on my part, I promise that the Sahib shall sleep safely in his house by night, and no thief shall break in to carry away his so rich treasures.'

The conversation ended itself on Mowgli's abrupt departure. Gisborne sat long smoking, and the upshot of his thoughts was that in

Mowgli he had found at last that ideal ranger and Forest-guard for whom he and the Department were always looking.

'I must get him into Government service somehow. A man who can drive nilghai would know more about the *rukh* than fifty men. He's a miracle – a *lusus naturae*[16] – and a Forest-guard he must be if he'll only settle down in one place,' said Gisborne.

Abdul Gafur's opinion was less favourable. He confided to Gisborne at bedtime that strangers from God-knew-where were more than likely to be professional thieves, and that he personally did not approve of naked outcastes who had not the proper manner of addressing white people. Gisborne laughed and bade him go to his quarters, and Abdul Gafur retreated growling. Later in the night he found occasion to rise up and beat his thirteen-year-old daughter. Nobody knew the cause of dispute, but Gisborne heard the cry.

Through the days that followed, Mowgli came and went like a shadow. He had established himself and his wild house-keeping close to the bungalow, but on the edge of the *rukh*, where Gisborne, going out on to the veranda for a breath of cool air, would see him sometimes sitting in the moonlight, his forehead on his knees, or lying out along the fling of a branch, closely pressed to it as some beast of the night. Thence Mowgli would throw him a salutation and bid him sleep at ease, or descending would weave prodigious stories of the manners of the beasts in the *rukh*. Once he wandered into the stables and was found looking at the horses with deep interest.

'That,' said Abdul Gafur pointedly, 'is sure sign that some day he will steal one. Why, if he lives about this house, does he not take an honest employment? But no, he must wander up and down like a loose camel, turning the heads of fools and opening the jaws of the unwise to folly.' So Abdul Gafur would give harsh orders to Mowgli when they met, would bid him fetch water and pluck fowls, and Mowgli, laughing unconcernedly, would obey.

'He has no caste,' said Abdul Gafur. 'He will do anything. Look to it, Sahib, that he does not do too much. A snake is a snake, and a jungle-gipsy is a thief till the death.'

'Be silent, then,' said Gisborne. 'I allow thee to correct thine own household if there is not too much noise, because I know thy customs and use. *My* custom thou dost not know. The man is without doubt a little mad.'

'Very little mad indeed,' said Abdul Gafur. 'But we shall see what comes thereof.'

A few days later on, his business took Gisborne into the *rukh* for three days. Abdul Gafur being old and fat was left at home. He did not approve of lying up in ranger's huts, and was inclined to levy contributions in his master's name of grain and oil and milk from those who could ill afford such benevolences. Gisborne rode off early one dawn a little vexed that his man of the woods was not at the veranda to accompany him. He liked him – liked his strength, fleetness, and silence of foot, and his ever-ready open smile; his ignorance of all forms of ceremony and salutations, and the childlike tales that he would tell (and Gisborne would credit now) of what the game was doing in the *rukh*. After an hour's riding through the greenery, he heard a rustle behind him, and Mowgli trotted at his stirrup.

'We have a three days' work toward,' said Gisborne, 'among the new trees.'

'Good,' said Mowgli. 'It is always good to cherish young trees. They make cover if the beasts leave them alone. We must shift the pig again.'

'Again? How?' Gisborne smiled.

'Oh, they were rooting and tusking among the young *sal* last night, and I drove them off. Therefore I did not come to the veranda this morning. The pig should not be on this side of the *rukh* at all. We must keep them below the head of the Kanye river.'

'If a man could herd clouds he might do that thing; but, Mowgli, if as thou sayest, thou art herder in the *rukh* for no gain and for no pay—'

'It is the Sahib's *rukh*,' said Mowgli, quickly looking up. Gisborne nodded thanks and went on: 'would it not be better to work for pay from the Government? There is a pension at the end of long service.'

'Of that I have thought,' said Mowgli, 'but the rangers live in huts with shut doors, and all that is all too much a trap to me. Yet I think—'

'Think well, then, and tell me later. Here we will stay for breakfast.'

Gisborne dismounted, took his morning meal from his home-made saddle-bags, and saw the day open hot above the *rukh*. Mowgli lay in the grass at his side staring up to the sky.

Presently he said in a lazy whisper: 'Sahib, is there any order at the bungalow to take out the white mare to-day?'

'No, she is fat and old and a little lame besides. Why?'

'She is being ridden now and *not* slowly on the road that runs to the railway line.'

'Bah, that is two *koss* away. It is a woodpecker.'

Mowgli put up his forearm to keep the sun out of his eyes.

'The road curves in with a big curve from the bungalow. It is not more than a *koss*, at the farthest, as the kite goes; and sound flies with the birds. Shall we see?'

'What folly! To run a *koss* in this sun to see a noise in the forest.'

'Nay, the pony is the Sahib's pony. I meant only to bring her here. If she is not the Sahib's pony, no matter. If she is, the Sahib can do what he wills. She is certainly being ridden hard.'

'And how wilt thou bring her here, madman?'

'Has the Sahib forgotten? By the road of the nilghai and no other.'

'Up, then, and run if thou art so full of zeal.'

'Oh, I do not run!' He put out his hand to sign for silence, and still lying on his back called aloud thrice – with a deep gurgling cry that was new to Gisborne.

'She will come,' he said at the end. 'Let us wait in the shade.' The long eyelashes drooped over the wild eyes as Mowgli began to doze in the morning hush. Gisborne waited patiently: Mowgli was surely mad, but as entertaining a companion as a lonely Forest Officer could desire.

'Ho! ho!' said Mowgli lazily, with shut eyes. 'He has dropped off. Well, first the mare will come and then the man.' Then he yawned as Gisborne's pony stallion neighed. Three minutes later Gisborne's white mare, saddled, bridled, but riderless, tore into the glade where they were sitting, and hurried to her companion.

'She is not very warm,' said Mowgli, 'but in this heat the sweat comes easily. Presently we shall see her rider, for a man goes more slowly than a horse – especially if he chance to be a fat man and old.'

'Allah! This is devils' work,' cried Gisborne, leaping to his feet, for he heard a yell in the jungle.

'Have no care, Sahib. He will not be hurt. He also will say that it is devils' work. Ah! Listen! Who is that?'

It was the voice of Abdul Gafur in an agony of terror, crying out upon unknown things to spare him and his grey hairs.[17]

'Nay, I cannot move another step,' he howled. 'I am old and my turban is lost. *Arré! Arré!* But I will move. Indeed I will hasten. I will run! O Devils of the Pit, I am a Mussulman!'

The undergrowth parted and gave up Abdul Gafur, turbanless, shoeless, with his waist-cloth unbound, mud and grass in his clutched hands, and his face purple. He saw Gisborne, yelled anew, and pitched forward, exhausted and quivering, at his feet. Mowgli watched him with a sweet smile.

'This is no joke,' said Gisborne sternly. 'The man is like to die, Mowgli.'

'He will not die. He is only afraid. There was no need that he should have come out of a walk.'

Abdul Gafur groaned and rose up, shaking in every limb.

'It was witchcraft – witchcraft and devildom!' he sobbed, fumbling with his hand in his breast. 'Because of my sin I have been whipped through the woods by devils. It is all finished. I repent. Take them, Sahib!' He held out a roll of dirty paper.

'What is the meaning of this, Abdul Gafur?' said Gisborne, already knowing what would come.

'Put me in the jail-*khana*[18] – the notes are all here – but lock me up safely that no devils may follow. I have sinned against the Sahib and his salt which I have eaten; and but for those accursed wood-demons, I might have bought land afar off and lived in peace all my days.' He beat his head upon the ground in an agony of despair and mortification. Gisborne turned the roll of notes over and over. It was his accumulated back-pay for the last nine months – the roll that lay in the drawer with the home-letters and the recapping-machine. Mowgli watched Abdul Gafur, laughing noiselessly to himself. 'There is no need to put me on the horse again. I will walk home slowly with the Sahib, and then he can send me under guard to the jail-*khana*. The Government deals out many years for this offence,' said the butler sullenly.

Loneliness in the *rukh* affects very many ideas about very many things. Gisborne stared at Abdul Gafur, remembering that he was a very good servant, and that a new butler must be broken into the ways of the house from the beginning, and at the best would be a new face and a new tongue.

'Listen, Abdul Gafur,' he said. 'Thou hast done great wrong, and altogether lost thy *izzat*[19] and thy reputation. But I think that this came upon thee suddenly.'

'Allah! I had never desired the notes before. The Evil took me by the throat while I looked.'

'That also I can believe. Go, then, back to my house, and when I return I will send the notes by a runner to the Bank, and there shall be no more said. Thou art too old for the jail-*khana*. Also thy household is guiltless.'

For answer Abdul Gafur sobbed between Gisborne's cowhide riding-boots.

'Is there no dismissal then?' he gulped.

'That we shall see. It hangs upon thy conduct when we return. Get upon the mare and ride slowly back.'

'But the devils! The *rukh* is full of devils.'

'No matter, my father. They will do thee no more harm unless, indeed, the Sahib's orders be not obeyed,' said Mowgli. 'Then, per-chance, they may drive thee home – by the road of the nilghai.'

Abdul Gafur's lower jaw dropped as he twisted up his waist-cloth, staring at Mowgli.

'Are they *his* devils? His devils! And I had thought to return and lay the blame upon this warlock!'

'That was well thought of, Huzrut;[20] but before we make a trap we see first how big the game is that may fall into it. Now, *I* thought no more than that a man had taken one of the Sahib's horses. I did not know that the design was to make me a thief before the Sahib, or my devils had haled thee here by the legs. It is not too late now.'

Mowgli looked inquiringly at Gisborne; but Abdul Gafur waddled hastily to the white mare, scrambled on her back and fled, the wood-ways crashing and echoing behind him.

'That was well done,' said Mowgli. 'But he will fall again unless he holds by the mane.'

'Now it is time to tell me what these things mean,' said Gisborne a little sternly. 'What is this talk of thy devils? How can men be driven up and down the *rukh* like cattle? Give answer.'

'Is the Sahib angry because I have saved him his money?'

'No, but there is trick-work in this that does not please me.'

'Very good. Now if I rose and stepped three paces into the *rukh* there is no one, not even the Sahib, could find me till I chose. As I would not willingly do this, so I would not willingly tell. Have patience a little, Sahib, and some day I will show thee everything, for, if thou wilt, some day we will drive the buck together. There is no devil-work in the matter at all. Only . . . I know the *rukh* as a man knows the cooking-place in his house.'

Mowgli was speaking as he would speak to an impatient child. Gisborne, puzzled, baffled, and a great deal annoyed, said nothing, but stared on the ground and thought. When he looked up, the man of the woods had gone.

'It is not good,' said a level voice from the thicket, 'for friends to be angry. Wait till the evening, Sahib, when the air cools.'

Left to himself thus, dropped as it were in the heart of the *rukh*, Gisborne swore, then laughed, remounted his pony, and rode on. He visited a ranger's hut, overlooked a couple of new plantations, left some orders as to the burning of a patch of dry grass, and set out for a camping-ground of his own choice, a pile of splintered rocks roughly roofed over with branches and leaves, not far from the banks of the Kanye stream. It was twilight when he came in sight of his resting-place, and the *rukh* was waking to the hushed ravenous life of the night.

A camp-fire flickered on the knoll, and there was the smell of a very good dinner in the wind.

'Um,' said Gisborne, 'that's better than cold meat at any rate. Now the only man who'd be likely to be here'd be Muller, and, officially, he ought to be looking over the Changamanga *rukh*.[21] I suppose that's why he's on my ground.'

The gigantic German who was the head of the Woods and Forests of all India, Head Ranger from Burma to Bombay,[22] had a habit of flitting bat-like without warning from one place to another, and turning up exactly where he was least looked for. His theory was that sudden visitations, the discovery of shortcomings and a word-of-mouth upbraiding of a subordinate were infinitely better than the slow processes of correspondence, which might end in a written and official reprimand – a thing in after years to be counted against a Forest Officer's record. As he explained it: 'if I only talk to my boys like a Dutch uncle, dey say, "It was only dot damned old Muller," und dey do better next time. But if my fat-head glerk he write und say dot Muller der Inspecdor-General fail to onderstand und is much annoyed – first dot does no goot because I am not dere, und, second, der fool dot comes after me he may say to my best boys: "Look here, you haf been wigged by my bredecessor." I tell you der big brass-hat[23] pizness does not make der trees grow.'

Muller's deep voice was coming out of the darkness behind the fire-light as he bent over the shoulders of his pet cook. 'Not so much sauce, you son of Belial! Worcester sauce he is a gondiment und not a fluid. Ah, Gisborne, you haf come to a very bad dinner. Where is your camp?' and he walked up to shake hands.

'I'm the camp, sir,' said Gisborne. 'I didn't know you were about here.'

Muller looked at the young man's trim figure. 'Goot! That is very goot! One horse und some cold dings to eat. When I was young I did my camp so. Now you shall dine with me. I went into Head quarters to make up my rebort last month. I haf written half – ho! ho! – und der rest I haf leaved to my glerks und come out for a walk. Der Government is mad about dose reborts. I dold der Viceroy so at Simla.'

Gisborne chuckled, remembering the many tales that were told of Muller's conflicts with the Supreme Government. He was the chartered libertine of all the offices, for as a Forest Officer he had no equal.

'If I find you, Gisborne, sitting in your bungalow und hatching reborts to me about der blantations instead of riding der blantations, I will dransfer you to der middle of der Bikanir Desert[24] to reforest *him*. I am sick of reborts und chewing paper when we should do our work.'

'There's not much danger of my wasting time over my annuals. I hate them as much as you do, sir.'

The talk went over at this point to professional matters. Muller had some questions to ask, and Gisborne orders and hints to receive, till dinner was ready. It was the most civilized meal Gisborne had eaten for months. No distance from the base of supplies was allowed to interfere with the work of Muller's cook; and that table spread in the wilderness began with devilled small fresh-water fish, and ended with coffee and cognac.

'Ah!' said Muller at the end, with a sigh of satisfaction as he lighted a cheroot and dropped into his much-worn camp-chair. 'When I am making reborts I am Freethinker und Atheist, but here in der *rukh* I am more than Christian. I am Bagan also.' He rolled the cheroot-butt luxuriously under his tongue, dropped his hands on his knees, and stared before him into the dim shifting heart of the *rukh*, full of stealthy noises; the snapping of twigs like the snapping of the fire behind him; the sigh and rustle of a heat-bended branch recovering her straightness in the cool night; the incessant mutter of the Kanye stream, and the under-note of the many-peopled grass uplands out of sight beyond a swell of hill. He blew out a thick puff of smoke, and began to quote Heine to himself.

'Yes, it is very goot. Very goot. "Yes, I work miracles, und, by Gott, dey come off too." I remember when dere was no *rukh* more big than your knee, from here to der plough-lands, und in drought-time der cattle ate bones of dead cattle up und down. Now der trees haf come back. Dey were planted by a Free-thinker, because he know shust der cause dot made der effect. But der trees dey had der cult of der old Gods – "und der Christian Gods howl loudly."[25] Dey could not live in der *rukh*, Gisborne.'

A shadow moved in one of the bridle-paths – moved and stepped out into the starlight.

'I haf said true. Hush! Here is Faunus[26] himself come to see der Insbector-General. Himmel, he is der god! Look!'

It was Mowgli, crowned with his wreath of white flowers and walking with a half-peeled branch – Mowgli, very mistrustful of the firelight and ready to fly back to the thicket on the least alarm.

'That's a friend of mine,' said Gisborne. 'He's looking for me. Ohé, Mowgli!'

Muller had barely time to gasp before the man was at Gisborne's side, crying: 'I was wrong to go. I was wrong, but I did not know then that the mate of him that was killed by this river was awake looking for thee. Else I should not have gone away. She tracked thee from the back-ranges, Sahib.'

'He is a little mad,' said Gisborne, 'and he speaks of all the beasts about here as if he was a friend of theirs.'

'Of course – of course. If Faunus does not know, who should know?' said Muller gravely. 'What does he say about tigers – dis god who knows you so well?'

Gisborne relighted his cheroot, and before he had finished the story of Mowgli and his exploits it was burned down to moustache-edge. Muller listened without interruption. 'Dot is not madness,' he said at last when Gisborne had described the driving of Abdul Gafur. 'Dot is not madness at all.'

'What is it, then? He left me in a temper this morning because I asked him to tell how he did it. I fancy the chap's possessed in some way.'

'No, dere is no bossession, but it is most wonderful. Normally they die young – dese beople. Und you say now dot your thief-servant did not say what drove der pony, und of course der nilghai he could not speak.'

'No, but, confound it, there wasn't anything. I listened, and I can hear most things. The bull and the man simply came headlong – mad with fright.'

For answer Muller looked Mowgli up and down from head to foot, then beckoned him nearer. He came as a buck treads a tainted trail.

'There is no harm,' said Muller in the vernacular. 'Hold out an arm.'

He ran his hand down to the elbow, felt that, and nodded. 'So I thought. Now the knee.' Gisborne saw him feel the knee-cap and smile. Two or three white scars just above the ankle caught his eye.

'Those came when thou wast very young?' he said.

'Ay,' Mowgli answered with a smile. 'They were love-tokens from the little ones.' Then to Gisborne over his shoulder: 'this Sahib knows everything. Who is he?'

'That comes after, my friend. Now, where are *they*?' said Muller.

Mowgli swept his hand round his head in a circle.

'So! And thou canst drive nilghai? See! There is my mare in her pickets. Canst thou bring her to me without frightening her?'

'Can I bring the mare to the Sahib without frightening her!' Mowgli repeated, raising his voice a little above its normal pitch. 'What is more easy if the heel-ropes are loose?'

'Loosen the head and heel-pegs,' shouted Muller to the groom. They were hardly out of the ground before the mare, a huge black Australian, flung up her head and cocked her ears.

'Careful! I do not wish her driven into the *rukh*,' said Muller.

Mowgli stood still fronting the blaze of the fire – in the very form and likeness of that Greek god who is so lavishly described in the novels. The mare whickered, drew up one hind leg, found that the heel-ropes were free, and moved swiftly to her master, on whose bosom she dropped her head, sweating lightly.

'She came of her own accord. My horses will do that,' cried Gisborne.

'Feel if she sweats,' said Mowgli.

Gisborne laid a hand on the damp flank.

'It is enough,' said Muller.

'It is enough,' Mowgli repeated, and a rock behind him threw back the word.

'That's uncanny, isn't it?' said Gisborne.

'No, only wonderful – most wonderful. Still you do not know, Gisborne?'

'I confess I don't.'

'Well, then, I shall not tell. He says dot some day he will show you what it is. It would be gruel if I told. But why he is not dead I do not understand. Now listen thou.' Muller faced Mowgli, and returned to the vernacular. 'I am the head of all the *rukhs* in the country of India and others across the Black Water.[27] I do not know how many men be under me – perhaps five thousand, perhaps ten. Thy business is this, – to wander no more up and down the *rukh* and drive beasts for sport or for show, but to take service under me, who am the Government in the matter of Woods and Forests, and to live in this *rukh* as a Forest-guard; to drive the villagers' goats away when there is no order to feed them in the *rukh*; to admit them when there is an order; to keep down, as thou canst keep down, the boar and the nilghai when they become too many; to tell Gisborne Sahib how and where tigers move, and what game there is in the forests; and to give sure warning of all the fires in the *rukh*; for thou canst give warning more quickly than any other. For that work there is a payment each month in silver, and at the end, when thou hast gathered a wife and cattle and, maybe, children, a pension. What answer?'

'That's just what I—' Gisborne began.

'My Sahib spoke this morning of such a service. I walked all day alone considering the matter, and my answer is ready here. I serve, *if* I serve in this *rukh* and no other: *with* Gisborne Sahib and with no other.'

'It shall be so. In a week comes the written order that pledges the honour of the Government for the pension. After that thou wilt take up thy hut where Gisborne Sahib shall appoint.'

'I was going to speak to you about it,' said Gisborne.

'I did not want to be told when I saw dot man. Dere will never be a Forest-guard like him. He is a miracle. I tell you, Gisborne, some day you will find it so. Listen, he is blood-brother to every beast in der *rukh*!'

'I should be easier in my mind if I could understand him.'

'Dot will come. Now I tell you dot only once in my service, und dot is thirty years, haf I met a boy dot began as this man began. Und he died. Sometimes you hear of dem in der census reports, but dey all die. Dis man haf lived, und he is an anachronism, for he is before der Iron Age, und der Stone Age. Look here, he is at der beginnings of der history of man – Adam in der Garden, und now we want only an Eva! No! He is older dan dot child-tale, shust as der *rukh* is older dan der Gods. Gisborne, I am a Bagan now, once for all.'

Through the rest of the long evening Muller sat smoking and smoking, and staring and staring into the darkness, his lips moving in multiplied quotations, and great wonder upon his face. He went to his tent, but presently came out again in his majestic pink sleeping-suit, and the last words that Gisborne heard him address to the *rukh* through the deep hush of midnight were these, delivered with immense emphasis: –

> 'Dough we shivt und bedeck und bedrape us,
>   Dou art noble und nude und andeek;
> Libidina dy moder, Briapus
>   Dy fader, a God und a Greek.[28]

Now I know dot, Bagan *or* Christian, I shall nefer know der inwardness of der *rukh*!'

It was midnight in the bungalow a week later when Abdul Gafur, ashy-grey with rage, stood at the foot of Gisborne's bed and whispering bade him awake.

'Up, Sahib,' he stammered. 'Up and bring thy gun. Mine honour is gone. Up and kill before any see.'

The old man's face had changed, so that Gisborne stared stupidly.

'It was for this, then, that that jungle outcaste helped me to polish the Sahib's table, and drew water and plucked fowls. They have gone off together for all my beatings, and now he sits among his devils dragging her soul to the Pit. Up, Sahib, and come with me!'

He thrust a rifle into Gisborne's half-wakened hand and almost dragged him from the room on to the veranda.

'They are there in the *rukh*; even within gunshot of the house. Come softly with me.'

'But what is it? What is the trouble, Abdul?'

'Mowgli, and his devils. Also my own daughter,' said Abdul Gafur. Gisborne whistled and followed his guide. Not for nothing, he knew, had Abdul Gafur beaten his daughter of nights, and not for nothing had Mowgli helped in the housework a man whom his own powers, whatever those were, had convicted of theft. Also, a forest wooing goes quickly.

There was the breathing of a flute in the *rukh*, as it might have been the song of some wandering wood-god, and, as they came nearer, a murmur of voices. The path ended in a little semicircular glade walled partly by high grass and partly by trees. In the centre, upon a fallen trunk, his back to the watchers and his arm round the neck of Abdul Gafur's daughter, sat Mowgli, newly crowned with flowers, playing upon a rude bamboo flute, to whose music four huge wolves danced solemnly on their hind legs.

'Those are his devils,' Abdul Gafur whispered. He held a bunch of cartridges in his hand. The beasts dropped to a long-drawn quavering note and lay still with steady green eyes, glaring at the girl.

'Behold,' said Mowgli, laying aside the flute. 'Is there anything of fear in that? I told thee, little Stout-heart, that there was not, and thou didst believe. Thy father said – and oh, if thou couldst have seen thy father being driven by the road of the nilghai! – thy father said that they were devils; and by Allah, who is thy God, I do not wonder that he so believed.'

The girl laughed a little rippling laugh, and Gisborne heard Abdul grind his few remaining teeth. This was not at all the girl that Gisborne had seen with a half-eye slinking about the compound veiled and silent, but another – a woman full blown in a night as the orchid puts out in one hour's moist heat.

'But they are my playmates and my brothers, children of that mother that gave me suck, as I told thee behind the cook-house,' Mowgli went on. 'Children of the father that lay between me and the cold at the mouth of the cave when I was a little naked child. Look' – a wolf raised his grey jowl, slavering at Mowgli's knee – 'my brother knows that I speak of them. Yes, when I was a little child he was a cub rolling with me on the clay.'

'But thou hast said that thou art human-born,' cooed the girl, nestling closer to the shoulder. 'Thou *art* human-born?'

'Said! Nay, I know that I am human-born, because my heart is in thy hold, little one.' Her head dropped under Mowgli's chin. Gisborne put up a warning hand to restrain Abdul Gafur, who was not in the least impressed by the wonder of the sight.

'But I was a wolf among wolves none the less till a time came when Those of the jungle bade me go because I was a man.'

'Who bade thee go? That is not like a true man's talk.'

'The very beasts themselves. Little one, thou wouldst never believe that telling, but so it was. The beasts of the jungle bade me go, but these four followed me because I was their brother. Then was I a herder of cattle among men, having learned their language. Ho! ho! The herds paid toll to my brothers, till a woman, an old woman, beloved, saw me playing by night with my brethren in the crops. They said that I was possessed of devils, and drove me from that village with sticks and stones, and the four came with me by stealth and not openly. That was when I had learned to eat cooked meat and to talk boldly. From village to village I went, heart of my heart, a herder of cattle, a tender of buffaloes, a tracker of game, but there was no man that dared lift a finger against me twice.' He stooped down and patted one of the heads. 'Do thou also like this. There is neither hurt nor magic in them. See, they know thee.'

'The woods are full of all manner of devils,' said the girl with a shudder.

'A lie. A child's lie,' Mowgli returned confidently. 'I have lain out in the dew under the stars and in the dark night, and I know. The jungle is my house. Shall a man fear his own roof-beams or a woman her man's hearth? Stoop down and pat them.'

'They are dogs and unclean,' she murmured, bending forward with averted head.

'Having eaten the fruit, now we remember the Law!' said Abdul Gafur bitterly. 'What is the need of this waiting, Sahib? Kill!'

'H'sh, thou. Let us learn what has happened,' said Gisborne.

'That is well done,' said Mowgli, slipping his arm round the girl again. 'Dogs or no dogs, they were with me through a thousand villages.'

'*Ahí*, and where was thy heart then? Through a thousand villages. Thou hast seen a thousand maids. I – that am – that am a maid no more, have I thy heart?'

'What shall I swear by? By Allah, of whom thou speakest?'

'Nay, by the life that is in thee, and I am well content. Where was thy heart in those days?'

Mowgli laughed a little. 'In my belly, because I was young and always hungry. So I learned to track and to hunt, sending and calling my brothers back and forth as a king calls his armies. Therefore I drove the nilghai for the foolish young Sahib, and the big fat mare for the big fat Sahib, when they questioned my power. It were as easy to have driven the men themselves. Even now,' – his voice lifted a little – 'even now I know that behind me stand thy father and Gisborne Sahib. Nay, do not run, for no ten men dare move a pace forward. Remembering that thy father beat thee more than once, shall I give the word and drive him again in rings through the *rukh*?' A wolf stood up with bared teeth.

Gisborne felt Abdul Gafur tremble at his side. Next, his place was empty, and the fat man was skimming down the glade.

'Remains only Gisborne Sahib,' said Mowgli, still without turning; 'but I have eaten Gisborne Sahib's bread, and presently I shall be in his service, and my brothers will be his servants to drive game and carry the news. Hide thou in the grass.'

The girl fled, the tall grass closed behind her and a guardian wolf that followed, and Mowgli turning with his three retainers faced Gisborne as the Forest Officer came forward.

'That is all the magic,' he said, pointing to the three. 'The fat Sahib knew that we who are bred among wolves run on our elbows and our knees for a season. Feeling my arms and legs, he felt the truth which thou didst not know. Is it so wonderful, Sahib?'

'Indeed, it is all more wonderful than magic. These wolves drove the nilghai?'

'Ay, as they would drive Eblis[29] if I gave the order. They are my eyes and feet to me.'

'Look to it, then, that Eblis does not carry a double rifle. They have yet something to learn, thy devils, for they stand one behind the other, so that two shots would kill the three.'

'Ah, but they know they will be thy servants as soon as I am a Forest-guard.'

'Guard or no guard, Mowgli, thou hast done great shame to Abdul Gafur. Thou hast dishonoured his house and blackened his face.'

'For that, it was blackened when he took thy money, and made blacker still when he whispered in thy ear a little while since to kill a naked man. I myself will talk to Abdul Gafur, for I am a man of the Government service, with a pension. He shall make the marriage by whatsoever rite he will, or he shall run once more. I will speak to him in the dawn. For the rest, the Sahib has his house and this is mine. It is time to sleep again, Sahib.'

Mowgli turned on his heel and disappeared into the grass, leaving Gisborne alone. The hint of the wood-god was not to be mistaken; and Gisborne went back to the bungalow, where Abdul Gafur, torn by rage and fear, was raving in the veranda.

'Peace, peace,' said Gisborne, shaking him, for he looked as though he were going to have a fit. 'Muller Sahib has made the man a

Forest-guard, and as thou knowest, there is a pension at the end of that business, and it is Government service.'

'He is an outcaste – a *Mlech*[30] – a dog among dogs; an eater of carrion! What pension can pay for that?'

'Allah knows; and thou hast heard that the mischief is done. Wouldst thou blaze it to all the other servants? Make the *shadi*[31] swiftly, and the girl will make him a Mussulman. He is very comely. Canst thou wonder that after thy beatings she went to him?'

'Did he say that he would chase me with his beasts?'

'So it seemed to me. If he be a wizard, he is at least a very strong one.'

Abdul Gafur thought awhile, and then broke down and howled, forgetting that he was a Mussulman: –

'Thou art a Brahmin! I am thy cow! Make thou the matter plain, and save my honour if it can be saved!'

A second time then Gisborne plunged into the *rukh* and called Mowgli. The answer came from high overhead, and in no submissive tones.

'Speak softly,' said Gisborne, looking up. 'There is yet time to strip thee of thy place and hunt thee with thy wolves. The girl must go back to her father's house to-night. To-morrow there will be the *shadi*, by the Mussulman law, and then thou canst take her away. Bring her to Abdul Gafur.'

'I hear.' There was a murmur of two voices conferring among the leaves. 'Also, we will obey – for the last time.'

A year later Muller and Gisborne were riding through the *rukh* together, talking of their business. They came out among the rocks near the Kanye stream; Muller riding a little in advance. Under the shade of a thorn thicket sprawled a naked brown baby, and from the brake immediately behind him peered the head of a grey wolf. Gisborne had just time to strike up Muller's rifle, and the bullet tore spattering through the branches above.

'Are you mad?' thundered Muller. 'Look!'

'I see,' said Gisborne quietly. 'The mother's somewhere near. You'll wake the whole pack, by Jove!'

The bushes parted once more, and a woman unveiled snatched up the child.

'Who fired, Sahib?' she cried to Gisborne.

'This Sahib. He had not remembered thy man's people.'

'Not remembered? But indeed it may be so, for we who live with them forget that they are strangers at all. Mowgli is down the stream catching fish. Does the Sahib wish to see him? Come out, ye lacking manners. Come out of the bushes, and make your service to the Sahibs.'

Muller's eyes grew rounder and rounder. He swung himself off the plunging mare and dismounted, while the jungle gave up four wolves that fawned round Gisborne. The mother stood nursing her child and spurning them aside as they brushed against her bare feet.

'You were quite right about Mowgli,' said Gisborne. 'I meant to have told you, but I've got so used to these fellows in the last twelve months that it slipped my mind.'

'Oh, don't apologize,' said Muller. 'It's nothing. Gott in Himmel![32] "Und I work miracles – und dey come off too!" '

Notes

ABBREVIATIONS

1st American   The first American editions of *The Jungle Book* and *The Second Jungle Book* (see the Note on the Texts).

Boas   Franz Boas, 'The Central Eskimo', in vol. 6 of *Annual Report of the Bureau of American Ethnology to the Secretary of the Smithsonian Institution* (Washington: Government Printing Office, 1888).

DK   Daniel Karlin's notes to *The Jungle Books* (London: Penguin Classics, 1987).

Elliott   H. W. Elliott, *The Seal-Islands of Alaska* (Washington: Government Printing Office, 1881).

Hobson-Jobson   Henry Yule and Arthur Burnell (eds.), *Hobson-Jobson: A Glossary of Colloquial Anglo-Indian Words and Phrases* (1886), 2nd edn. (London: John Murray, 1903).

JLK   John Lockwood Kipling, *Beast and Man in India: A Popular Sketch of Indian Animals in Their Relations with the People* (1891), 2nd edn. (London: Macmillan, 1904).

K   Rudyard Kipling, 'Author's Notes on the Names in *The Jungle Books*', vol. 12 of the Sussex Edition (see *Sussex* below), pp. 471–8.

NRG   *New Readers' Guide to the Works of Rudyard Kipling* (available through the Kipling Society's website www.kipling.org.uk).

OED   *Oxford English Dictionary Online* (www.oed.com).

ORG   R. E. Harbord (ed.), *The Readers' Guide to Rudyard Kipling's Work*, 8 vols. (Canterbury: Gibbs, 1961–72).

Sanderson   G. P. Sanderson, *Thirteen Years Among the Wild Beasts of India* (1878), 2nd edn. (London: W. H. Allen, 1879).

Sterndale, *Seonee*   R. A. Sterndale, *Seonee or Camp Life on the Satpura Range: A Tale of Indian Adventure* (1877), 2nd edn. (London: Sampson Low, 1877).

Sterndale, *Mammalia* R. A. Sterndale, *Natural History of the Mammalia of India and Ceylon* (Calcutta: Thacker, Spink, 1884).

Sussex *The Sussex Edition of the Complete Works in Prose and Verse of Rudyard Kipling* (abbreviated to 'Sussex Edition'), vol. 12: *The Jungle Books* (London: Macmillan, 1937).

THE JUNGLE BOOK

PREFACE

1. *Pudmini*: Appears in 'Toomai of the Elephants' as Petersen Sahib's pet elephant. It is interesting to observe that her brother, a baggage elephant in the Indian Army, bears the name of the last emperor of the Mughal Empire (Bahadur Shah II, 1775–1862), who was deposed by the British after the Indian Mutiny of 1857.

2. *Jakko . . . the Presbytes*: The genus *Presbytes*, referring here to langurs – white-bearded monkeys with long limbs and tails. They are identified with the monkey-god Hanuman and considered sacred by Hindus. Jakko Hill, highest of the Simla hills, is populated by a large number of monkeys, and has an old temple dedicated to Hanuman on its summit.

3. *Sahi . . . customs*: 'referring to three characters: Sahi the porcupine, the "savant"; an unnamed wolf; and a bear. Bear-dances were a common entertainment at Indian village fairs' (DK). In *1st American*, Sahi appears as 'Ikki'; see also note 20 to 'Mowgli's Brothers'. For 'Seeonee', see note 3 to 'Mowgli's Brothers'.

4. *One of the leading herpetologists . . . Thanatophidia*: Referring to a mongoose. A herpetologist is an expert on reptiles, while Thanatophidia (Greek *thanatos*/'death' and *ophis*/'snake') is a scientific name for venomous snakes. The phrase 'not to live but know' is a reference to Robert Browning's poem 'A Grammarian's Funeral' (collected in *Men and Women*, 1855).

5. *Empress of India*: A steamship of the Canadian Pacific Line, with regular services between Vancouver and the Far East. Kipling himself travelled to Japan on the *Empress of India* in April 1892, with his wife Carrie, whom he had recently married.

6. *A fellow-voyager*: 'a fellow-passenger' (*Sussex*); supposedly Limmershin, the Winter Wren, in 'The White Seal' (see note 3 to that story).

MOWGLI'S BROTHERS

First published in *St Nicholas* magazine, January 1894, with illustrations by W. H. Drake.

1. *Chil*: 'pronounced *Cheel*' (K). 'Rann the Kite' (*1st American*). *Chīl* or *cheel* is an Indian name for a kite, derived from 'its shrill thin scream, [which is] a constant and characteristic Indian sound' (JLK, p. 34).

2. *Mang*: 'the bat, is *Mung*, a made-up name' (K).

3. *Seeonee hills*: The Seoni district is on the Satpura Range, a chain of hills in central India. Kipling never visited Seoni, but learned about the place from Sterndale's *Seonee* and other sources. Note that Kipling uses an unusual spelling, as the standard one at that time was 'Seoni' or 'Seonee' (*Encyclopaedia Britannica*, 9th edn., 1875–89). He previously spelled it 'Seonee' in *The Light That Failed* (1890) and *The Naulahka* (1892). According to an early manuscript draft of the story (dated February 1893, and now in the Carpenter Collection at the Library of Congress, it was originally given to a family friend, Susan Bishop, who acted as a helper and nurse around the time when Kipling's first daughter, Josephine, was born), Mowgli's jungle was originally set in 'the Aravulli hills' in the state of Mewar in Rajasthan, north-west India. The opening line of this manuscript reads: 'It was about seven o'clock of a very warm evening among the Aravulli hills when the Father Wolf woke up from his day's sleep scratched himself yawned and spread out his paws one after the other to get rid of the sleepiness in their tips.' The first page of the Bishop manuscript is reproduced in Lucile Russell Carpenter, *Rudyard Kipling: A Friendly Profile* (Chicago: Argus Books, 1942), n.p.; the same page is also viewable on the Library of Congress website: www.loc.gov/exhibits/british/images/vc203a.jpg (last accessed 8 February 2013).

4. *Tabaqui, the Dish-licker*: 'the Jackal, is pronounced *Tabarky*. I think I made up this name myself (accent on *bar*)' (K); according to JLK, however, 'A sponger or parasite is *tabáqi kūtta*, a dish (licking) dog' (p. 264). This phrase is an expression of utmost contempt, especially because dogs were seen as, and associated with, outcastes (*pariahs*) in Hindu society.

5. *We call it . . . dewanee*: Hydrophobia (literally, 'fear of water') is another name for rabies or canine madness, transmitted through the bites of infected animals, notably dogs. Jackals were often

subject to hydrophobia, partly owing to their contact with wild or village dogs, and hence endangered the lives of cattle and humans. As JLK writes: 'The jackal afflicted with rabies is a deadly creature, and more common than one likes to think' (p. 280).

6.   *Gidur-log [the jackal people]*: Gidur-log 'means literally "Jackal people". *Gidur*, pronounced *Geeder*, is an Indian name for the jackal, and *log* – pronounced always *logue*, to rhyme with *vogue* – means people' (K). Please note that the square brackets used for glosses on names in 'Mowgli's Brothers' and subsequent stories are in the original. These 'editorial' interventions by Kipling are interesting, considering that the narrator of the *Jungle Books* poses as the 'Editor' of the stories.

7.   *Shere Khan*: 'pronounced *Sheer Karn*. "Shere" means "Tiger" in some of the Indian dialects, and "Khan" is a title, more or less of distinction, to show that he was a chief among tigers' (K).

8.   *Waingunga River*: 'a real river in Central India. It is pronounced *Wine-gunger* (accent on *gung*, I think)' (K). The modern spelling is 'Wainganga'.

9.   *Lungri*: 'pronounced as spelt. It means literally "Lame", as Shere Khan was' (K).

10. *thy master*: In India, an aged or lone jackal (known as *kole balloo*), who had been expelled from his pack, was said to 'devote himself to the service of some tiger': 'It is his business to discover and give warning of the whereabouts of any stray cattle or other animal he may find that will afford his royal master a meal, the remains of which, after the tiger has dined, he of course hopes will fall to his share' (Edward Balfour, *The Cyclopædia of India and of Eastern and Southern Asia*, vol. 3 (London: B. Quaritch, 1885), p. 877).

11. *below in the valley*: 'in the dark valley' (*1st American*).

12. *They say ... man-eaters become mangy*: It was widely believed that tigers developed mange, or became diseased, as the consequence of eating human flesh: 'Strange to say, it appears that human flesh is not wholesome for [tigers]; for their skins become mangy after they have taken to eating that alone. I have shot a "man-eater" from the back of an elephant, and I found that the skin was not worth taking' (Frederick Marryat, *The Mission, or Scenes in Africa* (1845; London: George Bell & Sons, 1895), p. 169). However, it was also common to attribute man-eating tigers' 'mangy' condition to their old age, and some even rejected the popular myth that man-eaters were always mangy. According to Sterndale: 'Old mangy tigers often take to man-eating,

which they find easy work, but lots of man-eaters I have seen have had very glossy coats; there is nothing in human flesh *per se* to cause mange or other disease' (*Seonee*, p. 72).

13. *Raksha*: '("The demon"), which Mother Wolf was when any one interfered with her cubs, is pronounced *Ruk-sher* (accent on *Ruk*)' (K).

14. *Sambhur*: A large deer of the elk species. Sterndale describes a stag *sambhur* as 'the king of Indian deer', admiring his size and majesty (*Seonee*, p. 89).

15. *Mowgli the Frog*: 'a name I made up. It does not mean "frog" in any language that I know of. It is pronounced *Mowglee* (accent on the *Mow*)'(K). Elsewhere Kipling writes: 'Mow rhymes with *cow*' (*All the Mowgli Stories* (London: Macmillan, 1933), p. 8).

16. *Akela*: 'which means "Alone", is pronounced *Uk-kay-la* (accent on *kay*)' (K).

17. *Baloo*: 'Hindustani for "Bear". Pronounced *Bar-loo* (accent on *Bar*)' (K).

18. *Bagheera*: 'Hindustani for a panther or leopard. It is a sort of diminutive of Bagh, which is Hindustani for "Tiger". Pronounced *Bug-eer-a* (accent on the *eer*)' (K).

19. *never kill or eat any cattle young or old*: In the Hindu religion, cattle are sacred and are never to be harmed or eaten. That is to say, Mowgli, by following the Law of the Jungle, unknowingly observes the law of the religion and human society which he was originally born into.

20. *Sahi*: Hindi name for a porcupine. In *St Nicholas* and *1st American*, the name of the Porcupine is Ikki, of which Kipling notes: 'I think I made this up. It rhymes with "sticky." (Ho-Igoo is a real native name for him)' (K). The name 'Ho-Igoo' appears in 'How Fear Came' (see p. 156 and note 11 to that story).

21. *Mor the Peacock*: 'Mao the Peacock' in *St Nicholas* and other editions, including *1st American* and *Sussex*. According to Kipling, 'Mao' is 'pronounced something like Mor' and 'is a native name for the Peacock' (K).

22. *kill thee in the jungle*: 'kill thee in the jungle, for fear of those that love thee' (*1st American*).

23. *the King's Palace at Oodeypore*: Oodeypore (more commonly spelled 'Udaipur') is a Native State in Rajputana (now Rajasthan). It is some 400 miles north-west of the Seoni district, which makes the story of Bagheera's journey to Seoni remarkable, even unlikely. Kipling visited Udaipur in November 1887, as a part of his month-long trip to Rajputana, and wrote of seeing in the

menagerie in the Durbar Gardens there 'a black panther who is the Prince of Darkness and a gentleman', alongside 'two growling, fluffy little panther cubs'. It was also in Udaipur that Kipling witnessed panthers being driven to be shot in the king's game preserve (*Letters of Marque* (1891), chapters 8 and 9).

24. *which is not long*: 'which is not long, as a rule' (*1st American*). 'The revision prepares for Akela being the exception' (DK).

25. *twelve seasons*: 'many seasons' (*Sussex*). 'Kipling perhaps wished to be less explicit about the improbable age which Akela is to reach by the time of "Red Dog"' (DK).

26. *sag [dogs]*: 'the Persian monosyllable for dog, "Săg" is often in a native mouth a more savage term of contempt than "Sūar", pig' (JLK, p. 264). See also note 4 above.

27. *slowly*: 'slowly, and thrusting out his lower lip' (*1st American*).

28. *us in the Pack*: In *St Nicholas*, this also reads 'us in the Pack', while 'us and the Pack' occurs in *1st American* and *Sussex*. 'In the original, Mowgli refers to himself as still "in the Pack"; in the revised reading, he already identifies with "men"' (DK).

29. *alone*: 'alone to the crops' (*1st American*). In the original version published in *St Nicholas*, Kipling went on to write after this sentence: 'Next month I will tell you how Mowgli kept his word, and laid down Shere Khan's hide on the Council Rock.' 'Tiger-Tiger', the story in which this occurs, indeed appeared in the following month, February 1894.

KAA'S HUNTING

First published in *To-day*, 31 March and 7 April 1894, with illustrations by H. R. Millar, and then in *McClure's Magazine*, June 1894, with illustrations by W. A. C. Pape. Also appeared as 'Mowgli among the Monkeys' in a US publication, *Kipling Stories and Poems Every Child Should Know* (1909). 'Kaa' in the title is 'pronounced *Kar*. A made-up name, from the queer open-mouthed hiss of a big snake' (K). The pronunciation guide in *All the Mowgli Stories* (1933) reads 'Kar, with a sort of gasp in it'.

1. *fubsy*: Fat and squat; plump.

2. *or revenged himself on Shere Khan the tiger*: Present in *To-day* but not in *McClure's* and *1st American*.

3. *Hathi*: 'pronounced *Huttee*, or say nearly so. One of the Indian names for "Elephant"'(K).

4.   *Bandar-log*: 'means Monkey People. Bandar is pronounced *Bun-der*' (K). See also note 6 to 'Mowgli's Brothers'. Kipling refers to a monkey as 'Bandar' in his poem 'Divided Destinies' (collected in *Departmental Ditties*, 1886), which narrates a conversation with a monkey in a dream. The word might also be seen as a parody of 'Bhadralok' ('respectable folk'), which in the colonial context referred to the Western-educated Bengali elite, also known as 'Babus'.

5.   *outcaste*: 'outcastes' (*1st American*); 'outcasts' (*Sussex*).

6.   *What the Bandar-log think now the jungle will think later*: 'Reminiscent of the phrase once commonly used: "What Manchester thinks today England will think tomorrow", a boast from the glory days of the Liberal Party, which was particularly strong in that city, and the *Manchester Guardian*' (*NRG*).

7.   *Aaa-ssp!*: 'Ah!' (*McClure's*); 'Aaa-sssh!'(*1st American* and *Sussex*).

8.   *Cold Lairs*: 'There are lots of old deserted cities in India which look very much like the Cold Lairs in the *Jungle Books*. It is called Cold Lairs because when any animal leaves its lair or den, the place becomes cold, of course. Same with men as animals' (K). Kipling visited the old deserted cities of Amber and Chitor during his trip to Rajputana in 1887 (see note 23 to 'Mowgli's Brothers'), and these, no doubt, inspired the descriptions of the 'Cold Lairs' in this story and in 'The King's Ankus'.

9.   *on level ground*: 'on rocky ground' (*To-day* and *McClure's*).

10. *when he was put down*: 'when he was put down by Mother Wolf's side' (*1st American* and *Sussex*).

Road-Song of the Bandar-Log

1.   *We've forgotten, but*: 'Now we're going to' (*1st American* and *Sussex*).

2.   *scumfish*: As the dictionary definition, 'To suffocate, stifle, choke (with heat, smoke, a bad smell)' (*OED*), does not make much sense here, it has been suggested that Kipling playfully uses the word to capture the quick movements of monkeys up in the trees; it can be seen as a kind of portmanteau, evoking several different words – such as 'skim' (like a flying-fish), 'jump', 'skirmish' and 'scum' (referring to the *Bandar-log*'s outcaste status) – and as an onomatopoeia imitating the sounds of the monkeys scurrying through the foliage. For further discussion, see *Kipling Journal* 243, 244, 246 and 247 (1987–8).

'TIGER-TIGER!'

First published as 'Tiger-Tiger' in *St Nicholas* magazine, February 1894, with illustrations by W. H. Drake. 'Tiger! Tiger!' in *1st American* and *Sussex*. The title is an allusion to William Blake's famous poem 'The Tyger' in *Songs of Experience* (1793): 'Tyger, Tyger, burning bright / In the forests of the night, / What immortal hand or eye / Could frame thy fearful symmetry?'

1. *When . . . Council*: In *St Nicholas*, 'Tiger-Tiger' immediately follows 'Mowgli's Brothers', but in the book editions 'Kaa's Hunting' is inserted between these two stories. In *1st American*, an extra sentence was added before this opening sentence to make the transition between stories smoother: 'Now we must go back to the last tale but one.' In *Sussex*, in which the Mowgli stories from the *Jungle Books* are rearranged in chronological order (see the Note on the Texts), Kipling places 'How Fear Came' between 'Kaa's Hunting' and 'Tiger! Tiger!', with the opening sentence: 'Now we must go back to the first tale.'

2. *a red and yellow mark on his forehead*: A caste-mark.

3. *Messua*: 'pronounced *Mess-wa* (accent on *Mess*)' (K).

4. *a man I must be*: 'a man I must become' in other editions, including *St Nicholas*, *1st American* and *Sussex*.

5. *for eight cents*: Not in *1st American* and *Sussex*.

6. *a long drink of milk*: In *St Nicholas*, Kipling then inserts in parentheses: 'this was new to Mowgli, but it tasted good'.

7. *He certainly . . . comfort the god*: These two sentences are omitted from other editions. In *St Nicholas*, 'much good silver' in the second sentence reads 'nearly seventy cents in silver'.

8. *Khanhiwara*: 'a real place on the map. It ought to be pronounced *Kan-i-war-rer*, I think' (K). A village in the Seoni district that is, according to Kipling in 'Letting in the Jungle', 'thirty miles' away from Mowgli's jungle (p. 189). It is more commonly spelled 'Kanhiwara', as it is in *The Second Jungle Book*.

9. *for the potter . . . is worse*: John Lockwood Kipling writes: 'here in India, by formal prescription, only the gipsy, the potter, the washerman, and such like folk, out-caste or of low caste, will mount or own the ass' (JLK, pp. 76–7). He also provides an illustration of 'the potter and his donkey' (p. 80).

10. *Buldeo*: Pronounced 'almost as it is spelt, but the *o* isn't sounded very much (accent on *Bul*)' (K).

11. *a Tower musket*: 'an old army musket' (*St Nicholas*). The Tower musket was a flintlock long gun of around 1800, so called

because it was tested at the Tower of London arsenal. By the time Kipling was writing this story, it had become an outdated weapon.

12. *Purun Dass*: '[pronounced] *Poor-un Darss*, a real native name' (K).

13. *a hundred rupees*: In *St Nicholas* and *1st American*, Kipling adds '[$30]'. *NRG* notes: 'at 1s. 4d. to the rupee, 100 rupees were then worth £6.13.4 (£6.66)', which 'would have been a large sum for peasants in India'.

14. *Mowgli's impertinence*: In *St Nicholas* 'Mowgli's insolence; for as a rule native children are much more respectful to their elders than white children'. This somewhat characterizes Mowgli as like a white child.

15. *come up to their noses*: 'In remote regions, where a European is seldom seen, [buffaloes] are occasionally inclined to resent his presence. There is something ignominious in a party of stalwart British sportsmen being treed by a herd of angry buffaloes, and obliged to wait for rescue at the hands of a herdsman's child, but this has happened' (JLK, p. 156).

16. *Rama*: 'the herd-bull of the buffaloes, is pronounced *Rar-mer* (accent on *Rar*)' (K).

17. *dhâk-tree*: Small bush or tree which grows in many parts of Indian jungles; known as 'the flame of the forest' as 'its deep orange flowers give a brilliant aspect to the jungle in the early part of the hot weather' (*Hobson-Jobson*).

18. *do not even low*: According to John Lockwood Kipling, Indian students at his colleges found it difficult to understand what 'lowing' was when reading Thomas Gray's 'Elegy Written in a Country Churchyard' (1751), in which 'the lowing herd wind slowly o'er the lea'; he explains that this is because 'Neither ox nor cow lows in India. Their grunting note is seldom heard and does not carry' (JLK, p. 142).

19. *but get down ... one after another*: In *St Nicholas* this reads: 'You can see them lie down in the muddy pools one after another'. In the remainder of this paragraph in *St Nicholas*, Kipling contin-ues to address 'you' rather than simply describing the herd-children as 'they': 'you hear one kite ... and you know that if you died'; 'Then you sing endless songs with odd native quavers'; '[you] play that you are a king and they are your armies, or that they are gods and you ought to worship them', etc. This creates a very different impression, as the use of 'you' inevitably invites the reader to identify with the herd-children while revealing the narrator's intimate relationship with the Indian scene that he is describing.

20. *then sweep down*: Mowgli's plan to set buffaloes against Shere Khan reflects a popular belief in India that buffaloes are fearless of tigers. As Sterndale puts it: 'Buffaloes will attack and drive off a tiger, and they not unfrequently save the lives of their keepers' (*Seonee*, p. 70). A herd of buffaloes was sometimes used by hunters to drive off an injured tiger (R. G. Burton, *A Book of Man-Eaters* (London: Hutchinson, 1931), p. 114).

21. *ladies'-chain*: A move in country dancing, in which two women give their right hands to each other and turn to change places and partners.

22. *He was dead*: 'He was dead, and his lame paw doubled up under him' (*St Nicholas*).

23. *one anna*: A unit of currency formerly used in India, equalling one sixteenth of a rupee.

24. *tulsi*: A species of basil 'sacred to Vishnu, cultivated by the Hindus as a sacred plant' (*OED*).

25. *dangling feet*: *1st American* and *Sussex* add: 'It was then that Mowgli made up a song without any rhymes, a song that came up into his throat all by itself, and he shouted it aloud, leaping up and down on the rattling skin, and beating time with his heels till he had no more breath left, while Gray Brother and Akela howled between the verses.'

26. *'Have I kept my word?' said Mowgli*: *1st American* and *Sussex* add: 'when he had finished'.

27. *became a man and married*: 'became a man and took service and married' (*St Nicholas*). This is a reference to 'In the Rukh' (see Appendix, p. 315).

Mowgli's Song

1. *Sleepest . . . behind*: A separate verse in *1st American* and *Sussex*.

2. *the hunter*: 'the hunter, the man' (*1st American* and *Sussex*).

3. *Waters of the Waingunga, Shere Khan*: 'Waters of the Waingunga, bear witness that Shere Khan' (*1st American* and *Sussex*).

4. *The water . . . Why?*: A separate verse in *1st American* and *Sussex*.

THE WHITE SEAL

First published in the *National Review*, August 1893. In writing this story, Kipling studied the works of Henry Wood Elliott (1846–1930), an American naturalist and artist, who was the leading authority on fur seals in Alaska; he must have read Elliott's *The Seal-Islands of Alaska* (1881), from which all the names in this story and many of the materials are taken, and also possibly his *Our Arctic Province: Alaska and the Seal Islands* (1886). These books are based on Elliott's research during his visits to Pribilof Islands in the 1870s. It is also important to note that in the early 1890s when Kipling was writing this story, Elliott, previously supportive of the fur-seal industry, became an ardent campaigner against indiscriminate commercial hunting both on sea and on land, having witnessed, on his return to the islands in 1890, that the seal population had been reduced to near extinction in less than fifteen years. His campaign eventually led to the signing of the North Pacific Fur Seal Convention in 1911, an international treaty on sealing which is said to have saved fur seals in Alaska. (See also note 34 below for further background information.)

Many names in this story are Russian due to the fact that the Pribilof Islands, situated in the Bering Sea off the west coast of Alaska, were discovered by Russian explorers in 1786–7, and belonged to the country till 1867 when they were sold with Alaska to the United States. Kotick the white seal also speaks Russian, and all the Russian phrases appearing in this story ('poltoos', 'Ochen Scoochnie!', 'Stareek') were taken from the glossary in Elliott's *The Seal-Islands of Alaska*.

1. *Novastoshnah*: One of the major fur-seal rookeries (breeding places) in St Paul (see the next note), which is connected to the rest of the island by a narrow neck of land. Kipling writes: 'I don't know how this should be pronounced. It is a Russian name' (K). According to Elliott, the word means 'place of recent growth', 'so used because this locality in pioneer days was an island to itself and it has been annexed recently to the main island of St Paul' (n.p.). 'North East Point' is the English name, not a translation.

2. *St Paul*: One of the Pribilof Islands – see headnote.

3. *a very quaint little bird*: 'a very odd little bird' (*1st American* and *Sussex*). Limmershin is supposedly a fellow passenger on the *Empress of India*, mentioned in the Preface (p. 4). 'Limmershin' is an Aleutian name for the wren that literally means 'a chew of tobacco' (Elliott, p. 174).

4. *Sea Catch*: '*Sea Catchee* is the Russian name for a full-grown seal' (K). Elliott gives the spelling of 'Seecatch', which Kipling playfully anglicizes as the name of the father seal.

5. *Hutchinson's Hill*: A volcanic hill in the north-west of Novastoshnah which, according to Elliott, 'with its low, gradual slopes, trending to the east and southward, makes a rocky foundation

secure and broad, upon which the great single rookery of the island, the greatest in the world, undoubtedly, is located' (p. 16).

6. *holluschickie*: The Russian name for young non-breeding male seals. The plural form of *holluschak*, a bachelor seal (Elliott, p. 173).

7. *Matkah*: 'pronounced *Mut-ker* (accent on *Mut*), means a mother seal' (K). It may be noted that male seals in nature possess numerous wives in their harems; this contrasts with Kipling's monogamous seal society.

8. *Lukannon Beach*: A sandy beach on the south of St Paul Island and a main breeding-ground of seals. Named after one of the Russian pioneers who visited the island in 1787–8.

9. *Otter Island*: A rocky islet, six miles south-west of St Paul. Elliott reports that the tiny island, 'surrounded by an unbroken mural precipice extending nearly all around', has only 'a broken, rocky beach and no sand' (Elliott, p. 16), and is therefore not fit as a nursery. Many thousands of *holluschickie* annually haul out in Otto Island (p. 16), as these non-breeding 'batchelor seals' are not allowed to come near the breeding-grounds.

10. *Kotick*: 'pronounced *Ko-tick*, means "baby seal" (accent on *Ko*)' (K).

11. *There never has been . . . a white seal*: Elliott writes that he saw 'only three albino pups among the multitudes of St Paul', and 'none on St George' (p. 47), another principal seal island in the Pribilof Islands.

12. *his flippers . . . by his side*: Said to be an error pointed out to Kipling by a newspaper interviewer in 1903, according to whom 'A fur seal sleeps with his fore flippers folded on his breast, not limp at his sides', to which Kipling is reported to have responded, 'Confound you' (*Kipling Journal* 58 (July 1941), p. 24). Kipling, however, did not change his wording in *Sussex*.

13. *Sea Pig*: 'Sea Pig, the Porpoise' (*1st American* and *Sussex*).

14. *the Stumpy-tailed albatross*: The short-tailed albatross, found in the North Pacific.

15. *the man-of-war hawk*: Popular name given by sailors to the frigatebird.

16. *never to stop . . . particularly a row-boat*: 'Because of the (increasing) practice of open-sea hunting of seals' (DK).

17. *Juan Fernandez*: An archipelago (rather than a single island) in the Pacific Ocean, off the coast of Chile. One of the islands was renamed 'Robinson Crusoe' in 1966, as Defoe's novel took its

inspiration from the life story of Alexander Selkirk (1676–1721), a Scottish sailor who became marooned on the island and lived there alone for four years. Another island in the archipelago was renamed after Selkirk (see note 28 below).

18. *the Horn*: Cape Horn, the southernmost tip of South America. Sailing around the Horn is notoriously dangerous owing to the high winds and tides, which have caused many shipwrecks.

19. *Kerick Booterin*: The 'first chief' of the native community when Elliott was visiting St Paul in the early 1870s. Booterin and his son Patalamon are both listed as resident natives in Elliott, p. 159.

20. *Aleut:* A native of the Aleutian Islands of Alaska. Most of the indigenous population of St Paul Island were of Aleut origin and traditionally hunted seals for a living; they became the major workforce in 'harvesting' fur seals under the supervision of the Alaska Commercial Company.

21. *Sea-Lion's Neck . . . Salt House*: Elliott provides a detailed map of Novastoshnah, on which these place names are marked. Sea-Lion's Neck is the south-western point of Novastoshnah, and about 1,200 metres away from there is the Salt House, where seals' skins were pickled in salt. The natives were paid forty cents for each skin that they delivered to the Salt House (Elliott, p. 156).

22. *Sea Vitch*: 'Russian for "Walrus"' (K); in Elliott, 'seevitchie'. The Walrus Islet is a small rock six miles away from Novastoshnah that is 'frequented by several hundred male walrus, to the exclusion of females, every summer' (p. 17).

23. *Sea Cow*: 'another name for what are called "Manatees" or "Dugongs" in the natural-history books' (K). More precisely, it is the 'Steller's Sea Cow' of the North Pacific, which was hunted to extinction in 1768 only twenty-seven years after it was first discovered by Europeans. That is why Sea Vitch comments, 'If he is living still'.

24. *Basking shark*: Elliott mentions 'carnivorous attacks of basking sharks and killer whales' (p. 63) as main threats to young seals, though the basking shark actually does not eat seals but feeds on plankton.

25. *Kerguelen Island*: An uninhabited island in the southern Indian Ocean, also known as Desolation Island, midway between South Africa, Australia and the Antarctic, where, according to Elliott, 'perhaps nine-tenths of all the oriental fur-seals' once congregated

(p. 7). The Antarctic fur seal on this island were hunted to near extinction in the eighteenth and nineteenth centuries, though the number has since recovered.

26. *Gallapagos ... the Cape of Good Hope*: 'All the islands and places mentioned in "The White Seal" are on the map. You had better look them up' (K). The islands are all listed in Elliott as seal-grounds in the Southern Hemisphere that were thoroughly wrecked by indiscriminate killing by fur-sealers. *Gallapagos*: Rendered 'Galapagos' (the modern spelling) in *Sussex*, this is an archipelago of volcanic islands off the coast of Ecuador, famous for Charles Darwin's visit in HMS *Beagle* in 1835. *Georgia Islands*: South Georgia and the South Sandwich Islands is a British territory in the Southern Ocean, east of South America. *Orkneys*: The South Orkney Islands, also located in the Southern Ocean, south-west of South Georgia, were discovered in 1821 by sealers. *Emerald Island*: First sighted in 1821 and marked on the map as halfway between Australia and Antarctica, this is one of many 'phantom islands' which have since been declared non-existent; in Kipling's day it was still believed to exist. *Little Nightingale Island, Gough's Island*: Little Nightingale and Gough Island are part of the British-owned Tristan da Cunha archipelago in the South Atlantic Ocean. *Bouvet's Island*: Bouvet Island, the southernmost island of the South Atlantic. *The Crossets*: The Crozet Islands in the southern Indian Ocean, 1,400 miles south of Madagascar. *a little speck of an island south of the Cape of Good Hope*: In the *National Review*, Kipling adds, 'called Royal Company Island'. This information was taken from Elliott (p. 7), and does not seem to be accurate, as the Royal Company's Islands, discovered in about 1840, were marked on the map as 400 miles south of Tasmania. In fact, this is a group of 'phantom islands', which were eventually removed from Admiralty charts in 1904.

27. *Cape Corientes*: Cape Corrientes is on the Argentine coast at Mar del Plata, where 'a small cliff-bound rookery ... is owned and farmed out by the Argentine republic' (Elliott, p. 7).

28. *Masafuera*: Isla Más Afuera, one of the Juan Fernández Islands, now known as Isla Alejandro Selkirk – see note 17 above.

29. *Copper Island*: Now Medny Island, one of the Commander Islands ('Komandorskiye Ostrova' in Russian) in the Bering Sea, which Elliott lists as one of only four islands with a fur-seal population in the North Pacific, the other three being Bering

Island, another of the Commander archipelago, and St Paul and
St George in the Pribilof Islands.

30.   *the Great Combers of Magellan*: 'the big waves that roll up from
the South Pole to the beaches and rocks of Patagonia' (K).

31.   *the Frog-Footman*: In the *National Review*, this is given as 'the
frog-footman with the letter in *Alice Through the Looking-glass*',
although the frog-footman, who exchanges a ceremonious bow
with the fish-footman on the receipt of a letter, appears in chapter
6 of Lewis Carroll's *Alice's Adventures in Wonderland* (1865),
rather than its sequel *Through the Looking-Glass* (1871).

32.   *been there*: 'been under them' (*1st American* and *Sussex*).

33.   *are not very clever, and they*: Not in *1st American* and *Sussex*.

34.   *where no man comes*: In the *National Review*, Kipling goes on
to write: 'Now there are two great countries squabbling to find
out which of the two shall kill seals off the island of St Paul's in
the Bering Sea; and while they are squabbling news has come in
that the seal-catch is small. It will get smaller and smaller, till at
last the two countries will be left with nothing to argue about.
Limmershin told me. Isn't it simple when you know all about it?'
The 'two great countries' mentioned here are the United States
and Great Britain, and the dispute between them was heating up
in the early 1890s, with Britain threatening to use force if the
United States attempted to arrest Canadian sealers in the Bering
Sea. Elliott, who had recently come back from the Pribilof
Islands with a new mission to protect seals (see headnote), played
a significant role in the negotiation process between the two
countries, by urging the need to restrict sealing to save seals from
extinction. 'The White Seal' was Kipling's literary intervention in
the dispute, and highlighted the conservationist view put forward by Elliott. The dispute was finally resolved in August 1893,
a few weeks after the publication of this story in the *National
Review*.

Lukannon

1.   *This is a sort of sad Seal National Anthem*: 'This is the great
deep-sea song that all the St Paul seals sing when they are heading back to their beaches in the summer. It is a sort of very sad
seal National Anthem' (*1st American* and *Sussex*).

'RIKKI-TIKKI-TAVI'

First published in *St Nicholas* magazine, November 1893, with illustrations by W. H. Drake. The title (and name of the character) is 'pronounced *Rikky-ticky-tar-vi*. Mongooses are as bold and clever as I have tried to describe, and they often come into a house or even into an office with people going in and out all the time, and make friends with men there. A perfectly wild mongoose used to come and sit on my shoulder in my office in India, and burn his inquisitive nose on the end of my cigar, just as Rikki did in the tale' (K).

1. *Nag*: 'pronounced *Narg*, is a native name for the Cobra. *Nagaina* (pronounced *Na-gy-na*; accent on *gy*) is his wife' (K).
2. *Segowlee*: Now Sugauli, a small cantonment in Bihar province, north-east India, near the Nepal border.
3. *Darzee*: 'which means "tailor", is pronounced *Dar-zy*' (K).
4. *Chuchundra, the musk-rat*: '[pronounced] *Chew-chun-drer*' (K). The 'musk-rat' is the popular name of the common musk shrew, 'an animal having much the figure of the common shrew, but nearly as large as a small brown rat', with 'a strong musky odour' (*Hobson-Jobson*). 'Chuchundra' is the Hindi name for this type of shrew.
5. *Marshal Niel*: Also spelled 'Maréchal Niel', a strong tea-scented climbing rose with deep yellow colour, named after Adolphe Niel (1802–69), one of Napoleon's marshals. Introduced in 1864, it was one of the most popular garden roses in the nineteenth century. The garden described in the story is said to be modelled after the bungalow 'Belvedere' in Allahabad which belonged to Kipling's friends, Professor Alex Hill and his American wife Edmonia Hill. Kipling lived there in 1888 as 'a paying guest'. *NRG* suggests that the name Teddy is possibly derived from 'Ted', the nickname of Edmonia, who was a close confidante of Kipling's in India.
6. *Brahm*: Or Brahma, the supreme god in Hinduism.
7. *Nagaina*: See note 1 above.
8. *wriggled*: 'flinched' (*1st American* and *Sussex*).
9. *Karait*: 'pronounced *Ker-ite* (accent on *ite*)' (K). The krait, one of the most venomous snakes in India.
10. *Chua*: 'pronounced *Chew-er*' (K). 'Chua' is the Hindi name for 'rat'.
11. *Coppersmith*: The popular name in India of the Crimson-breasted Barbet. JLK describes the bird as a 'noisy herald of spring . . . [whose] cry of "tock-tock" fills the air as completely as the sound of a brazen vessel' (p. 47).

Darzee's Chaunt

An archaic variant of 'chant', 'chaunt' in the poem's title was 'already a poeticism in Kipling's day, and hence suitable for Darzee's burlesque dignity' (DK).

TOOMAI OF THE ELEPHANTS

First published in *St Nicholas* magazine, December 1893, with illustrations by W. H. Drake. This story draws its inspiration from George Peress Sanderson's *Thirteen Years Among the Wild Beasts of India* (1878), which vividly describes the elephant-catching operations in India. Sanderson (1848–92), whom Petersen Sahib is said to be modelled on, pioneered a system of capturing a whole herd of wild elephants by driving them into stockades. A stockade is called a *keddah*, a word that was also used to mean the elephant-catching operation as a whole. In 1879 Sanderson was appointed as superintendent of the Government Keddahs at Dacca, and supervised a yearly expedition to capture and train wild elephants for the Government service. Kipling mentions 'Sanderson Sahib' in 'The Killing of Hatim Tai', a story about an elephant 'condemned to death by the Government, because he had stepped upon his *mahout*' (collected in *The Smith Administration*, 1891). Another important source of inspiration for this story is the myth of elephant 'ballrooms', recorded in John Lockwood Kipling's *Beast and Man in India* – see note 16 below.

1. *Kala Nag . . . served the Indian Government*: According to JLK, 'in consequence of the liability of the male to occasional fits of ill-temper from functional causes, it has been decreed that only females are to enter Government service' (p. 239). *NGR* comments that 'Kala Nag would have been recruited well before this decree'. 'Black Snake' (i.e. Kala Nag) and 'Radha Pyari' (seven lines later) are listed among other genuine elephant names in JLK (p. 217). (For more on elephant names, see note 21 below.)

2. *a ripe age for an elephant*: 'An elephant at twenty-five years of age may be compared to a human being of eighteen. He attains his full strength and vigour at about thirty-five, and has been known to live for a hundred and twenty years' (JLK, pp. 239–40).

3. *Afghan war of 1842*: Known as the First Afghan War (1839–42), which started with the British invasion of Afghanistan to set up a puppet regime, but ended in fiasco and massive British casualties. It was the first major conflict in Afghanistan which the

British fought to contain the Russian threat to the Indian Empire, signalling the start of the 'Great Game', a phrase used to describe Anglo-Russian rivalry for supremacy in Central Asia.

4. *little milk tusks had dropped out*: It was widely believed that 'the first or milk tusks of an elephant . . . are shed between the first and second year' (Charles Knight, *The English Cyclopaedia*, vol. 2 (London: Bradbury and Evans, 1866), p. 505), though some contemporaneous authorities, such as G. P. Sanderson, disagreed with this view.

5. *Emperor Theodore . . . Abyssinian War medal*: In the Abyssinian Expedition of 1868, more than forty elephants accompanied the Indian Army to Ethiopia, taking the sea route from Bombay. The expedition was to rescue several British hostages held by Emperor Tewodros (Theodore) II of Ethiopia in his fort in Magdala, and ended in the emperor's suicide before he could be captured by the British.

6. *Ali Musjid*: A reference to the Battle of Ali Masjid, the opening battle of the Second Afghan War (1878–80). Ali Masjid is the narrowest point of the Khyber Pass.

7. *Moulmein*: Now 'Mawlamyaing', a teak port and commercial centre of British Burma. When Kipling visited Moulmein in 1889 on a steamship, he saw elephants 'hard at work in timber-yards', and described the place as 'a sleepy town, just one house thick, scattered along a lovely stream and inhabited by slow, solemn elephants, building stockades for their own diversion' (*From Sea to Sea and Other Sketches: Letters of Travel*, 2 vols. (London: Macmillan, 1900), vol. 1, p. 231). Moulmein also provides the setting of George Orwell's essay 'Shooting an Elephant' (1936).

8. *Garo hills*: Heavily forested hills in Assam, in north-east India; one of the chief destinations of elephant-trapping expeditions of the Indian Government – see headnote.

9. *tusker*: A male elephant with tusks.

10. *mahouts*: Elephant-drivers.

11. *howdah*: A great chair or framed seat placed on the back of an elephant. The Rajas' ceremonial howdahs were lavishly decorated with gilt canopies and hangings, to symbolize their prestige and power.

12. *Cawnpore*: Now Kanpur, a town and important military station on the Ganges, 600 miles north-west of Calcutta, famous as the scene of a massacre of the British during the Indian Mutiny of 1857. Cawnpore is the setting of another of Kipling's elephant stories, 'My Lord the Elephant' (collected in *Many Inventions*, 1893).

13. *Petersen Sahib*: See headnote.

14. *Pudmini*: Acknowledged in the Preface as a source of material for 'Toomai of the Elephants'.

15. *annas*: A unit of currency formerly used in India, one *anna* equalling a sixteenth of a rupee.

16. *There are great cleared flat places . . . the elephants dance*: John Lockwood Kipling writes: 'Colonel Lewin tells me of a belief in the Chittagong Hill tracts, that wild elephants assemble together to dance! Further, that once he came with his men on a large cleared place in the forest, the floor beaten hard and smooth, like that of a native hut. "This," said the men, in perfect good faith, "is an elephant nautch-khana" – ballroom. [. . .] I confess to a deep envy of the Assam coolie, who said he had been a hidden unbidden guest at an elephant ball. [. . .] Let us believe, then, until some dismal authority forbids us, that the elephant *beau monde* meets by the bright Indian moonlight in the ballrooms they clear in the depths of the forest, and dance mammoth quadrilles and reels to the sighing of the wind through the trees and their own trumpeting, shrill and sudden as the Highlander's hoch!' (JLK, pp. 224–5). Colonel Thomas Herbert Lewin (1839–1916) was the Superintendent of the Hill Tracts of Chittagong from 1866 to 1875.

17. *Bapree bap!*: 'Oh, Father!'; 'a common exclamation of Hindus when in surprise or in grief' (*Hobson-Jobson*).

18. *Dihang River*: A name for the upper reaches of the Brahmaputra.

19. *guddee*: Throne of an Indian ruler.

20. *hog-bear*: 'Another name for the sloth-bear' (*Hobson-Jobson*), a nocturnal and omnivorous bear, known for its habit of digging for ants and termites.

21. *Hira Guj . . . Kuttar Guj*: 'Hira Guj (*Hee-ra*), Birchi Guj and Kuttar Guj are all true names of elephants' (K). Commenting further on the common names for elephants, JLK writes: 'The Sanscrit word *hāthi* [. . .] in popular use is less used by mahouts than the Pali, *gaj*, frequently compounded with weapons, flowers, etc., to make a name, as *Katár-gaj*, dagger elephant, *Moti-gaj*, pearl elephant. The Persian word *pil* is also used' (p. 217).

Shiv and the Grasshopper

1. *Mahadeo*: Another name for Shiv (Shiva), the third deity of the Hindu triad besides Brahma and Vishnu. Kipling's characterization of Shiv as 'the preserver' is interesting, as he is usually known as the destroyer and restorer.

SERVANTS OF THE QUEEN

First published as 'Her Majesty's Servants' in *Harper's Weekly*, 3 March 1894, with an illustration by F. S. Church, and in the *Pall Mall Magazine*, March 1894, with illustrations by P. Frenzeny. Most other editions, including *1st American* and *Sussex*, use 'Her Majesty's Servants' as the title. In *Sussex*, this was placed as the last story of the *Jungle Books*.

The story takes its inspiration from the Rawal Pindi Durbar, the meeting between the Viceroy Lord Dufferin and the Amir of Afghanistan (Abdur Rahman) in April 1885. Kipling reported on the durbar as a special correspondent of the *Civil and Military Gazette*. He wrote thirteen articles in all, which are reprinted in Neil K. Moran, *Kipling and Afghanistan* (Jefferson, North Carolina: McFarland, 2005) and as extracts in Thomas Pinney (ed.), *Kipling's India* (Basingstoke: Macmillan, 1986). These articles capture well the atmosphere and conditions of the camp. The story is closely based on the tenth article, published on 8 April 1885, which gives a vivid account of the military review described in the story, and of how the Amir was impressed by the spectacle.

The title echoes one of Kipling's verse headings for his father's book *Beast and Man in India*: 'The black bulk heaving where the oxen pant, / The bowed head toiling where the guns careen, / Declare our might, – our slave the elephant / The servant of the Queen' (JLK, p. 207).

1. *Rule of Three*: An arithmetic 'method of finding a fourth quantity, given three known quantities, which bears the same relation to the third as the second does to the first' (*OED*). Also known as 'the Golden Rule' for its extensive usefulness.

2. *Tweedle-dum . . . Tweedle-dee*: 'Tweedle-dum and Tweedle-dee' is a phrase used to describe two things that are so similar that it is impossible to tell them apart. 'Tweedle-dum' and 'Tweedle-dee' appear as characters in an English nursery rhyme, and also in Lewis Carroll's *Through the Looking-Glass* (1871).

3. *Pilly-Winkie . . . Winkie-Pop!*: This variant on 'Tweedle-dum and Tweedle-dee' echoes the chorus appearing in Kipling's poem 'The Song of the Banjo', composed in 1894: 'With my "*Pilly-willy-winky-winky popp!*" / (Oh, it's any tune that comes into my head!)'.

4. *Rawal Pindi*: One of the largest military stations in the Punjab, now a city in Pakistan near Islamabad.

5. *camels . . . ropes of the tents*: Kipling notes how camels are 'nervous and stupid creatures when they are all camped together.

They stampede at night sometimes for no reason, and fall all over the tents and horse-lines' (K).

6. *Vixen*: Kipling owned a fox-terrier of this name. 'Vixen' also appears as the narrator's beloved companion in others of Kipling's stories, such as 'My Lord the Elephant' (collected in *Many Inventions*, 1893) and 'Garm – a Hostage' (collected in *Actions and Reactions*, 1909).

7. *plowter*: A variant of 'plouter', 'to splash about . . . in anything wet or dirty' (*OED*).

8. *why didn't you stay*: 'why the pickets didn't you stay' (*1st American* and *Sussex*).

9. *Gun-bullocks*: Kipling wrote in his notes to *Sussex*: 'the bullocks and elephants of the big-gun batteries of 40-pound Armstrong guns are not needed now that machinery has come into fashion, and the batteries were abolished long ago' (K).

10. *my own account*: 'my own account, quietly' (*1st American* and *Sussex*).

11. *Blue Gums of the Back Blocks*: The blue gum is a species of *Eucalyptus* native to Australia; 'back blocks' is an Australian expression for the land of the remote and sparsely inhabited interior.

12. *kajawahs*: A pair of large panniers, carried by a camel, one on each side. Using *kajawahs* was an effective way of transporting the sick and the injured, as well as army equipment.

13. *Hapur*: A town about forty miles east of Delhi.

14. *Imagine . . . cocktail*: Ormonde (1883–1904) was a legendary English thoroughbred horse with an unbeaten record, and a Triple Crown winner in 1886. A 'cocktail' refers to a horse that is not entirely thoroughbred, and it would be really insulting for Ormonde to be called one by a ''bus-horse' – used for pulling omnibuses. In *1st American* and *Sussex*, this sentence reads instead: 'Imagine the feelings of Sunol if a car-horse called her a "skate".' Sunol (b. 1886) was a great trotter in harness-racing, bred and trained in California. She created a great sensation in 1891 when she beat the world record for the mile that had remained unbroken since 1885. A car-horse tows trams (or 'tramcars' in American English); and a 'skate' is a derisive term of abuse, meaning 'a poor, worn-out, decrepit horse' (*OED*).

15. *Malaga*: A city in southern Spain.

16. *Carbine, winner of the Melbourne Cup*: Carbine (1885–1914) was 'a very great Australian racer, who carried off all the big events in the racing line, many years ago' (K). Born in New Zealand

and competing mainly in Australia, the racehorse won thirty-three races in his life, including the Melbourne Cup, the most prestigious race in Australia, in 1890 in a record time.

17. *saying a poem*: 'saying a piece' (*1st American*); 'saying poetry' (*Sussex*).

18. *Pachydermatous Anachronism*: 'the (jocular) sense is "thick skinned good-for-nothing"' (DK). Pachydermata is an order of mammals in the classificatory system of Georges Cuvier (1769–1832) that includes elephants and other 'thick-skinned' (pachydermatous) animals, such as rhinoceroses, hippopotamuses, pigs and horses. The term in itself suggests 'anachronism' (i.e. 'existing out of its time'), as Cuvier's system, though still popular, was becoming obsolete by the time Kipling was writing. Sterndale in *Mammalia* compares Cuvier's with the modern system of classifying mammals.

19. *I can't trust my driver*: This echoes Sanderson's warning to European officers against entrusting native drivers with the elephants' health and management, as they are 'invariably grossly superstitious and ignorant' (p. 96).

20. *barking dog*: According to JLK, 'the elephant hates and fears dogs as much as some great men of to-day hate noisy newspapers, and with better reason. Nature, in furnishing the beast with a soft and tender trunk, has bound him down to keep the peace with all creation' (JLK, pp. 226–7). Vixen terrifies elephants in a similar manner in 'My Lord the Elephant' (see note 6 above).

21. *slued*: 'Swung round; variant spelling of "slewed"' (DK).

22. *Bonnie Dundee*: A tune used by most cavalry regiments of the British Army. The words of the song were originally written by Sir Walter Scott.

23. *An order was given*: 'There was an order' (*1st American* and *Sussex*).

Parade-Song of the Camp-Animals

1. *Elephants of the Gun-Team*: This echoes, and is set to the tune of, the famous marching song 'The British Grenadiers', which starts: 'Some talk of Alexander, and some of Hercules / Of Hector and Lysander, and such great names as these . . .'.

2. *Gun-Bullocks*: Also echoing and set to the tune of 'The British Grenadiers': 'Those heroes of antiquity ne'er saw a cannon ball, / Or knew the force of powder to slay their foes withal . . .'.

3. *Cavalry Horses*: Set to the tune of 'Bonnie Dundee'. See note 22 to 'Servants of the Queen'.

4. *Screw-Gun Mules*: This echoes and is set to the tune of 'The
    Lincolnshire Poacher': 'As me and my companions was setting
    out a snare / 'Twas then we spied the gamekeeper, for him we
    didn't care / For we can wrestle and fight, my boys, and jump
    from anywhere / Oh, 'tis my delight on a shiny night in the sea-
    son of the year . . .'.
5. *hair-trombone*: 'hairy trombone' (*1st American*).

THE SECOND JUNGLE BOOK

For additional annotations on the Mowgli stories, including glosses of
Indian flora and fauna and the pronunciation and origins of character
names, see the notes to *The Jungle Book*.

HOW FEAR CAME

First published as 'How Fear Came to the Jungle' in the *Pall Mall
Budget*, 7 and 14 June 1894, with illustrations by Cecil Aldin, and in
the *Pall Mall Gazette*, 14 and 15 June 1894, with the 'The Law of the
Jungle' as a verse epigraph heading the story. Also published as 'A
Strange Tale of the Jungle' in the *New York World*, 10 June 1894.

Hathi's story of 'how fear came' to the jungle echoes God's promise
to Noah: 'the fear of you and the dread of you shall be upon every
beast of the earth, and upon every fowl of the air, upon all that moveth
upon the earth, and upon all the fishes of the sea; into your hand are
they delivered' (Genesis 9: 2). Kipling's initial working title for the
Jungle Books was 'Noah's Ark Tales' (letter to Mary Mapes Dodge,
24 November 1892, in Pinney (ed.), *The Letters of Rudyard Kipling*,
vol. 2 (Basingstoke: Macmillan, 1990), p. 72).

1. *If you have read . . . remember that he*: 'You will remember that
    Mowgli' (*Sussex*). In *1st American*, 'stories' reads 'book'.
2. *Now everybody knows . . . best and ripest*: 'as many gardeners
    know to their cost, porcupines are most scrupulously dainty and
    epicurean as to their diet' (A. C. McMaster, *Notes on Jerdon's
    Mammals of India* (1871), quoted in Sterndale, *Mammalia*, p. 364).
3. *Bee-Rocks*: 'bees' nest' in the journal publications; 'probably
    changed [to 'Bee-Rocks'] to match the location in "Red Dog"'
    (*NRG*) – see note 21 to 'Red Dog'.
4. *who was quite sure*: 'who, in those days, was quite sure' (*1st
    American* and *Sussex*).

5. *hurt my Man-cub*: 'hurt the Man-cub' (*1st American* and *Sussex*).

6. *mohwa*: 'pronounced *Mow-er* to rhyme with *cow-er*, is a tree that bears sweet sticky smelly blossoms which some of the native tribes in the Jungle make into a strong drink. Its Latin name is *Bassia Longifolia*, I believe' (K).

7. *held him to be*: 'knew him to be' (*1st American* and *Sussex*).

8. *Tha*: 'pronounced *Tar*. A made-up name' (K).

9. *even ... to-day*: Not in *1st American* and *Sussex*.

10. *Mysa*: 'I made it up. Pronounce it *My-ser* (accent on *My*)' (K).

11. *Gonds ... Ho-Igoo*: The Gond is one of the aboriginal tribes of central India – 'a Dravidian people, many of them jungle-dwellers' (*OED*) – while 'Ho-Igoo' is a Gondi name for the porcupine. See note 20 to 'Mowgli's Brothers'.

THE MIRACLE OF PURUN BHAGAT

First published under this title in the *Pall Mall Gazette* and the *Pall Mall Budget*, 18 October 1894, with illustrations by Cecil Aldin. Also published in the *New York World*, 14 October 1894, as 'A Miracle of the Present Day'. 'A Song of Kabir' was first published as a verse epigraph heading 'The Miracle of Purun Bhagat'; the original title in the *Pall Mall* publications reads: 'A song of Kabir. (*trans.*)'. 'Purun Bhagat' in the story title is 'pronounced *Poorun Bhuggat*, [and] means "Purun the Holy Man"' (K).

1. *langurs*: 'pronounced *Lun-goors*, are the big monkeys of the Himalayas' (K) – see note 2 to the Preface.

2. *realized that the ancient order*: 'felt that the older order' (*1st American* and *Sussex*).

3. *get on*: 'get on in the world' (*1st American* and *Sussex*).

4. *the kingdom*: 'the little kingdom' in the *Pall Mall* publications.

5. *Pioneer*: A daily newspaper published in Allahabad. Kipling worked for this newspaper as an assistant editor from November 1887 until he left India in March 1889.

6. *confer ... the Grand Cross of the Star of India*: i.e. the Maharajah was made a Knight Grand Commander of the Order of the Star of India, instituted by Queen Victoria in 1861 after the Indian Mutiny of 1857, in order to honour loyal Indian princes and the British who served in India.

7. *the Order of the Indian Empire*: A junior order of the Star of India (see previous note), created by Queen Victoria in 1878, a year after she assumed the title of Empress of India.

8. *K.C.I.E.*: Knight Commander of the Order of the Indian Empire.

9. *game of General Post*: A rapid exchange of positions; derived from a popular parlour game, 'General Post', in which players are required to change seats simultaneously.

10. *Dewan*: The prime minister of a Native State.

11. *coco-de-mer*: 'the very big coconut shell that comes, I believe, from the Seychelles Islands, and does not grow in India' (K). The Seychelles are off the east coast of Africa, near Madagascar.

12. *Kala Pir . . . Jogis*: Kala Pir is a tribal deity 'worshipped in the low hills and throughout the eastern districts of the Punjab' (G. W. Briggs, *Gorakhnāth and the Kānphalā Yogṭs* (Calcutta: Motilal Banarsidass, 1938), p. 138). The Jogis ('Yogis' in *1st American*) are the followers of the Hindu god Shiva, and Kala Pir is thought to be a manifestation of this god.

13. *Rohtak to Kurnool . . . Samanah*: Rohtak is a city north-west of Delhi, and Kurnool (now spelled 'Karnal') is a town on the Grand Trunk Road, India's longest highway running 1,600 miles from Calcutta to Peshawar. Samanah, thirty miles south-west of Ambala, is described by Charles Knight as 'the ancient capital, now a heap of ruins' (*The English Cyclopaedia*, vol. 4 (London: Bradbury and Evans, 1867), p. 583). Purun Bhagat must have loosely followed the Grand Trunk Road, and then continued to Ambala.

14. *Gugger river*: A tributary of the great Sutlej River, which rises in the southern Himalayas.

15. *Kulu*: A district in the Himalayas, some seventy miles north of Simla. The Sahiba in *Kim* (1901) is a Rajput woman from Kulu.

16. *Sewaliks*: 'Siwaliks' (*Sussex*); the southernmost range and foot-hills of the Himalayas.

17. *Simla*: Hill-station and summer capital of British India at the foothills of the Himalayas, and the main setting of Kipling's first book, *Plain Tales from the Hills* (1888). With the modern spelling of 'Shimla', the city is now the capital of Himachal Pradesh.

18. *salaamed*: To salaam is to bow low, with the palm of the right hand placed on the forehead.

19. *Chota Simla*: 'means "Little Simla", the native quarter of the town of Simla' (K) – see note 17 above.

20. *borax*: Produced naturally in Tibet, Tibetan borax was imported over the Himalayas into India before being exported to supply the European market.

21. *Mutteeanee Pass*: Mutteeanee (now Matiana) is a town approximately forty miles north-west of Simla on the Himalaya–Tibet road. The Mutteeanee Pass is also mentioned in Kipling's poem 'The Truce of the Bear' (1898).

22. *Kali . . . Sitala:* 'pronounced *Kar-li*, is the name of an Indian goddess (accent on *Kar*)' (K). Durga, a multi-armed fighting goddess, and Sitala, the smallpox goddess, are often associated, or identified, with Kali.

23. *enormous hollow*: 'gigantic hollow' (*1st American* and *Sussex*).

24. *bannocks*: Home-made loaves, usually unleavened – a word used in Scotland and the north of England.

25. *Ladakhi*: From Ladakh, a lofty mountainous region of Kashmir at the back of the central range of the Himalayas, some 200 miles north of Simla.

26. *many-sided fields*: 'many sided plots of fields' in other editions.

27. *barasingh*: 'is native for "Big Horn" (pronounced *Burra Sing*)' (K).

28. *mushick-nabha*: A Pahari word for the musk deer (Sterndale, *Mammalia*, p. 494, which gives the spelling of 'mussuck-naba').

29. *Bhai! Bhai!*: *Bhai* is 'brother' in Hindi.

30. *Sona*: A word for the Himalayan black bear in the Lepcha language, according to Sterndale (*Mammalia*, p. 113).

31. *D.C.L.*: 'Doctor of Civil Law'.

32. *Mohiniwala*: Unidentified.

A Song of Kabir

Kabir was an Indian mystic, poet and religious reformer of the fifteenth century who sought to bring together Hindus and Muslims through faith in one universal God. He rejected the caste system and idolatry, and preached the spiritual equality of all humankind. His teachings gave rise to a religious movement called the Kabir Panth ('Path of Kabir') and were also incorporated into the Sikh Scripture. Kabir is mentioned too in the verse epigraph to chapter 14 of *Kim* (1901). A selection of his poetry was translated into English by Rabindranath Tagore and published in 1915 as *Songs of Kabir*.

1. *guddee*: Throne of an Indian ruler.

2. *bairagi*: A mendicant (Sanscrit: *vairāgya*) who is deemed to be free from human passions and worldly desires. The term is also used to refer to the crutch which such mendicants carry with them, as Purun Bhagat does (see '*bairagi* – his brass-handled crutch' on p. 167).

3. *sal and the kikar*: The wood of the *sal* tree is a common and valuable timber in India; also considered to be a sacred tree in both Hinduism and Buddhism, being associated with Vishnu and Buddha. The *kikar* '(*Kee-kar*) is a scrubby, spiny tree that belongs to the Acacia family (accent on *Kee*)' (K).

LETTING IN THE JUNGLE

First published in the *Pall Mall Gazette*, 12 and 13 December 1894, and in the *Pall Mall Budget*, 13 December 1894, with illustrations by Cecil Aldin, then in *McClure's Magazine*, January 1895, with illustrations by W. A. C. Pape.

1. *if you . . . Jungle Book*: Not in *Sussex*.
2. *Leave Man alone . . . Leave Man alone*: 'Leave the men alone . . . Leave the men alone' (*Pall Mall* publications and *McClure's*); 'Leave Men alone . . . Leave Men alone' (*1st American* and *Sussex*). In the next paragraph, 'smell Man again' is 'smell a man again' in the magazine publications.
3. *think of Man*: 'think of men' (*1st American* and *Sussex*).
4. *heliograph*: A device for transmitting signals and messages over a distance by reflecting sunlight with a mirror. In India, it was extensively used in military campaigns as well as in survey operations. The heliograph plays a key role in Kipling's humorous poem 'A Code of Morals' (collected in *Departmental Ditties*, 1886).
5. *Mowgli's four wolves . . . melting into the thorn and under-brush*: 'The four cubs . . . melting into the thorn and under-brush as a mole melts into a lawn' (*1st American* and *Sussex*).
6. *be a Man*: 'be Man' (*1st American* and *Sussex*).
7. *two days' old trail*: 'trail of overnight' (*1st American* and *Sussex*).
8. *Do men . . . said Gray Brother*: In other editions, including the magazine publications, it is Bagheera who asks this question: ' "Does Man trap Man?" said Bagheera.'
9. *Nilghai*: The largest Indian antelope, the adult male of which is noted for its dark blue colour. Kipling writes: 'pronounced *Neal-guy*. It means literally "blue bull", a wild antelope as big as a small pony (accent on *guy*)' (K).
10. *talao*: An artificial pond or lake (Hindi).
11. *Two nights ago*: 'Last night' in other editions.

12. *Kanhiwara*: 'Khanhiwara' and throughout the story (*1st American* and *Sussex*). See also note 8 to 'Tiger-Tiger!'.

13. *Who is Man ... the eater of earth?*: Daniel Karlin writes: 'Bagheera is quoting from the Old Testament, but the implication is ambivalent; of two possible texts, one contradicts his scorn of Man, the other confirms it' (DK). See Psalm 8: 'What is man, that thou art mindful of him? [...] Thou madest him to have dominion over the works of thy hands; thou hast put all things under his feet: all sheep and oxen, yea, and the beasts of the field'; and Psalm 144: 'Lord, what is man, that thou takest knowledge of him! or the son of man, that thou makest account of him! Man is like to vanity: his days are as a shadow that passeth away [...] Cast forth lightning, and scatter them: shoot out thine arrows, and destroy them.'

14. *dropped*: 'dropped like a dead man' (*1st American* and *Sussex*).

15. *thy woman*: 'the woman' (*1st American* and *Sussex*).

16. *Thy mother*: 'Thy lair mother' (*1st American* and *Sussex*).

17. *a Master-word*: 'the Master-words' (*1st American*); 'The Master-Words' (*Sussex*).

18. *Bhurtpore*: Also spelled 'Bharatpur', a princely state in Rajputana (now Rajasthan).

19. *a trap ... in the pit*: The pitfall method was a traditional way of catching wild elephants; it was considered to be 'most barbarous' (Sanderson, p. 75) by the British and was replaced by the Keddah system of driving the elephants into stockades – see the headnote for 'Toomai of the Elephants'.

20. *Sahi*: In *Sussex*, 'Ikki', while *1st American*, unusually, has 'Sahi'. See note 3 to the Preface.

21. *the buffaloes ... their wild mates*: According to Sterndale, wild buffaloes and domesticated ones are 'identically the same, and numerous instances have been known of the latter joining herds of their wild brethren' (*Mammalia*, p. 491).

22. *leeped*: plastered; from the Urdu (Hindi) word *līpna*, which means to 'wash with cow-dung and water' or 'to plaster'. Cow dung, mixed with water, was widely used for daily and ritual cleansing of the house as well as for plastering.

23. *Karela*: The bitter gourd.

24. *no heart*: 'no time' (*1st American* and *Sussex*).

25. *vines*: *1st American* and *Sussex* add: 'like the lances of a goblin army following a retreat'.

26. *no more to go*: 'no more to lose' (*McClure's*); 'no more to be robbed of' (*1st American* and *Sussex*).

Mowgli's Song Against People

1. *cess*: In India, 'a tax levied for a specific object; often with pre-fixed word defining the object ("irrigation cess", "road cess", etc.)' (*OED*).

THE UNDERTAKERS

First published in the *New York World*, 8, 9, 10 and 12 November 1894, and also in the *Pall Mall Budget*, 8 and 15 November 1894, with illustrations by Cecil Aldin, and the *Pall Mall Gazette*, 14 and 15 November 1894. 'A Ripple Song' originally appeared as a verse epigraph to the story in the *Pall Mall* publications with the word 'Translation' below the poem.

1. *Jacala*: The crocodile mentioned in 'Red Dog' and 'The Spring Running'.
2. *railway bridge*: In 1887 Kipling wrote two articles in the *Civil and Military Gazette* on the building of railway bridges over the Sutlej and Jhelum rivers at Chak-Nizam (collected in Pinney (ed.), *Kipling's India* (Basingstoke: Macmillan, 1986), pp. 206–23). These articles are said to have been the basis of 'The Bridge-Builders', published in 1893 (collected in *The Day's Work*, 1898), which depicts the Englishman's heroic struggle against the forces of nature in India through bridge-building. 'The Undertakers', published a year later, can be seen as a rewriting of 'The Bridge-Builders' from the animals' point of view, in which the fierceness of nature becomes equated with the threat (and memories) of native insurgency. See note 21 below.
3. *Mugger-Ghaut*: '[in which Ghaut is] pronounced *Gort*, means "the Crocodile's Ferry", or bankside' (K). The 'mugger' is a marsh crocodile, described in *Hobson-Jobson* as 'the destructive broad-snouted crocodile of the Ganges and other Indian rivers' and feared as a man-eater. (See also note 7 below.) As Daniel Karlin observes: 'the resemblance to the English term "mugger" (a street criminal) is a lucky accident' (DK).
4. *flying-foxes*: Fruit-eating bats.
5. *Adjutant-crane*: A large species of stork that is native to India and a scavenger. 'A bird so called (no doubt) from its comical resemblance to a human figure in a stiff dress pacing slowly on a parade-ground' (*Hobson-Jobson*).
6. *Ally Sloper-like*: Ally Sloper was a popular fictional character in British comic strips, who first appeared in *Judy* in 1867. He was

noted for his bulbous red nose and bald head, and for his disrep-
utable yet humorous conduct, such as 'sloping' (i.e. to abscond
without paying) through alleys to avoid his landlord and the
debt collector; it is from this that his name was derived.

7. *Gavial*: Also called a 'gharial', a member of the Crocodilia group
    of large reptiles that includes crocodiles and alligators. Kipling
    describes it as 'a sharp-nosed alligator, who does not generally
    eat men. The Mugger's nose is as blunt as a boot' (K).

8. *at Kasi to-day and Prayag to-morrow*: The proverb is unidenti-
    fied. Kasi and Prayag are ancient names for Benares and
    Allahabad respectively.

9. *'In August . . . remember!"'*: According to JLK, ' "The jackal born
    in August says of the September flood, I never saw so much water
    in all my life," is a popular snub for youthful conceit' (p. 279).

10. *he flies off . . . war-dances*: JLK also remarks: 'For grotesque
    devilry of dancing, the Indian Adjutant beats creation . . . there
    is an abandonment and lightness of step, a wild lift in each sol-
    emn prance, which are almost demoniacal' (p. 37).

11. *Gunga*: The River Ganges.

12. *Brahman*: 'Brahmin' (*1st American* and *Sussex*).

13. *Rewa . . . Chilwa*: Rewa, Mohoo, Chapta, Batchua and Chilwa
    are all 'names of fresh-water fish' (K).

14. *upland Jats – Malwais of the Bêt*: Jats are a people from northern
    India, while Malwais are natives of the Malwa (Malwah) region
    of the Punjab, which is also known as the Bêt, 'a rich farming
    district between two rivers [the Sutlej and the Jumna] in North-
    ern India' (K).

15. *kikar-scrub*: '(*Kee-kar*) is a scrubby, spiny tree that belongs to
    the Acacia family (accent on *Kee*)' (K).

16. *Wenham Lake ice . . . ice by machinery*: The ice from Wenham
    Lake in Massachusetts was a popular commodity in the nine-
    teenth century, and was shipped all over the world by the Tudor
    Ice Company of Boston. Wenham Lake ice dominated the ice
    trade until the steam-powered ice maker was invented and
    became widely available later in the century. The first ice factory
    in Calcutta was established in 1878.

17. *hunted them in my time*: The Mugger is referring to the 'Indian
    Mutiny' of 1857 (now also known as the First War of Indian
    Independence), in which Indian troops turned against British
    rule, and the British were killed in great numbers. The story that
    follows narrates the event from the Mugger's point of view.

18. *Sirhind, the waterless*: A level and arid plain in the Punjab between the Jumna and Sutlej rivers. The *Readers' Guide* speculates on the route which the Mugger took: 'Assuming [. . .] that the mugger started his overland journey from the Kashi Bridge near Ferozepore where it crosses the Sutlej he would have travelled south and east across the desert [i.e. Sirhind] until he reached the Jumna somewhere about or above Agra. Crossing the Jumna he would reach the Ganges via Etawah at Cawnpore or below where he would expect to find his harvest of Mutiny corpses, and thence down river to Allahabad, Benares, Patna and Monghyr, his eastern limit, a total journey of about 800 miles' (*ORG*, vol. 7, p. 3000).

19. *the Jackal knew . . . Mugger's family circle*: 'i.e. the mugger ate jackals on his journey; eating a creature establishes an ironic "blood-relationship" with it' (DK).

20. *Agra . . . Etawah . . . Allahabad*: These cities on the Jumna River were notable centres of the 1857 rebellion – see note 17 above.

21. *Arrah*: The scene of a dramatic siege during the 1857 rebellion (see note 17 above); as Kipling elsewhere puts it: 'Arrah was a place where ten white men and fifty-six loyal natives barricaded themselves in a billiard-room in a garden and stood the siege of three regiments of mutineers for three weeks' (*Land and Sea Tales for Scouts and Guides* (London: Macmillan, 1923), p. 8). Kipling published a story called 'The Little House at Arrah' in *Pioneer*, 24 February 1888.

22. *in red coats, not English*: i.e. native troops in the Indian Army, who turned against the British.

23. *Purbeeahs*: Sepoys (native soldiers) of the Bengal Army.

24. *the Martini*: 'an old make of rifle, firing black powder. The four-bore was a gun used for shooting elephants, very heavy, and firing a bullet about an inch in diameter' (K).

25. *one of the Englishmen . . . who had built the bridge*: The battle between the Englishman as a bridge-builder and the Mugger is reminiscent of 'The Bridge-Builders' (see note 2 above), in which the Mugger appears as the Mother Gunga, the goddess of the river, infuriated by the Englishmen's building of the bridge.

A Ripple Song

1. *Safe across*: 'Once across' (*Pall Mall Gazette*); 'Here, across' (*1st American* and *Sussex*).

THE KING'S ANKUS

First published in *St Nicholas* magazine, March 1895, with illustrations by W. A. C. Pape. There, it begins as follows: 'These jungle tales are told the same way that Baloo left the Bee-rocks – any end first; and you must take them as they come – just as the frog took the white ants after the rains.' This opening paragraph was omitted from the book editions. Chaucer's 'The Pardoner's Tale' has been suggested as one of the possible sources of inspiration for this story.

1. *Jungle Saying*: These lines are modelled on Proverbs 30: 15–16: 'There are three things that are never satisfied, yea, four things say not, It is enough: The grave; and the barren womb; the earth that is not filled with water; and the fire that saith not, It is enough.' Jacala is the crocodile mentioned in 'Red Dog' and 'The Spring Running'.
2. *the two hundredth time*: 'the hundredth time' (*St Nicholas*).
3. *Cold Lairs ... you may have heard*: See note 8 to 'Kaa's Hunting'.
4. *Salomdhi ... Bappa Rawal*: Bappa Rawal (AD 713–53) is the powerful Hindu ruler who founded the Mewar Dynasty in Chitor in southern Rajasthan. Kipling refers to Bappa's life and his legendary status in chapter 10 of *Letters of Marque* (1891), where he gives a short history of Chitor. James Tod's *Annals and Antiquities of Rajasthan* (Madras: Higginbotham, 1873), which Kipling consulted, mentions a Salomdhi, the ruler of the Magadha kingdom, as probably a contemporary of Bappa Rawal, and gives his genealogy (Chandrabija, Viyeja, Yegasuri) (vol. 1, n.p.).
5. *elephant-howdahs*: A howdah is a great chair or framed seat placed on the back of an elephant. See note 11 to 'Toomai of the Elephants'.
6. *Thuu*: 'pronounced *Thoo-oo*' (K).
7. *fifty yards away*: 'thirty yards away' (*1st American*).

QUIQUERN

First published in the *Pall Mall Gazette*, 24 and 25 October 1895, and then in *McClure's Magazine*, November 1895. Kipling never crossed the Arctic Sea, and the *Readers' Guide* attributes much of the background information he needed to write this story to 'an explorer who visited him in Vermont' (*ORG*, p. 3007), while R. A. Durand, in

A Handbook to the Poetry of Rudyard Kipling (New York: Double-day, 1914), p. 314, refers to Franz Boas's paper 'The Central Eskimo' (1888) as the original source of 'Angutivun Tina' (see p. 267 and the note on it below). Kipling seems to have closely followed Boas's accounts of Inuit life and mythology, but he must have also consulted other sources (the Arctic Circle was a very popular topic in nineteenth-century Britain), as many of the native words in the story do not conform to Boas's orthography.

The title 'Quiquern' 'is pronounced *Kwai-kwern*, and the places named in the story can be found on maps of the country inside the Arctic Circle. Look them up' (K). According to Boas, 'Qiqirn' is a 'spirit of which the natives are in great fear [. . .] a phantom in the shape of a huge dog almost without hair [. . .] If it comes near dogs or men they fall into fits and only recover when Qiqirn has left. It is exceedingly afraid of men and runs away as soon as angakoq [the village sorcerer] descries it' (p. 597).

1. *narwhal*: An Arctic whale, also known as sea-unicorn as the male develops a long straight spirally twisted tusk.

2. *blubber-lamp*: A shallow, boat-shaped lamp made of soapstone (see note 10 below), which burns blubber derived from seals or other marine mammals; also known as a soapstone lamp. It is used as a light source, as well as for cooking and heating.

3. *Northern Lights*: The Aurora Borealis – an aurora, or light display, seen in the skies in the north polar regions.

4. *Labrador . . . Ellesmere Land*: Baffin Land (now more commonly called 'Baffin Island'), the biggest of the Canadian Arctic Archipelago, is separated from the Labrador Peninsula in eastern Canada by Hudson Strait (which leads into Hudson Bay), by the Fury and Hecla Straits from Melville Peninsula on the north coast of Canada, and also by Lancaster Sound from North Devon (now called 'Devon Island') next to which lies Ellesmere Land (now 'Ellesmere Island'), off the north-west coast of Greenland. Baylot Island lies at the northern end of Baffin Land. Thus Franz Boas writes: 'Baffin Land forms a connecting link for three regions inhabited by Eskimo: the Hudson Bay Territory, Labrador and Greenland' (p. 415).

5. *Inuit . . . Esquimau*: Eskimo (Esquimaux), which signifies 'eaters of raw flesh', is the name given by European anthropologists to the indigenous people of the Arctic regions of Canada, Alaska, Greenland and eastern Siberia. They call themselves 'Inuit', a word which signifies 'people'; the singular form is 'Inuk', though

in English it is common to use 'Inuit' to refer to a member of the Inuit people.

6. *Tununirmiut*: The people of Tununirn, 'the country lying back of something' (Boas, p. 665), which is the northernmost part of Baffin Land (see note 4 above).

7. *Navy Board Inlet*: A body of water between Baffin Land and the eastern side of Bylot Island (see note 4 above).

8. *musk-ox*: A large ruminant found in Arctic America, with a thick shaggy coat and long curved horns.

9. *'woman-boats'*: A 'woman-boat' is an *umiak*, a large open Inuit boat, about ten metres long and often rowed by women. This is distinguished from *kayak* ('man-boat'), which is a canoe covered in seal skin.

10. *old soap-stone affairs*: i.e. cooking over a soapstone lamp. Soapstone is soft steatite (or talc), which can be easily carved to make utensils, such as pots and blubber-lamps (see note 2 above), and sculptures.

11. *valuable as pearls*: 'the front teeth of musk oxen are considered as jewels' (*The Private Journal of Captain G. F. Lyon* (1824), quoted in Boas, p. 592). Animal bones and teeth were much valued by the Inuit as powerful amulets.

12. *Exeter and Cumberland Sounds*: In south-eastern Baffin Land (see note 4 above).

13. *Bhendy Bazaar*: A famous market in Bombay (now Mumbai), noted for its lively and cosmopolitan atmosphere.

14. *the man who knows all about it by practice*: According to Boas, the Eskimo word for 'chief', *piman*, means 'he who knows everything best by practice' (p. 660).

15. *kit-foxes*: Small foxes. More properly, this should read 'Arctic foxes', as kit foxes, the smallest of the American foxes, live in deserts and grassland of the south-west of the United States and northern Mexico.

16. *in the buckle*: See note 22 below.

17. *Each beast . . . by his own separate trace*: According to Boas: 'The strongest and most spirited dog has the longest trace and is allowed to run a few feet in advance of the rest as a leader; its sex is indifferent, the choice being made chiefly with regard to strength. Next to the leader follow two or three strong dogs with traces of equal length, and the weaker and less manageable the dogs the nearer they run to the sledge' (p. 533).

18. *toodle-ki-yi*: 'the author's invented onomatopoeia' (*ORG*, p. 3001). Also, possibly a compound verb devised by Kipling: i.e.

toodle ('to hum or sing in a low tone') + *ki-yi* ('the howl or yelp of a dog' in American English (*OED*)).

19. *Angutivun . . . The Song of the Returning Hunter*: A real Inuit song, the words and music of which are recorded by Boas under the title of 'The Returning Hunters' (p. 653). See the note on 'Angutivun Tina' below.

20. *'Amna aya, aya amna, ah! ah!'*: A well-known female chorus, which 'women go on singing . . . for nearly an hour' (Captain W. E. Parry, *Journal of a Second Voyage for the Discovery of a North-West Passage from the Atlantic to the Pacific* (London: John Murray, 1824), p. 542; also recorded in Boas, p. 657).

21. *wolverine*: The largest of the weasel family.

22. *tutareang*: A buckle with two holes; 'One end of the thong is firmly tied to the buckle, passing through one of the holes, while the opposite end passes tightly through the second hole. The thong may be quickly opened by a strong effort on the part of the hunter, while it helps to keep him quiet' (Boas, p. 477). The buckle is used when 'the sealer expects to wait a long time', such as when 'only a few men go out hunting and famine is impending' (p. 477).

23. *hydrophobia*: Rabies – see note 5 to 'Mowgli's Brothers'.

24. *Great Bear*: Ursa Major, a prominent constellation in the northern hemisphere, the seven brightest stars of which form 'the Big Dipper' (or 'the Plough').

25. *the great Ten-legged White Spirit-Bear*: The white bear *tornaq* is mentioned in Boas, but there is no indication that it has ten legs. Neither does 'Qiqirn', a phantom dog (see note on the title above), seem to have 'extra pairs of legs', contrary to Kipling's description on p. 258.

26. *five miles*: 'ten miles' (*1st American* and *Sussex*).

27. *a Thing . . . that quivered all along the outlines*: 'a mirage, caused by the refraction of light in layers of air of varying temperature and density' (*NRG*).

28. *Baffin's Bay*: The sea between Baffin Land (see note 4 above) and Greenland.

29. *the Greenland side of things*: 'the Greenland side of the water' (*1st American* and *Sussex*).

30. *Melville Bay*: A large bay off the coast of north-west Greenland. (See also note 4 above.)

31. *helplessly*: 'helplessly in deep water' (*1st American* and *Sussex*).

32. *tons of rubbish*: 'tons of ice' (*1st American* and *Sussex*).

33. *nearly dark*: 'all dark' (*1st American* and *Sussex*).

34. *Lake Netilling at Nikosiring*: In the southern part of Baffin Land (see note 4 above).
35. *Imigen*: An island north of Cumberland Sound.
36. *Cingalese*: A native of Ceylon (now Sri Lanka).

Angutivun Tina

The title is rendered ' "Angutivun Tina" ' in *1st American* and ' "Angutivun Tina" ' in other editions, including *Sussex*.

1. *This is a very free translation of the Song of the Returning Hunter*: Sung by Kotuko in the story, this song appears to be Kipling's inspired invention. In 1899, Franz Boas and Henry Rink published a translation of the actual Inuit song (under the title of 'The Returning Hunters'), which reads as follows: 'Our husbands thus down there, as they have been hunting reindeer, as they have been regularly engaged in hunting, I shall have plenty of meat now' ('Eskimo Tales and Songs' in *The Journal of American Folklore* 2/5 (1899), p. 131). According to them, the song is 'sung by the women who stand looking out for [the men's] arrival' (p. 131), which strikingly contrasts with Kipling's version, in which the hunters after seal-spearing sing of their home-coming.

RED DOG

First published as ' "Good Hunting" ' in the *Pall Mall Gazette*, 29 and 30 July 1895, and in *McClure's Magazine*, August 1895, with illustrations by W. A. G. Pape. At the manuscript stage, Kipling was also contemplating 'The Little People of the Rocks' as a possible title.

1. *paying a just debt*: 'paying your debts to the last farthing' (*McClure's*); 'paying debts' (*1st American* and *Sussex*).
2. *afraid*: 'just a little afraid' (*1st American* and *Sussex*).
3. *the Mad Elephant of Mandla*: Sanderson writes: 'Of cases recorded of really vicious animals perhaps the most notable is that of the Mandla elephant, an elephant supposed to have been mad, and which killed an immense number of persons about five years ago. It is said to have eaten portions of some of its victims, but it probably only held their limbs in its mouth whilst it tore them to pieces' (p. 53). The elephant was shot in 1871 by Captain A. Bloomfield, whose own account of the mad elephant is collected in Dhriti K. Lahiri-Choudhury (ed.), *The Great Indian Elephant Book* (1999). Mandla is about sixty miles north-west of Seoni.

4. *Great Famine*: Possibly the Great Famine of 1876–8, one of the most widespread and prolonged of the nineteenth-century Indian famines.

5. *caught in a pit*: 'once more trapped in a pit' (*1st American* and *Sussex*). (See also note 19 to 'Letting in the Jungle'.)

6. *masterless*: 'masterless, white-toothed, deep-chested' (*McClure's*); 'masterless, full-voiced' (*1st American* and *Sussex*).

7. *Phao, son of Phaona*: Phao is 'pronounced *Fay-ou*: he was son of *Fay-owner*. A made-up name' (K).

8. *with strange feelings*: Not in *1st American* and *Sussex*.

9. *Pheeal*: 'pronounced *Fe-arl*, is the noise that a jackal sometimes makes when he is following or going before a hunting tiger. It is, men have told me, quite different from his regular cry and not nice to listen to' (K).

10. *The Four . . . turned into stone*: 'The Four stopped at once, bristling and growling. Mowgli's hand went to his knife, and he checked, the blood in his face, his eyebrows knotted' (*1st American* and *Sussex*).

11. *despairing bay*: *McClure's* goes on to add 'like a bell tolling on a wrecked ship'.

12. *Dhole*: 'is *Dole*: and is one of the native names for the Wild Hunting Dog of India' (K).

13. *Won-tolla*: 'is pronounced *Woon-toller* (accent on *tol*)' (K). According to Sir Walter Elliot (1803–87), a Scottish naturalist who worked in India, 'Sometimes a large wolf is seen to seek his prey singly; these are called *Won-tola*, and are reckoned particularly fierce' (quoted in Sterndale, *Mammalia*, pp. 234–5).

14. *The Dekkan*: Now spelled 'Deccan', 'part of the big Central Plain of India. Look it up on the map' (K).

15. *heavy and strong*: *1st American* and *Sussex* add: 'for all that they eat lizards in the Dekkan'.

16. *one striped ape*: *1st American* and *Sussex* add: 'and sure am I in my stomach that Shere Khan would have left his own mate for meat to the dhole if he had winded a pack across three ranges'.

17. *sleep*: 'gain' (*McClure's*); 'meat' (*1st American* and *Sussex*).

18. *Chikai, the little leaping rat*: Probably a species of Jerboa-rats, desert rodents which leap with their hind legs.

19. *milk-tushes*: Milk-tusks – see note 4 to 'Toomai of the Elephants'.

20. *after moonrise*: 'after moonset' (*1st American* and *Sussex*).

21. *weatherworn rocks . . . Little People of the Rocks*: Kipling's note on 'Bee rocks' reads: 'There are some rocks above a river near

Jubbulpore in India where wild bees have lived for many years. Nobody goes near them if he can avoid it, for sometimes they attack and kill men and horses' (K). He is here referring to the 'Marble Rocks' at Jubbulpore over the Narmada River, a beautiful gorge and famous sight-seeing spot, where visitors were often attacked by a swarm of bees. Jubbulpore (now spelled 'Jabalpur') is about eighty miles north of Seoni. 'Bee Rocks', as they are referred to later in the story (as well as in 'How Fear Came'), are said to have been inspired by the photographs of the Marble Rocks taken by Kipling's friends the Hills who visited there (*ORG*, p. 3031). These photos are in the Carpenter Kipling Collection in the Library of Congress at Washington.

22. *they did not know*: 'they did not know the Law' (*1st American* and *Sussex*).

23. *who had . . . that buck*: Not in *1st American* and *Sussex*.

24. *Kaa's head . . . whispered*: 'Kaa's head was close to Mowgli's ear; and it was a little time before the boy answered' (*1st American* and *Sussex*).

25. *the sole of his foot*: *1st American* and *Sussex* add: 'and singing to himself'.

26. *that meant revenge to the death*: 'that meant they were going to stay till he dropped out of the tree' (*McClure's*); 'that meant they were going to stay' (*1st American* and *Sussex*).

27. *monkey-fashion*: '*Bandar-log* fashion' (*1st American* and *Sussex*).

28. *naturally rushed . . . smelt the blood*: 'naturally rushed after it' (*McClure's*); 'instinctively rushed after it' (*1st American* and *Sussex*).

29. *stringing out*: 'tailing out' (*1st American* and *Sussex*).

30. *The Little People . . . late blossoming flowers*: As Daniel Karlin observes, there is an 'echo . . . of Keats, a favourite of Kipling': 'to set budding more, / And still more, later flowers for the bees, / Until they think warm days will never cease, / For Summer has o'er-brimmed their clammy cells' ('To Autumn', 1819).

31. *They are unhurt*: Not in *1st American* and *Sussex*.

32. *down and down to the rocks*: 'down to the deep eddies' (*1st American* and *Sussex*).

33. *The Little People . . . help wolves*: 'The Little People go back to sleep. They have chased us far. Now I, too, turn back, for I am not of one skin with any wolf. Good hunting, Little Brother, and remember the dhole bites low' (*1st American* and *Sussex*).

34. *and I shall see well*: Not in *1st American* and *Sussex*.

35. *wild-eyed lahinis*: 'anxious-eyed lahinis' (*1st American* and *Sussex*). 'Pronounced *Lar-hee-ney*, is a made-up name for she-wolves (accent on *hee*)' (K).

36. *bites low*: 'bites at the belly' (*1st American* and *Sussex*). Sterndale refers to the general opinion that 'the wild dog endeavours to seize the quarry by the flanks and tear out the entrails' (*Mammalia*, p. 241).

37. *went the same*: 'went without ceasing' (*1st American* and *Sussex*).

38. *worked their way to his aid*: 'worried their way to his side' (*1st American* and *Sussex*).

39. *wearied and afraid*: 'cowed and afraid' (*1st American* and *Sussex*).

40. *dare to run*: 'care to run' (*Sussex*).

41. *there was time to breathe . . . turn a dhole aside*: 'there was time now and again to breathe, and pass a word to a friend, and the mere flicker of the knife would sometimes turn a dog aside' (*1st American* and *Sussex*).

42. *the lair-father . . . this lair-father kills thee*: 'the Outlier . . . this Won-tolla kills thee' (*1st American* and *Sussex*).

43. *There is no more for thee*: 'There is no more to say' (*1st American* and *Sussex*).

44. *Now . . . to my kind*: Not in *1st American* and *Sussex*.

45. *raised*: 'lifted the bodies aside and raised' (*1st American* and *Sussex*).

46. *the last of the dying dholes*: 'the remnant of the flying dholes' (*1st American* and *Sussex*).

47. *dholes . . . stand before them*: 'dholes, whose boast was that all Jungles were their Jungle, and that no living thing could stand before them' (*1st American* and *Sussex*).

Chil's Song

1. *Chil!*: 'For Chil!' (*1st American* and *Sussex*); likewise in the two subsequent occurrences of this line.

THE SPRING RUNNING

First published in the *Pall Mall Gazette*, 26 and 27 September 1895, and in the *Civil and Military Gazette*, 27, 28, 30 September and 4, 5, and 7 October 1895. Also published as 'Mowgli Leaves the Jungle for Ever' in *Cosmopolitan Magazine*, October 1895, with illustrations by W. H. Drake.

1. *hungry*: 'angry' (*1st American*).
2. *Ferao*: 'the scarlet woodpecker, is pronounced *Feer-ow*; a made-up name meaning "Come back again", like Spring does' (K).
3. *against the need*: 'against the spring' (*Cosmopolitan*).
4. *Listen to Ferao*: 'Listen to Ferao, and be glad!' (*1st American and Sussex*).
5. *Unhappy as he was*: 'Forgetting his unhappiness' (*1st American and Sussex*).
6. *Hai mai!*: Literally, 'Oh, my Mother!', an idiomatic exclamation in Hindi.
7. *as if it had been new game*: Not in *1st American* and *Sussex*.
8. *and I will see*: 'as I did in the old days, and I will see' (*1st American and Sussex*).
9. *Why ... Red Dog?*: 'Why did I not die under Red Dog?' (*1st American and Sussex*).
10. *to cast the skin*: 'to blot out an old trail' (*Cosmopolitan*).
11. *And this is ... Mowgli's stories*: 'This is the last of the Mowgli stories, because there are no more to be told' (*Cosmopolitan*).

The Outsong

1. *spathe*: a large bract or floral leaf, enveloping the flower cluster of certain plants, such as arums and palms.
2. *ways of Man*: 'worth of Man' (*1st American and Sussex*).

APPENDIX

IN THE RUKH

First published in *Many Inventions* (1893). Reprinted with the sub-title 'Mowgli's Introduction to White Men' in *McClure's Magazine*, June 1896, with eleven illustrations by W. A. C. Pape. In *McClure's*, Kipling introduces the story as follows:

This tale [. . .] was the first written of the Mowgli stories, though it deals with the closing chapters of his career – namely, his introduction to white men, his marriage and civilization, all of which took place, we may infer, some two or three years after he had finally broken away from his friends in the jungle [. . .] Those who know the geography of India will see that it is a far cry from Seeonee to a Northern forest reserve; but though many curious things must have befallen Mowgli, we have no certain record of his adventures during those wanderings. There are, however, legends.

The *rukh* in the title is a 'forest reserve' in the vocabulary of the local government of Punjab, the term being 'generally applied in the Punjab to Government or other lands specially set apart for the growth of fuel or grass' (*Calcutta Review* 46/92 (1867), p. 276). Starting in the mid-nineteenth century, the Indian Government made a series of land reservations (*rukhs*) to create government forests, in order to meet the growing needs for timber and other resources. 'In the Rukh' celebrates the Imperial Forest Department's hard work in fostering and managing the reserved forests, and this is where Mowgli makes his first appearance. The *OED*, till quite recently, had given the Hindi word *rūkh*, which means 'tree', as the etymology of the term, but it is in fact derived from the Punjabi word *rakkhna*, to keep or to set apart, as is the term *rakkha*, a protector or guardian.

1. *tyre*: From the Tamil *tayir*, the common term in southern India for curdled milk, similar to yogurt. In Hindi, it is called *dahi* (*Hobson-Jobson*).
2. *reboisement*: Reforestation (from the French).
3. *spindling pine*: 'unhappy pine' (*McClure's* and *1st American*).
4. *the rules of Nancy*: From 1867 to 1886, the officers intended for the Indian Forest Service were sent to study at the National School of Forestry at Nancy in France. Even after 1885, when the forest school at Cooper's Hill, near London, was opened to take over the training, the trainees were required to spend several weeks in Nancy as part of their studies.
5. *blue gum*: A species of *Eucalyptus*, native to Australia.
6. *poll and lop*: To cut off the top of a tree and trim the branches.
7. *recapping-machine*: 'A small hand-operated machine for inserting new percussion caps into spent shot-gun cartridge cases' (*NRG*).
8. *Calcutta Botanical Gardens*: Originally founded in 1787 by the East India Company, the Calcutta Botanical Gardens developed into a leading centre of botanical research and gave guidance on Indian forestry; it also acted as a distributor of plants and seeds in India.
9. *shikar*: A shooting and hunting game.
10. *devilry*: 'blood's lust' (*McClure's*).
11. *sal trees*: See note 3 to 'A Song of Kabir' ('The Miracle of Purun Bhagat').

12. *koss*: A measure of distance in India, varying from one to three miles depending on the locality.

13. *clomb*: An archaic past tense of 'to climb'.

14. *He was old . . . and not a little mangy*: See note 12 to 'Mowgli's Brothers'.

15. *shikari*: Hunter.

16. *lusus naturae* : A freak of nature; from the Latin – 'a playing or sport of nature'.

17. *grey hairs*: 'gray hairs' (*Many Inventions*, 1893). In most of the earlier editions of the *Jungle Books*, including the first English and American editions, Kipling used the spelling 'gray' rather than 'grey', while in the Sussex Edition (1937–9), from which 'In the Rukh' in this current edition is taken, 'gray' was changed to 'grey' throughout; hence 'Gray Brother' became 'Grey Brother' in the Sussex Edition. According to *OED*: 'In the twentieth century, grey has become the established spelling in the UK, whilst gray is standard in the United States.'

18. *jail-khana*: Prison.

19. *izzat*: Honour of oneself and one's family: an important part of the cultural code of the Muslim community in India.

20. *Huzrut*: From the Arabic, *Huzur*, 'Your Highness'.

21. *Changamanga rukh*: The oldest and largest man-made forest in India, some fifty miles south-west of Lahore, plantation of which started in 1866. Berthold Ribbentrop (see the next note) was in charge of drafting a working plan of the Changa Manga plantation.

22. *The gigantic German . . . Head Ranger from Burma to Bombay*: Muller is said to be based on Berthold Ribbentrop, a German forester who joined the Indian Forestry Service in 1866 and acted as the Inspector-General of Forests to the Government of India from 1889 to 1900. He is the author of *Hints on Arbori-culture in the Panjab* (1873) and *Forestry in British India* (1900). According to an interview that Ribbentrop gave to a newspaper, the *San Francisco Call*, on 8 September 1895, he knew Kipling's father very well and met Kipling when he was working as a journalist in Lahore. He also mentions how Kipling had called him the 'Gigantic Head of the Indian Forest' in his story. It has been suggested that the name 'Muller' may be a reference to the eminent German philologist Friedrich Max Müller (1823–1900), famous for his work on comparative religion.

23. *brass-hat*: A high-ranking staff officer.

24. *Bikanir Desert*: Bikanir (or 'Bikaner'), a district in the north-west of Rajasthan, is part of the Great Indian Desert, or Thar Desert.

25. *'und der Christian Gods howl loudly'*: A reference to the German poet Heinrich Heine's poem 'Almansor', collected in *Buch der Lieder* ('Book of Songs'; 1827): 'And they wildly fall together, / Pale turn all the priests and people, / Crashing falls the dome upon them, / And the Christian gods wail loudly' (trans. E. A. Bowring, *The Poems of Heine* (London: Longman, 1859), p. 82). This is the last stanza of the poem, in which Almansor, a Moor converted to Christianity, has a dream in which Cordoba Cathedral, formerly the Grand Mosque in the heyday of Islamic rule in Spain, which still bears inscriptions from the Koran, dramatically crashes down, no longer able to bear the Christian yoke. The poem thus gives expression to the power of non-Christian religions, hitherto suppressed by European rule.

26. *Faunus:* The Roman god of woods and protector of flocks, identified with the Greek god Pan; usually represented with the horns and legs of a goat, and often playing pipes.

27. *Black Water*: In Hindi *kālā pānī*, a term used by Hindus for the sea. It was believed that those who crossed the Black Water would lose their caste.

28. *Dough we ... a Greek*: A loose quotation from the seventh stanza of 'Dolores' (1866) by Algernon Charles Swinburne. The original reads as follows: 'We shift and bedeck and bedrape us, / Thou art noble and nude and antique; / Libitina thy mother, Priapus / Thy father, a Tuscan and Greek.'

29. *Eblis:* From the Arabic *Iblīs*, the Devil in Islamic mythology.

30. *Mlech:* From the Sanskrit *mleccha*, outcaste or outsider; according to *OED*, the word originally meant 'a non-Aryan or person of an outcaste race; a barbarian' in ancient India, and later came to refer to 'a person who does not conform with conventional Hindu beliefs and practices; a foreigner'.

31. *shadi:* 'Wedding' in Hindi.

32. *Gott in Himmel!:* 'God in Heaven!' in German.

read more

PENGUIN CLASSICS

PLAIN TALES FROM THE HILLS
RUDYARD KIPLING

'You are all liars, you English'

Plain Tales from the Hills, Rudyard Kipling's first collection of short stories, established his reputation and brought India to the British imagination. Including the stories 'Lispeth', 'Beyond the Pale' and 'In the Pride of His Youth', they tell of soldiers, wise children, exiles, forbidden romances and divided identities, creating a rich portrait of Anglo-Indian society. Originally published for a newspaper in Lahore when Kipling was a journalist, the tales were later revised by him to re-create as vividly as possible the sights and smells of India for readers at home. Far from being a celebration of empire, these stories explore the barriers between races, classes and sexes, and convey all the tensions and contradictions of colonial life.

Part of a series of new editions of Kipling's works in Penguin Classics, this volume contains a General Preface by Jan Montefiore and an introduction by Kaori Nagai discussing Kipling's portrayal of the relationship between India and England, the role of the narrator in his *Plain Tales*, and the revisions that he made to them.

Edited with an introduction by Kaori Nagai
Series Editor Jan Montefiore

PENGUIN CLASSICS

THE MAN WHO WOULD BE KING: SELECTED STORIES
RUDYARD KIPLING

'They tell me that one never sees a dead person's face in a dream. Is that true?'

Rudyard Kipling is one of the most magical storytellers in the English language. This new selection brings together the best of his short writings, following the development of his work over fifty years. They take us from the harsh, cruel, vividly realized world of the 'Indian' stories that made his name, through the experimental modernism of his middle period to the highly-wrought subtleties of his later pieces. Including the tale of insanity and empire, 'The Man Who Would Be King', the high-spirited 'The Village that Voted the Earth Was Flat', the fable of childhood cruelty and revenge 'Baa Baa, Black Sheep', the menacing psychological study 'Mary Postgate' and the ambiguous portrayal of grief and mourning in 'The Gardener', here are stories of criminals, ghosts, femmes fatales, madness and murder.

Part of a series of new editions of Kipling's works in Penguin Classics, this volume contains a General Preface by Jan Montefiore and an introduction discussing Kipling's reputation and influence, the ambivalence of his writing and the fascination with 'otherness' expressed in his short works.

Edited with an introduction by Jan Montefiore
Series Editor Jan Montefiore

PENGUIN CLASSICS

JUST SO STORIES
RUDYARD KIPLING

'The rhinoceros took off his skin and carried it over his shoulder as he came down to the beach to bathe'

The Camel gets his Hump, the Whale his Throat and the Leopard his Spots in these bewitching stories which conjure up distant lands, the beautiful gardens of splendid palaces, the sea, the deserts, the jungle and its creatures. Inspired by Kipling's delight in human eccentricities and the animal world, and based on bedtime stories he told to his daughter, these strikingly imaginative fables explore the myths of creation, the nature of beasts and the origins of language and writing. They are linked by poems and scattered with Kipling's illustrations, which contain hidden jokes, symbols and puzzles. Among Kipling's most loved works, the *Just So Stories* have been continually in print since 1902.

Part of a series of new editions of Kipling's works in Penguin Classics, this volume contains a General Preface by Jan Montefiore and an introduction by Judith Plotz exploring the origins of the stories in Kipling's own life and in folklore, their place in classic children's literature and their extraordinary language.

Edited with an introduction by Judith Plotz
Series Editor Jan Montefiore

THE STORY OF PENGUIN CLASSICS

Before 1946 ... 'Classics' are mainly the domain of academics and students; readable editions for everyone else are almost unheard of. This all changes when a little-known classicist, E. V. Rieu, presents Penguin founder Allen Lane with the translation of Homer's *Odyssey* that he has been working on in his spare time.

1946 Penguin Classics debuts with *The Odyssey*, which promptly sells three million copies. Suddenly, classics are no longer for the privileged few.

1950s Rieu, now series editor, turns to professional writers for the best modern, readable translations, including Dorothy L. Sayers's *Inferno* and Robert Graves's unexpurgated *Twelve Caesars*.

1960s The Classics are given the distinctive black covers that have remained a constant throughout the life of the series. Rieu retires in 1964, hailing the Penguin Classics list as 'the greatest educative force of the twentieth century.'

1970s A new generation of translators swells the Penguin Classics ranks, introducing readers of English to classics of world literature from more than twenty languages. The list grows to encompass more history, philosophy, science, religion and politics.

1980s The Penguin American Library launches with titles such as *Uncle Tom's Cabin*, and joins forces with Penguin Classics to provide the most comprehensive library of world literature available from any paperback publisher.

1990s The launch of Penguin Audiobooks brings the classics to a listening audience for the first time, and in 1999 the worldwide launch of the Penguin Classics website extends their reach to the global online community.

The 21st Century Penguin Classics are completely redesigned for the first time in nearly twenty years. This world-famous series now consists of more than 1300 titles, making the widest range of the best books ever written available to millions – and constantly redefining what makes a 'classic'.

The Odyssey continues ...

The best books ever written

PENGUIN CLASSICS

SINCE 1946

Find out more at www.penguinclassics.com